GATE
— OF THE —
DEAD

DAVID GILMAN enjoyed many careers,
including firefighter, soldier and photographer
before turning to writing full time. He is an
award-winning author and screenwriter.

www.davidgilman.com
www.facebook.com/davidgilman.author

Also by David Gilman

MASTER OF WAR

DEFIANT UNTO DEATH

MASTER OF WAR
GATE
OF THE
DEAD

DAVID GILMAN

HEAD OF ZEUS

First published in the UK in 2016 by Head of Zeus Ltd

9 7 5 3 1 2 4 6 8

A CIP catalogue record for this book is available from
the British Library.

ISBN (HB) 9781781852903
ISBN (XTPB) 9781781852910
ISBN (E) 9781781852934

Printed and bound in Germany by GGP Media GmbH, Pössneck

Head of Zeus Ltd
Clerkenwell House
45-47 Clerkenwell Green
London EC1R 0HT

WWW.HEADOFZEUS.COM

For Suzy,
as always

... as skilled in war as any man could be, wonderful men at planning a battle and seizing the advantage, at scaling and assaulting towns and castles, as expert and experienced as you could ask for ...

Bascot de Mauléon, man-at-arms, relating the skills
of men of the Free Companies to Jean Froissart,
fourteenth-century French chronicler

CHARACTER LIST

*Sir Thomas Blackstone
*Christiana, Lady Blackstone
*Henry: Blackstone and Christiana's son
*Agnes: Blackstone and Christiana's daughter

THOMAS BLACKSTONE'S MEN
*Sir Gilbert Killbere
*Gaillard: Blackstone's Norman captain
*Meulon: Blackstone's Norman captain
*John Jacob: Blackstone's captain
*Perinne: wall builder and soldier
*Elfred: master of archers and bower
*Will Longdon: centenar and veteran archer
*Jack Halfpenny: archer
*Robert Thurgood: archer

GERMAN KNIGHTS
*Werner von Lienhard
*Conrad von Groitsch
*Siegfried Mertens

GASCON KNIGHTS AND MEN-AT-ARMS
Jean de Grailly: Captal de Buch, Gascon lord and English ally
*Beyard: Jean de Grailly's captain
Gaston Phoebus: Count of Foix

FRENCH KNIGHTS

John, Lord of Hangest: French protector of the French royal
family at Meaux

Loys de Chamby: French knight at the siege of Meaux

Bascot de Mauléon: fought with the Captal in Prussia and then
at Meaux

*Sir Marcel de Lorris: minor French lord, mentor to Henry
Blackstone

ENGLISH NOBLEMEN, KNIGHTS AND SQUIRES

Henry of Grosmont, Duke of Lancaster

Ralph de Ferrers: English Captain of Calais 1358–61

Sir Gilbert Chastelleyn: knight of Edward III's royal household

Stephen Cusington: Edward III's representative.

*Roger Hollings: a squire

*Samuel Cracknell: messenger, sergeant-at-arms.

*Lord Robert de Marcouf

*Sir Robert de Montagu

ENGLISH RULERS

King Edward III of England

Edward of Woodstock, Prince of Wales

Isabella of France (Isabella the Fair), dowager Queen of
England

FRENCH RULERS

King John II (the Good) of France

The Dauphin: the French King's son and heir

The Duchess of Normandy: the Dauphin's wife

Charles, King of Navarre: claimant to the French throne, King
John's son-in-law

Philip of Navarre: Charles of Navarre's brother.

ITALIAN NOBLEMEN, KNIGHTS, CLERICS, MERCHANT AND SERVANTS
Galeazzo Visconti: ruler of Milan
Bernabò Visconti: ruler of Milan
Marquis de Montferrat: Piedmontese nobleman
Pancio de Controne: physician to Edward III's father.
*Niccolò Torellini: Florentine priest
*Paolo: Torellini's servant
*Fra Stefano Caprini: Knight of the Tau
*Brother Bertrand: monk
*Oliviero Dantini: silk merchant of Lucca

ENGLISH PHYSICIAN
Master Lawrence of Canterbury: Queen Isabella's physician.

MAYOR OF MEAUX
Jehan de Soulez

LEADER OF THE JACQUERIE UPRISING
Guillaume Cale

* Indicates fictional characters

1358

BLACKSTONE'S ROUTE

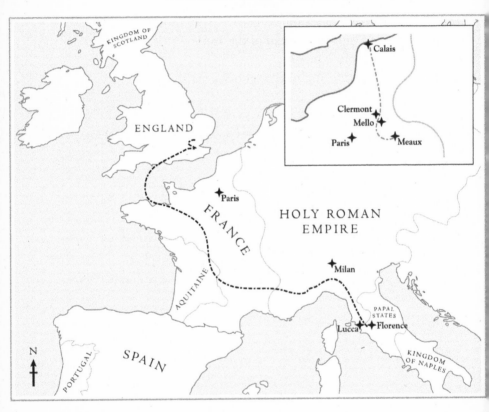

KINGDOM OF
SCOTLAND

ENGLAND

Paris

FRANCE

HOLY ROMAN
EMPIRE

AQUITAINE

Milan

PAPAL
STATES

Lucca   Florence

KINGDOM
OF NAPLES

PORTUGAL   SPAIN

N

Calais

Clermont
Mello
Paris   Meaux

WINTER–SPRING: ITALY TO ENGLAND

SUMMER: ENGLAND TO FRANCE

PART ONE

CITY OF SPEARS

CHAPTER ONE

The screams echoing down the stone walls sounded as if souls were being cast into the devil's fire pit. Mercenaries hurled burning torches into buildings and cut down those who tried to escape. The town was aflame and its citizens had no chance of survival against the invaders who had descended from the mountains like a river of blood. The mixed force of German and Hungarian killers hurled aside the flimsy defences. Small knots of men tried to defend their homes but were overwhelmed. Some were hamstrung and forced to watch the violation and murder of their families. The horror made men beg for a quick death. None was given.

These humble townspeople had dared protest at their winter supplies being seized without payment by mercenaries returning to Milan through the mountain passes. As the column of troops made their slow progress home their commander had left men behind in Santa Marina. A lesson needed to be taught, so the slaughter began. The mercenaries took to the task as savagely as any battlefield barber-surgeon hacked off a gangrenous leg. No artisan or farmer could stand up to the might of these soldiers contracted by the Visconti, Lords of Milan, and there would be little chance for another mercenary force to oppose them. To the south of the town ran a broad river fed by the mountain snows. Cold, and in places deep, it formed a natural barrier to anyone attempting to relieve the stricken town. Men would have to traverse narrow mountain tracks into Santa Marina, and such an approach would be seen. No one would dare risk traversing goat paths by night.

Except Thomas Blackstone and a hundred of his handpicked men.

3

* * *

Five captains each had twenty men behind them; each group was led by a scout who trailed a hemp rope held by every man to guide them along different paths through the darkness. When daylight came they slept hidden among the boulders and scrub from which they could spy out where their route would take them that night. Step by stumbling step – tripping and cursing beneath their breath, ignoring the cuts and wounds to hands and legs – they finally reached the near bank of the river that skirted Santa Marina's southern edge on the third night, guided by the campfires of the thirty or more tents encamped between river and town. Beyond these mercenary billets the town still smouldered, and the dull crimson glow of deep-seated fires tinged the night sky. Shrieks still reverberated down the streets. There could be no more than about seventy men left in the town. The odds favoured Blackstone.

'Bollocks,' said John Jacob, Blackstone's English captain, as he lay in the grass peering across the river. 'Wet feet.'

'And arse,' said Sir Gilbert Killbere, who was at Blackstone's other shoulder. 'Sweet Jesus, Thomas, did you have to bring us this way? That's a hundred paces across if it's a yard.' He rolled onto his back and pulled his helmet free. The going had been hard enough up until now. He dragged a grubby paw over his grizzled stubble.

Blackstone lay watching for shadows moving between the tents. There were few to be seen and he guessed that most of the killers would be in the town. The campfires burned brightly enough to cast their glow across the river. His attack would be exposed to anyone who came out of a tent and looked the wrong way. No matter how quickly his lightly armed men could move, a boulder-strewn river would take time to cross.

'The river won't flood for months. It'll be waist-deep at worst. Where's Will?' he said.

There was a scuffle of movement behind them in the reeds that grew on the shore.

'Here,' answered Will Longdon. He belly-crawled closer and peered over the low bank. 'Ball-ache time, Sir Gilbert. That mountain water will be bloody cold,' he said.

'Aye, for short-arsed archers like you,' said the veteran knight.

'The fires will guide us in,' said Blackstone. 'Deploy your archers, Will. Three hundred yards downstream. That's the shallowest part and those who escape us will run for it come first light. Half the men there, half here. Snap shut like a wolf trap.'

He looked down the line of men who lay on the embankment. Gaunt from lack of sleep, dirt-engrained faces, fists clutching sword, axe or mace ready for the slaughter. The firelight's glow caught their eyes. They looked frightening enough to scare the scales off a devil's imp. Without another word Blackstone clambered to his feet and, as one, the men followed. He waded into the shallows, finding what footing he could among the stones underfoot. The near-darkness made the crossing even more difficult but Blackstone and his men had forded more dangerous rivers in the past – times when French crossbowmen had loosed a sky full of quarrels down onto them – but still they had gone on and beaten their enemy. No man who had ever made that journey would think this to be anything more than an inconvenient, cold soaking. They would warm soon enough when they started to kill.

The gentle sloshing of men's feet soon gave way to silence as they waded waist-deep into the river and the sound of their passage was hushed by the water gurgling over the shallows. Blackstone glanced left and right at the ragged line of men who followed him. Spear and sword were used to steady themselves against the current. Once he was satisfied that they were all across, he pushed his way through the grass and reeds that gave them the final few moments of flimsy cover.

The sixty fighting men slipped silently between the tents, quickly pulling back the flaps to see if any mercenaries slept. Blackstone and others ran on, ignoring the grunting cries of men who thought themselves safe in their blankets. The closer he got to the town, the louder the screams he heard.

Blackstone ran into the first square. Bodies lay strewn: smashed heads, slit stomachs, dark streams of blood glistening on the cobbled surface; men, dogs, women and children – all had been put to the sword. A dozen soldiers taunted a man with their spear points as he crawled on all fours, a mass of entrails billowing below him. They jabbed and cut at him, inflicting ever more pain and misery. They guzzled wine from clay pots and laughed at the man's agony. Left and right, narrow alleys echoed with similar cries. Torches flickered here and there, their light throwing night demons up against the walls as the Visconti men heaved women from doorways and butchered children who ran screaming for their mother's skirts.

One of the soldiers half turned as he heard the sound of pounding boots. Thinking they were men from the tents coming into town to enjoy the slaughter, he grinned, but his leer gave way to a look of puzzlement as he squinted into the uncertain light at the charging, silent men. By the time he realized they were not his own his warning scream was too late. Blackstone's men fell on them with a suddenness that gave no time for defence.

'Left!' Blackstone ordered, moving around the men's bodies, running towards the sound in one of the alleys. The wounded townsman rose to his knees, bloodied hands holding his entrails, blinded eyes lifted to a bearded giant of a man, as tall and broad as Blackstone, a man he would never see and who swiftly cut his throat in an act of mercy.

'Meulon!' Blackstone shouted. 'Five men! Over there!'

The throat-cutter looked quickly to where several men in another side street had turned towards them. The half-obscured killing in the square had alerted them but like their fallen comrades their moment of uncertainty lost them any advantage they might have had. They fumbled as they saw that the men who attacked looked more vicious than their own kind; fear made them falter. By the time they advanced against the intruders they were shoulder to shoulder in the narrow confines of the alleyway and no match for lunging spears followed by axe and sword blows.

Blackstone wore an open-faced bascinet and his men's clothing was little different from that of the men who had attacked and torched the town. Some wore greaves to protect their legs and pieces of armour on their shoulders and upper arms; all had a mail haubergeon beneath a jupon bearing Blackstone's coat of arms – a gauntleted fist grasping a sword blade like a crucifix – cinched at the waist with a belt from which hung a fighting axe and dagger.

Halfway down another narrow passage a woman clawed and kicked against her attacker as a second man relieved himself against a wall, a burning torch in his free hand. He looked over his shoulder as the darkness from the alleyways seemed to move. He turned and pushed the torch forward and then felt the warmth flood against his leg. By the time he had dropped the torch and fumbled for his sword John Jacob had swung his blade in an upward arc and taken the man between the legs. The pain from his slashed genitals made him bend double, grasping the bloody mess, and another of Blackstone's men swung his axe down across the man's exposed neck. Blackstone rammed the soldier attacking the woman, throwing him off balance, then smashed Wolf Sword's pommel into his snarling mouth. Bones and teeth cracked, the man's head snapped back, and Killbere's sword lunge took him in the throat. Blackstone's men moved forward; all ignored the half-naked woman.

'How many with us?' Blackstone shouted as he came into another small square where twenty or so men were using a horse trough to beat down a heavy chestnut door, its iron hinges the size of a war shield. More bodies lay scattered, blood smeared the walls and the square's flaming torches illuminated the carnage.

'Enough!' answered the veteran knight who pushed past Blackstone, eager to kill.

'Gilbert! Wait!' Blackstone shouted. There were only nine men with them as the others were fighting running battles in the streets behind them.

Those who assaulted the doorway turned and in a heartbeat saw that they were superior in numbers to their attackers.

Blackstone's feet slithered on blood-wet stone, and by the time he'd recovered his pace two or three men had gone past him after Killbere. Swords clashed; ill-timed strikes sparked against the cobbled street. Some of Blackstone's men picked up fallen shields and came shoulder to shoulder to form a wall against the erratic attack. Blackstone could see that Killbere was in danger on his exposed left flank. The older man would soon go down. Blackstone ran towards him, but three men lunged from a doorway where flames licked the wooden stairwell behind them. The force of the attack pushed him back against a wall as he parried their blows. He half turned, letting the first man's momentum carry him stumbling past into the wall. Blackstone reached down and pulled a fallen shield onto his exposed arm. A sudden flurry of blows from the other two men hammered down on the metal rim but he ran his weight against them and the look in their eyes told him what they saw: a snarling apparition as the shadows contorted his face. He beat them back. One turned and ran; the other sidestepped, swung and cut at him with his arm raised. Blackstone rammed Wolf Sword's hardened steel deep into the exposed armpit, then shouldered the dying man aside. The man on the ground rolled clear, abandoned his sword and ran into the safety of an alleyway.

Blackstone turned to try and catch sight of his friend but Killbere was obscured by two hulking frames: the two Norman spearmen, Meulon and Gaillard, who had brought their men from a side street and boxed in the now helpless mercenaries, seven of whom backed into a corner and threw down their weapons.

'Mercy!' they cried, some going down onto their knees.

Before Blackstone could stop his men they had cut into them. Two survivors cowered back, their arms raised in a futile attempt to shield themselves from the coming blows.

'Wait!' Blackstone ordered.

Killbere turned a blood-splattered face towards him. Blackstone knew his own would be similarly smeared by the fighting.

'Spare them?' asked Killbere incredulously.

Blackstone's men parted as he strode through them. 'For now. Get up,' he ordered. Over his mail one of the men's jupons bore the insignia of his lord, a viper swallowing a child.

'I know Visconti's blazon,' he said and turned to the second man, whose blood-splattered covering revealed a partial image. The cloth was so faded and worn that the image could barely be seen. A crown sat on what appeared to be a woman's head. But instead of arms there were outspread wings, and where there should have been legs were eagle's talons. For a moment the image of those talons clawed at his memory. He knew that coat of arms. He had seen it in the heat of battle.

The men trembled from the exertion and fear of the fighting. Their death was moments away and no man, even barbaric mercenaries such as they, wished to die unshriven.

Blackstone laid Wolf Sword's blade tip against the insignia. 'Who is this you serve?' he said.

The sharp point, although only laid gently on the cloth, caused it to tear. The man pushed himself back against the wall.

'Werner von Lienhard,' he answered.

Blackstone said nothing; his men were waiting for him to push the blade through the man's chest so they could be about their business of stripping whatever wealth could be found on the men they had killed.

Then he spoke. 'Your German lord. Where is he? North with Visconti's other troops? Or with the column?'

'Milan,' the man said, his voice croaking from lack of water.

'How many men in the column?' Blackstone asked.

The two men looked at each other and shrugged, shaking their heads with uncertainty.

'A few hundred, lord.'

'Their route home?' Blackstone said.

'Through Vani del Falco. We were to follow them.' The man went down on one knee and his companion quickly followed. 'Mercy, lord. We will do whatever you ask of us. Spare us and we will serve you.'

Killbere's sweat-streaked face glowered with impatience at Blackstone. 'We have more to kill, Thomas. We can't stand here all night talking to these vile bastards.'

Blackstone lowered his sword. 'I'll spare them,' he said. 'But bind their arms and keep them safe.'

'Bless you, lord! Bless you!' the men blurted.

Killbere fell in step beside Blackstone as he strode across the square. 'You've a reason for this?'

'It will be dawn soon. Those we didn't kill will have run for the river. Organize the men, Gilbert. Find as many of the townspeople as you can.'

'Thomas, you're thinking up more trouble for us. Sweet suffering Christ. We've bled enough. We've lost men tonight.'

Blackstone turned to face the man he respected more than any other. Killbere had fought for his King, had stepped in front of the English army and urged them to stand shoulder to shoulder against the French. And yet he had chosen to follow Blackstone into exile and serve him.

'Gilbert, trust me.'

The older man hesitated, and then nodded. Fatigue and exasperation were getting the better of him. He muttered something incoherently under his breath and turned away to do Blackstone's bidding.

CHAPTER TWO

A harvest of white-fletched arrows stood proud from the bodies of those men who had tried to escape. Will Longdon's archers had unleashed their shafts in a storm that would have brought terror and incomprehension to those attempting to evade Blackstone's swordsmen in the town. The bowmen could bring down their target at three hundred paces; at two hundred, illuminated by the campfires, the retreating men simply ran into a curtain of arrows that fell from the night sky. The archers held their positions until Blackstone sent word for them to cross the river into the field of slaughter and protect his flank in case of any possible counter-attack. Longdon's men gathered their bloodied arrows, their bodkin points easier to draw free from their victims' punctured flesh than any broadhead. Arrows were a valuable resource, and these yard-length shafts fashioned from ash, as thick as a man's middle finger and flighted with goose feathers, were difficult to replace in any quantity. Once the archers had gathered the arrows they scavenged food and drink from the campsite and then, content with their night's work, they settled into their defensive positions and began to straighten and repair the fletchings. A decent arrow would repay its fletcher's skill by killing more than once.

Dawn brought with it the acrid stench of spilled blood as the breeze tugged at Blackstone's banner that now fluttered from Santa Marina's bell-tower. Villagers emerged from cellars and hiding places; others returned cautiously from the wooded hills and caves that surrounded the town. By nones they were gathering their dead, laying out the corpses in one of the small piazzas where donkey carts stood ready for them to be loaded for burial.

11

'Thirty-two of Visconti's men dead in the field, another thirty-seven here,' reported Meulon to Blackstone.

'Most of the bastards took fright when they saw you running out of the darkness,' said Perinne, one of Blackstone's longest-serving Frenchmen. 'The sight of you and Gaillard could curdle a mother's milk.'

The weary men leaned against the church wall; some sat with their backs pressed against it, cleaning their weapons. They had found bread and cured meat and drank wine taken from the houses.

'How many did we lose?'

'Nine. Two won't see out the day.' John Jacob told him the names of each man lost in the night's fighting. Blackstone knew them all, though some of the names could not be given a face. No matter. They had fought as expected and would be buried in Santa Marina's graveyard with a prayer said over them by their priest.

'Where was the priest hiding?' Blackstone asked.

'The bell-tower,' said Gaillard.

'Should have had Jack Halfpenny bring down the black crow,' said Killbere and spat.

'Will's a better bowman,' said Gaillard.

'Jesus, it doesn't matter who, you Norman oaf! Any damned archer would have done!' said Killbere. 'Thomas, what's next? Back home for a hot bath, some mulled wine and a soft-breasted woman? I'm in need of sustenance.'

'Not yet, Gilbert. We've work still to do.' Blackstone raised his arm and gestured to the soldiers across the square. The men herded the survivors forward. They stood on steps and walls and gathered in cobbled alleyways. Looking down at their dead they waited in silent obedience, not knowing what demands would be placed upon them by this new group of mercenaries. The priest was brought forward.

He had spent thirty-eight of his sixty-one years being shunted from village to village. He was a troublesome priest who railed against levies imposed on the *villani* by bishops and landlords, but who, five years before, had found himself blessed by being sent to

Santa Marina. Bypassed by the pestilence, they believed that God had given them life for a reason other than to have their labour abused by low payment from those who bought their food. It had been the priest who had encouraged the villagers to make a stand and demand better payment. It had been he, he reasoned, who had brought this act of retribution down upon them.

'Your banner flies from my church,' he said to Blackstone. '*Défiant à la mort*. I know enough of the language to understand it. The next time these men attack they will tear down the church stone by stone to reach it. But I will defy them. In God's name and in the name of Sir Thomas Blackstone. These people of Santa Marina will offer prayers every day for you and your men.'

Killbere hawked and spat, then sighed, arms folded across his chest, his lack of interest plain for the priest to see.

'All of you,' the emboldened priest said.

'There will be no further attacks against you. My banner guarantees it,' said Blackstone.

'It's better than a thousand armed men protecting you,' said Killbere, wishing to add emphasis to Blackstone's reputation.

Blackstone turned the priest's shoulders so he could face the townspeople. 'How many people died here?'

The old priest shook his head. 'Three hundred, perhaps. I cannot yet say. We have not searched all the houses for their bodies.'

'And those who live?'

'The same number. I pray more.'

'Listen to me, old man! Those who attacked you were only part of a column that is making its way back to the safety of their own territory. These villagers know the mountains. Will they fight?'

Killbere and those within earshot looked momentarily startled, as did the priest, whose shock was more apparent. Townspeople or villagers did not fight armed men. No peasant ever raised a hand against professional soldiers. Words failed the old man; his jaw opened and closed, his eyes widened.

'Will they fight?' Blackstone said again. 'My men and your people can ambush those who caused the slaughter here. An ambush will not kill them all, but we'll take plunder, which will be shared with you. Horses, weapons, cloth, coin, supplies, carts and mules. It will provide some degree of recompense. We can isolate them and kill at least a third of them. As many of them as they slaughtered. You know these people. Speak to them. They say no, and my men and I return home within the hour.'

He pushed the recalcitrant priest forward until his sandalled feet stood in pools of blood that had seeped from the bodies laid in the square. He fumbled his words, uncertain how to rouse the townsmen to strike back – and then a lifetime of preaching sermons came to his aid. His voice carried across the square, urging the people to join Blackstone and his men and smite down those who had brought such grief and sorrow to their town.

'Thomas, you've a March hare for a brain at times. These peasants can barely wash their own arses,' said Killbere.

Blackstone looked at the men, who obviously shared Killbere's doubts. The priest had come to a faltering stop. No voices were raised to join the fight. But they had not moved away. They were waiting for something more.

'They know every hill and crooked mountain path; they can throw rocks and loosen boulders. They can snare hundreds of men in the ravines and fall on them with staves and pitchforks. We can kill even more, and if we do those bastards will not come this way again and these people will be free. They will be respected by those who would wish to treat them otherwise.'

Killbere stood closer to Blackstone. He raised his mouth to Blackstone's ear and in barely a whisper said, 'Thomas, you are no longer a stonemason living in a village under Lord Marldon's juris-diction. You are more than that. You always have been. You cannot give them false hope for such freedom. They have not fought the wars you have endured,' he said. He spoke the words in kindness.

Blackstone placed a hand on his friend's shoulder. 'I will always be that stonemason, Gilbert. I'm a common man and that can never change. I can give them the fury to fight.'

'How?' said Killbere.

Blackstone gestured to two of his men who stood guard at a doorway. They dragged out the two surviving mercenaries. Blackstone made his way into the square, the guards manhandling the frightened men to him.

'You have a chance to reclaim your lives!' he called out. 'We came here because we are paid men! *Condottieri!* And you have seen that we can inflict a greater slaughter on them even though there were fewer of us! Come with us today and I, Thomas Blackstone, will give you revenge! Seize it!'

He grabbed the two terrified men.

'Sir Thomas, you said you would spare us!' one of them begged.

'I did,' Blackstone answered. 'Now it's up to them.'

He threw them into the square where they stumbled and fell over the corpses. The men slipped in the gore, then stood like wounded beasts surrounded by a pack of wolves. One raised his hands in supplication. Nothing happened. No one moved. The two men carefully tried to back away, stepping over the bodies of women and children. It seemed they had a chance to escape. And then a villager's angry voice cried out. It was a shriek of agony so piercing it shocked the crows from the roofs. Another voice joined the cry. And another. A cacophony of pain rose up from the crowd. No words were spoken, no blasphemous curse, no threat issued. Just howling anguish that chilled the blood and held all those who were witness to it rigid with expectation.

Then someone in the crowd threw a stone that struck one of the mercenaries. He went down on one knee, but staggered to his feet again. Both men tried to retreat, but the howl of anguish became a roar of hate. Another came forward with a stave as a woman pushed her way through from the other side of the square brandishing a fire iron; within moments others surged across the corpses of their own loved ones towards the helpless men, who tried to run. Their cries for mercy were drowned. They fought with their fists, but went down beneath the flailing attack. Soon the men were dead, battered beyond recognition.

Thomas Blackstone had gifted the villagers with blood-lust.

* * *

The townspeople ran across tracks that were little more than scars in the hillside. They ran as if in a swarm – no single track confined them; instead they swamped the hill, picking their way along routes used since their ancestors first grazed goats high in the mountains.

Blackstone kept up as best he could, but these sure-footed peasants were used to steep climbs and twisting tracks and he and his men were forced to stop, gasping for breath, by the time they had reached two-thirds of the way up the steep incline.

The men's heaving lungs were raw from exertion, but if they stopped too long their limbs would seize and make the final push to the summit more difficult.

'They're like fleas on a dog's back,' said Perrine. 'We're going to lose sight of those up front. God knows what sort of fuck-up they'll make when they find the column.'

'He's right,' said Killbere. 'Thomas, you should take the archers and some of the others to get up there with them. I'm too slow, so I'll follow those breaking off to the right. It's less of a climb and they must be working their way around the hilltop to flank the column.'

The men hawked the phlegm from their lungs and throats, bent double to ease their pain.

'I'll take thirty men with Sir Gilbert,' said John Jacob. 'If you can get the higher ground with Will Longdon's lads, then you'll cause the Visconti's men pain and give those mad bastard peasants a chance not to get themselves slaughtered.'

'Virgin's tears,' said Longdon and then smiled. 'You men-at-arms always expect us archers to do the hard grind.'

'It's a mark of our esteem for your killing skills,' said Killbere sarcastically, ready to move on, determined to show the younger men that he was fit enough to lead the flanking assault.

'Pick your men,' said Blackstone and turned to run up the mountainside.

Longdon gritted his teeth, settled his war bow into its linen bag across his back, and followed his sworn lord and friend. The archers clambered after them as Killbere and Jacob pointed to others, gesturing that they should join them. Talking took too much air from their lungs; air sorely needed for this last leg-punishing run uphill.

It would have taken the better part of a day for a column of mounted men, laden with slow-moving carts and supplies, to reach the defile that ran between the curving passes. The men and women of Santa Marina took less than three hours using muscle-tearing shortcuts. Soaked in sweat, Blackstone pulled free his helm and pushed his head beneath a brook that tumbled cold water between the rocks.

'Shit!' said Jack Halfpenny as the archers sank to their haunches. 'I've barely the strength to spit, never mind draw my bow.'

'On your feet,' ordered Longdon. He was hurting as much as the next man, but needed to have the archers ready for whatever Blackstone asked of them. There was little chance of controlling those townsmen bent on revenge; there was no one to lead them or to take command. 'They've blood in their nostrils, Thomas. Like a crazed war horse. You'll not stop them now.'

'They'll cause damage all right,' said Blackstone. The townsmen were moving downhill across both sides of the road. They did so in silence; no cries echoed along the defile from them and the column had not yet looked up to see their approach. The column had split in two; its vanguard was already moving out of sight around the distant curve, but the main force lumbered along with the wagons. With most of the cavalry at the front they would be hard pressed to counter-attack.

To his right Blackstone saw armed men appear from around the shoulder of the hillside. It was Killbere and John Jacob with the others, who were now a thousand yards away and on the far side of the road. Blackstone had to get his archers onto the left flank along the contour line.

'There's more to do, lads,' he told them.

17

'There always is, Sir Thomas,' said Robert Thurgood. The archer was a newcomer, along with Jack Halfpenny. Neither was yet twenty years old. Lean and wiry, their size belied their ability to draw a powerful English war bow. Both men came from the same village and had tramped across France with the Prince of Wales during his great raid that ended in the slaughter at Poitiers. As children they had stood at the butts and watched the older boys practising archery. Of the two it was Halfpenny who first felt the strength of a bow in his hand and the squirming joy in his chest as the shaft loosed. Thurgood was more interested in shirking work on the lord's estate and was known for an aggressive temper that had seen him punished on more than one occasion. Jack Halfpenny showed his friend how an accomplished archer earned respect and attracted village girls at a county fair. When they presented themselves to Blackstone's captains, the scarred knight himself tested their skills and heard their testimony and Halfpenny convinced the legendary knight to allow them to join his company. Halfpenny had stood silently while Thurgood spoke of battle and killing; of how the English and Welsh archers were the greatest of men and the jewels in the King's crown. Then Halfpenny spoke of the body of the yew bow in his hand and the waxed cord pulled to his cheek, of how the power of the loosed arrow gave flight to a part of him that he could not explain, but that he knew it was a gift from God. Those words gave the two friends the opportunity to join the renowned Thomas Blackstone. Like all fighting men they were hungry for booty if it was to be had, but Killbere was as hard a taskmaster as any they had served before Blackstone. 'And best we get to it before Sir Gilbert thinks we're no better than women gossiping at a bathhouse,' Halfpenny gasped.

The track that followed the contour was level enough for Blackstone and his fifty-three men to cover the distance and, once the lumbering wagons below reached the turn in the road, the villagers began hurling rocks from the slopes. The sudden assault caused chaos. Men who had been slumped half-asleep in the saddle from the dreary pace of pack mules and ox-drawn wagons were flung into panic.

The archers formed their line, bent their bows and fixed their bow cords. Arrows were readied.

'Wait,' said Longdon to his bowmen, watching Blackstone gather the half-dozen men-at-arms, ready to plunge downhill into what would surely become a frantic fight for life as the men below realized they were cut off from the vanguard. Santa Marina men and women were forcing iron bars under unstable boulders; others put their weight behind rotting trees, tipping them into an increasing avalanche of debris onto the mercenaries.

Cries of alarm mingled with frantic commands from those trapped, whose horses bolted, slipped and went down as riders fought to control the panic. Footsoldiers rallied quickly and began to clamber uphill towards their attackers. Unarmed peasants would soon turn tail.

Blackstone watched as the mercenaries regrouped. They were trained to turn and attack an ambush. If the villagers held their ground then Killbere and the others would have the advantage as the Visconti men tried to fight uphill. The mercenaries' lumbering *carroccio* was an ox-drawn wagon bedecked with their commander's banners – a command post worth seizing – and which now made it difficult for those ambushed to make any quick response. The oxen that pulled the war wagon sat squarely in the middle of the road, helping to further divide the main force.

The *carroccio* swayed, unsettled by the frightened oxen as men ran past and the wagonmaster hauled on their reins. The breeze unfurled the flags enough for Blackstone to see the Visconti viper twist and curl, as if in that moment swallowing a child.

Blackstone wanted that banner. He raised Wolf Sword in command and heard Will Longdon bark his order to the archers.

'NOCK! DRAW! LOOSE!'

The creaking war bows, their waxed hemp drawn back, were as much a part of Blackstone as the muscles in his body. When the twanging bowstrings gave flight to the bodkin-tipped arrows,

Blackstone ran as if propelled from the straining heartwood of yew.

Shock reverberated through the mercenaries who had clambered up the opposite hill. They were about to wreak slaughter on defenceless peasants, uncertain why the armed men who stood yards behind had not advanced to engage them. And then they understood. Arrows thudded into them, the force of their impact driving through bodies cloaked in mail. Men fell and writhed, contorted in agony. Many were dead within seconds, gasping those last few breaths, choking on blood as heart and lungs were pierced. Those who survived the first arrow storm faltered, then turned back, seeking out the archers. Another terrifying hammer blow fell on them. And then Killbere advanced through the stunned villagers who had never before seen what violence archers could inflict.

Blackstone ran hard. Those on the track had realized they had been outflanked and turned to face the attack. Now they had armed men in front and behind and they could see that the archers were firing further down the trapped column as riders tried to make their escape. Blackstone saw Killbere and Jacob in the centre of an extended line as they hacked their way downhill. Meulon and Gaillard speared and jabbed as the townsmen and women scurried behind the killing, finishing off wounded men with knives.

The Visconti men were being overwhelmed by the ambush and the weight of townsmen who still hurled rocks and beat them with staves and scythes as they went down. The peasants raised their voices again: men shouted; others screamed. Blackstone and Perinne were confronted by four men who had formed a wall of shortened lances. Neither had a shield and, armed only with swords, they would not be able to get past the five-foot-long sharpened lances. Perinne bent and picked up a rock and threw it into one of the men's faces. He stumbled back. Blackstone followed the Frenchman's lead and hurled sharpened flints at the men, who seemed surprised that their ranks could be broken in such a manner. Trying to avoid the rocks they raised their shoulders and turned their heads, which made their lances waver and gave Blackstone a way forward. Once behind the lethal points he and Perinne cut down the panicked mercenaries.

Enemy riders spurred their mounts into the attack, and three of Blackstone's men went down, but the mercenaries could see there was no escape unless they made a break through the archers' storm and tried to rejoin the vanguard that lay beyond the boulder-strewn curve in the track. As one of the riders charged forward, Blackstone and Perinne grabbed a lance, bent their backs into it and took the horse deep in its chest. The rider fell amidst thrashing hooves and Perinne nimbly danced to one side and plunged his knife into the injured man's throat.

As the pitiful screams of horses began to fade along with those of dying men, one of the cavalrymen rode through the chaos and snatched the Visconti banner. Defeat would bring its own penalty from his master, but to salvage the flag from the hands of their enemy might purchase some grace. Blackstone picked up a fallen shield and fought through men disorientated by Killbere's advance. As he rammed home Wolf Sword's blade into the back of a man who had turned to face Jacob and the others, he knew it was too late to reach the battle flag. He watched the rider spur his horse into a gully and then found scrub that would hinder those on foot. The fluttering viper took flight.

Survivors turned to escape when they saw the flag carried away. They had to run the gauntlet of peasants and Blackstone's men, but some made it into the forest to find their way across the blocked road. Blackstone heard Killbere's voice demanding those who surrendered to be spared. Ransom would be paid, so they were worth more dead than alive. Reluctantly the peasants did as ordered. The fierceness of their own assault now diminished.

The tumult settled into the stillness that always followed a battle. This had been little more than a skirmish, but Blackstone's men had attacked a column of the enemy three times their own number and, with the help of those from Santa Marina, defeated

21

the main force of well-trained mercenaries. Close to three hundred enemy dead lay scattered on the road and hillsides and as the peasant women went among the corpses to strip them of clothing, belts and weapons, their men turned the great ox-carts around and loaded their plunder. Sacks of grain, cloth, saddles and bridles, bags of coin and armour. Some of the loose horses ran wildly on the slopes; others stood eating grass. All told, more than two hundred of them would be caught. Twenty-eight townsmen were dead, half again wounded. Blackstone had lost only three men.

A town had been saved; revenge inflicted; plunder taken. And those who had suffered the defeat would know it was Thomas Blackstone, *condottiere* of Florence, the outlawed English knight, veteran of Crécy and Poitiers, who had inflicted it upon them.

CHAPTER THREE

Blackstone and his men wintered in their own place of safety in the mountains, guardians to the rich city of Florence that lay to the south. Italian lords despised the foreigners among them, who fought with such savagery as to revolt any citizen of a civilized state. They were reviled, but also respected for what they could do. These men seemed impervious to harsh weather; they would fight through winter snows or the worst of summer heat. Fighting was their reason to live and reward for their efforts would come in this life rather than the next.

Santa Marina's misfortune had been caused by a broken treaty. A bad debt had needed to be collected by the Visconti in Milan, and although the city republics contracted their *condottieri* to work within the confines of their own territory, agreements were occasionally made between opposing forces to allow an enemy to cross another's territory. There were times when it suited opponents to agree a safe passage as those who gave the indemnity might one day require the same permission in return. Florence had agreed to let the Visconti recover money owed from an unpaid ransom. Conditions of payment were agreed, a fair price would be paid for any damage to crops or livestock along the way, but when the Visconti forces were returning home they had altered their route and the rearguard of the column, foraging for fresh supplies, entered Santa Marina, where they argued with the townspeople about the price of the food they wanted to buy. Knowing the viciousness of these men and that they had deviated from their journey home raised an alarm that brought Blackstone and his men to enforce the terms of agreement. However, by the time

Blackstone received the news it had already been too late for most
of those in the town.

Now the history of the battle he and his men had fought those
months before had been written by monks in their scriptorium, and
the Battle at Santa Marina had covered the townsmen with glory.
The deeds of Thomas Blackstone and his mixed force of English,
Welsh, French and Gascon, already known for their belligerence
in battle, were now inscribed on parchment, though in the writing
the fight became more about the courage of the townspeople and
less about the *condottieri*. Some rumours even blamed Blackstone
for instigating the violence. Such gossip eventually reached the
ears of his men.

'We are obliged to fight by our contract,' said John Jacob as
they sat around the fire in Blackstone's quarters. The Englishman's
strength and courage had been tested many times and never found
wanting. He had been honoured in the past by Blackstone choosing
him to carry out tasks that might deter lesser men. Years before he
had led men up a castle's sheer walls to help rescue Blackstone's
family. John Jacob's men soon learned to trust the stalwart fighter.

'Aye, there's a code of law and we'll be forfeit if we don't,'
Killbere agreed.

'If another bloody town gets into a shit pit, we'd do better to
negotiate a settlement with the bastards who started it. Why fight
to the death?' said Will Longdon. 'No harm in making a few florins
on the side. Lift a few sacks of grain, take some horses – they'd
only be nags, but it all adds up. And I'll wager there's always a
few men in the town with something worth having.'

'We were supposed to rescue the town, not ransom it,' said
Jacob.

Will Longdon poked the burning logs with a fire iron. 'I've a
right to my opinion, and if I see an opportunity where we can gain
without risking injury or death, then we should take it. Ransom
rather than kill. A man who surrenders forfeits all property.'

'Will's right,' said Blackstone.

'I am?' Longdon said, unable to keep the surprise from his voice.

'But not about Santa Marina,' Blackstone told him. 'There's no negotiating with Visconti's men. They'll never show or ask for quarter. You have to kill them first.'

Killbere sat with his feet outstretched towards the flames. His cloak was pulled around him and he wore a fur-lined velvet cap, said to have come from the land of the Russians. This cap had once graced the head of a merchant from Bologna who had thought to travel through the mountain passes to Lucca.

'We are paid well for what we do,' he said. It sounded as though his words were tinged with regret.

'Winter rations always make you discontented,' said Blackstone. 'Though we've eaten well these past few months. There's been plenty of forest boar.'

'Which has started to taste like old goat. I don't much care for these Italian winters, Thomas. The truth is I don't much care for any of it. The wine is weak and the peasant food barely enough to put flesh on a cur's ribs.'

'But the women here have the flesh,' said John Jacob. 'They give me warmth and comfort.'

The others murmured their agreement as Meulon bent to stack more logs on the fire. His great frame shielded the heat. 'Spring is here, Sir Gilbert. The sun already gives us warmth.'

'And you tell me you don't hunger for something other than that?' answered Killbere. 'You and Gaillard. I hear you talking about Normandy. Sweet Mother of God, we are all homesick and that's the truth.'

It was always difficult getting the men through winter. No matter how much raiding or defensive work they did, the season ground every man down.

'We are alive, fed and paid without question,' added Gaillard. The other captains nodded their agreement. How often did lords of their manor or even their sovereign neglect to pay their fighting men?

'Paid by clerks who keep a tally. As if we were shepherds,' said Killbere.

'Who leave us well alone,' answered Blackstone. 'The Florentines ask little of us. We choose who we raid. Who we fight and when. We give our loyalty; they give us money.'

'And there's always a bonus to be had somewhere along the way,' said Jacob. 'We captured seventy whores from that brothel in Monte di Castellano last summer.'

'And we give a firm hand when it is needed,' added Gaillard lamely.

The men laughed.

'Gaillard, your calloused palm would take the skin off a pig,' said Will Longdon.

'I didn't mean the whores. I meant keeping other bastards in check,' Gaillard retorted.

'We know that, my friend,' said Meulon, 'just that your mouth was a pace behind your brain.'

The conversation was running dry. They had complained enough.

'The day's routine awaits us,' said Jacob, getting to his feet.

Routine. The very word was a heavy burden, but one that the captains used to keep short-tempered soldiers out of trouble.

A sentry's cry echoed up from the streets below.

And then a dwarf on a white donkey rode into view.

CHAPTER FOUR

Thomas Blackstone hated cities. To him they were forests criss-crossed with animal tracks where violent beasts waited in shadows. An enemy was best confronted on open ground. He gazed down at the bristling towers clustered behind high walls from where he camped in the mountains north of the Italian city-state of Lucca. The air was heavily scented with wild jasmine and yellow-flowered gorse. The city shimmered in the unexpected heat of the spring haze.

Lucca. A place of enormous wealth. And treachery.

'It's a trap,' said John Jacob, sucking a piece of meadow grass, gazing down across the vast plain.

'They'll snare you, Thomas,' agreed Elfred, his master of archers, pointing towards the distant city. 'You'll be gutted and hung from them walls and we won't be there to stop it. Damned if you can't see it for what it is. Damned if you can't.'

Blackstone nodded. Elfred was getting old but he had seen enough killing and stupidity on the battlefield to smell a disaster lying in wait.

'Meulon?' Blackstone called to the Norman who had been at his side for these past twelve years, who stood like a sentinel, one foot resting on a boulder, his helmet and piecemeal armour at his feet. The bear of a man pulled his fingers through his beard. He had taken to tying its length with a leather cord. His mane of hair and heavy-set eyebrows, under which his dark eyes stared, made a startling image, enough – it sometimes seemed – to make an enemy falter. A fatal mistake. He turned to Blackstone.

'You have more enemies than wild bees on summer flowers,' he said. 'You cannot take men inside with you. And even you cannot

27

take a city's garrison single-handed.' He looked at the others who nodded their agreement.

Perinne, like others among them, had sworn loyalty to Blackstone years before when they fought in Normandy and killed the mercenary leader Saquet. He rubbed a hand across his scarred scalp. 'Do not go. It means nothing to refuse.' There was no shame in turning away from a place where a man could be snared like a rabbit.

Blackstone looked at the half-dozen men lounging outside the sweet-smelling cow byre where dung and spring grass gave a pungent, comforting odour. Seasons of Italian sun, wind and rain had burnished their skins and highlighted the scars that had been earned fighting at his side. Each was a trusted companion as well as a captain to his soldiers. Blackstone and his men had forged their way through the Alps less than two years before when he was exiled by the English Crown. The slaughter at Poitiers had been a great victory for the English, but Blackstone's blood-lust to slay the French King in revenge for the brutal killing of a friend had offended King Edward's son, the Prince of Wales. He and Blackstone were the same age – men whose destiny had been entwined in battle years before. They had had an uneasy relationship then: a King's son who owed his life to an archer. A common man knighted on the battlefield from whom an uncommon fighter had emerged. Sir Thomas Blackstone was the scourge of the French and anyone else who challenged him. However, his determination to kill King John had blinded Blackstone to the demands of his Prince, who then stripped him of everything – his towns in France and his stipend to feed and arm his men. And in the aftermath of the battle Blackstone's terrible, long-hidden secret had been revealed and had caused his wife and children to be taken from him.

These men served him; some had known him as both man and boy. Others had benefited from his loyalty and friendship. Each was expected to speak his mind. One of the men pushed himself deeper into the shade of an olive tree. As with the others, the hard life of serving Thomas Blackstone showed in Will Longdon's lean and sinewy body, but like any English archer, he had muscle packed across his back and shoulders. Few men could pull the 160 pounds' draw weight of a bow – and none had done it better than Blackstone himself, before his arm had been snapped by a German knight at Crécy. The soldiers of the greatest army in Christendom had been slain in their thousands. Crécy's slaughter was a memory etched on their souls as jagged as a battle sword's chipped edge.

'Pissing against the wind is a drunkard's foolishness,' said Longdon. 'A clear-thinking man would do no such thing. We've fought long and hard, and now you're about to drop your hose and bare yourself to a scabby bunch of bastards who have more money than bed lice in a mattress and servants aplenty to pick snot from their noses. Piss on them, aye, but do it upwind. We could burn down one of their gates and slit a few throats. That'd take their mind off you skulking through them alleyways. And I'll wager there'd be a few silver and gold rings to be had,' said the veteran archer who served as Elfred's centenar. A hundred English war bows were under his command, archers who had been drawn by the reputation of Sir Thomas Blackstone when he had contracted his men's fighting skills to Florence.

Near enough a thousand men stood at Blackstone's back now, straddling hilltop towns and fortifications that barred any incursion from the north and west of Florence. A protective barrier of sword, spear and bodkin-tipped, yard-long arrows, behind which Blackstone's men leaned their weight.

The centuries-old ruined tower that offered shelter for their horses also half concealed another soldier. Like the men in the grass it was hard to tell if he was a knight or a common soldier. Each wore a mail coif to protect head and shoulders over padded jerkins with Blackstone's armorial device – a symbol more potent than many a priest's admonition. Pieces of armour on thigh, arm and shoulder gave each of the seasoned fighters agility. Over the years they had taken prized weapons from those they killed, but their greatest weapon was the reputation that went before them.

'The dwarf is an omen!' Killbere said as he stepped from the ruin's shade. He dressed no differently from the others, despite his seniority and the fact that he was a knight of long standing, and had been Blackstone's sworn lord when the young Englishman had first gone to war. Killbere's beard had silken threads of white; his hair, cut close to his scalp, was peppered with grey. He was a ferocious fighter well able to rally men to hurl themselves against an enemy of greater strength. 'Superstition goes hand in hand with the mystery of Christ and his angels.' He grinned at the lounging men and then turned his gaze to where the saddled donkey stood tethered in the olive grove. Sitting patiently like a child, but with an old man's face, the dwarf was dressed in a fine cloth tunic with bone buttons. A soft velvet cap sat jauntily on the misshapen head, which seemed too big for his stunted body, and a pair of fine, hand-made boots graced the feet now dangling from the rock where he sat. Dwarfs were common enough in rich households: they seemed to have a calming effect on horses, and men of wealth and status often had an entourage of these small men dressed in fine livery.

'Dwarfs can be bad luck as well,' said Elfred, and spat. 'Devil's imps.'

'Good luck, too, though, 'specially when he serves a priest,' countered Will Longdon. 'And a rich one at that.'

'You'd as soon lie in a graveyard with a whore than believe in the power of the devil,' said Perinne.

'Only if it were a priest's whore for good luck!' Longdon answered. 'And I'd rattle her bones enough to wake the dead!'

The men laughed, but they all glanced uncertainly towards the dwarf, who seemed unconcerned at their deliberations. He had delivered his message from his master – the Florentine priest Niccolò Torellini, who served the Bardi banking family – and what these men did was of no concern to him. He waited, as would any servant, out of earshot and disinterested, for Sir Thomas Blackstone's answer.

'Father Torellini saved my family before Poitiers. He secured them sanctuary with the Pope at Avignon,' Blackstone told them, glancing at John Jacob, who had accompanied Blackstone's wife Christiana and the children on that ill-fated journey and who had slit the throat of the man who had raped her.

'He did,' John Jacob agreed. 'And like Sir Thomas says, we've sold our sword to his master and been paid well. We're of great value to them here.' He hesitated. 'Still,' he said, looking at Blackstone, 'it must strike you as odd that a priest from Florence is now hiding in a church in Lucca, an enemy city. And sends for you.'

'His own master, Bardi of Florence, pays our contract. What cause is there for him to betray me now?' asked Blackstone.

'Unless someone's made him a better offer for your head,' said Killbere. 'These are different than the lords we served in England or France,' he added, nodding acknowledgement towards the Frenchmen among Blackstone's command, 'they at least swore fealty and held a sword in anger. These rich cities buy their protection from us, and others like us, and we do the killing and the dying. Money-men should never be trusted, Thomas. They serve a different god from the rest of us.'

Killbere stood in the middle of the men and levelled his gaze on the younger man. He placed a hand on his shoulder in friendship and concern. 'You're an outlaw, Thomas. There's many a man who believes that killing you would please the Prince of Wales. Italians have dealings with the Kings of Europe. If it were up to me I'd have the dwarf on a spit and burn the truth out of him. We'd soon see where the truth lies. Devil or priest's messenger, you'd soon know.'

Blackstone looked again at Lucca's towers, looming like a barrel of spears within the city's walls, each one proclaiming its owner's power. Rich and wealthy families built their towers on a piazza, with a house attached and another tower on another corner, securing their safety. Streets were controlled by rival gangs who made their allegiances to wealthy households, wriggling loyalties that slithered through dark alleys where enemies plunged knife and sword into unwary victims. But the Lucchese were known for buying off their enemies and allowing themselves to be protected by stronger city republics. They were shielded by a powerful allegiance with Pisa and Milan, enemies of Florence. Capture Thomas Blackstone and a vital blow would be struck against the Florentines.

Blackstone was as superstitious as the next man. There was a god to be feared, but he wore a silver talisman of a pagan Celtic goddess around his neck. The medallion of Arianrhod had been pressed into his bloodied hands years before by a mortally wounded Welsh archer during the street fighting in Caen – and she had protected him ever since.

'The dwarf is an omen,' warned Gaillard.

Blackstone considered the men's trepidation. He smiled. 'Like the Valley of Lost Souls,' he said to them.

'Oh, blood of Christ, Thomas,' groaned Killbere.

The others uttered no comment but each made a small gesture of embarrassment or winced at the memory that Blackstone had evoked.

When Blackstone had brought his men across the Alps and down into Tuscany they had made camp in the scented hills on their approach to Florence. As darkness fell a flickering light appeared, soon joined by a dozen more, and then thirty and then a hundred. They appeared from bush and tree, floating towards the men. Struck with a terror of the supernatural, the men had watched in silent awe. Legend said that the valley had once been a place of great slaughter and was haunted by a thousand souls who had died without the comfort of sacrament or priest. Dispossessed, they searched for unsuspecting travellers to become their host. Blackstone had felt the chilled blade of fear cut down his spine as the flickering lights swarmed: *revenants*, the walking dead, unshriven ghosts desperate to take over a man's body and to be reanimated by demons. Men drew in breath and unsheathed swords, making the sign of the cross as they prepared to defend themselves against the malevolent spirits. Blackstone and his company were in a strange land and he knew that if unknown curses and myths were to halt them at every turn they would be no use as fighting men. As his men held back Blackstone stepped into the blinking lights and let them swirl about him. Men swore and prayed in the same breath and begged him to turn back. Blackstone reached out a hand into the pulsating light. He watched one settle and then closed his fist.

A flaming torch revealed a small fly crushed in his hand. No blood or blister showed, no wound or incision, no entry into his body to take over his soul. They soon learnt that they were nothing more than fireflies and, as everyone knew, fireflies were simply the souls of unbaptized children seized by angels. The men's embarrassment knew no bounds until drink and fighting had cleansed them of it.

If the dwarf had not been sent by sorcerer or enemy to lure him into the city of towers, then Father Niccolò Torellini needed his help.

Killbere knew the argument was lost. 'At least let me come with you. I speak this Tuscan tongue better than most.'

'You have as much skill with the language as Will Longdon who curses in it fluently,' Blackstone answered. 'I'll go alone and the rest of you will wait in the hills for two days and then go back to the men. One way or another you will know what happens.' He glanced towards the dwarf. 'Hold him. If it is a trap, pay him a gold florin and let him go.'

'What?' said John Jacob. 'Free the dwarf with a reward if you're taken?'

Killbere smiled. He knew how Blackstone thought. 'And then we follow him and kill the sons of whores who laid the trap.'

CHAPTER FIVE

There were several gates into the city from which the garrison soldiers on the high walls could clearly see the approach roads across the open plain that might bring an enemy. Danger lay outside the walls. Money had bought safety for the Lucchese. A law had long since been passed that stopped any of the ambitious men in the city from building their fortress-like villas within six miles of the city. The oligarchs were allowed their tower houses within and their villas in the hills. No private army could ever be gathered close to Lucca, which blunted any ambitious merchants' power-hungry desires.

Soon after dawn threw its light across the great plain, Blackstone waited with Killbere and Meulon in the foothills, identifying which gate might offer him the best chance of entering the city. Their breath plumed in the chilled air: there had been a frost, but it would soon melt in the warmth of the early spring sunshine.

'Avoid the south-east port, Thomas,' Killbere said as Blackstone pulled a coarse cloth shirt over his head. 'That's the road that leads to Florence. They'll have extra eyes there. Go further around the walls to the Gate of the Foreigners. There will be many wishing to enter the city. The Duomo is close by. It's a good landmark from which to get your bearings.'

He saw where Killbere pointed. A steady stream of farmers was already using the narrow road to trundle their produce into the city. And they seemed to be moving through the high gates without being stopped. From where they stood they could see three of the approaches into Lucca. Traffic was moving slowly on the other two roads where small overladen carts of caged livestock, escorted by men and women bearing baskets of produce, were backed up as sentries at the gate impeded their advance.

'They may have extra eyes, Gilbert, but they're not searching too closely. It's the other ports into the city they're checking. If it is a trap they're expecting me to avoid the road from Florence. I'll go in there.'

Elfred and Will Longdon had relieved a peasant farmer of his heavy bundle of firewood, paying him more than its worth. Despite its weight and size Blackstone could have carried twice as much with ease, but as he got closer to the imposing towers that flanked the high gates, he bent his back and altered his stride to a shuffle.

From beneath his cowl he glanced furtively left and right. The huddle of people jostling towards the entrance to the city, and their constant chatter and shouts as they greeted each other and barracked the soldiers to let them through, all helped to conceal the stooping figure carrying the oversized load of wood. There were others with similar loads: fuel to feed the cooking fires and furnaces of the smelting guilds. Others trundled handcarts laden with caged ducks and chickens, pitted wheels rumbling over the uneven road, jostling for a place as pig herders swore and flicked their grunting charges with switches. The walls were over thirty feet high, built of cut sandstone, deep and unyielding, with blocks of limestone spaced horizontally between them that accentuated the curve of the arch. The watchtowers were higher still. A massive double archway, itself twenty feet or more in height, held the double gates and portcullis. If an army made an assault, Blackstone thought, it would take more siege engines than he had heard of in Italy to smash through. He saw crossbowmen on the walls, but their weapons were held casually, without intent. They were garrison soldiers, unused to close-quarter battle. The only weapon he carried was a knife in his waistband that would be lethal in his hands, but the confines of the city's passageways meant that garrison troops could overpower and kill him if they were numerous enough.

35

At the entrance of Porta San Gervasio he reached the narrow footbridge that spanned the canal: it was only a few feet wide. He felt the worn timbers of the lowered drawbridge beneath his feet. This was the most dangerous moment. Farmers were funnelling into the archway, pressed shoulder to shoulder, close to the sentries on either side. The stone-lined stream was as ancient as some of the city's Roman walls and men and women were plunging folds of material into the water, tanning the fabrics. Two of the women tanners began to argue, their voices pitched high in anger as one grabbed yards of fabric from another, and in the tussle a length of cloth fell into the stream. No sooner had one of the women reached for it than she slipped and the situation quickly escalated; a man pulled the second woman away and slapped her hard. The queue of farmers shuffled almost to a halt as two of the sentries strode towards them to restore order. Blackstone edged forward, taking advantage of the distraction. A woman in front of him struggled with a heavy hand basket as she was jostled. She cursed to another, but Blackstone quickly lifted the basket and muttered an offer to help. His back was so bent his face barely reached her chest; the cowl kept his scarred face from view. By the time she had muttered her thanks and begun a diatribe against the amount of time it took to get into the city these days, the line had quickly passed under the raised portcullis. The sentries looked past him, their eyes scanning the crowd, uninterested in a peasant bent double, or his woman companion who chattered like a caged bird.

The fetid narrow *chiassi* swallowed the crowds, each alley filtering the peasants away to the different piazzas where they would set up their stalls. Blackstone straightened his back. The sky was pierced by tower after tower, a forest of neatly cut stone blocks of granite and limestone, built up with narrow clay bricks that soared skywards. Some had covered balconies at their summit; most had four- or five-storey houses attached to them. He admired the thinking behind them, for there were no outside stairs from which to gain access. A perfect defence, unless an enemy managed to hurl a torch through one of the first-floor windows.

The dwarf had scratched an outline of the ancient city in the dirt. No street bore a name, only the churches, built by the wealthy, who claimed a piazza as their own territory and would then build a private chapel across from their homes, only a few paces away, so they could walk quickly into its sanctuary without fear of assault from rival gangs that supported other families. Blackstone was quickly lost. He cursed to himself. He needed the sky and the touch of breeze on his face to find his way.

Follow your nose, the dwarf had instructed him. Beyond where the iron pots are made, he was to go past the nearest church, then there would be the stench of leather workers; the guildsman's church would be at his right shoulder, another piazza lay to the east, with the place he sought pressed against the north wall. The figure of Christ would beckon him. That was where Father Torellini waited.

The hard-baked dirt street led to a darkened passage. He eased the rope supports from his shoulders, dropped the bundle and stepped clear. Glancing down through the funnels of shadows, he saw light penetrating onto small piazzas, some of them barely thirty feet wide. A darkened doorway led into a courtyard, from which he heard voices tumbling from the rooms above. And something else – a steady rhythmic sound that he realized could be heard throughout the alleyways and streets. He looked up at open windows that allowed what little air there was to pass through the buildings. The heat and stench of thousands of people crowded into a walled city, woodsmoke from the fires, the foulness of open drains and the acrid smell of small foundries clung like a miasma to the confined walls. The rhythms he heard fought against themselves like a confused sea of sound. He remembered Torellini had told him there were more than three thousand looms in the city, so great was its world trade in silk. No wonder the Lucchese could buy their way out of conflict. That was what he heard. Looms: the heartbeat of the city. It seemed that every floor of every house released the sound of its promise of wealth. Blackstone felt a breeze waft down an alleyway to his right. That's where the foundry smell came from.

Instinct guided him. Where each *chiasso* broadened into a square, groups of armed men lounged idly. Some sat with their backs against the wall, others leaned, talked, gestured, argued or laughed. Some taunted others across the piazza, trading insults. But the violence was confined to verbal abuse. These were family gangs, holding their own territory. Blackstone avoided them all, sometimes retracing his steps, finding another passageway, leaving behind another cacophony of metal being beaten into pots. The city reminded him of Paris, though Lucca, as far as he could see, had no wide streets; however, guildsmen were belligerent no matter in what bramble patch of a city a man found himself. Trespass and you would feel their resentment at the end of a club or knife.

A dancing bear, chained by a ring through its nose, reared up as a crowd quickly stepped back, amazed at the size of the beast. Coins tinkled in appreciation, and acrobats turned somersaults in the air. A flurry of activity made him press his back into an alcove. A dozen armed young men full of bravado were pushing people aside as they made their way towards him. Was this the trap or a belligerent personal feud between gangs to be settled? There was no point in risking discovery, so he pushed open the door at his back. Voices and laughter echoed from walls that held sconces lighting the steps leading below. Blackstone quickly closed the door and followed the passage downwards. He turned into a basement with an arched roof and sturdy pillars that supported it. Washed-out images on the walls proved to be ancient frescoes of men and women. Fragrant oils clung to the Roman bricks so neatly laid that his stonemason's eye recognized the work of a master builder centuries earlier. Figures moved in the half-light; a splash of water, a woman's squeal and a man's voice bellowing with laughter. The air was heavy and he realized why the fragrance was so strong – it was to diffuse the heavy smell of human sweat. Something touched his arm, making him turn quickly. A woman gazed up at him. She wore a fine silk drape over one shoulder, her breasts exposed. They pressed against him.

'This place welcomes every man who can pay, but there are those present who would object to a man of low class being here. Men of more affluence usually honour us.'

She had spoken quietly, as if not wishing others in the shadows to hear, or notice the roughly dressed man who had entered the brothel.

Blackstone listened for any intrusion from the street, but the gang of malcontents had passed by. 'Where am I?' he asked the woman.

She raised an eyebrow and glanced to where a middle-aged man lay on a narrow bed with a woman straddling him. The dim light caught the sheen of sweat on his balding head and the dewdrop of sweat from her breasts.

'I know what this place is, but where am I in the city?' he said.

'A stranger? Up to no good? Are you a cut-purse or do you have business on a farm stall?' she answered, taking a step back, her voice taunting him.

She faltered at Blackstone's silence; his gaze frightened her. She pulled the drape across her breasts, holding it at her throat. 'You are beneath the walls of the ancient city.'

'How close am I to the church that shows Christ with the angels?'

She almost sneered. 'You're a pilgrim? And you end up in here? We can show you paradise, stranger.'

Blackstone snatched her arm and pulled her to him; the silk fell noiselessly to the floor. She was close enough now to see his scarred face. 'Where is it?' he whispered. Oil lamps were being lit, the cellar becoming brighter and the shadows more threatening as others realized there was an intruder.

She gave in quickly, her arrogance crushed by fear. 'The Church of San Frediano is the only one... I think...' she muttered.

'Where?'

She seemed confused. Men of God, or those who sought His comfort in a church, were usually more meek than threatening. 'Follow the streets opposite... to the right... and then you will see the city walls... then keep going to your left. It's there.'

He released his grip; she stepped back fearfully and bent to pick up the silk drape. When she raised her head he was gone.

Blackstone sensed he was nearing the church that gave sanctuary to the priest. He used the shadows and alleys like an animal wary of danger that could leap out at any corner but he was unaware of the black-cloaked figure who had followed him since he entered the city. The cloaked man's fist rested on his sword's hilt.

As the sun arced its way across the clay-tiled roofs and its rays sought out the darkened squares, Blackstone stepped into the brilliance of a broad piazza. Stallholders clung to its edges as crowds jostled to buy food from their tables. Men and women dressed in fine clothes of colourful silk, some escorted by two or three personal bodyguards, strolled along another street that bisected the square. Beggars came and went among the crowds. Occasionally coins were dropped into the outstretched palm of one sprawled in a doorway. Charity was a fine thing. The rich only paid beggars so that their own sins in this life could be accounted for by the poor in the next. Those Lucchese with money gazed at the shops cut into the walls, the T-shaped narrow doors, flanked on each side by an unglazed window displaying their wares. A shopkeeper stood back in the cool shadows, hands clasped in gratitude as one of the wealthy citizens entered the doorway.

Blackstone stayed in the narrow alley at the corner of the piazza, taking in all that went on before him. Nothing seemed out of place, but it was the perfect ambush site. Across the piazza the gleaming white limestone church stood squarely before him. Above its pillared entrance was a magnificent mosaic façade, rich in hues of gold and blue, that spanned the upper width of the church. It showed the Ascension of Christ flanked by two angels and beneath his feet the twelve disciples.

It was two hundred arrow-long paces to the church's door.

He waited.

A man at one of the stalls bent down to lift a copper pot. With barely a tilt of his head his eyes looked in Blackstone's direction.

When he straightened, his gaze went past the woman customer extending her hand with money.

Blackstone glanced left.

Two men stood examining pockmarked pewter plates. But their faces had turned away the moment their glances met. Hands reached beneath cloaks. These were the professionals. They would have paid others less able to strike first.

It was a trap. It needed no prediction from his friends. He expected it.

Three, then. Were there more?

Christ's eyes gazed down with benevolence. Reach out and ascend to the glory of my Father's house, he seemed to implore.

Blackstone kissed the silver goddess.

If there were more assassins waiting he could not identify them.

Cut a clear path through the crowd, he told himself. Halfway, sidestep to the right; the copper-pot stallholder was the closest.

Kill him first.

The others would rush him. The crowd would scatter. Chaos. Go down on one knee and strike upwards. Gut the second man low. Hamstring the third. Panic would do the rest.

Blackstone had to reach the Church of San Frediano and its sanctuary.

He strode into the piazza and felt the sun's warmth. The glare from the pale stonework creased his eyes. He gripped his knife, holding it down at his side.

There were five assassins waiting to kill him.

CHAPTER SIX

Blackstone eased himself through the milling crowd, edging his shoulder towards the stallholders on the right-hand side of the piazza. The heavy church door was open to allow the citizens of Lucca access to pray. The darkness that lay within might conceal those wishing to cause him harm, but it was more likely that the killers would ply their trade outside the sacred place.

Out of the corner of his eye he saw the furthest two men ease their way into the crowd from his left-hand side, and the man who had pretended to sell the copper pot was already less than six paces away, his eyes intent upon his victim. That alone marked him as an amateur, unused to killing with stealth. A common thug hired to do a butcher's work.

The other two assassins still had to negotiate the shuffling crowds, but Blackstone knew the moment he killed the first man they would rush him – but that too would aid him. They would be forced to push people aside and be hindered by them – and he would kill them easily.

The first man bared his teeth, his body turned slightly, left shoulder forward, ready to strike upwards with the knife held low in his right hand. Blackstone turned his back on the other two men and pushed himself into his attacker. His left hand grasped the man's wrist in a crushing grip before he could strike, and in the instant before he plunged his knife into the man's ribs, piercing lungs and heart, he saw his eyes widen in surprise that his attack had been foiled and in pain as the bones in his hands cracked from the strength of the man he had come to kill. A stonemason's grip.

Blackstone embraced the body, letting the dying man slip onto the ground, and then twisted to meet the rush of the attack coming from behind him. For a few moments there was no reaction from the crowd: a man had fallen; another eased him to the ground. They stepped around Blackstone and the dead man; it was only when the other two killers began to push their way through that people called out in alarm and warning. By then Blackstone was on one knee, letting the first man stumble over him as if caught by undergrowth. Blackstone lunged, slashing the man's hamstring; he crumpled to the ground screaming in agony as he dropped his weapon and clutched at the wounded leg. His shrieks were quickly silenced as Blackstone's knife went into the hollow of his throat.

Now those immediately around Blackstone realized that there was killing being done. Cries and shouts of panic spread across the square as people milled, not knowing which way to turn to escape. Blackstone was already pulling a woman aside as the second man swept down his sword. He had used both hands, a high guard above his right shoulder, but the momentum that carried him forward made his strike clumsy. Blackstone sidestepped, his knife now in his left hand, and, as the man passed him less than an arm's length away, let his blade and the man's own momentum do their work. The man's throat was cut, blood spurted; he dropped the sword and grasped the pulsing wound as he staggered and fell and then squirmed, gurgling, gazing upwards, seeing the vision of Christ beckoning him.

The chaos spread like the plague. Blackstone moved towards the church. He made no attempt to run, as he had no desire to alert any witnesses to his escape. He suddenly caught a glimpse of a gaunt-faced man who swirled past him feet away – his black cape billowing with an embroidered blazon on its back that looked like the symbol of an axe with a pointed shaft. He checked his stride, turned and saw the cloaked man wield his sword. Beyond him, a burly man, leather apron pulled tight across his broad body and the look of a blacksmith about him: thickset bare forearms; face pitted with soot; a gnarled hand clutching a falchion raised

43

ready to strike, its short, curved cutting blade a weapon to hack and maim. He was less than six paces away and, had the swirl of the cape not caught his eye, Blackstone's back would have been towards the assailant.

The gaunt man braced, drew back his sword on the barrel-chested man. It was a simple killing. The blade rammed into the man from below his heart, the sudden agony throwing back his head, eyes wide, falchion clattering onto the paved square. Blackstone's mystery saviour quickly withdrew his blade, turned to Blackstone. His eyes darted over Blackstone's shoulder in warning. Blackstone spun, instinctively sidestepped and saw the fifth assassin. He was little more than a youth and fear and desperation creased his face. His clothes were threadbare; the long-bladed knife he wielded might have been fine for slicing meat for the stew pot, but useless in a struggle. Then Blackstone fell heavily, his feet slipping in blood. The boy slashed down, yelling to give himself courage as Blackstone twisted away.

The black cloak smothered his vision as the Samaritan stepped over him. Blackstone saw the blade strike the boy, heard a pitiful whimper of pain that was a final exhalation of breath.

Blackstone stood and faced the stranger who had saved his life. The man's wiry frame belied his strength and agility. Gaunt cheekbones projected below brown eyes of a piercing intensity. Whoever this man was he was older than Blackstone, closer in age to Killbere. Fighters who had angels at their back had either the devil or God in their hearts.

'Hurry,' the man said and turned for the church.

The small door into the church gave way to a cavernous, vaulted interior. The piazza's glaring heat and the blood that flooded across the pale stones were banished. The cool embrace of the ancient church suddenly chilled Blackstone. Stools and benches were few. Prayer here meant that most worshippers would feel the hardness of the flagstones on their knees. Penance was delivered with ease. The gloom gave way to darkness in the side chapels from which the altar's muted light beckoned. The church was empty except for an elderly woman who knelt in prayer. When she heard the scuff of boots and the closing of the door, she turned, saw the two men, made the sign of the cross and, pulling her shawl further over her face, shuffled away, leaving Blackstone and his Samaritan alone.

Blackstone's saviour unclipped his scabbard and prostrated himself full length before the altar. Blackstone could now clearly see the emblem blazoned on the cloak, but still did not recognize the woven double-bladed axe with its pointed shaft. He waited, still wary, letting his eyes adjust. From slashing assault to a house of sanctuary was little more than a dozen paces. Was anyone waiting in the shadows, knife in hand, willing to risk excommunication for the mortal sin of murder in a church?

The black-cloaked swordsman got to his feet and stepped away towards a marble font. He waited, scabbard point to the floor, hands resting on the pommel of his sword, like a tomb's guardian. His eyes, though, stayed on Blackstone.

No sound of movement reached Blackstone. He wiped the blood from his hands across his tunic; then he took a dozen paces from the entrance where he knelt and crossed himself, glancing at the silent Samaritan. He would not prostrate himself – to kneel before the unseen God was humility enough when assassins lurked. From the darkness someone whispered his name. Blackstone turned and saw the familiar figure of Father Niccolò Torellini emerge from a side chapel beyond the pillars.

Torellini was the proof that Fate had entwined an English King, a French lord and an Italian priest with influence. Blackstone had learnt, years after the event, that this had been the same man of God who had cradled his mutilated body on the field at Crécy. After the battle Blackstone had been given into the care of Jean de Harcourt and trained as a man-at-arms, and then he and his family had been hunted by mercenaries led by Gilles de Marcy – the Savage Priest. It was Torellini who had given Blackstone's family safe passage to the Pope at Avignon, and in return Blackstone accepted the task of warning the Prince of Wales that he and his exhausted army would stand alone against the might of the French King. Much good it did the French. Sir Gilbert Killbere, Elfred, Will Longdon and the others had stood at Blackstone's shoulder and, despite the odds, defeated the French at Poitiers.

'Thomas,' the old man whispered again, a sigh of both gratitude and relief. He barely came up to Blackstone's chest, but he took the Englishman's arms and Blackstone lowered his scarred face to be kissed on each cheek.

'I knew you would come,' he said, and led Blackstone further into the cool shadows. The silent guardian followed twenty paces behind.

Father Torellini eased Blackstone onto a bench.

'Here, sit here, Thomas. I prayed for your safety.' His eyes settled on the silver image of the figure with outstretched arms that hung around Blackstone's neck. 'You still pray to a pagan goddess,' he said, though not as a criticism.

Blackstone smiled. 'I see her as one of God's angels.'

'Good answer. One day I will believe you,' said Torellini and waited for Blackstone's inevitable question.

Blackstone half turned so he could watch the swordsman. The man remained expressionless, but Blackstone's instinct told him that if a shadow moved or a breath of air touched his cheek, the sword would be in his hand.

'Who is he?' Blackstone asked.

'His name is Fratello Stefano Caprini. He is here to ensure that you live long enough to embrace your destiny.'

'He saved my life. There were two assassins I hadn't seen. He's your man? A soldier of Florence?'

'He's God's man. A warrior of the Lord. You saw his coat of arms?'

'The axe? Yes,' Blackstone answered, though there was a nagging memory that he had seen it before.

'It is not an axe, Thomas. It is the Tau. A symbol of the letter that was the first word of Christ. He is one of the Cavalieri del Tau.

A military order of hospitallers. These *fratelli* care for pilgrims and the sick.'

'And outlawed Englishmen,' Blackstone said. Then he remembered a time when he and his men had come across a dead Franciscan monk found after a routiers' raid, butchered and staked to a tree. Around his ankle was a piece of twisted hemp that bore a small wooden cross similar in design. It had been of no significance to the killers, but Blackstone had noticed it when they buried him. He nodded in thanks to the swordsman, but got no response.

'Why did you send for me?' asked Blackstone.

CHAPTER SEVEN

Samuel Cracknell lay hidden in a room of a merchant's house in Lucca. He had sailed from England several weeks earlier, bound for Genoa, from where he would be given safe passage to Florence. There he was to seek out Father Torellini who served the Italian banker, Rodolfo Bardi, friend and lender to the English Crown. The priest would ensure that word reached Sir Thomas Blackstone and Sergeant-at-arms Cracknell would then deliver the message whose wax seal bore the arms of Edward, King of England.

The ship, an unwieldy cog, almost foundered, but the ship's master saved his vessel, only to lose it when two enemy Pisan ships appeared. The feud between Pisa, Florence and Genoa was an ongoing conflict and although Genoa traded with the world, Pisa ruled the southern waters of the Tyrrhenian Sea. Cracknell had thrown his cloak and tunic, bearing the insignia of a messenger from the court of Edward III, King of England, into the churning sea when the ship was seized west of Genoa. By a miracle his captors did not find the folded parchment he carried or the gold coin sewn into a hem. Cracknell lied to save his life, telling them he was a servant to an English wool merchant, travelling to Genoa to secure a contract and that his letters of authority had been lost in the storm. He bore no emblem or ring of office; he displayed no obvious signs of wealth; he was worth no ransom. It was a grave risk, but one that had to be taken. Had he admitted his true status they would have tortured him and discovered that he carried a letter for the English *condottiere* contracted by Florence who secured the mountain roads between Florence and Pisa. He risked death because he was worthless to them, unless they sold him into slavery. Every minute he still drew breath would offer him a chance to escape.

The ship's master knew his identity and could have traded the secret for his own safety, but when his captors decided Cracknell was worthless – and moments before they pulled a knife across his throat – the seaman cursed the sons of whores who lived like sea lice feasting on unarmed merchantmen and head-butted the nearest Pisan guard. It cost him his life but it gave Cracknell the chance he needed. He leapt overboard and made good his escape. The crossbow bolt that struck his shoulder was a lucky shot; falling at the end of its trajectory and weakened by the distance, it penetrated his shoulder muscle but lacked the force to shatter bones and sever vital arteries. Desperation drove him inland, where finally his wounds and exhaustion left him crumpled by the roadside.

The vagaries of fate might have left him to die where carrion crows would soon feed on him, but he was found by devout Christians, servants of a Lucchese merchant travelling home, who dressed his wounds and took him to their master.

The silk merchant, Oliviero Dantini, faced a dilemma. He found the sealed message, wrapped in a pig's bladder to keep it dry, stitched into the man's clothing. His fingers barely resisted the urge to slit open the folded parchment and violate the royal seal. But a lifetime of deliberation stopped him. He fingered the shiny document, smelling its musk of sweat and salt and the subtle aroma of ink.

Cracknell slipped in and out of consciousness and begged that word be sent to Father Niccolò Torellini in Florence. Dantini's words soothed and comforted his distress until finally the man admitted he was a messenger from the English court. No thief then, Dantini realized. The man had travelled several hundred miles to bring word to a friend of England. Who knew? Perhaps even a friend of the King.

Others would be on the same journey. One man with a letter would not be the only one bearing such a message. Others perhaps by land. Or by another ship. If he, Dantini, were to contact the Florentine then he would have the opportunity to ingratiate himself with those who had influence with the English King. On the other hand Lucca was an enemy of Florence and allied to Pisa. Where was the profit and loss in this situation? Christian duty had been fulfilled, but commerce and politics made other demands that had to be served.

There was also the danger that the authorities in Lucca would discover that the man he harboured was not simply an injured traveller who might have been waylaid and wounded by brigands.

Why, he had asked Cracknell, did he need Father Torellini? But the Englishman fought the pain and shook his head. He refused to succumb to the infected injury that was slowly sucking his life away, or the persuasive questioning of the merchant who leant close to his face and lowered his ear to listen for a whisper of explanation. 'Father Torellini' were the only words he murmured as he slipped in and out of consciousness.

The fever caused by his wounds would soon kill him and the merchant knew he had to make a decision quickly. Checks and balances. Dantini never made less than 150 per cent profit on any deal. Influence was a desirable commodity that could be traded.

He watched as the physician did what he could to ease Cracknell's pain. He dressed the wound and bled him, then eased drops of hemlock between his lips. If Dantini had not spent time in Bruges, had not conversed in the English courts with other merchants, had not understood and spoke English, he would have let the wounded man die without another thought. But then his fever made him ramble and Oliviero Dantini heard him mutter: *Torellini... find Torellini... and... Sir Thomas... Blackstone.*

The mention of the Englishman's name made him catch his breath. A mixture of fear and excitement dried his mouth.

He knew the risk was worth it. Florence and Blackstone's sword were blessed by the Pope. The great divide between the city republics meant loyalties shifted as soon as one alliance was dropped and another formed. Lucca had Pisa's protection. To have saved King Edward's messenger and delivered the man's sealed orders to the influential priest – that would give him greater access to the English court. And Edward was known to reward those who showed loyalty. Like any business transaction, this situation required some thought – and guile. Those in Pisa and Milan would be generous. The English *condottiere* was a prize that could be better than gold and someone had already tried to claim the reward in the piazza. Who it was he did not know but it had been a brutish and clumsy attempt.

The trick was to kill Thomas Blackstone, but without being seen to be involved.

Blackstone waited with Torellini until the priest finally unclasped his hands. He had twisted and held them in a rare sign of anxiety during the telling of what he knew about the Englishman now sheltering in Dantini's house. The light was fading; they would soon be in darkness.

'I was fearful that when I sent for you I was drawing you into a trap, which is why I asked Stefano to watch for you.'

'Who knew I was coming into the city?'

Father Torellini shook his head. 'This merchant made no mention of your name, only that the King's messenger had a document for me. I knew, as did Stefano.'

'Then this Dantini seeks reward for the service.'

Torellini nodded. 'The merchants of Lucca have houses in Bruges. They travel the courts – England, France and Spain, the Holy Roman Empire – they take news of who says what to whom and what alliances seem fragile. They speak many languages; it's how the likes of Edward learn what is happening in the world.'

'It's unlikely the men in the square were simple cut-purses. I had nothing they could want except my life.'

The priest reached out and touched Blackstone's shoulder. 'Are there any of your men who would betray you? Anyone?'

'Not one,' Blackstone said, barely able to keep the irritation from his voice.

'Thomas, I understand. But a new man perhaps? A woman you lie with?'

51

Blackstone shook his head. Only those closest to him knew of the clandestine meeting.

'Your dwarf,' Blackstone said. 'You sent him to me. He knew.'

'Paolo? No, no, he has served me for thirty years. I sent him to you when I left Florence. He never came here; he would know no one. I was told to come to this church, and when I got here the local priest gave me the name of the man I must seek out.'

'Whoever is responsible will show his hand again. Are we to stay here for the night?' Blackstone asked.

'No, we go to the house.'

'We can't stumble around without torches, and the city patrols will be on us.'

'No need for torchlight. There is a man being sent who can see despite the darkness.'

By nightfall the city was so dark Blackstone could not see his hand in front of his face. When night fell the Lucchese shut down their looms as master and servant alike went to bed. Candles were expensive and used sparingly.

Blackstone held the guide's rope as he stumbled along uneven streets; behind him Father Torellini took his length of rope, as did Stefano Caprini at the rear. The only sound in the narrow streets was the *tap-tapping* of the blind man's stick as he led the three men through *chiassi* known to him since childhood. Each brick and stone on the building's flanks told him where he was in these narrow passageways, some barely wide enough for Blackstone's shoulders to pass through.

Blackstone could hear Father Torellini's laboured breath and then, as they made their way beneath the black cowl of an archway, Blackstone sensed they had stepped into a small piazza. The moonless, heavily clouded night sky was a different shade of darkness and the black shadows loomed upwards like malevolent giants gazing down on the intruders. The blind beggar stopped and the men behind him stumbled into each other.

'Thomas, what is it?' the priest whispered.

Blackstone made no reply and eased his arm against Torellini in a gesture of assurance. The old beggar grunted and Blackstone heard his hand rasp against the stone wall. And then he struck the wall three times so that the sound echoed around the open space. He paused and then made the same signal again. No one spoke. Then, in the building opposite, Blackstone heard what sounded like a large piece of canvas being moved followed by the creaking of shutters as a first-floor window opened. He could make out a figure lowering a ladder into the street below. The scrape of timber against stone and the final dull sound as it touched the ground made the old beggar grunt again, this time in satisfaction.

No instructions were needed. The blind man tugged the rope free from their hands and tapped his way into the darkness.

'We're here,' Blackstone said.

CHAPTER EIGHT

Oliviero Dantini sat in a darkened corner of his apartment that spanned the breadth of the townhouse. Below him were two floors of looms standing silent. If he secured the trust of the Florentine priest, then betrayed his Englishman later, it would place sufficient distance between him and the act. Had he not put himself at huge risk? he would tell the English Court. Had he not done as much as he could? He would kneel before the priest, expressing his humility, and the priest would bless him. And the first step of his new journey would be taken not only with the English but here in Lucca.

He could rise to the office of *podestà*: there was power and influence to be wielded as chief magistrate. God knows he had lent the city enough money over the years, and his influence with the farmers and peasants in the *contado* would grow – though how anyone could choose to live beyond the city walls was a mystery to him. He had extended the hand of financial friendship to the drapers' guild, and helped to provide cheap cloth for the market. Becoming chief magistrate would allow him to settle scores with rival families. He might even be able to exert influence on communal councils and shape the rural statutes that protected local interests. Lucca was a city-state, its people bovine creatures cosseted by the city walls since Roman times; as the city grew, more walls were built and financial inducements ensured Pisa's protection. Now that trade with England and Flanders demanded even more silk, Dantini could already see himself in the *palazzo della podestà*, wearing the chief magistrate's magnificent gowns. Or perhaps not? Doubt entered his mind. Power should not be seen but rather felt. No, he decided, the common populace would respect the show. And he could build more wealth, and wealth would buy title, and then he could pay for his own *condottieri*. A small army outside the walls exerting their strength...

His thoughts were interrupted by his servant's announcement. 'The priest is here, master.'

'Then allow him to enter. Does he need help?' he answered impatiently.

'There are two other men with him,' answered the servant.

Fear suddenly stripped away all ambition. He waved a hand impatiently. 'Be certain it's the priest. Make sure! If it is... then... lower the ladder fully. Bring him to me. Go. Go!'

He touched his fingers to his brow. It was a cool night but the sweat glistened. He dabbed his face and waited in the half-lit room as he heard the outside curtain being drawn and the shutters opened.

He crossed himself and muttered a prayer. If his worst fear was realized, the priest was bringing a dark angel into his house.

Father Torellini identified himself and was beckoned to climb the ladder.

'I'll go first,' Blackstone told him and shuffled forward with the priest's hand on his back for guidance; as he reached the ladder he palmed the knife in his hand. To go through the darkened window into an unknown room was to accept an assassin's invitation. He clambered up and then, readying himself for violence, felt the tension ease from his shoulder as a muted, warm glow seeped from the room. Against the far wall stood a servant holding a candle with his hand shielding the light, casting everything else in the room into shadow. Blackstone could see that behind the servant stood a man, clearly the master of the house, who held one hand across his chest, gripping the folds of his cloak. The figures were barely recognizable, their features almost hidden in the soft light. Blackstone quickly took in what little of the room he could see. It was large and almost devoid of furnishings. Broad planks formed the floor, stout beams the ceiling. There were wall hangings, but he couldn't make them out. He stepped over into the room and, without taking his eyes from the servant and his master, extended his hand through the window.

'Come on up,' he said quietly, and heard the creak of the priest's weight on the ladder below.

When the two men joined him in the room the servant passed the candle to his master, who still seemed nervous of the strangers in his house. The servant quickly pulled up the ladder, and then drew an outside canvas covering, held across the opening on an iron rod. He closed the wooden shutters, trapping what little light there was in the room.

The merchant stepped forward nervously. Here was the man so many had tried to kill. The shadows heightened the merchant's fear. The dimness served to accentuate Sir Thomas Blackstone's fearful aspect. Thank Christ the Lord Almighty and the blessed Virgin Mary that he had not been involved in the killing in the piazza because who else could know of Blackstone's association with the priest, or that the Florentine was in the city or that the Englishman would come to Lucca? That Dantini protected the English messenger would surely convince Torellini and Blackstone that he was uninvolved in that attempt. Italy swarmed with paid mercenaries to protect city-states. Some were greater than others. But this *condottiere* who protected Florence was taller than he imagined. This was no squat, muscled man like other thugs and killers he knew of; his height alone gave him authority. Dantini realized that he had involuntarily stepped forward, raising the candle holder so that he could see the tall man's face. The stubble clung to the running scar like scrub on the side of a dusty road.

'Sir Thomas,' he said in almost a whisper, flustered for the moment; his hand trembled, making the feeble light flicker. He bowed, keeping his eyes averted longer than necessary, desperately hoping that the killer in his midst would not savage him or his family. 'I did not know you would be with Father Torellini,' he managed to say without too much hesitation.

'Someone did. I met them in the piazza,' Blackstone answered.

Dantini raised his face – his innocence in the matter must be seen. 'Terrible news, Sir Thomas. Terrible.'

'For them. And whoever paid them,' said Blackstone, staring down the merchant.

Before Dantini answered, Torellini stepped forward. 'I am Father Torellini, and these men serve as my protection.' He spoke with the authority that Church and State gave him. 'You take a great risk.'

Dantini sighed with relief, thankful that the priest seemed to be on his side. 'I do, yes, indeed, that is true. A great risk...' he said, almost stumbling over the words, uncertainty suddenly clouding his thoughts again. All his skills of negotiation in trade, of buying cheap and selling dear, all his years of usury and cunning fraud, seemed to desert him. How many times had he watched men less able than himself succumbing to his skills? The wealth of the Lucca silk trade gave him power over those who desired it. Be they kings or queens, upstart noblemen and their whores or common wool farmers, Oliviero Dantini had outsmarted them all.

He recovered his composure and gestured to the doorway that led to another room.

'I will wait by the window,' said Caprini. 'Best to see who else might be in the streets at this time of night.'

Blackstone nodded and followed the others as the servant quickly ran forward and opened the ornate carved doors that led to a more sumptuous apartment where furnishings and carpets softened the broader-planked floors and stone walls. All the windows were shuttered, and Blackstone realized that without a ground-floor entrance, access to these tower houses with their interconnecting rooms was possible only by a ladder lowered into the courtyard. Those that had towers attached, like this merchant's house, were well-defended strongholds in a city plagued with family rivalries. Blackstone had taken an instant dislike to Dantini. There was a slyness about him. His posture kept changing: one moment he was gesturing with his arm as they strode across the luxurious apartment as if about to tell them of its wealth and finery; the next his shoulders slumped like a whipped servant as Blackstone demanded, 'Where is the King's messenger?'

Another room. A bed, woven carpet and drapes, a woman who cowered in nightgown and cap. As old as the merchant himself, and fatter. The wife of a rich man in a sumptuous bed surrounded by drapes. She looked defiant, but made the sign of the cross and lowered her gaze when she saw Father Torellini.

'Yes, yes. Blessings, sister,' Blackstone heard the priest mutter tiredly behind him.

Oliviero Dantini led them to a central staircase that ascended into the tower. Another candle was lit as the servant went ahead and cast light up into landings with oppressively dark chestnut beams and flooring.

'I had the best physician. Trustworthy, I assure you. I paid him well,' Dantini said breathlessly as he took the steps, eager to let it be known that he had spared no expense despite the citizens of Lucca's reputation for miserliness. 'Here. A safe room. He is here,' he added as the servant waited at the next landing by a doorway. He gestured impatiently for the man to open the door.

'Let me speak with him, first, Thomas. Who knows what delirium he may suffer,' said Torellini.

Blackstone stepped back and let him go into the room. Dantini shifted nervously, but his anxiety calmed as a servant girl stepped forward carrying a tray of wine glasses. The girl was no more than fourteen or fifteen years old, but composed and self-assured. Her eyes were lowered respectfully, Blackstone thought, in obedience to a master who probably took such a beautiful girl to his bed. Her plain linen dress showed her slender neck and shoulders; her fair hair and blue eyes gave her an almost angelic air.

Dantini took a glass of wine and noticed Blackstone watching the girl, who remained unmoving, waiting until her master's guest took his wine.

'Georgian,' Dantini said, leering over the rim of the goblet. 'From the Black Sea. A better choice, I have always thought, than the Tartars they bring in. Such ugly creatures. Beauty, Sir Thomas, should always be at the centre of a man's desires. In all things. Don't you agree?'

'Does she speak?' asked Blackstone, ignoring the question.

'No, no. They have a foul guttural tongue. They learn quickly enough to remain silent with a strap laid to their backs. Cheaper than hiring Italian servants. Why pay exorbitant wages when you can buy a slave for fifteen florins?'

A woman's voice called from the lower floors. 'My lord? My lord?' An exclamation of concern.

Dantini winced. 'My wife. Forgive me, Sir Thomas, I must assure her that no harm will befall us this night.'

For a moment he considered dismissing the servant girl, but changed his mind, thinking that she would amuse the Englishman. Perhaps he might even offer to buy the tender-looking girl and in that instant he regretted telling Blackstone that she had cost fifteen florins at the Pisa slave market. He scurried downstairs to attend to his wife's anxiety.

Blackstone gently lifted the girl's chin. She looked at him defiantly. He understood that look and the feelings that lay behind it. Her breasts looked firm, their nipples pressing through the undershift and linen dress. It was not difficult to understand how such innocence could be desired. Though by now, of course, innocence had long since fled the girl. He laid a hand on her shoulder and with the lightest of touch turned her so that he could see the nape of her neck and the smooth skin between her shoulders. The tips of flat welts, new and old, criss-crossed her back. He knew the full strike of the belt would go down to her buttocks. Somewhere on that tender white skin would be a mark burned into her flesh to denote her slavery. Probably no bigger than a small coin, it would pucker in a pink eruption. Either her thigh or her breast, he thought. It made no difference. The flesh healed, but slavery was death to the soul. He turned her to face him again. He took the purse from his belt and placed it on the tray. The girl's eyes widened, but Blackstone smiled and calmed her fear. Dantini's footsteps echoed up the stairs.

'Go when you can,' Blackstone said quietly, hoping she might understand his intent even if she did not comprehend the words he spoke. He made a child-like gesture of his first two fingers walking.

She caught her breath and then quickly took the purse from the tray.

Dantini puffed his way to the landing. 'You don't care for wine, Sir Thomas?' he said. 'Or... anything else?'

'Nothing.'

'Of course. As you wish. I am here to serve,' he said and waved the girl away, unable to avoid watching her buttocks clench and sway as she moved downstairs. He smiled apologetically at Blackstone, who gave no sign of sharing the moment of pleasure.

The door opened. The merchant stepped aside, allowing Blackstone to bend beneath the door frame and enter the room, which had a cot, a pitcher of water and a bowl, and the wounded man who lay half raised on the pillows. His linen shirt was bloodstained, his left arm bound in a sling. Cracknell held a knife in his good hand; sweat ran into his eyes. He blinked and shook his head, his hair flicking the sweat away. The air was oppressive. It stank of urine and infection – a stench that was no stranger to Blackstone.

'He was unconscious. I prayed for him and bathed his face, and no sooner did he awake than a knife was in his hand,' explained Torellini, who turned and raised a hand to calm the wounded man. 'I am Father Niccolò Torellini, my son. We have found you. You are safe.'

Cracknell gave an audible sigh of relief and lowered the knife.

Blackstone looked at him. He had seen poison creep into men from their wounds, and this man was no different, with his pallor and palsy, and his struggle for breath. He knew they had reached him with barely enough time before he died. And die he would. No physician could cure whatever happened to the blood and heart of a wounded man. It needed good luck and God on your side. And both, it seemed, had abandoned the King's messenger. It was only his courage and duty that had kept him alive this long.

Blackstone eased the merchant from the room, pushing the inquisitive but obedient man onto the landing, then closed the door behind him. Whatever was said in the dying man's room was for Father Torellini and Thomas Blackstone.

'What is your name, my son?' asked Torellini.

'I am Samuel Cracknell. I have... a document that... must... reach... Sir Thomas. Only... he can read it. I have your word, Father?'

'I will not give it to him...' Torellini said quietly and smiled at Cracknell's sudden uncertainty. He laid a comforting hand across the man's. 'He is here. He has come to see you himself. You can give him the document with your own hand.'

The priest moved away from the bedside and took the branch of candles from Blackstone, who pulled the footstool closer to the dying man's cot.

Cracknell peered through the shadows that played on Blackstone's face. Was he ready to give the vital message to this man dressed as a commoner?

'You're Sir Thomas?' he asked uncertainly.

Blackstone nodded, turning his face so that his scar might be seen more clearly. Like a doubting child Cracknell raised an uncertain finger and traced the scar without touching Blackstone's face.

His eyes narrowed as a moment of indecision intruded on his fevered mind. Battle-scarred veterans were ten a penny. 'You once knew a King's messenger, did you not?' he asked, determined to make sure that Blackstone was who he said.

'I did,' answered Blackstone. 'Some years ago. A good man. I sat with him as I sit with you. And he was taken by the French King's men in my place.'

'And you would remember his name?'

Blackstone remembered it well enough from back then, when the Norman lords teetered on the edge of rebellion and Blackstone was taught the art of killing with the sword. Normandy, a dozen years before. Christiana his wife-to-be, Henry and Agnes his

61

children yet to be born. Names, and the feelings that came with them, crowded his memory like a winter forest, skeletal boughs reaching out to scratch his conscience.

'His name was William Harness. A brave, good man who was wounded by French villagers. I made sure they paid for their viciousness to him.'

Cracknell sighed, as if releasing a great weight. 'We know that story well. Every man who rides into foreign fields... for... the King... knows it... as will their children.'

His hand grasped Blackstone's wrist to help him half turn and reach beneath the mattress. He pulled out a document, folded twice vertically, its thin ties wrapped around and crossed. At its crease was a dark red globule of dried wax, its heart pressed with the royal seal. The parchment had a greasy sheen to it, and a smear of blood had dried into its grime.

'One thing more, Sir Thomas. Use your knife... and cut away the stitching that holds the cord for my hose... here...' Cracknell said, touching his waist beneath his shirt.

Blackstone carefully lifted the cloth, felt the cord in the man's waistband. His fingers touched a coin stitched into the seam. He carefully separated a few stitches and eased out a gold coin. Cracknell nodded.

'I was told... that should also... be placed in your hand.' He grimaced in pain, his breathing now more laboured. 'My duty is done, Sir Thomas... Don't... don't linger in this... place. You are in danger, my lord.'

Blackstone dampened the cloth rag in the bowl of water and wiped the man's brow. 'I'm always in danger, Master Cracknell.'

CHAPTER NINE

Footfalls scuffed the wooden stairs into the tower. Blackstone eased Father Torellini aside and gripped his knife. Whispers filtered through the door frame, followed by a gentle tap. Blackstone opened the door and saw that there were two men, both dressed similarly to Stefano Caprini. Cloaked Knights of the Tau.

'We should take him from this place, Sir Thomas,' Stefano said. 'I sent word to my brother monks. Our hospital is close enough and no one will question us.'

Blackstone glanced at Cracknell – the man was close to death.

'Even so,' Stefano said, understanding the Englishman's thoughts, 'he will be under the hospitallers' care...' He lowered his voice to barely a whisper, ensuring the dying man did not hear him. '... until he dies, and then we will bury him in our graveyard. Has he fulfilled his duty to you?'

Blackstone nodded.

'Then you can do no more for him, Sir Thomas.'

'Stefano is correct, Thomas. Let me administer the sacrament,' urged Father Torellini. 'Now that he has done his duty the will to live will slip away from him.'

Blackstone looked back at the royal messenger who had clung to life so that he could carry out the King's wishes. He nodded. 'You and Stefano attend to him, Father,' he told them and eased opened the document, tilting the parchment to the candlelight and read the neat script: *Do as this man commands – no harm will befall you.*

Ten words that demanded Blackstone's obedience.

* * *

'Wait,' he said and pushed between the priest and the knight. He quickly knelt at the cot and shook the dying man. 'Master Cracknell.' He shook him again but there was no response.

'Thomas. He is beyond words now,' said Father Torellini.

Blackstone kept shaking the man, his free arm stretched back to give the document to the priest so he could see for himself. 'I need his words, Father. He's the voice of the King.'

Cracknell's breath was slow and heavy, easing him away from the flickering shadows. Blackstone gripped the man's shoulder and squeezed the wound. Cracknell's breathing faltered.

'Thomas. In God's name, mercy,' Father Torellini said, stepping forward to restrain Blackstone, but was in turn held back by the Tau knight.

'Pain awakens a man from the darkest places,' said Caprini.

Once again Blackstone pressed into the injury. Cracknell groaned. Now Blackstone forced his fingers into the suppurating wound itself, and the man gasped in agony, his eyes staring wildly, as his upper body curled from the cot. Blackstone held him, easing him gently back onto the pillows, and pressed a beaker of water to his lips.

'Sir Thomas...?' he whispered, uncertainly.

'Master Cracknell, listen to me. You have information I need. What were you told, that you should pass on to me?'

Cracknell's eyes focused, his mind searching for an answer. 'Nothing, my lord. No instructions for you.'

'I am to follow your command,' Blackstone said. 'Did you not know what was written?' he asked, already aware that no messenger would be privy to the contents of what they carried, but hoping that a personal message from the King to the outlawed knight might be an exception.

Cracknell shook his head.

'You were given nothing for me?' Blackstone repeated, knowing there was little else to be asked.

'Nothing,' came the answer.

Blackstone felt the frustration squirm within him. Cracknell must know something.

'Think of when the document was handed to you. The royal clerk, the Chancellor, whoever it was, what did he say?'

'To... Genoa... and then Florence... under escort... and safe passage to Florence and... Father Torellini.'

'More than that. You carry a command for me but you do not yet know it. It lies in the words that were spoken to you. Father Torellini would have sent for me had you reached Florence and there I would have questioned you as I question you now. Clear your mind and think.'

Cracknell's eyes darted through the layers of pain and time, searching desperately for the answer, seeing the royal clerk place the folded parchment into his hand. Watching his lips, hearing his orders.

'I was to board ship... at Portsmouth... from where you first... sailed to war... but... was commanded to return before... the King's tournament...'

'The King holds a tournament many times a year,' Blackstone repeated. 'Those are his pleasures.' It seemed a mystery he could not unravel. Was there any meaning in those instructions?

Cracknell smiled, as if finally understanding the subterfuge that had been his to carry. 'There can be only one... at Windsor... St George's Day, Sir Thomas... it can be no other...'

Blackstone laid the palm of his hand on Cracknell's face, as he would on a child's. 'It can be no other,' he said gently.

Blackstone waited out the night. Sitting in the high tower's darkness, watching the late-risen moon come and go behind clouds, throwing shadows from the city towers across the rooftops. Here and there in the distance a dull glow seeped upwards from the darkened alleyways as the night patrols of armed young men went about their business. Fireflies who sought out the living.

He heard muffled whispers from Torellini and the Tau knight and then the weary footfall of the older man as he climbed the night-black stairs.

'Thomas?'

'Here. By the window.'

A cloud shifted and the moon briefly illuminated the unshuttered opening. The priest sighed. 'I see you.' He sat on the top step. 'Cracknell has died, his soul cleansed by absolution. The *cavalieri* are swaddling his body. At first light they will take him to their graveyard. When the city gates are opened they will accompany a handcart carrying his body. You will pull the cart, Thomas – no soldier will question us then.'

Blackstone nodded, even though Torellini could not see his response. Where in this labyrinth had he been betrayed, and by whom? A wounded man washed ashore and by chance brought to a merchant's house. Who knew of the meeting? The merchant, Father Torellini, and the dwarf who had ridden with the message to Blackstone.

'Why does an English King use you?' he asked the priest.

'Edward has always had strong links with us,' Father Torellini answered.

'Because the bankers of Florence fund his war chest? It's more than that.'

Blackstone sensed the hesitation in the priest's answer.

'There is a history between us, Thomas. It goes back further than you can imagine. Before you were born. I serve one of the greatest men in Florence, and before him others served King Edward's father. It goes beyond the business of lending money.' He paused, evidently reluctant to continue.

The darkness was Blackstone's friend. Like a confessional it eased men's souls and loosened their tongues. He remained silent, listening to the priest's breathing.

'There is a Genoese family, the Fieschi. Cardinals and diplomats, used by the King's father,' Torellini said. 'And, like them, there are other Italians, such as my master, Bardi of Florence, whose family have been confidants of both royal father and son. The King has strong ties with us. His physician was Pancio de Controne, who helped the King open dialogue with other Italian bankers. Edward appointed Nicholyn of Florence to the royal mint. We share a –'

A lifetime of vows suddenly silenced him.

Blackstone listened to the old man's intake of breath, as if catching himself on the brink of an indiscretion.

'A secret?' Blackstone suggested.

'Yes. An intïmacy of trust.'

It was obvious that was all the priest was going to say.

In the city of fifty thousand souls a dog barked, others took up the challenge and then fell silent again. Blackstone knew little of King Edward's life. He had been a village stonemason who could read the sheriff's proclamations; an archer arrayed for war; a man-at-arms blessed with the strength to harness the rage within him. A King was divine.

'He trusts you to reach out to me,' said Blackstone.

'Did you understand the message?'

'I think so. I can't be certain. But I believe I am being summoned to England before the final week of April when Edward holds his tournament on St George's Day.'

Torellini was silent for a moment. 'I have heard that the King has granted a pardon to those who travel to the tournament. Foreign knights and princes are to be welcomed to fight there.'

'Not for me, Father. No pardon is granted to a man exiled by the King's son. But this message must have something to do with it.'

'Then it's nothing more than guesswork.'

'It's all I have.' He felt the embossed coin between his fingers. 'And Cracknell was told to give me this.' He reached across the wall opening, the brightness of the moon showing the gold coin held between finger and thumb.

'A double leopard,' said Father Torellini when he saw the embossed coin.

'Worth all of six shillings when it was in use. Why send me a coin that can't be traded except to be melted down?'

67

Father Torellini teased the coin in his fingers. Why indeed? A coin taken out of circulation many years before and now sent to a fighting man who had enough money to buy passage home, a *condottiere* whose contract with Florence meant that if the King needed Blackstone's men at his side then the Florentines would risk engaging ships and crews for them to be transported to England. But no such request had been sent to Florence. No, the gold coin was a symbol of royal authority showing two heraldic leopards crouched each side of King Edward on his throne. It was a deliberate reference to the throne of King Solomon described in the Old Testament. The image that told his subjects that theirs was a wise King.

'Ah...' Torellini sighed. 'I knew there was something wrong.'

Before Blackstone could question him, the priest gathered his garments and turned on the stairs. 'We need candlelight, Thomas. Come!'

Refusing to explain, Torellini scuttled down the stairs as quickly as he could, with an air of anticipation verging on excitement. 'Be patient, be patient,' was all he would say to Blackstone's questions.

When they descended to the first floor Father Torellini instructed the merchant to provide a dozen candle holders. Eager to please, Dantini hurried his servant, quietened his wife's protests and ushered Blackstone and the priest into his private chamber. The outer curtains were drawn and the shutters closed, sealing the light of a dozen candles within the room. Torellini dismissed the merchant and arranged the candle holders on a table, and then unfolded the parchment.

'The document you received is not what you think.' He brought the royal seal into the light. 'Do you see?'

Blackstone studied the seal's imprint. A monarch on horseback, a crowned helm, shield and sword. The horse's forelegs raised, the King posed as if his sword arm was ready to strike.

'I do not,' said Blackstone. 'It's the King's seal. I've seen it before on an archer's leave of absence from the battlefield.'

'A king's Great Seal is broken when a new monarch is crowned,' said Torellini, biting a knuckle as he worried about his explanation and whether his thoughts could even be true. 'This' – he tapped the document – 'this seal shows the King with crowned helm and three lions on the horse's caparison. Edward's seal does not. Edward's shield is quartered with the fleur-de-lys; his father's was not.'

'I've seen the seal before,' Blackstone insisted. 'This is the King's seal.'

'No, Thomas, this is his father's seal.'

Blackstone remained silent for a moment. Neither man spoke.

'I don't understand,' said Blackstone. 'If his father's seal was broken when Edward took the crown, then how can this be his?'

'A copy is always held by the Chancellor of the time,' the priest said, 'and, Thomas, if the King wished to send you a personal message, he would not use the Great Seal. He would hide such a message from his advisers. He would use his signet as a secret seal for such a private document.'

He held the gold double leopard out to Blackstone; the dull glint of light caught the figure of the King. 'This carries a Latin inscription. Has that pagan goddess you wear around your neck supplanted Our Lord Jesus Christ in your life? Do you know the bible's teaching? Were you taught it in your village?'

'Only enough to bear the sting of the village priest's switch before he absconded to the whorehouses of France. I cannot read Latin.'

'No matter,' said Torellini as Blackstone took the coin. 'The inscription translates to: "Jesus passing through the midst of them went on his way."'

Blackstone felt the blank despair of ignorance.

Father Torellini smiled and patted his arm. 'The book of Luke refers to Jesus passing through a hostile crowd of Pharisees. Do you see, Thomas, for those who are superstitious these words are a charm against thieves and the perils of travel. You have been sent a token to protect your journey home.'

He pressed the coin into Blackstone's hand, using both of his own to close the Englishman's big fist. 'There are enemies waiting for you; their assassins have already tried here. This is only the beginning.'

CHAPTER TEN

Blackstone's men waited, impervious to the chill wind twisting down through the valleys from the Apuan Alps. The sun's spring warmth returned only when the wind shifted and the forests suffocated its bitterness. Killbere had posted men as outlooks, but it was Blackstone's battle-scarred bastard horse that first gave warning of his master's approach. It snuffled the air, its whinny alerting the men. Within minutes Blackstone's lone figure clambered up a jagged ravine, through gorse and olive trees, an unexpected route for his return.

John Jacob cuffed one of the sentries. 'The dumb beast has better sense,' he chastised the man.

Blackstone pulled off the cloak and hood, and then his linen shirt, wiping the sweat from his body. The chill wind prickled his skin. Elfred undid a blanket roll and gave him a fresh shirt. 'You insult my horse, John. He's not dumb. He can turn against lance and sword, he can trample and kill along with the best of men and his eyes are better than my own.'

'We'd be best served if we had a few more like him, Sir Thomas,' said John Jacob, giving the shamed sentry a glaring scold.

'Well?' demanded Killbere.

'You were right. It was a trap,' Blackstone answered as he finished dressing, hooking the ties across his padded jacket.

'Damned if it wasn't obvious. But you haven't been in a whorehouse while our balls have been shrunk to walnuts in the night's cold, have you?' he said, handing Wolf Sword to its master.

Blackstone took a half-eaten apple from Will Longdon's grubby fist and bit hungrily. He had not eaten in hours.

'It's my pleasure, Thomas, to sacrifice life and limb in your service but that apple was paid for with coin from my own purse. No theft or threat was involved in its taking,' Longdon said.

Elfred jabbed him with the fletched end of an arrow. 'Sir Thomas to you, you insolent lying bastard. I saw you steal that apple.'

'That was another, you old blind fool. And I have known *Sir* Thomas since he got his feet wet invading Normandy and his blade wet killing those who got past *your* archers intent on killing our King.'

'Aye, and it was likely your poor rate of fire that let them!' Elfred said to the gathered men who jeered the hard-done-by Longdon.

Blackstone tossed the core to his horse, ignoring Longdon's outstretched hand. 'You can fill your belly later,' he said and walked to the horse, which raised its ears and snorted. He put his boot in the stirrup, and pulled on the opposite rein to stop the belligerent beast from turning and biting him, contesting his right to mount.

The men got to their feet to follow Blackstone to their mounts. Elfred looked enquiringly at Killbere, who had been Blackstone's first sworn lord many years before. He was ignored. This was not the time for questions. Blackstone had learnt something and he would tell them in his own time.

The hilltop town of Cardetto, from which they commanded the surrounding countryside, was a day's ride away. Towers and long-abandoned fortified houses on surrounding hills had been repaired since Blackstone and his men wrested them from a marauding band of routiers who savaged villager and merchant alike on the mountain tracks. The brigands had had no leader strong enough to hold the towers, and after they had burned a nearby monastery and slaughtered the monks, Blackstone and his men hanged twenty of the mercenaries in plain sight, and killed another forty who refused to yield their ground. Blackstone was a war leader who brutally imposed his authority, and his enemies had heard of it. Florence paid the bills and Blackstone's men held the heights like sharp-eyed eagles. There had been no idle time between skirmishes. Every man had carried stone to those hilltops to rebuild and reinforce the ruins – Blackstone among them. Florence's enemies employed other mercenaries to replace those Blackstone had killed, but they ventured no further than the boundaries of their own territory. It made no sense to fight unless they had no choice.

A cowl of smoke from Lucca's fires hovered over its roofs and towers like a malignant spirit. Blackstone was glad to be free of its claustrophobic narrowness. The anticipation of returning to England, despite the danger that awaited, thrilled him. He turned in the saddle.

'Meulon, Gaillard, Will and John. Go down the mountain the way I came. Two miles south and one east is a shepherd's hut. Father Torellini and a frightened silk merchant are there – one man guards them. Give him respect: he's a knight. Escort them to me.'

The men mounted, ready to do his bidding.

Will Longdon pulled a face. 'Another knight to obey and a damned priest to try and save our souls,' he moaned quietly.

Killbere hawked and spat. 'You're an archer! Your soul is beyond redemption. You should hope for a quick death so no priest has to wrestle with the devil for it. Get to it!'

As the four men spurred their horses, Killbere turned to Blackstone. 'He has a point, Thomas. And a silk merchant to boot? Is there a ransom for him?'

'There's a way home. And if we use our wits we will live long enough see England again.'

CHAPTER ELEVEN

Hours later Blackstone and his men made their way through the defile that led up to their village. Flags wavered against a clear sky as Blackstone's troops signalled each other from their mountain stronghold. The defensive line across the mountains had been unbroken these past fourteen months, the men's bellicosity cooled by the winter snows and Blackstone's regime of ongoing fortification.

A stone-paved track led up through the village, whose houses tumbled down the hillside towards the broad spread of the valley below. The town dominated the main roads of the area: a strategic position of considerable importance. The Romans had seen its value and so did Blackstone. Its alleyways connected houses where his men lived with their women, sharing the town with the *villani* who had been abused by others before Blackstone came with his men. Those who had held Cardetto before were allied to the Visconti of Milan, the northern lords who were growing ever more powerful. Pisa had funded these mercenaries in return for a guarantee that Lucca and Pisa would be protected against anyone from the south fighting for Florence. Protection soon turned into savagery. With no one willing to challenge them the mercenaries' cruelty was inflicted on the villagers. There were more than four hundred of these killers: Germans and Bretons, with a hard core of Hungarians, who were the vilest of men and who committed the worst atrocities, news of which spread across the mountain villages like a gorse fire on an August day. The surrounding *villani* fled for their lives, but these peasants' cries for help made little impression on the Lucchese. Their city was safe. Its gates were closed. Those who scraped a living in the mountains were hardy, adaptable; they would build new hovels elsewhere, was the Lucchese's argument. The communes closer to the city walls were safe. Food supply would not be interrupted; fuel would be brought in daily. Vicious slaughter was far removed from the day-to-day existence of the city dwellers.

'It is impossible to seize the village,' Blackstone's paymasters had told him. 'The streets are steep and houses clutter the *chiassi*; there's barely room for a donkey to pass between the buildings.'

Blackstone saw the difficulty and had taken a dozen men to reconnoitre the mountain slopes that rose up from the impassable ravines on either side of the village. Abandoned hovels, sheepherders' huts and ancient towers long broken down for their stone had been left to the wild grass and brambles. Their positions were no threat to anyone foolish enough to attack Cardetto, but once the village was seized, those places would be like an eagle's wings, broad shields to a sharpened beak.

He made certain that the mercenaries in the village saw his intent. For several days his men stood behind their shields, blocking any escape from the village. His archers wedged themselves in the rock crevices on either flank. Every man lit three small fires to give the impression that there were more of them than their enemy believed. By night more than two thousand fires flickered across plain and hill.

Blackstone waited, letting the defenders' nerves fray a little more each day. Let them wait, he had told his captains, they have food, they have water, but they do not have our advantage, that of knowing when the conflict will come. Blackstone would attack when the time was right.

The snow stayed high on the mountaintops, the low winter sun throwing spear-long shadows to the front of Blackstone's men. These lower slopes were tinder-dry as the east wind flayed gorse and men alike. Their muscles ached and the cold stiffened their grip on axe and sword.

Killbere stamped his feet and pulled his hands beneath his cloak. 'We need to take this goddamned place, Thomas, before my balls crack and drop into my boots. A good fight will stir the blood.'

Blackstone shook his head. 'Tomorrow, Gilbert. Ready the men for tomorrow.'

'Another day? Sweet Jesu! They'll barely be able to crawl into the place.'

'They will run, and they will fight through the streets. House to house. They'll do it because I'll do it.'

'Well, I'm getting too damned old to run! I'll do my killing at a more leisurely pace.'

'I want you to stay here and attend to the rearguard.'

'You taunt me, Thomas? I'll not be denied my share of the blooding!'

Blackstone nodded and remained silent. A look that was almost one of pity.

The colour flushed into Killbere's face. 'You take the centre, I'll take the right flank.'

'Very well,' Blackstone answered. 'If you feel it's not too steep a climb for you.'

It was only Blackstone's smile a moment after he had spoken that stifled the older man's impending retort. 'Aye, well – you just remember who saved your ignorant backside when you were a boy. Who stepped forward at Crécy and the whole army stepped after me? Who stood at the hedgerow at Poitiers shoulder to shoulder with you and took the French bastards full on? If it had not been for your blood-lust for the French King I would not have had to follow you into banishment! You've a short memory since that damned German knight beat you around your thick skull at Crécy. We should go at them today. Why wait?'

Blackstone turned to face the men who waited two hundred paces behind them. 'You always told me to choose my ground when I fought. Can you feel that? The wind is turning. From the north. It will be at our backs tomorrow and it will scour through that village. That's when we light the fires and let the smoke choke and blind them. And that is when we follow and kill them.'

* * *

They built up fires and dragged brush and wood onto them, smothered them in tufts of bog grass, laid wet sacking across the flames. Choking smoke funnelled up through the narrow streets, smothering the buildings. A thick plume that would soon be seen as a funeral pyre.

Inside the hovels mercenaries boarded up their windows, lay down on dirt floors, covered their faces with rags, poured what water they had over themselves, ignoring the women and children's screams. As the wind twisted smoke through the village Blackstone and his men followed in its wake, pounding up stone-laid steps, racing for the top through empty streets, not giving the defenders a chance to organize themselves. Blackstone and his men were silent, making no effort to break down doors and kill, their pounding feet the only sound. The more men up the hill, the less chance of being repulsed. As the mercenaries finally gathered their wits and pushed open their doors they were greeted by sudden violence as groups of Blackstone's men surged up behind him and slaughtered them.

Blackstone reached the top of the hill where three houses stood proud of the hovels below. Twenty men were behind him as they put shoulders and shields to flimsy doors. No one had ever dared attack this place before; no one could have even reached the lower streets – no one had thought of using the north wind as an ally.

Meulon and Gaillard kicked a door down and met a rush of resistance. Their size and weight held the mercenaries who threw themselves forward, but the narrow doorway limited their attack. The two Normans thrust their spears into throat and groin, forced others back as their men killed the squirming mercenaries and then boxed another four into a corner. The small room stank of death. Swords were no match for spears and another house was taken. As the Normans jabbed and cut their way forward Blackstone forced his way into the second house, John Jacob and his men the third. Blackstone had Perinne at his side and Will Longdon at his back. A dozen archers crowded the alleyways, spilling into any space that allowed them to use their bows in the narrow confines and to search out a target in window or door. Some of the mercenaries turned their backs to run, but cloth-yard shafts pierced spines and hearts. Inside the house children screamed, a woman wailed, men yelled in defiance. Blackstone called Will Longdon's name as he felt the wood splinter beneath his shoulder. Shield held high, he was in the squalid, half-lit room, where smoke still clung to daylight. A broad-shouldered man stood with six others. Blackstone could see he was the brigands' leader, armour on his chest and arms. One of his men kicked a woman to her knees, grabbing a handful of hair. The snarling mercenary held the mother's child and put a blade to its throat. He grimaced, saying something in a guttural voice that Blackstone did not understand. No need to. He would kill the small boy. In an instant Blackstone turned on the balls of his feet, away from the threat, going instead for the man who held the woman. Wolf Sword scythed down, cleaving the man from neck to waist, severing the hand that held the woman's hair and whispering through a handful of her dark locks. So quickly had he turned and struck, so instinctive was his attack, that the mercenary leader's gaze followed him – and did not see Will Longdon behind Blackstone's shoulder and the drawn-back arrow that would pierce his left eye a heartbeat later. The child fell and the mother scrambled for him. Blackstone stepped over her as she slid below the attacker's feet, drenched in blood, slithering through the gutted man's entrails to reach her wailing child.

By the time she had curled her body about him the remaining men were dead.

Strong hands pulled her to her feet. Will Longdon's rough voice shouted a command to quieten her screaming and passed the shivering woman back through the men to those outside for safekeeping. Blackstone put his foot on the mercenary leader's chest, pulled free the bodkin-tipped arrow from the skull and gave it back to his archer.

'Well shot, Will,' Blackstone said, loosening Wolf Sword's blood knot from his wrist.

'A poor aim, Thomas,' said Longdon, taking the bloodied shaft.
'I was aiming for his right eye.'

'It was good enough,' said Blackstone.

The village had been taken.

CHAPTER TWELVE

Father Torellini sat astride his horse and gazed up at Blackstone's village. Smoke curled from roof holes; coloured cloth and linen shirts fluttered like flags on washing lines strung between the houses. He could see that at every turn of the narrow passageways armed men stood vigilant. Across the hillsides signal flags bent in the breeze on top of the long poles as Blackstone's men passed information. Torellini did not understand what they meant but perhaps these lookouts were giving assurances that no one followed in their wake. And scattered around the fringes of the town were the usual camp followers: prostitutes, barbers and servants, those willing to serve a warlord, being paid for their services and enjoying the protection he might afford them.

Condottieri were loyal to their company and the men who led them. Father Torellini knew merchant families and rich citizens who gathered family around them for protection, and these men were bound together by similar loyalties. Blackstone had his *casa*, the household of men who served him, be they knight, squire, man-at-arms or archer – nothing would break their ranks. And Blackstone was different from most other commanders. He did not seek fine silks, rich food, or *collaterali*, those ostentatious trumpeters paid to announce a commander's status.

Before the pathways began their ascent through the houses a dry stone wall had been built as a redoubt, a first defence to hamper anyone clambering across the broken ground trying to use the shelter of the ditch that ran along the foot of the village – which, he guessed, would flood in winter. Father Torellini sighed with grim satisfaction. Not only had Blackstone created an obstacle for an enemy foolish enough to try and attack from that position, but he had also made the graveyard serve his purpose of defence. Father Torellini's eyes scanned the mounds – more than fifty of them at first glance. The wooden crosses, bound together with hemp, marking each grave were yet more obstacles for an enemy to overcome. Three paths led away from where his horse stood: to the left and right, trails that would be used by travellers; the third would take him straight ahead, up through the village. At the centre of this crossroads was a gibbet. There was no body swinging from it today, but when Blackstone executed anyone the death would proclaim to all those who paid their toll that the Englishman commanded these roads.

A simple stone shelter had been built on the approach path, barely big enough for half a dozen men to stand in, but its purpose was not a sentry position. It housed a crucifix, and a fine one at that; the figure of Christ in his torment was solid silver against the dark heavy wood to which it was nailed. Blackstone had given his men a place to remember their Lord God. Next to it stood another stone hut, a hermitage where an ageing mendicant monk offered his blessings to each of Blackstone's fighters. The Holy Mother Church forgave them their sins. A man could go to war knowing his soul had been cleansed.

Blackstone turned in the saddle and looked at Torellini, as if he could hear the priest's thoughts echoing across the hillsides. He smiled. He knew what his men needed and that prayer and forgiveness gave comfort not only to them but to those who paid Blackstone to fight for them.

'We took the crucifix from a merchant from Siena who tried to slip past us on his way to Lucca,' said Blackstone.

'And the graveyard is sanctified?' Father Torellini asked.

Blackstone nodded towards the old monk kneeling before his saviour. 'We found him wandering the hillsides. Too much sun, but he's devout, so I had him sprinkle some holy water. He can chant as many prayers a day as he wants. I can't hear him.'

Blackstone urged his horse forward while Father Torellini watched the monk muttering incessant prayer, spittle dribbling into his matted beard.

'And where would he get holy water from?' the priest called after him.

'We stole it,' Blackstone answered.

Village boys ran forward to take the men's horses as Blackstone and his captains walked up the twisting passages. Elfred and Will Longdon each took one of the silk merchant's arms, their pace and strength aiding the frightened man up the steps. His questions about his abduction had so far been unanswered: his only consolation was that the *cavaliere*, Fra Stefano Caprini, followed them up the tortuous streets. One who protected pilgrims would surely not allow Blackstone to murder or torture him. Torellini's dwarf trailed at the rear as Meulon took it upon himself to carry the priest on his back to the top.

'And a donkey carried the holy man,' mocked Will Longdon.

'And the donkey will kick your balls if you get too close,' said John Jacob, striding past them both, catching up with Killbere and Blackstone.

'Your loose tongue will lash you to death one day,' Elfred added, puffing with effort.

'A man should have some joy in his life. Not that you'd know anything about that, old man,' he answered, then grinned at Oliviero Dantini's worried face.

'You understand?' said Longdon.

The man nodded.

'Good. Happiness is the next best thing to godliness and godliness is only on my lips and in my heart when I'm shit-scared of getting killed. But happiness is with me all the time providing I can torment these miserable Norman bastards. It's a simple life.'

'You stupid whoreson, he has no idea what you're talking about,' Elfred moaned. 'Get a move on.'

'Course he understands. Even rich men like a joke, don't you?' he said, grinning again at the confused silk merchant. Longdon unslung his covered bow to jab at Meulon, but before he could stretch out his arm he smelled the stench of sweat at his shoulder. Gaillard looked down at the smaller man, nudging him aside. The two Normans had fought together before Blackstone had even arrived at their master's castle after Crécy.

'Be careful, little man,' Gaillard said. 'You trip on these steps and that war bow might go up your arse and out of your big mouth.'

Longdon was, like most of the others, smaller than the two hulking Normans, whose stature was matched only by Blackstone, but he was as muscled as any archer who could draw a war bow. The years with Blackstone meant that men from different countries fought together without rancour, but for Will Longdon, Frenchmen – Norman or not – belonged lying face down in the mud with an English arrow between their ribs. He was not afraid of either of them and swore by God's blood that if ever the humour left him he would strike low and fast with his archer's knife and geld the bastards. The fear that held him back was Blackstone's retribution. His sworn lord valued those close to him.

He quickened his pace, stepping past Meulon, dragging both merchant and Elfred with him. 'Heaven favours the strong of heart, Meulon, but you'd best hope the good priest has a prayer an English God can understand.'

What Dantini took to be ruffians came out of their houses and greeted Blackstone and their captains as they made their way through the twisting streets. The silk merchant had never seen such rough-looking men. Their appearance frightened him. They wore barely any armour, preferring leather doublets tied with broad belts that held knives and swords; some wore a metal breastplate, others a thigh piece on their exposed fighting side. They looked filthy and all were unshaven. Some chewed food and spat into the gutter; others pushed women back into the darkness of their houses when they tried to peek out and see the warlord and his

men return. Yet others loitered like the gangs on the corners of his own city, but these men were a different breed from the young men of rival families in Lucca. He averted his eyes from their gaze, feeling like a lamb trying to creep through a pack of wolves.

Their eyes followed him.

No one smiled.

It was with relief that he finally stepped into the small piazza at the top of the town. Four houses squared off the area and the house at the head of the square was one storey higher than the two-storey houses that flanked it. Women came out of the buildings to greet Blackstone's captains. Whores or wives or both, Dantini did not know, but he noticed that when Blackstone pushed open the door to the bigger of the houses and stood back to allow Father Torellini to enter, no woman came out to greet him.

Dantini stood helplessly, trying to take in what was going on around him. Nothing was as he had ever witnessed before. His attention was caught by the lower rows of stone on the base of the house next to him and without thinking his fingers reached out and caressed the uneven etched grooves. The marks were not from the hand of any stonemason or sculptor. He was suddenly startled as one of Blackstone's men grinned at his uncertainty and drew an arrow from his belt. He rubbed its point into the groove and then made a small gesture with the arrow.

'Sharpens up the heads nicely,' said the man.

Blackstone turned back from the door and faced the men.

'John, have the dwarf and our rich friend put into separate rooms. Guard them. Treat them well. Food and water. A woman if they want one.'

Dantini felt the sweat drying on his spine, a shiver of discomfort that was not fear. 'Sir Thomas!' he called impulsively, and wished he had not spoken when those in the square turned their gaze upon him.

Blackstone waited as the merchant found the courage to continue and realized he might soon be the laughing stock of these barbarians.

'I... I would like to bathe.'

'Of course,' Blackstone answered. 'You'll have hot water brought to your quarters or you can join me and my men in the bathhouse.'

Dantini was caught by surprise. The Englishman had a bathhouse. His mén washed. 'I would... prefer to bathe alone,' he answered lamely. The alternative was too unpalatable for words.

'And you shall have a clean linen shirt, Signor Dantini. It will be of sufficient quality not to irritate the skin. We took it from a baggage train going to Milan.' Blackstone paused and waited for the merchant's reaction. 'The man who wore it won't be needing it any more.'

His comment had the desired effect. Dantini's jaw dropped. And then Blackstone added, 'We ransomed him. He lives in a palace and has many more.'

The men in the square laughed – and Dantini could do little more than smile thinly at being the butt of the Englishman's humour.

'We don't kill every merchant we meet,' Perinne added. 'Only those who can't take a joke.'

Blackstone ushered Torellini into his house as one of the Normans, the one called Gaillard, pointed to one of the houses.

'Your room is there.' And then as an afterthought: 'You want a woman?'

Dantini shook his head vigorously. 'No, no. I do not.'

'I didn't think so,' Gaillard said, and placed a hand, which seemed to the diminutive Italian to be the size of a pig's thigh, against his back and gently nudged him towards the door.

What sport would be had with him? he wondered. What conclusion would Thomas Blackstone reach as to who had betrayed his presence in Lucca?

It had been impossible to ignore the gibbet at the crossroads.

CHAPTER THIRTEEN

Blackstone settled Father Torellini onto the straw mattress, which was half propped like a chair. Woven grass mats covered the baked clay tiles and the stone walls held the heat from the fireplace where Blackstone stacked more split logs. The mountain oak would burn long and warm. Torellini looked around the sparsely furnished room. It was a soldier's quarters: a roughly hewn table and bench in front of the window and a cot with blankets on the opposite side of the room. He had been told there was a privy at the back of the house and that the drains took water and waste below the piazza and into the ravine on one side of the town. Another deterrent. Climbing through excrement would take a particular type of soldier – probably only the likes of Blackstone himself would consider such a route in attack. The town's foundations had been built by the Romans, which was why there were sufficient wells for the town to survive even if besieged.

A couple of women brought hot food and extra blankets for the older man. The women were not unattractive and the broad hips and tantalizing breasts swaying beneath their half-tied shawls reminded the old priest of a time when he had tasted the pleasures of the flesh.

The two men ate in silence watching flames devour the logs.

'Those women are not yours,' Torellini said matter-of-factly.

'No,' said Blackstone, shoving another mouthful of goat stew into his mouth.

'Uh-huh,' muttered Torellini.

'What does that mean?' Blackstone asked.

Torellini pulled a piece of gristle from his teeth and threw it into the flames. 'A man like you needs a woman. All men like you need women.'

Blackstone glanced at this priest who had cradled his torn body at Crécy, taken his wife and children to safety before Poitiers, and who served God and the wealth of Florence.

'I lie with one when I need to,' he answered. 'I make sure they are looked after. No one here is taken against their will.'

'You've taken no wife either, nor bred more children,' Torellini said, making it sound like casual conversation, as if he had no care for Blackstone's domestic arrangements.

A gust of wind swirled around the piazza and flapped the tanned pigskin stretched across the window opening.

Blackstone scraped the plate, wiping it with a crust of bread. He filled his mouth, as if camouflaging the words. 'I have a wife and children,' he said. 'What other sins would you have me commit?'

'I have an interest. I apologize. Yes, I remember them.'

'So do I,' Blackstone grunted, pushing himself up from where he sat cross-legged before the fire.

'You have heard nothing these past years?'

'They're somewhere in France. That's all I know. They are lost to me, but what happened in Lucca is not. You have more important things to worry about than my family. I'm going to find out who betrayed me.'

Steam smothered the room's ceiling, making heavy rivulets of condensation trickle down the old plastered walls etched with men's names. How long had names and comments been scratched into the wall? A thousand years? More? Latin and Tuscan, Hungarian and German, words Blackstone could neither read nor understand. Bored and angry men leaving their mark, telling the world they had been there, wanting little more than sex and money and a full belly to sleep on.

At some time in history someone had painted images onto the walls that curved into arches supporting the ceiling's tightly laid Roman bricks. They haunted the walls like ghosts in the plasterwork, tints of blue and terracotta, broken faces like scarred fighters on a fractured background.

The square bath was big enough for a dozen men to sit chest deep. Women had boiled copper pots, crushing scented herbs into the bubbling water, then warmed bolts of linen cloth for the men to dry themselves.

The bathhouse was used only by Blackstone and his closest companions – those who had fought at his side over the years and who commanded his men. John Jacob, Elfred, Meulon and Gaillard sweated in the humid air. Will Longdon, linen cloth wrapped around him, lay stretched out on the clay tiles. Sir Gilbert Killbere, as always, declined to share anyone's water. An old warrior did not consent to bathe with those he commanded and these men still respected his rank and privilege. Had it not been Thomas Blackstone they followed they would stand in Killbere's shadow and face the enemy.

A mongrel born and bred. Blackstone's own words echoed from the past. How in Christ's name he kept the strictness of command in place, yet could still bathe in the same soup water as them, Killbere never understood. But Blackstone did just that. A fine line separated familiarity and obedience. So be it. But Sir Gilbert would bathe on his own terms.

'I have been summoned to England,' Blackstone told them.

They looked surprised, but each man kept his thoughts to himself. No one spoke. Their sworn lord would explain his own reasoning when it suited him, but the silence was only a few seconds old before Will Longdon expressed his opinion.

'That is to be welcomed, I would say. We've done no fighting here worth speaking of. Defending these mountains is one thing, but it's not anything to move the blood around a man's body. The men's arses are growing as fat as sows, even though you keep building these damned walls halfway up towards the heavens,' he said, nodding towards Blackstone. 'England, eh? My dick quivers at the thought. It means there's summat afoot with the French.'

'Your cock has no connection to your head, you ignorant

bastard,' Killbere growled. 'It would rise like a flagpole if a damned goat fluttered her eyelashes. It has a mind of its own! Sweet Jesus on the Cross, Thomas, you've a hundred archers commanded by a village idiot.'

'Aye, but he's my village idiot,' Blackstone answered. 'And with Elfred's wisdom at his back he's brought down enough death to carve a path for us through our enemies.'

The men in the bath nodded in agreement, breaking into smiles at Killbere's belligerent antagonism. He too knew that men needed prodding, that a kick up the arse from him was a welcome sign of respect for those who would stand at his back.

'That is a fact,' said John Jacob gravely. 'And cannot be denied, Sir Gilbert. It should be written that death has been unleashed by a village idiot.'

All the men except Meulon laughed and splashed water on the already dry Longdon, who complained bitterly and would have showed them his backside had Blackstone and Killbere not been present.

'You have already been betrayed, Sir Thomas,' Meulon said, 'and a summons to England might be another trap.'

'It's a command from the King,' said Blackstone. There was no need to explain Torellini's questioning of the Great Seal.

'Forgive me, Sir Thomas, but we have seen how kings behave. King John butchered my first master, Lord de Harcourt, and Edward's son outlawed you on pain of death,' Meulon answered.

'Because Thomas tried to kill a King! You do not strike down the divine, Meulon, whether he's French or not,' said Elfred.

'I am Norman and Sir Thomas knows where my heart lies. I would have slain Jean le Bon myself given the chance,' said Meulon. And then as the memory was caught: 'We lost too many good men to the house of Valois. A cause needs to be great for that to happen again.' He looked Blackstone. 'Isn't money a good enough reason for us to stay here?' He turned to the others, and shrugged. 'What do I know? I'm a common man who follows Sir Thomas. Where you go, I go.'

Elfred clambered from the bath and wrapped the linen sheet around him. The heated water still steamed and it was an opinion long held that too much of it could weaken a man. 'According to the quill dippers we have two hundred and forty-five lances; that's several hundred and thirty-five men. Are we to march them home? We are contracted to Florence.'

'The contract is only held for six months at a time,' said John Jacob.

'And we've had three contracts,' said Meulon. 'They will want Sir Thomas for as long as he is prepared to stay.'

'They'll find others,' Gaillard said. 'Will Longdon is not wrong, Sir Thomas. Our fighting days are few and far between. Our enemies stay in their own territory. They take their payments and have no wish to die fighting us.'

There was muttered agreement between them.

'For now we keep this news to ourselves,' Blackstone said. 'The men will be told in the next few days. But Meulon is right – we must discover who betrayed me. And why.'

John Jacob shrugged. 'It can only be one of three men. Your priest, his dwarf or the merchant. Only they knew in what church you would meet.'

'It was not Father Torellini,' Blackstone said in a tone that would accept no argument.

'Throw the bastards over the cliff,' said Will Longdon. 'Whoever bounces is the guilty one.'

'You would make a fine priest yourself with such skills for determining a man's guilt,' said Blackstone. And then explained what he wanted done.

When the others had left and as Blackstone dried himself, Killbere remained, keeping stubbornly silent.

'You can say what's on your mind now they've gone,' said Blackstone.

'And what good would it do me?'

'Your counsel has always been considered. I never treat it lightly.'

90

'And your stubbornness is a defence that cannot be breached.' Killbere wagged a finger. 'Very well! You're too trusting, Thomas. Fate places Torellini in your life. He once served you; he took your family to safety and commissions us all with money from a Florentine banker. A banker! They pay for war and profit from dying men's misery. They would sell their mothers into slavery if it turned an extra florin. Who is to say they have not made agreements with the Visconti? Who is to say the King himself has not subscribed to a deal? Our good King, and I bless and honour his name, is tight with the Italians. As good a fit as sword and scabbard. The priest could be playing you at the behest of *our* King and *his* master.'

Blackstone waited patiently but the knight only scowled in frustration.

'He serves me still, Gilbert. Trust me. He did not betray me.'

91

CHAPTER FOURTEEN

Paolo the dwarf stared out of the window across the clay-tiled rooftops. He knew his master was with the scarred-face Englishman and that Father Torellini was probably being held as was he – not guarded as prisoners, but given quarters as reluctant guests until the Englishman decided what was to be done. There was little reason for them to try and escape, and if there were, how far would anyone get down those twisting streets? Dogs would soon alert the mercenaries in the houses. No, he decided, they were safe enough. There was no fear within him, only the stoic patience of a life-long servant. Father Torellini was a priest of enormous influence. And he knew of his master's connections with the English court. There would be no question of harm coming to either of them.

When he had first set eyes on Thomas Blackstone he saw a man as tall as a mountain, a giant who could smite an army as a thrashing storm destroyed fields of corn. That was his legend. And the diminutive man could well believe it. He had obeyed his master and ridden into Blackstone's camp. No one killed a dwarf. Everyone knew that was bad luck. And Father Torellini had been correct. A mixture of superstition and respect for the Florentine priest secured him safe passage.

The door to the room creaked open. One of the mercenaries from the village, a vicious-looking man whose foul breath made him recoil, held a plate – a grimy thumb pressed into the piece of bread as he brought him food and wine. There was wood for the fire and the skins and blankets provided adequate warmth on the straw mattress. He tore off the soiled piece of bread and hungrily mopped up the peasant food. He had taken the offer of a woman and instructed her to wait outside. There was no point in sharing his food with a whore. He swilled the wine and belched, letting the firelight hold his gaze until he felt ready to call her into the room. When she entered she kept her eyes averted, either through subservience or fear of being had by a dwarf. It was something she knew nothing of. The men who usually paid her were assorted; they had calloused hands, blemished bodies and often black stumps where teeth should be. But they were men. Hasty and quick to be done with her. None had ever harmed her, because word of that would reach their sworn lord. One of the Hungarians who had joined Blackstone's company had punched her a year ago, drunk and feeble with lust. He was stripped and lashed. Afterwards, insulted by the whipping, he raised a knife in anger against the one that was called John Jacob, but a great bearded Frenchmen caught the man's hand, broke his arm and slashed his throat. He was a throat-cutter, that one. Everyone knew that. Except the ignorant pig Hungarian. But the dwarf? Had he been told no harm should be inflicted on the whores? Best not to challenge him. She kept her eyes lowered.

He pointed to the mattress and she obediently lay down and lifted her skirts, her face averted as he stripped naked, wanting her to see his muscled body. A dwarf was no different than any other man and, before Father Torellini had rescued him, he had wrestled other dwarfs for those whose tastes ran to such entertainment.

He lifted her breasts free, and turned her face towards his own.

'Do as I tell you,' he instructed.

She was well fed, and her belly and breasts wobbled with satisfying enticement as he exerted himself against her. She showed little interest in his efforts so he slapped her face hard to elicit anger and fear, and then she behaved and did everything he told her to do. A dwarf commanded little respect in the world but a village whore was barely worth her keep. When he finished with her she wiped her hand across her face, smearing her tears. As he buttoned his shirt he heard her mutter something beneath her breath. A curse, was it?

'What did you say?' he demanded.

She shook her head. He grabbed her hair, twisting it so that she could not move.

'What did you say!' he asked again.

More tears. Her hand trying to break his grip – gasping – begging for him not to hit her again.

'The merchant...' she said, stumbling to find the words through her pain.

'The merchant? The one here?'

She nodded.

'What about him? Have you opened your legs for him as well?'

'Pay me and I'll tell you,' she said defiantly.

He slapped her again and reached for his knife. 'You don't bargain with me, you slut. What about him?'

'All right, all right...' she begged. 'He says he has evidence. That he can prove you betrayed Sir Thomas.'

He released her. His own fear suddenly tightening its grip.

'Not so!' he said.

She cowered, easing her dress over her breasts, then pulling her hair back from her face. 'I heard it from one of the men. The merchant is frightened. That's all I know.'

'Get out!' Paolo said.

Had he not taken the whore he would not have discovered the information that now threatened him. Had Dantini already spoken to Blackstone? He weighed the odds in his mind. It was late. The village slept, the darkness challenged only by the occasional fleeting glimpse of the moon behind shifting clouds.

Dawn would bring its own reckoning.

The silk merchant's room was no less spartan than the dwarf's. Food and wine and wood for the fire had been provided, but fear had taken his appetite, and the warmth from the fire made little difference to the chill that crept into his bones. He pulled his cloak tighter about him. They had offered him a woman. Sweet merciful God, he was in the hands of barbarians. He,

Oliviero Dantini, who had stood in the courts of kings, being offered a village whore.

'Take your opportunity while you can,' one of Blackstone's English soldiers had suggested when he laid the plate of food down on the rough-hewn table. 'There's a chance you'll swing tomorrow.'

That which gripped the silk merchant's throat was no physical hand squeezing the breath from him; it was a terror that struck from within.

'I am the one who saved the messenger. I paid the physician, I sent for the good Father. It was I who took the risk!' he blurted to the disinterested mercenary.

'I don't know anything about that. I just heard that the dwarf has proof it was you what laid the trap. He's having a good time with a whore, he is. He'll be all right. That's all I know.' And then, as if trying to bring cheer to the frightened merchant: 'The food's not bad if you've the stomach for it.'

'I must speak to Sir Thomas!'

'He won't get you any better food. He eats the same as every other man.' He grinned, knowing full well it was not the food the merchant wanted to contest. 'The town is asleep. Tomorrow is soon enough,' he said and closed the door on the man's stricken face.

Never had Dantini felt so alone. The thoughts he had entertained of benefiting from Blackstone being killed in Lucca had been only fleeting. Thoughts could not condemn a man. They were known only to him and God. The Almighty would not punish him for *thoughts*! Untrue. Every priest and monk told how evil thoughts were like a whip to Christ's flesh. But, Dantini argued with his mind, he paid the Church! He paid the priests! He paid for his sins! He bought forgiveness! He fell to the floor in prayer, arms resting on the bench, his knees pressing into the wooden planks to feel the pain of contrition. He hid himself in prayer without any thought to time, and had no idea how long he spent muttering every benediction known to him since childhood. As a distant monastery bell woke its monks for vigils, there was a creak of a wooden floorboard outside his door.

* * *

Paolo had clambered across the rooftop to the next building. His physical strength and agility served him well as he swung down onto the external steps of the house where Dantini was lodged. The floorboards creaked as he stepped into the passageway, but he soon found the firmness of a beam beneath the planking and his lightness helped him move quickly towards the room where a faint glimmer of firelight and the soft whisper of prayer filtered beneath the door. With the palm of his hand he pressed the door gently, letting it ease away from him, its leather hinges making a barely audible protest. It went unnoticed by the man in the near darkness whose back was to him, hunched deep in prayer and whose whispers continued unbroken as he stepped closer, knife in hand.

He saw the murder clearly in his mind's eye. The kneeling man was the perfect target. The merchant's cloak and clothing would be too thick and of too good a weave to penetrate without a struggle, so he would pierce the man's throat and then his heart. He would steal the rings from his hands and let the killing be blamed on a godless mercenary. Keeping his eyes on the humbled figure he turned the knife, stepped forward and raised it. The figure before him seemed to shudder momentarily – four more paces and –

'Oh Paolo, I prayed it was not you,' said Father Torellini.

The dwarf faltered, stunned by the suddenness of his master's words. Father Torellini half turned, pulling the merchant's cowl from his head and showing his features to his servant's dumbfounded face. Paolo dropped the knife. He could not kill the man he had served these past thirty years. He had not even time to show remorse. Darkness behind the door came to life as Thomas Blackstone stepped forward and clubbed him to the ground.

CHAPTER FIFTEEN

Betrayal was worth a few hours of torture, insisted Blackstone's captains. There might be a greater conspiracy to uncover.

'Brand him and hang him over coals,' said Will Longdon. 'A slow roast to give him a taste of what awaits him in hell.'

Gaillard shrugged. 'For once I agree with him, lord,' said the Norman to Blackstone and the gathered men. 'He must suffer. Impale him and plant him at the crossroads.'

There was a murmur of agreement among the half-dozen men who sat around Blackstone on the roof terrace of his quarters. Killbere poked a finger into Gaillard's shoulder. There was no give in the muscle, but Killbere was concerned only with making his point.

'You would have Sir Thomas behave like the Hungarian barbarians? You are a pious shit, Gaillard. You pray before the Virgin yet you would ram a spear up a man's arse and have the world see what kind of men we are!'

'Then burn him, Sir Gilbert,' said Meulon in an attempt to save Gaillard's distress at being picked on.

'Aye, burn him and hang a crucifix around his neck,' said Killbere, 'and for what? Witchcraft?'

'He's a dwarf, he could be Satan's imp,' suggested Perinne, and made the sign of the cross.

Killbere turned to Blackstone, who stood with his back to them all, gazing across the valleys and mountain peaks. Beyond the white mountain of marble in the distance lay his way home.

'Thomas? These men would damn us all by their thirst for revenge. You mutilate the dwarf at your peril. It's bad luck, for God's sake,' Killbere implored Blackstone. 'Have the priest deal with him. Damnation will cast him out into his own wilderness.'

Blackstone turned to face the same men who had warned him against going into Lucca. 'Elfred? How far back does your memory go?'

'Sir Thomas?' queried his master of archers, uncertain what his lord meant.

'I was a boy when we went into France. We young archers served each other well enough; you were the voice of reason for us. We soiled ourselves and retched blood because of our fear, but you and Sir Gilbert held us together. You forged us, my friend, but you raised no objection when Sir Gilbert hanged John Nightingale because he'd fallen asleep at his post. Remember?'

'I do. Aye. He let the enemy burn the barn where we slept. We lost many a good man that night.'

'And afterwards your rank gave you responsibilities that meant men died under your command.'

'It did.'

'Then you are the senior man here after Sir Gilbert. What would you have us do with the dwarf?'

Elfred's mouth dried. His uncertainty was plain to see as he looked to each of the men sheepishly. 'It can be bad luck; Sir Gilbert's right about that. God made these small men, full formed and no different than us, but He made 'em right enough, and His purpose is known only to himself... Perhaps it'd be better to give the small man a chance...'

Unease crept through the men. 'A chance?' said John Jacob. 'You mean mercy?'

'Aye. Somehow. That's what I do mean,' Elfred answered.

'And that would square us with God, you reckon?' Will Longdon asked.

'It might,' Elfred told him.

John Jacob rubbed a calloused hand across his stubbled head. 'All right. Put him to the stake, and I'll garrotte him before we light the kindling. That's mercy enough.' He looked to his sworn lord. 'Sir Thomas?'

Killbere spoke before Blackstone could answer. 'I say again, kill this dwarf and bring down a lifetime of bad luck on us all.'

'That's superstition, Gilbert,' said Blackstone.

'And I believe it, as do you in that pagan Welsh goddess you wear around your neck.'

Arianrhod. He swore by her protection. Blackstone met the great knight's stare with his own. 'He has to die, Gilbert. There's no mercy here for a traitor. It will be by my hand. Any misfortune will be mine and mine alone.'

The threat of torture and Father Torellini's imploring made Paolo confess more than his sins. He had sold the information of where Blackstone would be in Lucca to Englishmen who had stopped him on the road to Blackstone's camp. They were men of rough trade but they did not seem to be mercenaries. Paolo swore they were English and not German, like the mercenaries who held ground further north. And they knew about the messenger, but not of his whereabouts or whether he still lived.

It had been a simple bargain. His own life, and that of his master's, for the prize that was Blackstone. Any word of the betrayal and Father Torellini would also die. He could not have known that his master had sought the help of a guardian Knight of the Tau to watch over Blackstone in the city.

Paolo begged for his life. He had gone to kill the merchant in order to protect his master, so great was his love for the man who had cared for him for more than half his life. Had the silk merchant held proof against the dwarf then sooner or later Father Torellini would have died beneath an assassin's blade. The dwarf's entrapment had been a simple bait laid by Blackstone to see who would attempt to commit murder in order to save himself. His men had watched and waited and when Oliviero Dantini submitted himself to prayer and Paolo had gone to kill him, Blackstone had taken the Florentine priest into the room and snared his trusted servant.

Paolo had been stripped to shirt and breeches and knelt, tied beneath the silver crucifix in the stone shelter. The mendicant monk stood beyond the crossroads, wild hair and beard like a biblical prophet, chanting a liturgy of garbled prayer as he gazed up at the Englishman who strode towards them. The villagers gathered behind him, but none ventured any further than where the houses ended.

Superstition gathered them like a dog penning sheep.

Only his captains followed, willing to share their sworn lord's decision.

Tears welled in Father Torellini's eyes. He rested his hands on his servant's head. 'My trusted Paolo, you sold Thomas Blackstone's life. You would have had a great man slain in order to save me. I cannot save you, but I absolve you of the sin and will pray for your safekeeping in heaven.'

The dwarf wept.

'Courage,' Torellini whispered, and gathered him in his arms as he would a child. 'Courage,' he said again and stepped back as he saw Blackstone approaching.

Paolo nodded and tried to control his fear as Father Torellini wiped the tears from his servant's face.

Blackstone stepped inside the shrine, and without a word to either man seized the rope that bound the dwarf's wrists and pulled him outside. Father Torellini crossed himself and muttered the benediction as Paolo scurried to keep up with Blackstone's long, unfaltering strides towards the gibbet. Like a child being taken from its parent he kept looking back to Father Torellini, who stood outside the shelter, hands clasped in prayer.

Paolo's gibbering words were a mixture of regret and desperation, imploring Blackstone to look after his master, whose life might still be in danger, as might Blackstone's. Paolo only ever wanted to serve his master. Nothing more. Nothing less.

'Forgive me, Sir Thomas. What I did, I did for Father Torellini,' he said as Blackstone put the noose around his neck.

It was to be no easy death. No scaffold for a drop that would snap his neck, instead a choking, kicking strangulation awaited him.

'You served him well,' Blackstone told him. 'I forgive you.' His words seemed to have a calming effect on the condemned man. Blackstone hauled on the rope.

CHAPTER SIXTEEN

The cold wind had swung and now blew from the north, and the men gathered their cloaks around them as they looked down across the village rooftops. The mountain passes were secure but Blackstone had not yet told them of his plans. He had spoken to Torellini and shared his thoughts. It was plain to see that the Englishmen who had accosted the dwarf in Lucca were looking for the King's messenger, knowing Blackstone would obey the command issued. Whoever had sent these men knew the connection between Father Torellini and Thomas Blackstone.

What was also plain to see was that there were too many bad omens connected to this matter, a common opinion held by Blackstone's captains. Nor was Blackstone immune from superstition. On his way to Lucca that day to meet the priest, a flock of crows had settled to peck grit from the roadside. These grey-backed harbingers of doom differed from the birds in England or France. Theirs was no cawing cry, but more of a growling warning. It gurgled in their throats, like a witch's cackle. It was a warning he had heeded and his guard had been up. Now storm winds blew hard. By nightfall the lash of hail beat against the clay roofs.

'I for one will be happy to leave this place,' said Killbere, easing a log into the fireplace as the others sat around the long plank table eating their supper. 'We've become little more than paid whores to rich merchants. We no longer fight an enemy, we skirmish and kill other whores who are paid by other rich bastards. There's no glory to be had. There's no sovereign to serve. Thomas, we should wrest ourselves from here. Be gone. Look how many administrators we are obliged to carry now. Tell the coin-counters and the bookkeepers and the clerks and the victuallers that they no longer have us as little more than names in their ledgers!'

'Are we to take nearly a thousand men to England?' John Jacob asked.

'No, we are still contracted to Florence,' said Blackstone.

Killbere pushed himself back onto the bench, elbowing Elfred along. 'A contract is only worth the paper it is written on. Our word and our loyalty lie with the King and if he has called for you to return then the way is clear. God, King and country, Thomas.'

'I have no country, Gilbert. I am outlawed.'

Meulon, who rarely offered an opinion, spoke up. 'Sir Thomas, those of us here would not wish to be left behind if you think to go alone.'

It was obvious he spoke for all at the table.

'Gilbert, are there men in your opinion who could command in our absence?' Blackstone asked.

'A dozen or more. If any of us fell they would step forward. Ask anyone here – they will say the same. A captain dies and another must be able to take his place. It's how we trained them.'

'And if I take a hundred men, how many will desert?'

The men looked among themselves.

'No more than a few,' said Longdon. 'I have a handful of archers who would sell their souls. Each company has like-minded men.'

'Pay them off and pay them well. Then choose thirty archers, and each captain ten men of your choice. Promote your best men to command those who stay. Our contract will not be forfeit.'

'You've a plan for us then, Sir Thomas?' Perinne asked, knowing there was no need for an answer.

Oliviero Dantini sat and waited for Blackstone's proposition to be set before him. Father Torellini watched his nervousness, offering no sign of comfort or understanding of what he had endured. The hanging of the dwarf had been a terrible sight and he could easily see himself suffering the same plight if he was not circumspect about what he said and did. A deal was to be made, that had been clear when he was summoned from his quarters.

'I've learnt that you not only commission ships for your trade from Pisa, but also from Genoa, who is their enemy,' Blackstone said.

'Of course; it is business,' he answered nervously. 'The Genoese sent mercenary crossbowmen to fight your King, Italian ships paid for by the French, but trade finds its own route.'

'I want a hundred men taken to France. The Florentines cannot commission ships without alerting my enemies. You will pay for ships from Genoa.'

Dantini swallowed hard. That would require a great outlay of money. His mind toyed with the options that were open to him. The Englishman could kill him without hesitation, but what purpose would that serve? So it was likely that if he could make a deal then he would live and might even make a profit. It would not be wise to agree and then betray Blackstone's plans, because then the day would come when a knife would find his throat. Hire the ships then, use these men to escort a valuable cargo, because that would ensure his wealth would be protected. And then Torellini would send word secretly to the English court that the merchant of Lucca had not only saved the life of his messenger but also helped Blackstone and his men to return. A profit would be made and his reputation enhanced.

His eyes flickered with the thoughts.

'You know how this would benefit you,' Father Torellini said.

Had it been that obvious? He nodded. 'I do. You and one hundred men,' he said to Blackstone.

Blackstone took Father Torellini and the Tau knight to his men. 'There are French and English knights and squires among our company. The men will vote on who shall lead them. Sir Gilbert knows of my plans. He will sail from Genoa to Marseilles and then ride on to Calais with a hundred men.'

'My lord? And you?' said Meulon.

'I go overland,' Blackstone answered, knowing his own misery at being aboard a turbulent ship would never be repeated if there was a choice to be had. 'You and Gaillard will not be going to England.'

Meulon's bearded face crumpled. 'You would leave us here?'

'No. You travel with me and meet up with Sir Gilbert when I cross to England.'

The Norman slapped the table. He could wish for nothing more.

'Safer for two Normans to be in France and await my orders with the others,' said Blackstone. 'Fra Caprini will also ride with me, and John Jacob, and Will.'

'North through Visconti territory? And then the Alps?' Elfred said, unable to keep the doubt from his voice. What Blackstone proposed was almost impossible. 'Most of the passes will be closed.'

'The monks at the abbey will get us through, just as they did when they brought us here,' Blackstone said.

'Sir Thomas, that was autumn. Now, after the winter snows, it will be hard going.'

'It can be done,' Father Torellini said. 'The monks keep the route clear. There are ropes spiked into the rock. If a man does not freeze to death he can get through.'

Will Longdon forced a grin. 'I don't mind boats, Sir Thomas. A few bowmen might be useful aboard ship.'

'The risk is great either way,' Sir Gilbert told them. 'Storm or blizzard, both can kill you just the same. And I've seen you flounder across many a river from the day we went into France. You have never yet learnt to swim. Your death is only of value if it's in the service of your sworn lord.'

'I don't much like the cold, is all I was saying, Sir Gilbert,' Longdon replied.

'And you say too much too often,' said Killbere. 'You'll go where you're sent and you'll keep your bow cord dry and your fletchings covered from the snow. God help Sir Thomas and those who travel with him, but your hunting skills might be all that stands between them and starvation.'

'And Will can poach with the best of them,' said Elfred.

'And get himself hanged for it one day,' said John Jacob.

Caprini rolled out a map and laid his finger along a curving line that snaked through mountains and plains across the border into France. 'The Via Francigena is the pilgrim route from Rome to Canterbury.'

The men gathered closer to the map. Some of the territory they knew from their patrols and fighting with Florence's enemies, but the route that Caprini traced was not familiar. It meandered along valleys and skirted towns, through deep forests and across what looked to be narrow ravines. Some of the place names they had heard of, particularly further north where the route would take them between mountains and sea.

It would be an arduous journey. A laden army might travel twenty miles a day with a good road and plenty of sweat; a King's messenger ninety if there were fresh horses every twenty miles or so. A pilgrim on foot could manage twelve miles or more a day. The men knew without asking that Blackstone would push them to cover the distance back to England in a month with good fortune on their side. It was sixty miles from Lucca to Aulla, and that would take them far enough north for the turn west and the hundred more to take Blackstone past Genoa through the mountains.

'We separate at Genoa,' said Blackstone. 'Sir Gilbert takes the main force by ship to France; I'll go through the mountains with half a dozen men and Fra Caprini as my guide.'

'The *fratelli* of Tau are sworn to protect pilgrims on their journey,' Father Torellini said, explaining to the others. 'They know every turn. Sir Thomas could not be in safer hands.'

Will Longdon snorted. 'Aye, but if the Visconti hear of it Sir Thomas will be trapped on a mountain pass. Half a dozen men? What chance then?'

'The fewer the better,' Blackstone told him. 'And there's a rumour, already being whispered by servants of a certain merchant in Lucca, that one of the Englishmen killed in the piazza might be an outlaw called Blackstone. His body and that of other unnamed men who died that day have already gone into a communal grave, smothered in lime. It might hold off those still interested in my death, but they will watch those boarding the ships at Genoa.'

'Well... I still foresee trouble,' argued Will Longdon uncertainly. 'A hundred men leaving without their sworn lord?'

Gaillard looked pitifully at him. 'Your brains are too near your arse. If Sir Thomas had been killed in Lucca then perhaps some of his men would return to France and England.' He looked hopefully to the knights, trusting he was correct.

Killbere gestured at Longdon. 'It's a fine day when a Norman has to explain a simple matter to an English archer.'

Longdon bristled. 'I understood it all, Sir Gilbert. Sometimes it's important to see that others grasp it as well.'

Caprini rolled up the canvas map. 'We will not visit any town or village on this journey. We will rest and be fed at monasteries and abbeys along the way. There is more than one route on the Via Francigena. And I know them. I have sworn to take Sir Thomas through the mountains and across France to Canterbury.'

Blackstone said, 'We will not go north of Aulla on the Via Francigena. That takes us too close to the Visconti. Our enemies will be watching, but they wouldn't dare strike against Genoa. Once past the city we will shadow the same road that brought us here using another pilgrims' route. When we reach the Alps the Marquis de Montferrat will give us safe passage. And if my enemies believe I still live, then when a hundred men set sail they will think I am aboard.'

Killbere tapped the map. 'Gascony is ours, Calais is ours. Once Sir Thomas is in England we will wait under English protection for our orders.'

Blackstone looked at each of his captains. He saw their concern for the venture, but they had never been unwilling to go forward into danger. It was not possible for such men to refuse.

Father Torellini blessed them as they prepared to leave. Saddle panniers, blanket rolls and personal weapons were all they carried.

Each wore a cloak over his tunic and a helm and shield strapped to his horse's pommel. Those who would travel beyond Genoa and across the mountains took no pack mules for provisions. With favourable roads and a relentless journey Blackstone and his escort should reach Calais in little over a month's time – if he was not discovered. Now that Dantini had agreed to engage the ships he would be taken with Killbere as surety for the ship's commission. Blackstone had permitted the dwarf's body to be taken down and buried and now his business at Cardetto was almost finished. The captains were chosen; Elfred would remain as master of archers. He made no objection to being left behind. He could still draw a war bow along with the best of men, gristle and muscle had not deserted him, but he was better suited for command now that old wounds and age hampered him from making a strenuous journey. There was to be no man taken who would slow their pace.

Father Torellini took Blackstone aside. 'Thomas, you will arrive in England not knowing why you have been summoned. Englishmen have already tried to kill you here – who knows what alliances have been formed or who wishes to claim your death?' He looked across at the gathered men who waited for their sworn lord. 'You have often survived because God has willed it. And no doubt you believe your pagan goddess has shielded you from greater harm. But you have always looked forward and seen the lie of the land and then chosen your place to fight. Now you must look to the future because your enemies will be hidden from you and you must find a way to kill them before they kill you.'

Blackstone ruffled the donkey's ears; the sturdy beast would carry Father Niccolò home to Florence. He gathered the reins for the priest. 'They will make themselves known one way or another. If it is in combat I will have a chance; if it is an assassin I may not.'

Torellini took the reins and placed his hand on Wolf Sword's hilt. 'Thomas, when you were close to death at Crécy you clutched this sword to your chest. None could prise it from your grip. Now the years have run by like the wolf mark etched on its blade. The half-cut silver penny pressed into its pommel is a memento of your wife – these are unyielding strengths that you carry, but your sword may not be enough to save you in the future. Perhaps now is not the time, but you must look to those who serve you, those who are closest to you, and ask yourself who might be prepared to betray you as I was betrayed.'

Blackstone looked uncertainly at the priest, and then to his escort. Meulon and Gaillard, oxen of men in battle and hard with loyalty. John Jacob fought fiercely and had helped save Blackstone's wife and children, as had Will Longdon that day on the alpine pass when Blackstone slew Gilles de Marcy, the Savage Priest.

'Those men carry my life with them, Father.'

'Of course they do but...' The priest brought his hands to Blackstone's shoulders and faced him squarely. The scarred face gazed down at him, and Father Niccolò Torellini made his point again. 'Think of battle. What you know of your enemy's intentions brings victory. Let my words be your companion for the future. Who among these men might betray you? Because your enemies already know your intentions.'

CHAPTER SEVENTEEN

The two surviving Visconti brothers, Galeazzo and Bernabò, Lords of Milan, were separated by two years in age. The dynasty had spread across swathes of northern Italy and these inheritors of ruthless ambition were more determined than their ancestors to increase their power further.

Guile, cruelty, avarice and murder were the tools they used to further their ambitions and these Vipers of Milan barely needed protective walls around their cities, so great was the terror they inflicted. Galeazzo, the elder of the brothers, was a man who appreciated art and culture and encouraged it when not devising slaughter and war. Debauchery was left mostly to his brother Bernabò. A mad bastard. A dangerous and insane bastard, according to those who dared to whisper the truth. Galeazzo held a dozen towns to the west and south; the more violent Bernabò much the same to the east, but his raiding parties, consisting of the most vicious mercenaries he could find, patrolled wherever they pleased within their vast tracts of territory. Occasionally Bernabò's men overstepped the mark in Galeazzo's lands and the two brothers would argue bitterly, threatening each other with death, until finally Bernabò would trade his men's trespass for gold and gifts and take pleasure in a week-long torture of those who had transgressed – a mere sideshow of impatient entertainment, given that both brothers were renowned for the *quaresima*, when they tortured victims for forty days.

And now they were arguing again. As his brother ranted Galeazzo felt unsure whether his life was being threatened.

'You ignore our inheritance!' Bernabò spat. 'You squander it! I embrace it!' he bellowed. 'It is not written in any document but we have it in our blood, so don't lecture me, brother! I will get dressed when I am good and ready. Sex and violence embrace me as I embrace them.' Bernabò had invited his brother to a banquet to celebrate a moment that might allow them some advantage in their war against the papacy, yet had failed to appear at his own dining table. Galeazzo had sent a nervous servant to search out his brother, but the man had returned bloodied and so he had taken it upon himself to go up to Bernabò's bedchamber. The sight of the half-dozen naked women who lay across cushions and bedding told him the preceding days had passed in orgy. Bernabò stood equally naked in the middle of the room, a bottle in one hand, the other scratching his balls. His beard was matted with food and wine and now flecked with spittle as he pointed an accusing finger at his brother. The incoherent rage built to dangerous levels and the deranged lord's roaring was made more frightening when some of his hunting mastiffs raised their howls from the yards below. Bernabò kept hundreds of the beasts. Many were savage beyond control and would be set loose on helpless villagers when Bernabò rode out. And woe betide any houndsman who allowed one of the beloved dogs to be injured. The offending houndsman was tortured to death.

Galeazzo was not prepared to be insulted but he had come to his brother's palace with fewer guards than usual. To fight his way clear would be futile. Especially if the dogs were set free. Three years before the two men had killed their brother, Matteo – whose vile behaviour exceeded even their own – when his actions threatened the Visconti empire. Better to cut away the diseased limb than have it infect the body. Was this a ploy for Bernabò to murder him or just a ranting taunt from a man whose excesses could not be sated? Galeazzo was even-tempered, which made him the more dangerous, but he had been no stranger to the same excesses in his own youth. He had once fornicated with his aunt and several other lovers at the same time and that drunken week was still a blur. The only clear memory he had was that she murdered her husband before he killed her.

'We need a proper war! A real war against the fucking Pope!' Bernabò yelled. 'We took Bologna from him, we should take Florence! Take those Tuscan bastards and burn them over coals. Burn every last fucking brick down.'

Galeazzo threw a silk robe to his brother. He was safe. It was to be an overweening rant, something that he had calmed and controlled before. Bernabò had indulged in such displays since the Pope had threatened to excommunicate them. Such a threat made little difference to Galeazzo: he had bargained away his soul years before. But Bernabò's hatred was greater.

The ongoing hostilities against the Papal States had in the past secured them riches from the success of their own *condottieri*, but there were few gains to be had these days. Bernabò pulled on the robe but left it untied as he slumped onto the bed next to a drunken whore.

'She has the best arse of them all,' he grinned, the temper gone almost as quickly as it had arrived. He slapped the woman's rear and then bent and kissed the inflamed mark. He sighed and rolled his shoulders, letting the tension ease.

'Florence is too beautiful to destroy,' said Galeazzo, sitting on a stool by the fire. He tipped a half-empty bottle to his lips. 'Art and sculpture define our civilization.'

'Fucking and killing define our civilization!' roared Bernabò and laughed until his face turned red with apoplexy, which made Galeazzo think for a moment he would choke and fall dead to the floor. But Bernabò wheezed and spat and then sighed with great satisfaction. 'We can hurt them – a little at least. Chop one hand off. Maybe an arm,' he said.

'What are you talking about?' Galeazzo said wearily, hunger pangs from his missed dinner beginning to feed his irritability.

Bernabò mouthed a word, making his lips exaggerate it.

Galeazzo was amused enough to smile. 'What? You drunken fool.'

Bernabò put a finger to his lips. 'We can only whisper the name,' he said, making a game of it.

'Am I to guess? What? You've poisoned the Pope? You've sent him a whore with the plague? You've pissed in the Arno?'

Bernabò stuck out his tongue like a finger from the orifice, then curled it back to his lips. 'Bl-a-ck-st-one.'

One man stood between them and Florence and that was the Englishman. There were others like him – he had only a small number of men, fewer than a thousand on contract. But they held ground that could not be taken. The attrition for the Visconti and their allies would be too great should they ever try. Besides, they were not ready to attack Florence. Not yet. But they would be, one day, and if Thomas Blackstone were not there to help defend the city it would be an advantage.

Their own mercenaries had fallen foul of the Englishman on a number of occasions, but none of his actions had threatened their well-being. Despite his reputation it was obvious that Florence did not have the manpower to come after them. Last winter Blackstone's men had slain hundreds of theirs who had been stupid enough to raid a small, worthless town in the Tuscan hills. They had paid the price and their commanders had returned to Milan and Pavia in shame. It should have been in fear – for retribution awaited them. These men would have done better to desert and make their home elsewhere. They had broken an agreement made with Florence and trust had been left lying in the bloodshed on those hillsides. Now there could be no further incursion to collect debts and Santa Marina had fallen under the protection of Blackstone. To strike back would be costly and pointless for such a worthless heap of stones. The Visconti executed two of the four commanders who had ridden in the vanguard that day, but spared the others. One was a German who sold his services and those of his men to the Visconti and despite the loss that day they considered him valuable. Had they had any romantic inclination towards chivalry they would have called von Lienhard their champion. No one had bested him in any challenge. The other commander was a favourite cousin – albeit a bastard relation. The Visconti were no strangers to the murder of family members, but in this instance to have killed him would have caused yet another rift among the clan and neither brother was ready for another internecine war. When the time was right alliances would be made and Florence and its treasures would be taken. The Vipers' spies were in brothels and churches, city-states' council chambers and bedrooms of the perverted, embedded like ticks in a dog's skin.

'What do you have?' Galeazzo asked, wanting the stupid game to end.

'An English courier came through the mountains. He carried no letter of safe conduct. He died...' Bernabò grinned. '... after a while. He had destroyed the sealed document he was to deliver before my men caught him, but he had been sent to Bardi's priest in Florence.'

'Torellini?'

Bernabò nodded.

'So the English reach out to the priest. So what? It means nothing. They deal with the bankers there.'

'There's more. Blackstone is leaving Italy. There was another messenger who sailed south.'

'You have him?'

'I have my assassin.'

'Even he cannot reach the Englishman,' said Galeazzo. 'We don't even know if Torellini made contact with him.'

The twisted face smirked, his quivering tongue flicking from his lips like a snake. 'Yes we do.'

Galeazzo held on to his patience. 'Enough, brother. Tell me what you have.'

'A runaway slave.'

The assassin was an aberration, especially to Bernabò Visconti. The killer led a chaste life, never knowingly seen with man or woman for the pleasures of sex. Bernabò didn't care. The self-imposed restraint was a ligature that choked distraction. His was a life that took gratification from death. If ever Bernabò Visconti felt the emotion of love, it was for this man – his perfect assassin.

The killer was expert in waiting long, patient hours until the perfect moment to slay his victim presented itself. Sometimes the strike was quickly taken, shocking in its audacity, other times he would infiltrate the inner circle of the man who was to die, a master of simple disguise that made him both visible but unsuspected. He was versed in all weapons, accomplished with sword and mace, but he favoured the knife. It was a special knife, the hilt and grip crafted for balance, long enough in the blade to penetrate, sharp to sever and small enough to conceal. The great craftsmen of Pistoia were renowned for such skills and it was always their knives that he used. He knew in particular of one old man who was renowned as a master blade maker.

Years before he had travelled to the small town, which lay between Florence and her enemy Lucca; it was a place where men killed frequently in vendettas, encouraged by the Florentines to wage their vicious feuds within their own streets and piazzas, keeping their violence away from Florence. He had visited secretly, not wishing to be seen in the streets, despite no one being aware of who he was or what his skills were. A stranger's face was always noticed in these small towns and suspicion hung in the air, ready to turn, as quickly as the spin of a coin, into a brutal assault in case such a stranger had been brought in as an assassin. Avoiding the narrow streets he went to the Ceppo hospital, where he offered his skills in herbal medicine to those who suffered wounds and other ailments. He had been taught how to staunch cuts that went to the bone and suture the wounds and then to apply the balms and herbs, the knowledge passed down to him by his mother, and her mother before her. After a month he disappeared, and no one knew where.

Undetected, he had gone beneath the hospital into the labyrinth that led below the city walls and several hundred yards later emerged in a side alley, so narrow that a loaded donkey could not pass through it. No sound of beaten metal came from behind the studded door that hid the small foundry where the blade maker produced his *pistolesi* – the daggers so favoured by assassins. Instead there was the sound of files and rubbing stones, grinding away at the blades. It was a slow, laborious task that required concentration to shape the bevelled centre of the knife and painstakingly smooth away its edges. He slept in the foundry, unwilling to leave until the knife he wanted was ready. It had been cut from a piece of steel and measured for its balance, its double-edged blade taking weeks to shape, its bevelled edges crafted and ground by the master's apprentice – then taken to the charcoal fire that glowed with deep red heat and thrust into Satan's domain to be tested by his heat. He never forgot the sight as the steel was prodded gently to harden: a process that demanded not only skill but years of experience. The charcoal had not to be too hot or it would ruin the steel, and if the blade became too yellow or blue then it remained too soft. Only when it turned a rich crimson along its whole length did the master have his assistant quench it in a vat of olive oil. It was the oil that sealed its strength. The cool blade was cleaned, slowly rubbed clean of the fire's deposits by a grinding stone, coarse at first and then finer. Once that was done it was placed on a griddle above a lesser-heated fire, allowing the embers to heat the metal gradually until it turned the colour of mountain honey. It was this that tempered the blade into hardened steel. Yet again it was quenched and once more ground and burnished until the metal gleamed.

The chestnut grip was carved to shape and bored end to end, then held in a vice and when the dagger's narrow tang was heated it was pushed through the small crossguard and into the wood forming a perfect fit. A young child, whose small fingers could bind thin strips of cured leather, wound and glued the grip. The dagger's blade was no more than the length of a man's palm from wrist to fingertip. It was an object of beauty to the Visconti's assassin – a blade so finely honed it could sting through the slender gaps of the best armour, and its bevelled edges so sharp it could slash a man's throat so that he did not know it until he choked on his own blood.

Unlike those who contracted him, especially the cruel Italian lord to whom he was bound by blood, he took no delight in the killing of a victim, felt no visceral thrill in making the final cut. Sending a soul to meet its judgement was an act that transcended the brutality of torture. Not for him the skills of tearing flesh and extending suffering; his pleasure came from the perfection of the kill and the deception of making the victim believe that the man sent to kill him was an ally. Suffering could be achieved in different ways. Take that which a man loves and then take the man himself once he knows he has lost it.

This killer was not known by face, except to the one corrupt lord. Throughout the Italian city-states a whisper sent out for his talent would, like a bee gathering pollen from flower to flower before returning to its hive, gain momentum and eventually reach him. He had never failed to kill his victim, and usually within plain sight of others. It was his ability to kill quickly and often with flair, and then to disappear like a phantom, that enhanced his legend. There was no name attached to him, no one place of residence. It was suspected that he lived in comfort, given the rumours that he only killed those of importance: merchant, politician or soldier – anyone whose influence had begun to encroach on another's power. That there could never be any link to those who hired him and the death of their adversary meant they had a golden cage of security – better than any Peruzzi or Bardi bank.

His appearance could change; his short hair meant his head could easily be covered by black cloth pulled tightly over his scalp. He wore no adornment or material that might warn his victim. He was a lithe man, slender as an acrobat, his practised muscles stretched across a torso that carried no fat, no sign of indolence or indulgence in fine sweet foods. When contracted to follow and slay a quarry he wore no boots, leaving his feet bare for purchase on marble floor or dirt street. He bound his legs and wrapped his torso in finely woven black cloth, with no leather belt to creak when he moved, rather a thin, corded rope to hold the material around him. He had learnt to control his respiration so that his breath would not plume in the chilled winter shadows, and he would not be heard to inhale as he lunged, or exhale as he struck.

Like a dancer he could turn on heel or toe.

One cut.

Then dance away.

Now, he was already in place. His orders were simple. Infiltrate Blackstone's men, lie in wait, become unseen, and when the time was right inflict great pain and suffering on the Englishman. Make him scream in agony so that his pain ripped out his heart and he died a slow death.

CHAPTER EIGHTEEN

Fra Stefano Caprini led the way along mist-hidden tracks that made the going slow over the next few days. Rivulets slithered down the rock faces as if the stone that protruded from the forest's banks wept from being held by ancient roots that clawed them back to the earth.

Breath feathered the air as the horses made their way steadily at the walk, nose to tail. Saddle-creak and jingling bridles were the only sounds that broke the silence as they clumped along the dirt pathway. Over the centuries the Via Francigena had been scraped from the countryside and in most places allowed only two men to walk abreast, which meant that riders could travel only in single file. Despite the closeness of the man in front and the dripping wet from the overhanging trees, Blackstone's men stayed alert during these passages through narrow confines. Saddlebags scraped the embankments; riders bent low over their pommels to avoid low-hanging branches. None voiced his tiredness or irritation at being hemmed in by the landscape. As they cleared a bend the valley mist was swept away, as if by the hand of God, and sucked further into the deep valleys. Nine hours after daylight had pierced its way through the hills they heard a solitary church bell's desolate tolling.

Across the saddle of land was a bell-tower and some stone buildings, big enough to house a dozen or more monks. A wisp of smoke went up and then bent as the air took it in the mist's wake.

'Little more than a monastery cell,' Caprini said, turning in the saddle to Blackstone, who nudged his belligerent horse alongside his guide. It snuffled and champed the bit, yanking its head. Blackstone gave a firm tug of the rein to settle it.

'Perhaps a dozen monks who work the fields and tend the livestock, so we will sleep with the horses in the stable. Food for us and the last of the winter silage for the horses,' the Tau knight continued, pointing to the low wooden thatched building on the other side of the tower. 'This is our final resting place before we climb into the foothills and seek out our guides through the pass.'

'You know this place?' Blackstone asked.

'I have not been here for ten years. It's grown. It used to be little more than a hermitage.'

Blackstone studied the lie of the land. The small plateau had been divided into sections. Low stone walls had been laid to protect their small *potager*. A meagre diet for a gruelling life. A goat was tethered; that would be for milk, not meat. It flicked its ears as a donkey brayed defiance. Probably at being kept in such miserable company as that offered by the hermit monks, Blackstone thought. The monks would grind what flour they could buy or trade and bake rough-crusted bread, but no such tantalizing smells accompanied the wisp of smoke.

This was the third similar refuge they had stayed in over the past nine days. They had made steady time, though too slow for Blackstone's liking, since bidding farewell to Killbere and the men south of Aulla. No threat had been made against them, no challenge offered as the company of men skirted village and town.

'When you reach Bordeaux,' Blackstone had told Killbere, 'go north, find the causeway to Saint-Clair-de-la-Beaumont; it will still be held by Jean de Grailly's troops. There's a church nearby and a monk there by the name of Brother Clement. I gave him my silver when we took Saint-Clair.'

Killbere's eyes widened. Blackstone raised a hand to stop his friend's inquisition. 'I promised Our Lord Jesus that day if he carried me safely ashore off that barrel of a cog then I would give over my plunder.'

Killbere scratched his beard. 'You are a man of conflicting habits, Thomas, but you're a man of your word, for which I and no doubt the Lord are grateful. And now I understand why you would rather have the ground beneath your feet than a rolling deck.'

Killbere considered what was being asked of him. Normandy was a dangerous place, more so since King John had been defeated and taken prisoner at Poitiers. Thousands of routiers were raping and burning across France. Knights lost their demesnes and Norman strongholds changed hands through siege or corruption. And the King's son was trying to keep Paris out of the clutches of the avaricious Charles of Navarre, who still had designs on the French Crown. The whole place was an angry hornet's nest.

'And if de Grailly has forsaken the place?'

'His men will hold it. It's too vital to lose.'

Killbere was agitated. 'I don't trust monks at the best of times. Halfwits, illegitimate cast-offs and self-serving, lying thieves who would strip a corpse in the name of the Almighty. God forbid they should seek a legitimate trade in the world.' He held a finger to the side of his nose and blew the snot free. 'Why not go further into Normandy and use those at Chaulion? It was your citadel and you gave the monks there more than a few pots of silver.'

'No. The Prince took my towns from me. His men would send word if you approach. Go to Brother Clement. See if he has spent my gift wisely; if he has then use him to find a safe route for you and the men. He'll be trustworthy and in my debt.'

Killbere had gazed down from the hills towards Genoa. There was sanctuary within sight at the Romanesque churches of Commenda di San Giovanni di Prè, a place that had protected pilgrims and fighting men since the time of the Crusades.

'You'll not reconsider? There's a straw mattress and hot food down there. God's blood, Thomas, a damned boat ride is better than a saddle-sore arse even if you retch it over the side. You might not get through those mountains. Take the boat with us.'

Blackstone turned his horse. 'Gilbert, I would rather face Satan and his devils with one arm tied behind my back than surrender to his kindred spirits lurking beneath those waves. Get to Calais. Await my orders.'

There was no more to be said and now, days later, hungry, wet and tired, Blackstone eased himself from the saddle and listened to the Tau knight's caution.

'This is a route seldom used, Sir Thomas. These monks prefer solitude and prayer. Such a community may not always express kindness to fighting men.'

Blackstone knew monks could be belligerent bastards if they were not there to serve pilgrims and receive payment for it. 'We pay our way, Stefano. I'm not here for conversation or prayer.'

Blackstone made a slow, cautious approach. Once they left the cover of the trees they would be seen, even by any devout monk who went about his work with his head full of prayer. Movement was a concealed fighting man's greatest weakness. He held the men at three hundred paces, the tree shadows making their numbers indistinct to anyone below. One of the monks raised his head from hoeing the stony ground and shielded his eyes from the low sun. His voice carried as he called to his brother monks.

'Armed men.'

Other monks appeared, carrying implements from the buildings and the fields behind the tower. They made no attempt to come together; there was no sense of them standing shoulder to shoulder as brothers who shared a sacred and remote hilltop religious cell. They stayed where they were.

'Fra Caprini,' Blackstone said. 'Go forward, tell them we mean them no harm. Once they see your blazon they'll know it's the truth.'

The Tau knight nodded. 'If I am uncertain of our reception I will call you in with my right hand. Otherwise the left.' He spurred his horse forward, leaving Blackstone and the men waiting.

John Jacob brought his horse alongside. 'Seems safe enough,' he said, letting his eyes sweep across the plateau and broken hills to snow-capped mountains beyond.

'So it seems,' said Blackstone, unable to keep a nagging doubt from his voice. Most of those below had moved towards the shelter of the buildings. Others had gone inside. A natural fear of armed men approaching was understandable.

Gaillard and Meulon eased around in their saddles to look at Blackstone.

'Good place for dismounted men to be at a disadvantage once we get down there, Sir Thomas,' said Meulon. 'Those low walls and livestock fences could hinder a fight when we're on foot.'

'Or be used to hide an ambush,' added Gaillard.

'I see that. And something else. Will?' he called, bringing the archer forward. 'Put your eye past those hillside walls. Up the slope, past those boulders.'

A bird of prey curved high in the sky, using the mountain air to gain its height.

'What do you see?' Blackstone asked.

'The ground is scuffed, as if men and horses have gone up,' said Longdon.

'Donkeys or goats, perhaps?' Jacob asked.

'Perhaps,' said Blackstone. 'I see one donkey fenced and a goat tethered. Poor monks won't have more livestock than that.'

'Can you see the ground birds?' said Will Longdon. 'Further still. Way beyond. Raven or crow. I can't be certain.'

'I can't see them,' Jacob said.

'Look beyond the slope, and the rocks, the ground falls away into a dip and then rises to the right, and falls away again, like a wave. In the curl of the wave there's movement.' He looked to Blackstone, who nodded in confirmation. An archer's eye was keener than most.

'Carrion feeding. A bird of prey in the sky. There's little food to be had this time of year. A few spring rabbits? A deer that's fallen to its death?' Blackstone said, knowing it was unlikely.

'They would be in the forest. Might be a dead bear or wolf though,' said Jacob.

'Then there would be more birds,' said Longdon.

'Could also be dead men,' said Meulon.

Blackstone watched Caprini speak to the monk in the distance.

123

There was still only one of them doing the talking: the one who had called out at their approach. The others had gone back inside the buildings or were standing near doorways or alongside a pig pen or wood store. Chickens clucked in the hen house.

'It's been a slow journey. If word has got here before us that this was our route, this is the last chance our enemies would have to stop us.' He turned in the saddle. 'Will, take Halfpenny and Thurgood. Ease the horses back. Dismount, and in case they can see you make it seem that you think one of the horses is lame. Walk one of them back, around that corner out of sight. Tether him and the three of you move downhill through the trees and find a place to cover us.'

'Aye, Thomas,' Will Longdon said and turned back.

'We'll ride in then?' said Jacob.

'Soon as Caprini signals. Let's not make it obvious that we doubt who's down there. We are weary travellers, exhausted by the journey. Gaillard, slump forward, you're sick. Tell the men. Be ready.'

They waited and then Caprini turned in the saddle and waved them in with his right hand.

Danger.

They eased their horses down the gentle slope towards the monks, hunched in the saddle like men who had been riding for days without sleep. Men who might be lulled into thinking they were safe.

Caprini understood. As Blackstone pulled up his horse a dozen paces away he touched the monk's shoulder. 'The brothers here are a silent order. But he will speak on their behalf.'

Blackstone considered the monk's appearance. Dirt-caked habit, hands calloused and grimy. If the other monks were as lean and strong as this monk appeared to be, then it showed that their life here was hard and demanding. The man's face was stubbled and his tonsure had not been shaved for days. Perhaps so remote a place made the act of washing less important. Caprini turned to the monk and gestured to Blackstone. 'These men are exhausted, Brother. They need nothing more than sleep and food for the night.'

Gaillard slumped across the saddle's pommel. Without the monk seeing, Meulon jabbed him in the ribs making him groan. John Jacob's eyes widened. Not too much acting, he was trying to say. Meulon shrugged.

'And I have a man sick,' said Blackstone.

The monk nodded. He showed no trace of concern at the arrival of the armed men. No sign of nervousness that these riders were not pilgrims of Christ. 'All are welcome here. But...' and as he hesitated Blackstone saw his eyes shift like a stallholder bargaining a piece of cloth, '... we are poor recluses. Some payment, no matter how small, would be welcome as a charity.'

Caprini glanced backwards as Blackstone as the others dismounted. Blackstone stayed where he was, head bowed into the cowl of his cloak.

'We have gold florins and enough silver coin to pay for a king's hospitality,' said Caprini. 'We carry funds from Florence to the Marquis de Montferrat so that he might keep the pass through the mountains safe.' He carried the lie well. He lowered his voice so that only the monk could hear him. 'They will cause no harm. Drunk and tired men sleep the sleep of the dead. This was the safest route I could find for them.'

'Then you are welcome,' said the monk. 'How many men?'

'There are six of us, Brother,' said Blackstone, looking at Caprini, whose eyes quickly scanned the dismounted men. Will Longdon and two others were missing. Perinne was already dismounted, fussing at his saddle strap, his eyes searching the compound for any untoward movement that might warn of a trap.

Caprini nodded to the monk. 'As you can see. Six.'

Blackstone hoped that when he sent Longdon into the trees they had been far enough away from the sanctuary not to have been noticed. The monk looked at the weary men, but also let his gaze go past them up the track and across the treeline. There

125

was no sign of movement. He seemed satisfied. 'Then we will accommodate you as best we can. Here in this remote place we seldom see travellers. One, perhaps two, at a time. But we shall do what we can. Two men can sleep in the dormitory, another in the stable. The sick man should be taken to the kitchen for warmth. We will do what we can for him.' He pointed to the three different areas where the men should tether their horses, then turned and gave a barely noticeable nod to one of the other monks near the woodshed. A tip of the chin that John Jacob noticed.

'Monks, my arse,' he whispered to Blackstone as they walked their horses towards the shelter. 'They're separating us. Easy pickings, Sir Thomas.'

He and Blackstone led their horses where they were instructed. A warning look from Caprini was acknowledged. The horses jostled; the Tau knight muttered: 'Be cautious. This man's dialect is not from these parts.'

The uncanny silence of the mountain foothills was broken only by the horses' shifting weight and the screech of the raptor high in the sky. Even the chickens had fallen silent, perhaps because of the hunting bird's distant threat. In the stillness the men tied off their horses and eased the saddles from their backs. Each man knew that Blackstone and John Jacob were already positioning themselves for an attack that might come from behind the low wall or the building's darkened doorway. They appeared unconcerned yet eyes and ears sought out the moment that they knew must come. They were vulnerable – but alert.

Meulon made a fuss of getting Gaillard down from his horse, easing his friend so that he sat, back against the wall, but with his spear laid at his side. Then Meulon took his time untying the panniers, looking across his horse's withers to where one of the monks had stepped out of sight.

It took six heartbeats before the attack started.

At the edge of the sanctuary seven armed men broke cover, their feet pounding into the damp earth like a war drum that signalled several things to happen at once.

The tethered goat jerked at its restraint, alarmed as a monk stepped from behind a wall and swung an axe at Meulon. He parried with his spear shaft and Gaillard went quickly onto one knee and rammed his spear point up through the man's lungs and heart. Meulon put his boot into the gasping man's chest as Gaillard pulled his haft free. The two Normans recovered quickly, turning as screams suddenly echoed from the running men being cut down by Longdon and his archers in the forest. Three armed men broke through, turning the corner of the furthest building, swords raised, their faces contorted with fear and disbelief that their own ambush had failed, knowing that there was no escape. They attacked with the desperate belief that all fighting men carry with them: that they will not die – not this day. John Jacob caught sight of the Italian knight as he squared himself to face the oncoming attack.

'He needs help,' he grunted as he and Blackstone shouldered their horses aside, forcing the animals between themselves and the armed monks who suddenly appeared from the doorway. The bastard horse objected and swayed its weight against Blackstone, throwing him off balance and making him step back. A crossbow bolt whipped through the air where he had stood a moment before. One man carried a fighting axe in each hand, the other a sword, and as the crossbowman threw aside his now useless weapon he snatched up a spear that had been hidden at the corner of the building. They lunged – aggressive men who made no sound; who kept their eyes on their intended victims. John Jacob was at Blackstone's shoulder to help block the swordsman, which hampered the double-handed axeman.

Blackstone ignored Jacob's words. Caprini would have to deal with his own attackers. The stocky Perinne hacked down a monk who wielded a falchion, swinging his blade with such force it cut through the man's heavy clothing, its keen edge slicing into ribs, lungs and heart. Blackstone and Jacob parried blows from wild-eyed assailants. Madness; men of God attacking with such violence. Fleeting thoughts flashed through Blackstone's mind. A planned ambush to stop him reaching England or fighting men disguised as monks to rob exhausted pilgrims? Every man was battling for his life.

Caprini stood his ground. He caught the first man's strike on the crosspiece of his sword, turned and slashed his knife hand across the attacker's face. Blinded, he fell squirming, ignored by the Tau knight, who altered his stance, dropped to one knee and took the second man in the groin. The charging man's weight forced Caprini down with him, but by then Meulon and Gaillard were at his back. Meulon's spear hooked into the attacker's collarbone and the screaming man was hoisted like a fish snatched from a stream. Meulon kicked down onto the man's neck, cracking bones, and wrenched his spear shaft free. The other man had faltered in his attack. The two giant men shielding the Tau knight were a terrifying sight and the man's courage failed him. He turned and ran. He did not see the three archers emerge from the trees and bend their backs into their war bows. The hiss of the arrow shafts through the air was unmistakable. The fleeing man turned, desperately seeking the arrows in the sky in a vain attempt to avoid them. By the time he saw them, two had pierced him: one through the chest, one the thigh. The third thudded into the ground less than half a shaft's length away. He squirmed, muscles contorting, a shattered body trying to deal with its agony. By the time the archers reached him he was dead.

As Blackstone killed the third man he looked across at Caprini. The moment was held like a stitched tableau. Figures lay dead; the Tau knight stood over a writhing monk and then rammed his blade into his chest to strangle a final terrified scream.

'So much for them being a silent order,' John Jacob said, smiling as he wiped his blade clean on a handful of straw.

The archers finished off two or three men who lay in the dirt, arrow shafts embedded in them.

The killing had taken less time than it would to toll the bell a dozen times.

Blackstone's men stood their ground. Were there others?

'Will?' Blackstone called.

'No more down here!' Longdon shouted.

Blackstone turned to where the two Normans stood with bloodied spears. Both shook their heads. 'It's finished, Sir Thomas.'

'No one inside. This was all,' said Perinne.

Nine monks lay dead. Seven more bodies lay sprawled. These men were dressed little differently than Blackstone's own men. Fighters. Brigands perhaps.

'Strip them!' Blackstone ordered.

CHAPTER NINETEEN

There was no need for Blackstone to order the others to take up a defensive position. Will Longdon placed Halfpenny and Thurgood where anyone approaching could be ambushed as Jacob searched the buildings. Meulon, Perinne and Gaillard stripped the monks as the Tau knight accompanied Blackstone to where the carrion crows had been spotted.

The two men rested a moment, catching their breath in the cold air, then looked back to where the slaughter had taken place. The naked corpses quivered like maggots as Blackstone's men dragged them into the centre of the killing field.

'Could they have been monks?' Blackstone asked.

'It is possible. Men have been known to lose themselves when they live such isolated lives,' Stefano answered. He paused for a moment. 'Who among us has not experienced madness?'

Blackstone remained silent, but the remark struck home. Ram a bodkin-pointed shaft into a man's chest and the shockwaves of pain tear through his body. As did the knowledge that when he fought he was possessed. Of what... he was uncertain.

'And you?' he said, looking carefully at the Italian knight, whose gaze had not left the bloodstained sanctuary.

'I have been in that place. And I swore to Our Lord Jesus that if he delivered me from it I would serve pilgrims and those who fought for Him.'

'Then why help me? I'm no pilgrim. I wear a pagan goddess at my throat.'

Caprini smiled. 'You are a man of reputation. Others fear you. Not I. You are unknown to me as a man. But when Father

Niccolò Torellini asks that you be helped, then I know you to be a deserving man who must be in the service of God.'

Blackstone continued uphill. 'I do not know God. I serve my King and my men. Have no expectation of me other than that,' he said.

Stefano Caprini sighed with the comfort of knowledge. 'You are as Father Torellini predicted. But whether you know it or not, there is a goodness within you that can only come from suffering torment of the soul.'

Blackstone turned and pointed a finger at him. 'Do not preach to me about who I am. Do not think you understand what I do or why I do it. I kill. And I do it well. That is all you need to know about me.'

The two men faced each other for a moment longer, and then the older man dipped his head in acknowledgement. He was not cowed by the younger, stronger man, but his own code of behaviour demanded he make amends. 'I apologize. It is not my place to speak of such things.'

Blackstone had no doubt that this knight had fought his demons and won, but his own would always shadow his life. They made him who he was.

He held them close.

Like old friends.

Shallow graves had been turned and picked at by scavengers. Wild beasts had torn the earth back and feasted on what remained of the men buried there. Bones were separated from torsos, a few – thigh bones and ribs – lay scattered across the alpine grass. There was little depth to the soil for burial so rocks had been placed over the corpses in an attempt to protect their sanctity, but they were inadequate against the wild creatures.

There were no markers or headstones.

'Why would anyone bring their dead up here?' Caprini asked, looking at the place, which probably held twenty or thirty graves. 'They have a graveyard near the sanctuary.

'To hide them from visitors,' Blackstone said, tugging at an exposed piece of cloth and easing out its remains.

'Then these are the bodies of monks murdered by brigands who took their place to kill pilgrims.'

What was left of the dead man's skin beneath his threadbare clothing barely concealed his bones. Blackstone eased a skull aside with the toe of his boot. The matted mass that was once the man's hair slipped away. He bent down and poked at the remains with his knife.

'Look for yourself,' said Blackstone and went to another grave, one that was better covered with stones. He pushed aside the rocks and scraped away the dirt covering.

Caprini looked up from where he was examining the skeleton. 'That grave is sacred.'

'Not up here,' said Blackstone, exposing the skeleton's skull. This corpse had the remains of a cap and wispy strands of hair that clung to it. He flicked away the head covering with the tip of his knife. 'These are not monks. They're pilgrims, slaughtered by monks.'

Caprini looked in disgust at the graves. Blackstone was already walking past him.

'Men of God who were placed here to give sanctuary to those on the journey to Canterbury and Rome, murdering innocent pilgrims,' said Caprini, as if the shame was his own.

'Priests torture witches and non-believers. The Inquisition will burn a man's soul from his body. What more is there to understand? I'll have the men cover them up.' Blackstone paid no more attention to the Italian's concerns and turned away.

'Do not condemn the Church because of these vile creatures,' Caprini called after him. 'These men were sarabaites, the most detestable of monks. They are loyal to the world and without an abbot to shepherd them they pen themselves in the fold of lust and wantonness. They affront God with their tonsures. They follow no Holy Rule, only whatever strikes their fancy. Better that we should stay silent than speak of them.'

'Then you can offer prayers for those they betrayed and slaughtered. I'm happy knowing I cast them into the fires of hell.'

The naked bodies of those who had once made vows of holy orders lay in a ragged line. Meulon pointed at them. 'There are no battle scars on any of them. There are a few healed wounds. Nothing that a farm tool couldn't inflict. Did you find anything up there?' he said.

'Murdered pilgrims. These bastards cut their throats or smashed in their skulls.'

Gaillard crossed himself. 'Shit.'

'John, call in Will and the others,' he said to Jacob. 'What of those who came from behind us?' he said to Meulon.

'They're fighting men all right. Scars on their backs from whippings...'

'Or penance,' said Gaillard.

'Gaillard, for Christ's sake. They're brigands, probably deserters. If Sir Thomas is right then these men worked with the monks. Chances are we came on them before they had time to organize themselves,' said Meulon and looked to Blackstone. 'Am I right?'

Blackstone nodded. 'These buildings yield nothing but what you would expect from dirt-scraping monks, but if they're deserters they're Visconti deserters,' he said, showing them a couple of the bloodied jupons that bore the faded viper patch.

'Planned, do you think? Or chance?' said Jacob.

'Can't be planned,' said Blackstone. 'How would they know which path we took?'

'Unless they put men across them all?' Jacob said.

'Perhaps,' admitted Blackstone. He threw the jupons down. 'Search everywhere. Find their booty. Then drag them into that byre,' he ordered.

By nightfall their horses had been sheltered and fed. Fresh water had been drawn from the well and the men had washed themselves, combing the blood from their wet hair and then gathering at the fire that Jack Halfpenny and Thurgood had built up. Will Longdon had boiled eggs then slaughtered and plucked half a dozen chickens. He had roasted and seasoned them while the others had torn apart the monks' dormitory and found a cache of coins, gold rings and silver trinkets. Not all pilgrims were penniless. Meulon and Gaillard spilled everything onto a blanket and carried it out to where the men now sat around the fire.

'And there's wine,' said Longdon as he and Thurgood put down clay jugs and settled themselves to eat and drink.

'Some of it was off,' said Thurgood. 'Tasted like piss and vinegar.'

'Didn't stop him from drinking it, though,' said Halfpenny. 'He'll be shitting a sword's length by tomorrow.'

'No,' said Perinne. 'He has a copper-bottomed gut. I've seen him drink laundry water with scum on it.'

The others laughed and grunted in agreement, quickly silenced by the chicken's soft flesh on their teeth. A clear sky glistened with stars that blessed them and the hot food eased away the aches and pain of minor wounds from the day's killing. There was an added benefit of the cold night air: it kept the dead bodies chilled and slowed decomposition.

Stefano Caprini hovered at the edge of the circle of men. Blackstone also stood to one side. He had eaten barely enough to satisfy his hunger, but it was enough that he had not lost a man to the ambushers – and that satisfaction had quelled his appetite. The food was good and every man licked fingers and sucked bones from the tasty fowl. Will Longdon was a good man to have riding with you. He could provide food better than most men. If there was a bird to be snared or a deer to be brought down, Will would find it. Always had. And when he cooked there was never a man who did not enjoy his offering. His whore mother had abandoned him as a child and a washerwoman in a village had taken pity – and his mother's shawl as payment – and fed the boy. She must have been the one who taught him to cook, Blackstone thought, though he had never known for certain. Who among them knew the story of their own family? His own was vague – a French mother who softened the heart of an English archer and died giving birth to another son. Each and every man had his own story. One day they might even discover what they were.

'You cannot take this,' Caprini said, meaning the booty on the blanket.

Meulon looked up at him, but turned away and devoted his attention to the succulent chicken leg.

'Cannot?' said John Jacob. 'Or should not?'

Thurgood and Halfpenny looked blankly at the other men. Thurgood's nose had been bent out of shape by many an alehouse brawl; now it became as pinched as the rest of his features as he tried to understand what challenges were being laid down. The Italian knight seldom spoke. Jacob tossed chicken bones on the fire and glanced towards Blackstone.

'My men killed those who tried to kill them,' said Blackstone.

'It is tainted with blood,' insisted the Tau knight.

Will Longdon snorted. 'And my hands are dripping in chicken grease, but I'll lick my fingers and taste the dirt from the ground and the blood of those men. It's what comes to us from our efforts.'

Blackstone watched his men's reactions. For an outsider to come between them and their reward could turn into a dangerous situation and his rank would not help him. They were no longer in any king's army; they were company men who chose their own commanders.

Gaillard got to his feet, his size looming even larger as his shadow was cast by firelight. He faced the Tau knight, but then turned away, muttering, 'I need a piss.'

Blackstone understood his men. Gaillard was agreeing with Caprini, but did not wish to break ranks.

'We are travelling fast,' said Meulon. 'This is no time to start carrying extra weight. Another fight like this and the next thing you know we'd need a pack horse. Best to leave things as they are.'

The Norman might have been talking about the weather. He did not seem to be criticizing Will Longdon for wanting to take the booty.

'Hang on,' said Thurgood. 'You agreeing with the Italian? That what you're saying? I did my share of killing today, and reburying the poor bastards murdered by them monks. A few coins and trinkets won't weigh me down.'

It was John Jacob who spoke the truth plainly. 'It's tainted with pilgrims' blood, lad. We'll give it to a church when we next come to one.' It was said in a manner that brooked no argument.

Longdon saw the look in the man-at-arm's eyes. He barely spared a glance in the archers' direction.

'Why not?' said Longdon. 'Let's play the Good Samaritan and give to the poor bastards who really need it, eh?' The centenar knew his duty. Allowing dissent to fester was how a battle line could yield. Blackstone had taken a gamble giving Longdon a hundred archers to command in the company, and now even with two chosen men, they had been selected by him. He was still a rogue who would steal a pair of shoes from the dead, like any of them, but he would not allow one of his archers to cause discord, especially in such a small group of men whose objective was to get their sworn lord back to England.

'What? No. A pig's arse!' said Thurgood.

Longdon licked his fingers. 'Besides, your arrow was wide of the mark when those men made their run.'

'I used my knife!' said Thurgood defensively. Every archer knew when his strike was good or not. 'I sliced as many throats as any man here.'

Longdon got to his feet and gathered the corners of the blanket. 'You're not here to use your knife, lad. Any arsehole swordsman – other than them among us, of course – can do that. You're here to put your man down with an arrow. To make sure we don't have to go round cutting throats.' It broke the tension. By the time he had delivered his admonition the blanket was gathered and taken to Caprini.

Thurgood looked confused. It was true he had missed – once. But was that a good enough reason to be denied a share of the spoils? He looked from man to man who either smiled or shrugged. The matter was closed.

Blackstone stepped forward and threw his chicken bones into the fire. 'We'll let the Italian carry the extra weight. That's only fair, wouldn't you say, Robert?' he said, laying a comradely hand on Thurgood's shoulder.

The question made the archer clear his confused dissatisfaction quickly. 'Aye... I suppose it is, Sir Thomas.' Then, with a more definite assertion that he had made the correct decision: 'It's only right.'

Caprini nodded his thanks to Longdon as he took the tied blanket from him.

'You're bloody lucky Thomas is here, sir knight. Me? I'd have had the trinkets round my neck, the coins in my purse and the rings on my fingers,' said Longdon barely above a whisper.

Caprini showed no concern. 'But an English archer needs to hold his war bow and draw an arrow without impediment. To wear rings on your fingers would make you less effective. Surely?'

Will Longdon turned away and sucked his teeth. Smart-arse knights. They were all the same, wherever they came from.

By the time the morning sunlight touched the valleys, the men were ready to ride. The donkey and the goat were tethered behind one of the horses. Two more days would take them to the monks at the pass. The livestock would serve as a contribution for their help, along with the booty, which was now tied onto the donkey's back. Thurgood had been persuaded that a donkey was better suited to carry it than the Tau knight, who was needed to guide them. The men's safety was still in the knight's hands, it was argued. And look what that had brought them, Thurgood had moaned. Then all the more reason to make certain that the monks who would guide them through the pass should feel sufficiently rewarded, came the argument in answer. Thurgood tethered the goat and the donkey on a trailing rein behind his horse.

'And when we thirst, you can milk the goat for us,' said Halfpenny.

'That's if he can tell the difference between donkey and goat,' said Will Longdon.

As the men's humour jibed back and forth, Blackstone stood in the byre with John Jacob. The dead had already been thrown unceremoniously inside, their bodies covered with anything that would burn – mattresses, benches and stools and then finally armfuls from the woodpile – then tallow and oil was smeared and spilled.

Blackstone looked at the carnage. Two of the men waited outside with burning torches. Jacob gathered a handful of the brigands' clothing.

'You've seen these, Sir Thomas,' he said, pulling aside the cloth so that the stitched, though faded, badge on its left breast could be seen. 'Visconti men.' He did the same with another. 'But this livery I don't know. It looks German or Hungarian.' He rubbed his thumb across the raised colours, more bloody than the others, and even less distinct. 'These were men fighting for the Visconti. Now, why would they be here? In this godforsaken place? Killing pilgrims was the monks' business. If anything they got in these men's way.'

He tossed the clothing onto the pile. 'If they were after you they must have had men in place along the main routes of the Via Francigena. This must have been the last place they would have expected you to travel, but a good site for an ambush, expecting our guard to be down. From here we're moving into de Montferrat's territory. The Visconti have no cause to love him, but they're not likely to send men that far west on a hunting expedition for you. It's either coincidence – or these men here were waiting for you.'

And that meant betrayal.

'Burn them,' said Blackstone.

By the time they rode across the ridgeline the funeral pyre's black smoke had risen high into the sky, a signal to anyone beyond the horizon that if this had been a planned assassination, then whoever had tried to have Blackstone killed had failed. It would take days for the information to reach the men's paymasters. From hermit monk to itinerant pilgrim word would go through village and hamlet until it reached *condottiere* patrols. The truth would become rumour and then legend. Thomas Blackstone, the scourge of his enemies, would be seen as the English knight who slaughtered innocent monks who had offered him shelter and respite.

CHAPTER TWENTY

There were twenty-three passes through the Alps. Transalpine princes controlled those that led into their territory, routes that had been established when man first questioned what lay beyond the next mountain. Great warriors such as Hannibal had achieved the seemingly impossible and the legions of Rome had tramped beneath the great snow-capped sentinels. To the north was the St Gotthard, used by the Milanese to extend their influence – wealth, goods and banking – into the land of the Germans. Further south the Brenner gave the Venetians and Florentines access across France towards Flanders and England. Even in mid-winter people and carts could get through the passes using sledges. However, the underbelly of the Alps was the route Blackstone had secured when he fought 'La Battaglia nella Valle dei Fiori' and tore the citadel that guarded the route from the grip of one of the Visconti's captains. It was a treacherous pass that made men cleave to its ice- and snowfields. When the thaw came, the monks who guided travellers across those narrow paths would try to retrieve the bodies, but more usually the mountain held them close.

Except for hot food and a change of horses for his men, Blackstone declined further hospitality offered by the Marquis de Montferrat. Fresh mounts were given freely to the men, though Blackstone's war horse had the stamina and strength to continue. It was a creature like its master – able to ignore privation and the harshness of nature. They were well suited.

'Stay,' de Montferrat said. 'The snows have slowed travel this year. Even the monks have lost some of their own to icefalls. There are women here for your men – and it is paid for.' He smiled because he was making good revenue thanks to Thomas Blackstone and the Pope. When Blackstone had fought the Battle of the Valley of Flowers at the border and seized the citadel it gave de Montferrat control over a key route into Lombardy. The papal chamber and the city of Genoa paid the Marquis a hundred thousand florins to allow mercenaries through the mountains to inflict terror and destruction on the Milanese rulers and their German mercenaries. Genoa, like the Pope, was the Visconti's enemy.

'And I take tolls for those troops to pass by the castle you seized.' He raised a glass of wine in salutation. 'You need never pay for anything in my territory, Sir Thomas.'

Blackstone realized that the harsh weather that had swept across the north that winter might have claimed any other of the King's messengers – had they been sent. Samuel Cracknell had sailed from England, his ship clinging to the coastline. Misfortune had struck when it was blown off course and into the hands of the Pisans.

'Have you heard of anyone from England coming through the pass these past weeks?' he asked.

'Other than handfuls of routiers and foolhardy merchants thinking this was a land ripe for exploitation? None.'

Blackstone watched the Marquis's response. There was no guile or deceit in his answer. Perhaps there had been only one messenger after all.

'Only merchants, then,' said Blackstone.

Montferrat laughed. 'By the Holy Cross, you would think they'd know the Italians are masters at making deals. Those poor bastards haul themselves through the passes. They come to make money, and they are culled by disease and war, just like you mercenaries.' He paused. As much as Blackstone had studied his host, so too had de Montferrat watched his guest. Both men were paid for the services they provided to their paymasters. Why was Blackstone turning his back on Florentine money? 'No one goes back through that pass, not at this time of the year. Why else is it called the Gate of the Dead?' he said. 'Not from this *heavenly* land. Stay here and die here.'

The meaning was not lost on Blackstone. Italy's republics might be at constant war, but it was nothing like the ravaged country of France.

Montferrat picked remains of his food from a silver plate and tossed it to the dogs that lay gazing intently in the hope of scraps. 'You risk a great deal coming this far north. How you survived in Tuscany these years I don't know. The Visconti would like nothing better than to hang and gut you. You think the Hungarians are cruel bastards? Nothing compares to those brothers.' He kicked one of the hounds from beneath his feet. It yelped and slunk away. Montferrat leaned forward to make his point. 'When the Pope threatened to excommunicate Bernabò he had four nuns and a monk stripped and put in a cage. He roasted them alive. He hates the Church. And those who fight for it.'

'And you,' Blackstone said.

'And me. Though I'm little more than a gatekeeper these days.'

'You're a Piedmontese nobleman. You have influence and that gives you information,' said Blackstone.

Montferrat shrugged. 'A little,' he agreed, his attempt at humility fooling no one. He relented, knowing what Blackstone was asking. 'The word came that you had left the service of Florence and were returning to France, or at least those that were interested thought it to be France.'

Blackstone gave nothing away. How difficult could it be for rumour to spread like a plague?

'Or perhaps not France?' Montferrat said.

'Who knew?'

He shrugged again. 'I heard you were taking ship at Genoa. And if I heard then your enemies heard.'

'And who was interested?'

'The Visconti. The Germans. The Hungarians. Other company captains. French noblemen dispossessed by you. Italian merchants robbed by you. Those with a vendetta against you. The Virgin Mary, for all I know. You didn't crucify her son, did you, by any chance?'

Blackstone drank the last mouthful of wine and pushed the stool away from the table. 'My thanks for the horses and supplies. We'll leave after matins.'

'Thomas, you have made it this far; whoever wants you dead will have to wait until after you pass through the mountains. Because now they will know that you did not leave with your men at Genoa.'

Montferrat toyed with his eating knife. He could make money from informing Blackstone's enemies where he was going. But then he ran the risk of losing the Pope's largesse. And then, who knows, he thought, they might even use Blackstone to take back the citadel, pour thousands of brigands through the pass and lay siege to him.

'Your intentions are safe with me,' he said.

'I never doubted it,' said Blackstone. But the Marquis was uncertain, from the Englishman's smile, whether he meant it.

Snow whirled in turbulent vengeance against those who dared to trespass through the mountains. It sought out the ravines and rock faces, punishing guides trying to cross the divide as they pushed and pulled wicker sledges carrying their passengers. The Italian villagers earned good payment for taking travellers through the pass, but it was the monks from the monastery on the French side of the mountains who had served pilgrims for a hundred years and knew every handhold, and it was they whom Blackstone would trust to take his men back to where they had journeyed two winters before.

'The villagers' greed has already killed many this past week,' the leather-faced monk told Blackstone as they waited in the lee of the mountain. The monk looked younger than Blackstone's twenty-eight years, but Blackstone could not tell his age as he watched him coil a hemp rope in a great loop that he tied off and slung across his body. These monks could be twice the age they looked – perhaps the high mountain passes brought them closer to God's domain and He blessed them for their piety and courage.

He had told them his name was Brother Bertrand, a novice, born and raised in the mountain villages and taken as an orphan into the monastery when still a child. Now he added that the pass was icy on this side of the mountain because of the north wind that swept down from the higher peaks. Once they reached halfway it would be easier and the downhill approach would cause them less difficulty.

Blackstone studied the young man. He had a foolish grin stitched across his face. Did that indicate that he was in the hands of an idiot? Blackstone wondered. Young, old or idiot – did it matter? He was a mountain guide. The monk's wiry frame could mislead an untrained eye as to his strength – indeed, a life of fasting and prayer might weaken some men – but if he had climbed and travelled these mountains since going into the monastery, then his slight body would be as supple as a English archer's yew bow. A trustworthy guide to lead them back.

'You will do nothing, Sir Thomas, until I tell you. And then you will obey every word I say until we reach the other side,' said the monk. 'If a man falls he is in God's hands, not ours. We do not stop on the path. You remember it?'

Blackstone did remember. It was one of the most difficult passes to traverse, but when he had led several hundred men into Italy in fair weather it had been less challenging. He had lost fewer than half a dozen men during that journey. The ground had been dry, the autumn winds not yet gathered behind the peaks. The sun broke through that day like a divine light showing the way through the Gate of the Dead.

Not so now. The unpredictable gusts of wind could lift a man the size of Meulon and cast him down. There was no argument from Blackstone or those who had previously made the same perilous journey with him.

As the wind buffeted the mountainside the men kept as close as possible to the rock face. Their horses were blindfolded and weapons secured to the saddle pommels. Meulon held the reins of his horse tightly, his bare hand comforting its muzzle. Like the others it was hobbled so that its strides were restricted. Despite the horses being sturdy beasts and used to such difficult conditions, it was better to control any skittish behaviour. Horses were dumb beasts whose erratic behaviour could kill a man. Only once they had traversed the worst the pass had to offer would the hobbles be untied.

Each man wrapped sackcloth around his horse's hooves and his own boots for purchase. Those who wore their hair long tied back its length with cord and then pulled their helmets tightly onto their heads and tightened the straps or bound them beneath their chins with a strip of linen. Debris from a rockslide could stun a man and to lose your footing meant a frightened horse and a long drop into oblivion.

Thurgood cast a glance at his friend, Halfpenny. This pass was more dangerous than he had imagined. The two archers had come into Lombardy by a more northern route after they found their services as archers no longer needed after the English victory at Poitiers. Drifting with many others they had joined one of the routier companies and plundered southwards until they heard that Sir Thomas Blackstone had a few hundred men under contract for Florence. They were young men, easily swayed by the attraction of a good wage paid by Italian city-states, and the chance to share plunder when the company's terror was unleashed on the unsuspecting. Rape and murder suited them. However, they found it was different with Blackstone. They had to prove their worth. By good fortune they were accomplished archers and experienced fighters, who wore an English soldier's belligerence like a coat of arms. And their animal instincts soon understood that Blackstone's command was little different than being in the King's army. Ill discipline was not tolerated. Rape of the innocent was punishable by hanging, and looting a church could lose a man his hand.

There were enough women among the camp followers who would spread their legs, provided they were paid, and Blackstone's captains saw to it that they were. Any fighting between soldiers over a woman that ended in a killing was judged on the circumstances.

There were still those who would die over a whore. A drunken *condottiere*'s knife attack meant Blackstone's company lost a fighting man, so whoever did the killing was well advised to have a good enough reason or he would feel the weight of Blackstone's justice.

'North was better,' Thurgood said to Meulon. 'A decent road and space for cart and horse. This is too narrow.' He squinted into the white flurries that buffeted around the weather side. 'And too high.' He looked at Halfpenny. 'Shit might freeze, Jack, but if I fall I'll not be stuck like a turd on a rock for everyone to see. Put an arrow through me and knock me off my perch. Will you do that for me?'

Halfpenny's cap was bound around his head and chin. Before he could answer through gritted teeth, Meulon muttered his own reply. 'I could put my spear up your arse now and save us all the trouble later.'

Halfpenny's gagged laugh through the binding sounded like a dog being strangled.

'Piss off, Jack,' said Thurgood. 'And you, you French bastard,' he said, pointing at Meulon, 'can kiss my English arse.'

'Norman bastard,' said Gaillard. 'We're Normans. And you forget Meulon is one of Sir Thomas's captains.'

'And my centenar is Will Longdon. That's who I take my orders from.'

Meulon grinned. 'But you are travelling behind me today so you will do as I do and watch for my command.'

Will Longdon made his way down the line of stationary men and horses, muttering instructions as he passed each man. 'Sir Thomas says to tighten the girths, bind loose clothing, secure weapons.'

Thurgood snatched at his arm. 'Will, am I to follow Meulon? He farts like a horse. I'll be over the edge with his stench.'

Longdon snatched free his arm. He was in no mood for bleating men. 'Is your bow covered and tied?'

'Aye, but –'

'And the cords are stored and dry?'

'Of course,' said Thurgood, aggrieved a fellow archer was not standing up for him.

'Then cease mewling and get ready to move. Do what Meulon says. He's too mean and ugly to argue with.'

Longdon turned back. His limbs were already seizing up in the cold. He steadied himself against horse and man as the intemperate wind whipped a flurry of snow against him.

'In half a day the track widens, but if you can't hold onto your fear until then, I'll tie a rope around you and drag you along like a dog,' said Meulon.

Halfpenny stepped quickly between his friend and the Norman. Thurgood was handy with a knife and he was lighter on his feet than the big man. 'You wouldn't want that, Meulon, you're as big as a tree and he'd end up pissing on your leg.'

Halfpenny and Thurgood had only been with Blackstone's company for less than a year and wielded no influence over any of the captains, and they only had Will Longdon to vouch for them. It was the veteran archer's standing with Blackstone that brought them so close to this bodyguard of men. That and their skill.

Nothing more was said as the horses resumed their hobbled steps. Meulon glanced back at the belligerent Englishman, and the thought passed through his mind that for once he did not want an archer at his back.

CHAPTER TWENTY-ONE

Oliviero Dantini had journeyed with Sir Gilbert Killbere, a man who spoke little to him, even though Dantini could converse freely in English and French. They had placed him in the centre of the column of the hundred men to ensure his safety should any attack be made upon them. Dantini had already sent his commission to the Genoese for the ships needed to take these *condottieri* across to Marseilles. The silk merchant lived in the city, but his trade depended on prevailing winds and he knew that Thomas Blackstone had chosen a good time to send his men across the water. Had it been thought through, he wondered, or did the hulking Englishman understand the vagaries of weather? He had been treated with respect by Killbere and these mercenaries, but he had never longed so much for his home. His sensibilities were continually offended by their presence, for he was a refined and cultured man, used to the courts of England, Flanders and France, and being taken and held prisoner by Blackstone had scarred him as if scalded with molten lead. These men of war frightened him every step of the way and their surrounding him made him feel like a lamb being taken to slaughter. At night he found it difficult to keep warm despite the quality of his cloak and bedroll. Maggots of fear ate away at him beneath his skin so that he trembled like a carcass being devoured from within.

Not that he was given much time to rest, because the English knight set off before dawn and rode beneath moonlight until darkness forced him to stop. Dantini was exhausted, but the older man showed no sign of fatigue. They were racing against time, eager to be in France. Dantini felt dirty and unwashed and yearned for the softness of his bed and one of the slave girls who would do his bidding. In these desperate moments he even felt affection for his wife, whose unwavering duty towards him and their children did her great credit, but whose conformity and piety meant there was little pleasure to be had from sexual union with her. Despite these conflicting emotions his dignity forbade him to yield to his fear, and he was proud of that. He placed himself in the hands of God to whom he prayed each night. Killbere assured him that once the men were aboard the ships and his note of commission had been witnessed and executed legally then he would be given an escort home to the gates of Lucca. There was nothing for him to fear, other than his own timidity, Killbere said.

Timidity? More like disgust at the company he had been forced to share. Their word had been kept; he had not been robbed or injured in any manner and Blackstone's bond to him had not been violated. Was this a code these creatures lived by, or another layer of fear, greater than his own, of Thomas Blackstone's intolerance of disobedience? Argument filled his mind, a conversation with himself that was as confusing as these men's behaviour. There was nothing about them he admired. He saw them through disdainful eyes as ignorant, brutal killers who inflicted savagery for payment, though he confessed in his prayers before God to the contradiction that he was grateful to have fallen into the hands of the Englishman, Blackstone. And as the journey reached its end he knew that the powers in Florence would let the King of England know of his service to the Crown. That thought, at least, gave him comfort. Once home he would make immediate arrangements to travel to Flanders and from there let it be known that he wished to visit the English court. King Edward's reputation went beyond that of warrior king – he was renowned for refinement and opulence. Money could buy culture, not like these barbarians, who took their blood money and bought women and drink, who thought themselves men of significance because they had purchased a house with a vineyard and a woman to bed them. A sovereign such as Edward was a benefactor, a great, cultured man whose library was renowned, who appreciated art and music and who held those who served him in Italy in great affection.

When Dantini saw the billowing sails carrying the men's ships away, he commanded his escort to ride for Lucca. He denied himself sleep in his urgency to feel the safety of the city. Once he'd entered through the portal of San Donato he let his escort return to their mountain lair. The city troops closed the great gates behind him, the strongest bodyguard he could wish for. He left his horse and saddlebags with the ostler at the gates, having no desire to wait while a message was sent to his house for servants to come and attend him. They could get the bags tomorrow. He was saddle-sore and his body felt as though it had been on the rack. Even so, as he got closer to home he could barely keep himself from running along the Via del Toro towards the comforts that awaited him. He could almost smell the fragrance of the warm bath that would be drawn for him and then the smooth skin of the young slave girl as he commanded her into his bed – and then he would offer thanks for his deliverance in prayer. It was nearly curfew and he praised God that he did not have to spend another night beyond the gates of his beloved Lucca.

The city looms had fallen silent. Doors slammed closed as people went home, leaving only stray cats and ghosts to flit through the darkening streets. The household would not be expecting him. He raised the great iron door knocker to strike against its plate, three strident blows of authority that would have the house servant running downstairs, flustered and bewildered as to who it could be at this time of night. Church bells rang, the door opened and Oliviero Dantini stepped into hell.

For a moment he was about to chastise the servant for lighting an expensive oil lamp so early in the evening, but before he could utter a word he was yanked into the entrance hall where he fell heavily. As confusion turned to terror another man grabbed him and hauled him to his feet. The man had the strength to lift him bodily from the floor, even though his legs refused to support him. The shadows moved and from somewhere a hand slapped him across the face with such force that he saw lights burst from the pain behind his eyes and tasted blood in his mouth. The next thing he knew he was being forced up the steps into his living quarters. He tried to say something, but his teeth had been loosened and his tongue cut from the force of the blow. He whimpered, begging to know who they were and why they were doing this to him.

He realized the intruders were not dressed as commonly as the *condottieri*. Reality deserted him momentarily as he noticed with an almost detached expertise that the men's clothing was of high quality. They hauled him into his wife's bedchamber and he saw that she sat upright in bed, propped by pillows, with the children under each arm. In the dull glow from the candles in the room he could see there was a grotesque smile on each of their faces as they lay against the crimson bedding. He knew somewhere in the recesses of his mind that his wife had never purchased anything but the finest-woven, embroidered linen sheets of pure white. And then he understood that their smiles were gaping wounds in their throats. He gagged and vomited and felt the tears sting his eyes. The men let him lie in his own mess and then one of them kicked him over and threw the contents of his wife's piss pot into his face. He spluttered and wiped his face with his sleeve. One of the men bent down holding the oil lamp so that he could see his face and watch his lips move in case the blow had deafened him and so that he understood why he was being punished.

'Your slave girl, the one who ran, she was picked up and taken north.'

North. This killer was talking about Milan.

The man with the fine cloth jacket nodded, seeing that the fool understood. 'My Lord Bernabò Visconti does not allow disloyalty to go unpunished. Lucca is beholden to Pisa and Pisa has an alliance with Milan and Milan is Visconti. You helped his enemy escape. This is your reward. Every living creature in this household is dead.'

Oliviero Dantini fainted.

The men carried his body to the top of his tower slapped him

151

back to consciousness so he could know what was to happen – and then threw him into the street below.

By the time Killbere and the men lost sight of land as a following wind eased them towards France and Blackstone reached the first of the passes that would lead him home, the self-satisfied citizens of Lucca awoke to the slaughter.

No bounty paid for protection could ever be enough to stop the Visconti's wrath.

CHAPTER TWENTY-TWO

There was to be no respite from the clawing cold that scratched its way through their clothing. Brother Bertrand, however, seemed impervious to the weather and every few hundred paces turned to see that the tall figure of the Englishman followed faithfully in his footsteps, and behind him the Tau knight and the rest. The monks who led men across these dangerous passes lived in the monastery on the other side of the pass. It was a beneficiary of the Englishman's strength and courage; thanks to him it flourished. Those who passed through the citadel that guarded the pass on the far side were seldom enemies of the Pope, and those that were, were stopped by the soldiers in the stronghold. This safe passage meant the guides were not threatened. There were whores in the villages, but the god-fearing lord of the area, Marazin, forbade fornication and the women had been forced to move further away into the ravines and rocky defiles that scarred the foothills where – to his mind – they gathered like a pestilence. Soldiers who sought employment in Italy camped beyond the citadel and the women would come down to share their tents while their husbands took the soldiers' payment.

Brother Bertrand made the sign of the cross at the memory of his travels through the soldiers' camp, disguising his true intentions by administering comfort to a wounded man. It was a place of corruption, where sexual acts were commonly seen. He had stood beyond a lit tent and watched a woman's rump moving rhythmically astride a Gascon soldier, her breasts loose from her dress. The warmth that spread from Bertrand's groin brought saliva to his mouth and he understood the devil's insidious reach.

'Brother?' a voice carried on the wind. He turned and saw Blackstone close behind him, the war horse at the Englishman's shoulder. 'What is it? What's wrong?'

The images of the women in the valley had insinuated themselves into his mind and caused him to falter. The wind lifted snow from the ridges and lashed the men. He was glad of the mountain, praised God that its torment was his flagellation.

'There!' he shouted to Blackstone above the roar of the wind. 'You see it?'

Blackstone raised a hand in acknowledgement. The low cloud had shifted suddenly, offering a brief glimpse of the distant valley. It was green and lush, the snowline barely touching it. It was like a promised land after the harshness of the mountain. Once into the valley the men would make good time. By dawn they would be there.

'Keep going!' said Blackstone, holding the hooded horse in check. It trusted Blackstone's scent, but quivered when it felt Blackstone's own uncertainty. The narrow ledge and jagged rocks still awaited man or beast if they fell.

Blackstone had seen the novice's haunted glance. The man was used to travelling such dangerous routes so he knew it had nothing to do with fear. In that one instant Blackstone thought he saw within Brother Bertrand a desperation that cut deeper than the hardship of life in a monastery, alone with only prayer and hard work for comfort. Self-denial was a cross the man bore, visible in the fleeting moment of sadness that crossed his eyes. It took someone who knew that loss to recognize it.

Brother Bertrand nodded and carried on. He had prayed hard in his attempt to resist the soft musk smell of the woman who had offered herself once she had been paid by the Gascon soldier, but he had failed. He had abandoned himself to it, allowing himself to wallow in her sin. It was a delight that could not be imagined; a betrayal of every vow he had taken; a moment of submission to the flesh that scoured his mind and pierced his heart with shame.

The woman had taunted him for his excitement and inadequacy and then gone to others, telling them what he had said to her in an attempt to impress her. And it was they who had questioned and threatened him until he had confessed the truth of what he had told the whore. He was one of many guides – not the most senior, not the most trusted – just one of many who escorted men through the Gate of the Dead.

But this time he would return with Sir Thomas Blackstone.

Bring Sir Thomas down through the narrow defile before the land broadened past the citadel and nothing would be said of his fornication, said a hardened-looking man – a Gascon who curled a fist around Bertrand's habit, tightening it around his throat, as the other hand grabbed his privates and squeezed until the novice monk yelped in pain.

Now, as he hunched his shoulders against the wind, he thought through what he had to do. Once the Englishman was through the pass, they told him, he could go quietly back to the life he had chosen. Keep your mouth shut, they had threatened. Spend your life in silence. No one need know you brought him this way.

He smiled at the thought. A Judas act was the devil's joy. Contrition would put him on the side of the angels.

They settled the horses into a wider, sheltered area of the mountain road. Water spilled from crevasses, not yet a spring melt, but the setting sun played some of its warmth onto the mountains and the weary men who huddled close to their mounts. There would be no hot food that night, only a strip cut from a smoked ham and dry biscuit. But there was no threat on the remote pass from Blackstone's enemies, which offered some comfort.

'He's a funny one, that,' said Thurgood, pulling a blanket around his shoulders.

Halfpenny looked to where the Tau knight knelt in prayer; the blazon on his cloak had been their beacon as they followed him through the foul weather and now its shape was like a symbol of devotion in the shortening day. Mist and then snow, and the incessant wind, had forced them to go carefully on the treacherous path. Thank God the worst was over. The descent already offered them more warmth.

'Religious fanatics, them lot,' said Halfpenny, passing a piece of cut meat to his friend. 'Still, if any of us gets a bad one, something like a knife in the guts, then he'd give you the sacrament, so that's some use, I suppose.'

Thurgood chewed the cured strip of pig. 'They say they touch God in their prayers, or God touches them. Don't like that idea. Me and God are best kept at arm's length. Bad enough He knows what I'm thinking most of the time; don't want Him touching me. God touches a mortal man and he's a goner. Dead, I reckon, like being struck by lightning.'

'Which is God expressing Himself how He does best – striking down them that's unfortunate enough,' said Halfpenny.

'Aye. You're right. We'll sleep well away from him. There's lightning in these mountains and if he's spending half the bloody night in prayer then him being touched could spell pain and grief for us all.'

'He's a good fighter, mind,' said Halfpenny. 'I saw him back there and he can fight like a proper bastard, he can.'

The grumbling archers made the best of what they had. A stony path for a bed, a blanket and shoulder of rock to rest their heads. If it snowed they would lie, cramped and unmoving, until forced to start another day.

'Hard to think of him being a man of God,' said Thurgood finally.

'Worst kind,' said Halfpenny, rolling himself into his blanket and pulling his cap down tighter over his ears for as much comfort as he could get.

The two archers were not the only ones watching the Tau knight pray. The stony ground must have hurt his knees, but he knelt with barely a tremble from either the cold or the pain.

Brother Bertrand waited for his moment. Blackstone and his men slept, or were at least curled into what little warmth could be had beneath their cloaks and blankets. Caprini made the sign of the cross and kissed his fingers. The monk walked quickly; his feet, covered in rough-woven sacking and sandals, made barely any noise over hard stone, but even with the wind's ghostly howl in the high peak Caprini heard his approach. His hand was already at the dagger in his belt when Bertrand stopped and raised his hand in a gesture of submission.

'Brother, I need your guidance,' he whispered, loud enough to be heard by Caprini. 'And forgiveness.'

Blackstone awoke with a boot dug into his back. The clear, cold morning showed a smudge of pink on the snow-crested mountains. He peered up at the Italian.

'Get up, Sir Thomas,' he said and turned to where Brother Bertrand knelt in painful penance, head bowed, hands clasped in prayer, dried blood crusting a swollen lip.

By the time Blackstone had raised himself and eased out the cold cramp, others had stirred. It was eerily silent. The wind had eased in the night and, once it had blown the last of the cloud away, it had finally ceased, as exhausted perhaps as the men.

Will Longdon yawned and relieved himself against a slab of rock. 'His prayers have worked then,' he said, meaning the kneeling man, then shivered with pleasure and relief.

John Jacob kicked Thurgood and Halfpenny awake, and followed to where Blackstone had walked to the kneeling monk. The gathering men stood back and waited.

The Tau knight put the toe of his boot beneath the monk's chin. 'Open your eyes.'

As if from a deep trance Brother Bertrand blinked in the morning light. His tongue licked his cracked lips, dry from the night air and lack of water.

Caprini pointed at him as he addressed the men. 'He asked me to hear his confession. And that which is confessed is between him, me and God. Unless he tells you why I had him pray throughout the night and struck him to clear him of his sin.'

The men shuffled in the cold, hugging themselves for warmth, yawning and scratching from the night's privation.

'That is permitted?' asked Meulon. 'To admit what was said in confession?' The thought could worry any man devout in his belief that only God and priest would share knowledge of his sin.

Will Longdon hawked and spat, then rubbed his face to flush some warmth into the skin. 'Meulon, you're the best throat-cutter I've seen, don't tell me you're scared of God knowing it like the rest of us?'

'Fra Stefano isn't talking about how we live and fight, you dumb bastard, he's talking about what happens to a man's soul,' said the Norman.

'That's enough,' Blackstone ordered without anger. The last thing he needed at this time of day was two of his captains bickering like village women. He turned to Caprini. 'He's confessed to what? Being involved with the ambush?'

'I am not permitted to tell you,' said Caprini, and eased his boot again, toppling the monk over like a pot.

'He's had his hand down his braies like the rest of us, I'll wager,' said Thurgood. 'Self-pleasure is a sin for the likes of him.'

'And the only pleasure you get when a whore sees that face of yours,' Longdon told him. 'Be quiet.'

'Brother Bertrand,' said Blackstone, 'I've no time or patience for a monk's misdemeanours. I've a full bladder and a day's ride ahead. If you had a hand in our betrayal we'll cut your throat and be done with it. It'll be quicker and less painful than being flung onto the rocks below. What's it to be?'

The monk prostrated himself before Blackstone and began a litany of jumbled, almost incoherent words into the frozen ground.

Blackstone looked imploringly at Caprini, who shook his head. 'I am not permitted to tell you.'

'Get him up,' Blackstone said irritably. Jacob and Longdon hauled the burbling monk to his feet. 'Give him water,' he instructed Gaillard, who took a water skin from the nearest horse's pommel and dribbled water into the weakened man's mouth. He coughed and spluttered, and Gaillard tipped more over his head. The cold, almost frozen, water made him gasp.

'You heard my question?' Blackstone said.

The monk nodded vigorously.

And told them everything.

CHAPTER TWENTY-THREE

A month's ride away, across many horizons, an ailing woman lay on a bolstered couch, supported by cushions of the richest silks, finely embroidered by the most skilled hands. Her indigo velvet dress, smooth as brushed fur, exposed her arms to the man who stooped at her side. Her ladies-in-waiting hovered dutifully in the background as the physician eased away the silver bowl that held the royal blood. Master Lawrence of Canterbury had bled the King's mother for the second time that day. Despite her pallor he knew that the moment he left to ride back the seventy miles home that this ageing beauty would have her ladies attend her. They would apply make-up and comb her raven-black hair, now shot through with silver, and clothe her in the finest dresses, whose style would have come from Paris or Rheims. Her illness would not defeat her sense of fashion, nor her royal bearing. When he had first been honoured by the command to attend the dowager Queen he had been nervous. He had served the King, and his sovereign lord had then seen fit to make his skills available to the woman who, in her youth, had seized the crown of England in what many saw as a pretence to hold it in safekeeping for her son Edward. It was a history of intrigue and deception by a woman who to this day still held some power and influence behind the throne of Edward III. Master Lawrence had witnessed the affection still shared between mother and son, acts of kindness that denied the rumours that she had been exiled to one of her castles years before. The physician led a privileged life. Not only was he intimate with all that befell the royal family but he was an eyewitness to history, much of which would never be recorded by any scribe.

This woman who lay in his care would ever be known as Isabella the Fair, once Queen of England and renowned for her beauty and intelligence. She was born to be Queen and her lineage connected her to the royal houses of Europe. Married at twelve, how old would she have been when she gave birth to the future King of England? Sixteen perhaps? It was said her husband had lain with her as a matter of duty. Master Lawrence barely stopped himself from snorting with derision as his thoughts meandered back through time. How could any man not desire her? Unless they preferred the company of young men, of course. Edward II had defied the rumour that he was a weakling. Yes, he had loved art and music, but he was known to be a man of strength; known too, perhaps, as one who had failed in military conquest. And perhaps it was that which caused the ambitious Isabella to take a lover, though this did not stop her leading a life of piety and pilgrimage. Master Lawrence had witnessed her acts of compassion and charity, most of which had gone unrecorded and did not quell the intrigue and gossip and, he acknowledged, the fear that surrounded her life.

When her sixteen-year-old son seized back the crown of England with a small group of devoted young noblemen he showed that he had inherited some of his mother's political skill by having her lover, Roger Mortimer, sent to London for trial by Parliament. Had the boy acted on impulse and slain the usurper he would have been seen as little more than an emotional, uncontrolled youth. The physician felt a shudder down his spine. When Mortimer was judged guilty he suffered the unspeakable agony of being hanged, drawn and quartered. Through this baptism of blood and foresight, young Edward had taken the first step towards being a warrior king.

Isabella the Fair was banished from court, but not from England or her son's heart. She was granted castles and a pension of more than four thousand pounds a year. The old physician had heard that she spent more than a third of it on jewellery. She was a woman who would never present herself as anything less than a queen.

'What vile liquid must we drink this time, Master Lawrence?' she asked. 'Is there no improvement with the humour of my blood?'

'Some, highness. Among other prescriptions I recommend white, clear sugar. It will purify the chest and the kidneys, but it can cause bilious humours, so it will be mixed with sour pomegranates and a glass of theriac and barley water each hour.'

'That sounds disgusting.'

'But I am aware that my lady is an exemplary patient,' he said, knowing there was a degree of familiarity permitted. A degree.

'Your examinations are almost complete?'

'Almost, highness.'

'Good. We have business to attend to.'

He had seen the horseman ride in – a hard ride given the lathered horse – and the mud-spattered Lord Robert de Marcouf had paced the courtyard awaiting his audience with Isabella. So, the intrigue went on, Master Lawrence thought as he watched his assistants clean and bind the Queen's slender arm. He was at an age when he lanced his own curiosity as soon as he would a boil. Too much inquisitiveness could fester into a risk to life.

A Norman lord was at the gate: a man who lived among squirming snakes who had once plotted against the King of France. And now? What more could be done? The French King was Edward's prisoner. What need was there now for a nobleman who had sworn allegiance to Edward? It was no secret that the King used his mother for diplomatic missions to further England's influence. It was no secret to those close to the King that she had influenced his decision to invade France in the first place. What other intrigues she shared with the King the physician could not imagine. His was not a political life, for which he was grateful, and what he heard and witnessed from those in his care could prove fatal should he speak of it. To have his hand on the pulse that beat from the royal heart was as close as he wished to be. He had no desire to know what lay within its dark chambers.

Few words passed between the physician and his patient, often only simple pleasantries, sometimes questions from her that probed sharply like the instruments he used to open her veins – precise and skilled; questions that fed her information. She was ruthless, manipulative and one of the most beautiful women who had ever graced the royal palaces. Master Lawrence of Canterbury wrote his prescription.

Isabella allowed one of the assistants to wipe a smear of blood from her wrist. 'We have scoured books over the years,' she said wearily, 'written by noble and literate men who have searched for the alchemy of everlasting life. If your prescription is the elixir we have always sought, your weight in gold would be given to you… forever.' She bathed him in the smile that made him think of a seductress or a she-wolf – he had never determined which.

'My humble skills are recommendations to your apothecary, highness. I myself would wish no longer a life than God may grant me.'

'Then you would deny me life if it were in your power to give it,' she said.

He sighed. He had stepped into one of her bear traps yet again. 'Highness, you show me to be the old fool that I am.'

'And we tease you, Master Lawrence. We could not wish for anyone better to serve us.'

He bowed his head. Her gracious remarks always flattered him. 'May I suggest that I be housed nearby? In case I am needed again at short notice.'

The determined tone of her answer reminded him that her reputation was well earned. Her dark eyes flicked quickly at him – a change as sudden as a cloud passing over the sun. He feared rebuke – but an instant later she smiled and he could see how a man would submit to her desires.

'Master Lawrence, we are, as always, in your debt. You have a long ride home and we would not wish to keep you from your duties elsewhere. We thank you.'

It was a gentle dismissal. He bowed and left the chamber. Her glance towards her ladies-in-waiting was sufficient for them to hurry forward and help her from the bed so that she might be dressed in more fitting clothes to receive her guest.

'Is Lord Robert here?'

'He is,' one of the ladies answered.

'Then we must hurry. He has travelled a long way and it would be ungracious to keep him from a well-earned rest.'

Robert de Marcouf was a Norman lord with lands in England and, like Isabella, with spies in France. He was only a few years younger than the dowager Queen, but age and the damp weather of Normandy and England crept into his joints and found the old injuries sustained in a half-century of fighting. He was one of the few great knights of his generation still active: many others were ailing – or dead. His generation had seen the last of the huge pitched battles, but not the intrigue that often caused them. He waited patiently in an antechamber where a fire burned in the grate with a woven rug spread before it. There was but a single piece of furniture in the room: a wooden stool. He had ridden through the night and his limbs ached with fatigue, but the stool was not for his comfort. He bowed as Queen Isabella entered the room and sat on the simple stool, her back straight and her eyes unwavering, while her attendant ladies moved back against timbered walls that displayed paintings done, he had been told, by Italian artists. He knew she was ill; it did not take much to discover the truth when one had influence. She was a woman in her sixties who had never been anything but a queen. He knew she must be in pain, but she sat with her back straight as a blade as she watched him.

'What news, my lord?'

A servant approached him with a tray that held a glass of deep red wine. He could hardly wait to bring it to his lips and gulp its invigorating warmth. He shook his head at the servant, who retreated. It was always a test of wills with Isabella.

'Blackstone sent men by ship from Genoa. It was a feint. He went north alone with a handful of men,' said de Marcouf. 'He will use one of the passes.'

'Then he is on his way. What else?' she said.

'There are those at court who believe Thomas Blackstone has been summoned as an assassin to kill the Prince of Wales, given the animosity between them.'

Isabella showed no emotion, but her mind's eye saw how easy it would be for a determined lone knight accompanied by a few men to slip past those who wished to stop him.

'Is our grandson aware of this?'

'No.'

She considered the news carefully. 'Once he gets into France he would be nearly impossible to find. Killing him here in England would be easier. Can he be stopped?'

The Norman did not answer. Who could know? A legend could be killed as easily as a common footsoldier. One arrow. One knife thrust.

'Do you believe he will get through?' Isabella asked.

'Thomas Blackstone does not always use that sword of his to beat an enemy. If that was the case he'd have been dead years ago. He is not a blunt instrument like a poleaxe, highness. He uses his brain. That's what makes him so dangerous.'

CHAPTER TWENTY-FOUR

Fifty men waited in the trees that flanked the defile beyond the castle. The brutish Gascon who had threatened Brother Bertrand sat in plain sight on his horse for anyone approaching to see. Behind him fourteen others sat astride their horses so that no one could approach from their rear. The track, the hillside and the way forward were effectively blocked. And those who held the citadel in de Montferrat's name, barely five hundred yards away, would cause them no trouble.

They had waited on horseback since first light and if the guide had been as good as he said he was then he would have Blackstone through the pass before the sun's rays reached the snow-capped peaks. How many rode with Blackstone was unknown, but word had it that there were fewer than a dozen. The cold made the Gascon's nose drip. He snorted and spat away the moisture. Fewer than a dozen men following a man with a price on his head. Christ, how had he managed to get this far, let alone expect to reach England?

Horses shifted their weight, their muscles having stiffened as they stood still. The damned cold would seize a fighting man unless he could move – and to move might give away the positions of those in the trees. It occurred to him that Blackstone might even have an advantage. If he had been riding since before dawn then horse and man would be warmer than him and if Blackstone perceived any threat awaited him then the Englishman would try something. The last thing he wanted was Thomas Blackstone taking his own men by surprise. He swore beneath his breath. Perhaps this hadn't been such a good idea after all. Better to have

166

let them ride through the defile and onto the plateau. God, it was cold sitting and waiting. A man's mind could wander.

He wiped the cold tears from his eyes. Something moved in the distance. He peered through blurred vision, and swore, wiping them again with a rag pulled from his jacket. A lone horseman came forward at the walk. The misshapen head of his horse swayed as it snorted, pluming air like some kind of damned demon beast. It looked as malevolent as the man riding it, who rode without a sword in hand. Had he been the only one to survive? The Gascon looked behind him, and then to the trees. No one could have got round them.

The rider stopped and pulled off his helm, dragging fingers through his neck-length hair. Pulled back the hair so he could be identified. The Gascon peered but could not see the rider's face clearly enough. Damn! He wiped his eyes again. Whoever it was, he hadn't moved – just sat there and waited. The Gascon tentatively urged his horse forward at a walk.

The horseman raised a hand. That was plain enough to see and then he called across the hundred or more yards that separated them.

'No further! Come closer and you'll die.'

The Gascon stopped, uncertain now as to whether this horseman was indeed Blackstone. Would such a renowned knight ride a horse that looked like that? Take nothing for granted, his own sworn lord had taught him since boyhood. His horse snorted nervously, its ears pricked. Something was wrong. It involuntarily took another pace forward, and another before he reined it back – and as he did so a rushing sound made him look to the sky. He knew that sound. He jabbed spurs into the horse's flanks and yanked the reins, moving it no more than four strides from where it had stood. Three arrows thudded into the ground where moments before he had been.

Sweet Jesus. It was Blackstone without doubt and he would kill the leader of any group of armed men before asking questions and that would make it easier to draw out the others. Blood of Christ!

The Englishman might have slipped fifty archers into those rocks without his knowing it.

'Sir Thomas! Hold! I am Beyard! A captain to my Lord de Grailly, sworn men to your King! We mean you no harm!' he shouted, his voice echoing across the rockface.

He settled the skittish horse as Blackstone beckoned him forward. 'Come alone!' he called, recognizing the Gascon accent. De Grailly, the Captal de Buch, was one of the greatest knights and, like his ancestors, held the hereditary title of Master of Gascony; he was sworn to Edward.

Beyard spurred his horse. If Blackstone did not believe him he would be dead in the next minute. When he got to within twenty yards he drew back on the reins and pulled up the horse. Now he could see the scarred face. He glanced left and right. There was no sign of anyone else. Where were those damned archers?

'You bear his arms?' Blackstone asked. The man had no shield by which to identify him.

'I do.' He pulled back his riding cloak and showed the blazon of five scallops set against a black cross that were stitched on his jupon's chest. 'I have been here a week, Sir Thomas. More men have been at the next two passes. We've been waiting for you. No one thought you would risk going further north through Visconti territory, so we chose the lower three routes.'

'How many men in all?' asked Blackstone. 'This pass and the route to the coast.'

'Near enough two hundred.'

If the man was speaking the truth then Blackstone knew such a sizeable escort would get him through without being slowed by caution. 'And where did you think I was going?' he asked, making sure the man knew enough to be trusted.

'You have been summoned to England, Sir Thomas. That's all I know. But you're in danger. There are those who wish to stop you.'

'The Visconti's men?'

'Perhaps,' said Beyard. 'Men will fight for those bastards either side of these mountains, but no – I believe it is other Englishmen.'

Since Lucca, Blackstone had known that Englishmen were involved in trying to kill him, though there was no evidence that they had been sent from England. Perhaps they were mercenaries wishing to claim the prize?

'Call down your men from up there,' Blackstone told him, glancing up at the forests.

Beyard realized that Blackstone must have remained hidden since before dawn, watching the deployment of his men. He signalled and the horsemen eased their way down and made their way into the open ground where they could all be seen.

'Are they all my Lord de Grailly's men?'

'Most. Some Provençal.'

'And your Lord de Grailly?'

'On crusade in Prussia. A messenger was sent. My sworn lord would have been here himself; there's no doubt about that. He holds you in high regard, Sir Thomas. I brought what men I could.' He paused, still unable to see where Blackstone's archers where. 'Your archers, Sir Thomas? I don't see them, so how could they see me?'

'You went into position too early, Beyard. We watched where you stood. An archer knows his distances. You were one hundred and thirty-eight paces from where I intended to halt. They fell back another eighty. They knew exactly where to aim. You invited them to kill you.'

Beyard flushed with anger at his own stupidity. He had fought at Poitiers; he knew what English and Welsh bowmen could do. Blackstone rode up as behind him three archers ran from beyond the rocks. They came fast, running hard to be at Blackstone's side, carrying their bows in their hands, ready to stop and shoot again if so commanded. Behind these three men five mounted men spurred their horses. They came on almost silently and Beyard noticed for the first time that the ugly beast that Blackstone rode had muffled hooves, as did the others. Nine men. That's all Blackstone had brought with him for this perilous journey. At the rear came a floundering figure, his habit caked with dirt, his feet wrapped in sacking.

'He betrayed me, then,' Beyard said, nodding towards the figure of the monk whose flailing arms seemed unlikely to propel him along any quicker.

'Not really. The devil betrayed you.' Blackstone smiled at the Gascon's confused look. 'He tasted sex and he wants more,' he said as the breathless Bertrand reached the men.

'God's blood! Send him to Avignon then,' said Beyard. 'Priests and nuns there go at it like rabbits.

'No,' said Blackstone, nudging the bastard horse forward next to the Gascon's. 'Says he doesn't want to be a monk after all. Wants to be a fighter.'

'God help us. We had best warn the men. I don't want any trouble from them with the women.'

It was Blackstone's turn to be uncertain. Beyard gathered his reins. 'The whore said Bertrand had no experience – that he shot faster than an arrow. But he's hung like a donkey. There'll be a line of whores stretching from here to the coast to sample his pleasures. I doubt the rest of us will have much luck and I'll wager he'll not do much fighting.'

The Gascon bodyguard had secured the plateau so that no intruder would be able to strike at Blackstone. He accepted the hospitality offered by the allied castle and next morning would lead the men towards the safe havens across France prepared by Lord de Grailly's household. There would be little chance of attack now – not with the Gascon lord's protection to Calais.

Now that he was back on French soil he felt the pull of his family even more strongly. All he knew of them was that they were somewhere in the north, close to Christiana's guardian and friend, Blanche de Harcourt. Blanche had written to him – four letters in eighteen months. Four sheets of paper. The family was well. His son, Henry, placed with a knight of good standing to serve as a page. His daughter growing more beautiful every day. No mention of the bastard child, the result of his wife's rape, which by now must have been born. Barely a word about

Christiana. Had she taken a lover? Did she still speak of the deception that Blackstone had kept hidden from her during their years of marriage? Fate had twisted a knife into their hearts when the truth was finally revealed. He had been a young archer when he had flanked the French ambush in Normandy that day years ago. An arrow shot and an old knight dead. A knight whom he later discovered was Christiana's father. The truth had finally burst like a boil from the plague. There was no mention of her demanding a divorce in the letters. Four letters was all he had. The words conjured their images in his mind. He had wanted nothing more than to live free from war on his Norman demesne. It had been almost perfect until the King of France had set a rabid murderer after him and then the secret that he had borne for so long had been exposed.

Blackstone shuddered as his thoughts chilled him, emotions clawing his innards. Anger and despair ignited a longing for his family. It was this bleak place that brought the memories flooding back. He had inflicted his revenge here, had lost his wife here and gone through the Gate of the Dead to Lombardy with no expectation of ever returning. But somewhere in France was everything that he held dear.

Blackstone shielded the candle flame as he walked along the line of men settling themselves into the empty horse stalls. Blackstone's men would take the castle's hospitality while Beyard's men stayed vigilant outside. Now that he had passed safely into their care, no sneak attack from his enemies would catch them off guard.

'We should get drunk tonight,' said Will Longdon as he threw down his blanket.

John Jacob kicked straw into an acceptable pile, toeing aside horse manure. 'Will's right, Sir Thomas. Some decent ale after the food they gave us would warm the bones. There's a chill to this place.'

'Aye, John, I know. But it's more than a chill from these stone walls that creeps into us,' Blackstone said. Jacob and Will Longdon had scaled the slippery fortification above the lake at the back of the castle when they fought for his family's lives the year before last. 'No drink, though,' he said. 'We start early. And ale won't drive this kind of cold from your bones.'

There was a truth to the superstition that lost souls clung to places they had known when they were taken suddenly from life and Blackstone had been part of a great slaughter here. If only prayer and a thick cloak was enough to give some warmth to those who had done the killing. Blackstone promised himself that he would offer thanks to his guardian goddess, the naked figurine bathed in the candle glow at his throat. He moved along to where the horses were stabled and found the corner stall where the darkness held his own horse. Where others stood lifting a hoof as they slept, ears back and eyes closed, his horse faced him, ears pricked forward, eyes glaring through the flickering light. Did it ever sleep? He stood before the great beast, saw in his mind's eye the brand on its right leg and remembered the day it took a dozen men and ropes to hold it long enough so the mark could be made. Like all horses contracted to the Italians it was obliged to be branded. Right leg for stallion war horses and coursers, left for palfreys and mules. Everything was accounted for so payment could be made for its loss – horse and man each branded in his own way.

He reached out for the animal to take his scent and snuffle his palm. Its yellow teeth snapped, making him snatch his hand back in time to save his fingers. It was a beast of war that gave no favour unless it felt inclined.

Blackstone understood it perfectly.

As he went across the yard to his quarters he saw the dull candle glow from the chapel. His own candle was spent and the following wind urged him towards the chapel. That and something else drew him to its flame.

Caprini knelt in prayer, but turned quickly, knife in hand as the door creaked open. Blackstone saw the blade and the man relax when he was recognized.

'Forgive me,' said Blackstone. 'I didn't know anyone was here.'

Caprini crossed himself and got to his feet, tugging the cloak around him. He glanced at the crucifix and then back to Blackstone. 'I'll leave you to your prayers.'

'No need,' said Blackstone, 'I doubt He would listen.'

'Every prayer is heard,' said Caprini. 'Do not blaspheme, Sir Thomas. You may stand a hair's breadth from the devil's grasp but you have not been snatched into his lair. Not yet.'

'I have laid waste towns and slaughtered all those who resisted me. I have left widows and orphans across the breadth of two countries and their screams would drown out any prayer of mine.'

'Then pay a priest to say them for you.'

'There isn't enough money,' said Blackstone.

'Then you live without salvation.' Stefano Caprini nodded curtly and walked out of the chapel.

Blackstone glanced at the burning light and the shadows it threw across the silver-inlaid crucifix on the small altar. How many men had prayed here before battle for their salvation? He could never know – but he had sent many of them to meet it.

Caprini tightened the belly strap on his horse. 'You have no further need of me now,' he said to Blackstone, who had seen the black-cloaked figure slip away from the castle's chapel to the stables. He was going to leave as silently and mysteriously as he had arrived in Lucca.

'I have every need of a man who can fight as well as you,' Blackstone told him. 'And these men need spiritual comfort. A fighting man close to God's heart. We only have a horny novice with us now who has renounced his vows. He won't be much good for prayers.'

'Sir Thomas, you have been brought safely through the mountains. In three weeks you will be in England.'

'And will need men I can trust at my back.'

'I have sworn an oath to help those on pilgrimage.'

'You swore an oath to take me to Canterbury.'

The two men stared at each other. The older man shook his head and pulled down the stirrup strap.

'Do not play with words, Sir Thomas, they can cause more wounds than that sword of yours.'

Blackstone placed a hand on the man's arm as he gathered the reins. 'I don't know where Canterbury is,' he said. 'Go with God – and I'll follow in your footsteps. That should get me back to England.'

Caprini thought about it without answering Blackstone and then unfastened the saddle straps. 'Canterbury,' he said in little more than a whisper. 'An oath is an oath.'

Blackstone walked back into the night. The Tau knight was a strange creature, a man who yielded little of himself, as if the dark cloak shielded his secret past. And what man didn't? thought Blackstone. Caprini may have fought well, but Blackstone did not yet trust him. Better to have the devil you know at your side, he told himself.

The men gathered at dawn as the mist tried to escape the forest's embrace. Caprini and the other men waited respectfully as Blackstone's lone figure stood by the graveside of the young man who had sacrificed his life less than two years before. Time, and the passing of it, was a concept beyond Blackstone's understanding – but the lingering ache of separation was real enough. He missed his wife, his daughter and his son, and still mourned the loss of this boy who had tried to protect his family.

He had chiselled the memoriam with his own hand.

This stone marks the resting place of Master Guillaume Bourdin, esquire to the English knight, Sir Thomas Blackstone, cruelly slain in defence of the helpless by Gilles de Marcy, the Savage Priest.

A scaffold held the remains of the man Blackstone had killed that day. His skin, as taut and blackened as weather-beaten leather, clung to the skeleton that was spreadeagled in warning. The dead man's dark shield still hung from his neck, held by wire

that bit deep into bone. Words Blackstone had etched on it still
gave warning to those who passed.

*Here hangs the body of this cruel murderer, killed in single
combat by Sir Thomas Blackstone. So will all evil perish.*

Blackstone spurred the horse and heard the rumble of hooves
behind him. Ahead lay England and a King who had summoned
him. The mist whispered away on the breeze, but the ghosts in
that place lingered.

PART TWO

TOURNAMENT
OF KINGS

CHAPTER TWENTY-FIVE

Blackstone had never been to London; in truth, before going to war he had seldom travelled beyond his own village. Since then the streets of Rouen and Paris had been his only experience of big cities. He didn't like either, and his recent journey into Lucca confirmed everything he felt about being confined within a city's walls. He had no idea where Canterbury was in relation to London; it remained a place that existed only in his imagination and in stories – no doubt exaggerated – told by those who had been to the great place of pilgrimage.

They had travelled across France day in and day out, with long hours in the saddle, but often walking across difficult terrain, caring more for their horses than themselves. The further north they rode the more familiar the landscape became. He was close to home, or what had once been his home. Normandy was as blighted as the rest of the country by the roving gangs of routiers. Since King Jean le Bon had been captured at Poitiers his son had failed to heal the bankrupt nation. The Estates General in Paris had risen up and Charles of Navarre was a spectre that still haunted the Dauphin. Each lord's house that sheltered Blackstone told the same story: France was in tatters and King Edward was sucking the marrow from its bones with his ransom demands for the French King. Knights fortified their manor houses; others had moved their families into the walled towns or cities. Blackstone asked all those who gave him hospitality if they had heard of his wife Christiana and the Countess Blanche de Harcourt, who sheltered his family.

'The routiers are off down the Rhone valley from what we've heard. I pray they take their blight to others, as unchristian as that seems,' said one old knight, still loyal to King Edward's desire to rule France, who had offered them a frugal meal. 'The de Harcourt family is still divided. The Countess dispersed her band more than a year ago. She had torched the King's villages in revenge for what he did to her husband. Then...' He shook his head in weary despair at Blackstone and Caprini, who shared the honour of his table. 'Then, like the rest of us, she returned home to try and save what she could. As far as I know she went to her fief in Aumale. Safer up there. Wish I could get my people somewhere like it. But in truth there's been trouble everywhere. The Dauphin is losing what little control and support he has. No one knows what will happen. I'm sorry, Sir Thomas, I don't know where your family is.'

He heard the same answer many times over the month it took the men to make their way to the coast. At every hamlet he was reminded of the life almost lived with Christiana and the children and the villagers who had depended on the strength of his sword arm. Every turn made him wonder if his family were close by.

Blackstone parted company with Beyard three days south of Calais with thanks for the Captal de Buch's captain's protection. 'I have sent word ahead, Sir Thomas,' said the Gascon. 'The boat waits for you at Le Havre. Go cautiously. I cannot tell who waits for you on the other side.'

Blackstone and the others rode on, sleeping rough so that no one could identify his coat of arms, or remember the scar-faced knight. When he caught the scent of the salt marshes on the wind, Blackstone took leave of his captains.

'Gaillard and Meulon, you both know Calais. You and the others take lodging outside the city and wait until Sir Gilbert arrives. John and Fra Stefano and I will take a ship to England.'

'Good luck on the crossing, Thomas,' said Will Longdon. 'We'll find a priest and have him pray for calm sea and fair wind.'

'Then pay him double, Will,' said Blackstone, 'or there'll be more of me on the sea bed than arrives ashore.' The men laughed. Sea crossings were the devil's realm.

'We've Fra Stefano to help calm the waters,' said Jacob. 'The Lord won't ignore us.'

'I should you warn you, I am still paying for the sins I committed,' said the Tuscan knight. 'You would need to build a cathedral to find favour with God on my behalf.'

Blackstone embraced his men in farewell with an admonishment that Bertrand be allowed only one whore a week and for the rest of the time be kept from the brothels. His training in looking after equipment and horses was to continue and he was not to be given any other clothing than the habit he wore. It might prove advantageous to have a monk who could sniff out information in the town.

He would sniff out more than that, Will Longdon had suggested.

They watched as their sworn lord and his companions rode out of sight.

'I always thought Fra Stefano was as stiff as a monk's cock in a monastery. I never knew he had a sense of humour,' said Will Longdon as they turned for Calais's protection. 'I'd have warmed to him more had I known.'

Meulon eased his horse across a stream, heeling the uncertain beast into the shallows. 'There was no humour in him, Will. When we crossed the mountains, the seneschal at the castle said he had heard of an Italian by that name. A man from Tuscany who once murdered and raped his way across Italy. He made the Visconti look like children torturing a cat for fun at a village fair. He had more sin than all of us put together before he turned to God and good deeds.'

Longdon crossed himself. 'Sweet Jesus, you never thought to tell Thomas?'

'He knows,' said Meulon. 'Why do you think he's made him go to England? A man like that seeks redemption every day of his life. He's God's shield for Thomas.'

They were blessed with a southerly breeze and a gentle swell long before his men paid any priest. Near-darkness smudged the

English coast and it was night by the time they landed and guided their horses uphill through the fishing port towards the burning torches held by the men who waited for them. Blackstone's hand rested on Wolf Sword's grip. A voice cried out: 'Do as this man commands – no harm will befall you!'

John Jacob tugged his horse forward. Blackstone said quietly, 'Whoever sent these men is the same who sent Samuel Cracknell.'

'Maybe so, but I'd feel better if we knew who they were.'

'It would do us no good,' said Blackstone. 'They could give us any name they wanted. He must be close to the King, otherwise he couldn't know what was written.'

Blackstone moved closer to the torchlight to see the face of the man who had called out. There was little to be seen beneath the open-faced helmet and the man's greying beard. He offered no hand of welcome or friendship and his eyes showed no fear as Blackstone's shadow fell across him. His authority, Blackstone reasoned, was probably sufficient to give him such an unwavering gaze. Rank and privilege. Men whose authority would not be challenged. The six men who accompanied him did not seem anxious to draw their swords, so there was no threat intended. Not yet at least. The man's cloak was held with a silver clasp at his throat beneath its fur collar and he pulled it back so that Blackstone could see the cross of St George on his padded gambeson.

'What month and day is it?' Blackstone asked.

'The day after tomorrow is St Anselm's Day.'

April. They had reached England in time for the tournament on the twenty-third. Perhaps now the meaning of the King's command would become plainer.

'We ride through the night,' the man said. He glanced at Caprini. 'You're a pilgrim's comforter?' he asked gruffly, barely able to disguise his disdain. 'The Italian?'

'My companion,' said Blackstone as Caprini gave no sign of answering. Scratch a scab and it will bleed. Scratch a man with Caprini's pedigree and God's servant or not, he might take offence at such a dismissive question.

'And him?'

'John Jacob. My captain. He served the King in London and was trusted to take an emissary to the King's son before Poitiers. An *Italian* emissary. Held in high regard by the King. Trusted with secrets. As I trust these men.'

Blackstone's answer seemed satisfactory. Nothing more was said as the men mounted their horses. 'Forward!' the man commanded the escort who rode ahead to light the way.

'How well do you know London?' Blackstone said to John Jacob.

'Barely. I went across its bridge once – the big one with the houses on it – and I served at Windsor for a while. Then I was sent to France. You'll know when we're there. You'll smell it. The Thames is a sewer.'

They rode at a steady pace on country roads, alerting cur dogs as they passed hamlets and villages, but nothing more. No challenges were made and no horseman lunged from the forests. White-edged clouds slipped across the sky, then blanketed the moonlight, casting them back into darkness. Pockets of rain swirled across the land, lashing down and then scurrying away once man and horse were soaked. They reached the edge of the town whose castle dominated the landscape. The low-roofed houses were lowly subjects to its grandeur. A toll-bridge cottage yielded a man carrying a stave in one hand and a burning torch in the other. He seemed uncertain as the horsemen clattered towards him.

'Stay clear!' one of the front riders shouted, barely slowing his horse. The man stubbornly refused to move out of the way, forcing the horseman to halt.

'I answer to the Constable. This is the King's road and there's a toll,' he insisted. 'There's an ordinance and I must obey it.'

By the look of him he was little more than a local villein granted the privilege of minor authority. However, a small man with any kind of authority could cause a problem and if the knight who led them thought his rank would be obvious then he was mistaken.

The tollgate keeper peered into the gloom, trying to see who it was that forced his horse through the body of riders.

'A penny a cart, a farthing a horse,' he recited. 'Each way, that is.'

The cloaked man rasped out a command. 'Stand back now!'

The man's voice had the desired effect. 'My Lord de Marcouf!' he gasped, and bowed his head quickly, obviously recognizing the threatening tone. And no man of rank or wealth ever paid a toll. That was for the poor.

De Marcouf turned in his saddle and glowered at Blackstone. Now his identity was known and Blackstone understood. A Frenchman sent to escort Blackstone home. A King's messenger to Italy and Gascon and Frenchmen to get him to wherever this place might be.

'Sir Thomas,' said John Jacob. 'I don't know where we are, but this isn't London.'

'Nor Canterbury,' said Caprini as he slipped a knife into his boot.

Despite the distance they had travelled, the castle gates stayed closed and de Marcouf made no attempt to have them opened. A sentry would challenge them at this time of night and might even raise an alarm. Clearly de Marcouf wanted their arrival to be kept as quiet as possible.

Men ran from a stable yard as they dismounted.

'We go through the postern gate,' said de Marcouf, handing his reins to one of the men. Others began to lead horses away into covered stalls where oats and hay bags were already prepared.

'They've been expecting us,' said John Jacob.

'But keeping it quiet,' said Blackstone. He handed the bastard horse's reins to one of the stable boys. 'He bites and kicks. Keep him away from the others and don't beat him or I'll beat you.'

The boy's eyes widened. 'Yes, lord,' he said.

'Tether him and let him feed. Groom him, clean his hooves and make sure there's fresh bedding straw for him. Clean. Not swept of dung and reused, you hear?'

The lad nodded and coaxed Blackstone's horse away. Blackstone watched. The fellow knew how to deal with the big horse, bringing his shoulder in close to his neck and jogging forward making the horse stride with him, but keeping his hand and face well away from its yellow teeth.

The escort had carried extra reed torches for the night ride, but now even those spluttered with exhaustion. More were taken from the ostler and once again Blackstone and his companions were obliged to follow de Marcouf. One man went ahead as the others flanked Blackstone, Jacob and Caprini. The men set off, striding quickly through the darkened houses towards the castle walls and the meadow that lay beyond it. The town's houses snaked this way and that, a mixture of cob, thatch, wood and stone. Unpaved streets, muddy from the rain, clogged the men's boots, but the escort was intent on moving as quickly as they could through the darkened passageways. As they turned into a wheel-rutted path a cart blocked their way.

Instinct put Wolf Sword into Blackstone's hand. If this was the street that led to the postern gate then it was the most obvious place for an ambush. A scuff of a boot made John Jacob push his shoulder against the nearest soldier, the sudden action alerting everyone to the attack from the darkened street to the left. Crossbow bolts struck down three of the soldiers, their torches falling into the dirt, throwing a flickering light into the alleyway.

Blackstone saw that John Jacob had read the ambush perfectly and shouted a command to the startled de Marcouf. 'Go with him!'

The Norman was no stranger to reacting quickly and as Jacob grabbed one of the fallen torches and ran into the side street Blackstone broke to the right, finding purchase in the stony dirt, hunched, ready to ram anyone that lurked, waiting to attack. The first volley of quarrels and the narrow confines of the street and its darkness told him there would be little time for their attackers to reload their weapons. John Jacob and the others would kill quickly.

185

Caprini was already at his shoulder. Behind them curses and shouts of pain rang out as steel struck steel from Jacob's counter-attack. Blackstone threw a burning torch into the darkness and saw the glint of flame catch men's faces as they jostled towards him. They had chosen unwisely. These narrow streets meant only three men could fight abreast and there were four of them. In the dancing shadows Blackstone let the first two men attack, one a pace behind the other. They had created their own fatal disadvantage. Blackstone held the blow on Wolf Sword's crossguard and took a half-step back, letting the man's momentum put him off balance. He grunted, knees buckling, hand outstretched, sword arm useless. Blackstone twisted Wolf Sword, rammed it down into the man's spine. It pierced mail, grating the links, shattering bone. There was no cry as the man could not draw breath to utter one.

The weight of his body released the blade and Blackstone yanked it upward, letting the pommel strike into the second attacker's face. It struck him on the cheekbone between open helm and face. The force of the blow threw the man back on his heels, floundering as pain blinded him and stripped the strength from him. Blackstone followed through; he stepped across him, forcing the sword into the man's gullet. Caprini had moved quickly and lightly in a cold-blooded exercise in killing. Efficiently and almost without effort he parried the third man's strike and then opened his guard momentarily, letting his attacker think that the older man could not sustain the fight. Caprini blocked the blow that immediately came, held it at head height and rammed his knife into his assailant's exposed armpit. The man's gasp of pain shuddered from him, his knees sagged, but he had not yet gone down – stubbornly, desperately gripping his sword, fighting through the wound that had not yet killed him. Caprini supported the man's weight on his sword and then twisted the knife, tearing deeper inside the assassin's body. He sighed as if reluctantly letting life slip away from him. Caprini stepped aside and let him fall dead into the darkness.

The fourth man hesitated, snatched the fallen torch and used it as a weapon against the hulking shadow that came for him.

In desperation he threw the torch towards the scarred face but Blackstone's arm flicked it aside; the sparks and embers from the spitting tallow flared – a fatal distraction. The man's eyes involuntarily followed them, allowing him only two more breaths of life.

Caprini ran forward into the darkness, quickly going down onto one knee in case another silent enemy was waiting, but there was no further attack.

Torchlight bobbed towards them from the ambush site.

'Sir Thomas?' called John Jacob.

'Here, John.'

Jacob and the surviving soldiers strode quickly towards them, illuminating the killing scene. De Marcouf's men turned back and forth, torches high, ready for another assault. The Norman's blood-streaked sword glistened in the reflected light.

'Assassins. They bear no coat of arms, they serve no lord,' he said.

'Five men,' said Jacob. 'Three bows. They should've used more of them; they'd have brought us all down.'

'Four here,' said Blackstone. 'Nine men. Perhaps they were only expecting the three of us.'

John Jacob spat, and toed one of the bodies. 'Still wouldn't have been enough,' he said. And in the devil's firelight Blackstone saw his captain grin.

Sounds of the fight had alerted the castle guard and Blackstone heard men's feet thudding across the narrow wooden bridge straddling the castle moat that led to the pointed archway of the postern gate, the castle's side entrance to the town. They bore torches which gave enough light to see where the houses ended and the meadowlands began and the belly of a river curving around its one side. A great tower loomed up in the darkness from where sentries would have seen and heard the attack in the streets. Once through that gate and in the confines of the castle there would be no escape. If there were any chance of freedom then being in a place unknown to him would make evasion from a determined enemy more difficult. Rivers often denoted boundaries and they in turn revealed landowners and loyalties.

'Wait,' said Blackstone as de Marcouf strode towards the stronghold. 'What river is this? Where am I?'

The Norman stopped and faced him.

'It is the Lea. And this is Hertford Castle. North of London, Sir Thomas. You have been summoned here with as much secrecy as possible. It was my duty to protect you and I thought I had taken sufficient measures. I offer you my apologies.'

Blackstone was none the wiser as to where he had been brought, but he knew of the knight who had escorted them. 'Lord de Marcouf. Your demesne was east of Paris and you supported Charles of Navarre rather than your French King. I remember your name mentioned by my friend Jean de Harcourt. Are we to be imprisoned here?'

De Marcouf looked at Blackstone and the two men who flanked him either side. A part of him was grateful that there would be no conflict between him and the hardened fighters who stared him down.

'Follow the command sent to you,' he said. 'Men should not question a royal summons.'

'Not all men are outlawed,' said Blackstone. 'And I have already been attacked more than once.'

De Marcouf and his escort faced the three men. The older man was senior in rank and Blackstone was being impertinent.

'You were escorted safely across France by my doing and commanded so by those who summoned you. Even an outlawed knight must show some gratitude by extending his trust,' said de Marcouf irritably. Bad enough that a man of his age had spent so long in the saddle and then been forced to fight at close quarters within spitting distance of the castle, now this bent-armed, scar-faced barbarian was questioning him.

Blackstone dipped his head in respect and acknowledgement, then followed the column of torchlight through the castle grounds.

He had little choice but to go where his fate took him. The bailey inside the curtain wall had timber-framed buildings built closely together – most likely used by officers of the court, he thought, and somewhere in that labyrinth were the royal apartments. This place overwhelmed any lord's manor that Blackstone had previously known. It was a King's country palace and comprised all that went with it: chapel, great hall, kitchens and offices, everything the sovereign would need when hunting away from London. Despite the poor light his mason's eye saw enough of the stone and flint walls to know they were several feet thick. And, like a cage door trapping an unsuspecting wolf, the imposing walls of the gatehouse held the portcullis. Blackstone's trepidation gnawed at him. Being brought halfway across Europe to meet the King in a castle away from London meant it was to avoid the prying eyes of his court. Father Torellini had warned him that the King would usually send a summons through his Chancellor, so had he been brought here as a safeguard against conspirators? If so, it had not worked. Nine men lay butchered in the dark streets as proof.

'If it was the King who wanted us dead, Sir Thomas, our heads would already be on the end of a pole,' said John Jacob quietly. 'But we might still get a bird's eye view over these walls by morning.'

'No doubt it's a fine view,' said Blackstone as they ducked below a low arch into a darkened passage.

The chapel bell rang for matins.

It was morning.

Forty-nine days since they had tried to kill him in Lucca.

CHAPTER TWENTY-SIX

Isabella the Fair wore the plain garments of the Franciscan Poor Clares beneath her velvet dress, the simple linen, dry against her skin, denying the comfort and sensuality of better cloth. She had watched them take Blackstone into the antechamber and now gazed through the screen's latticed woodwork as he stood without moving while de Marcouf paced back and forth. Both men showed the signs of a hard journey and she knew about the ambush. Her life had been spent watching men, and hers was a calculating intellect that saw through the hubris so many carried like a battle flag. Some were devious enough to be used to undermine an enemy or to gain power. She had once fallen for a man as strong as Blackstone and together they had seized the crown from her husband, the second King to bear the name Edward. His chivalrous attributes had been admirable and he had been a lover of music, poetry and art, but it was she who had the steel in her blood. Her husband had had strength enough but there had also been uncertainty in him, which some took to be timidity; his tenderness meant he had failed to grasp the importance of waging a war and securing peace on terms that suited the conqueror. The steel had been inherited by her son, the third Edward, and how willingly he had wielded it, snatching back his rightful crown from his regent mother and her lover, who had paid the price with a mutilated death while she was banished from court. Twenty-eight years had passed since that fateful day. Now there was no passion, only age and pain – and a mind that could still reach into men's lives and manipulate their destiny.

Blackstone had still not moved. A sentinel guarding the gates of an unknown land. It was time to bring this warrior knight into plain sight.

The potion she had taken eased the pain that was so insistent these days, but her poise did not desert her as she sat on a high-backed chair, supported by cushions, warmed by the fire in the grate. She had prayed, as she did several times during the day and night, and, looking at the man who bent his knee before her, wondered if Sir Thomas Blackstone was the answer to some of those prayers.

She let him stay on his knee longer than would normally be required. Behind him de Marcouf had already been given permission to stand. The old knight would have knelt on broken glass had she demanded it, but loyalty needed to be rewarded with gentleness. She waved away her chamberlain, the constant companion who saw to it that all was as it should be in the Queen's household. What was needed now was privacy, and God knew there was precious little of that rare commodity to be had.

'All right, enough of that,' she said, without any hint that gentleness might still find any refuge in her. 'What took you so long? Were you waylaid with whoring and theft?' she added in a bitter accusation.

Blackstone stood before her. The morning light softened her features, brushing away age, letting his imagination see how beautiful she must have been in her youth. John Jacob was outside and Caprini had gone to pray, while he, after three hours, had been ushered in to await the dowager Queen's presence. More bells rang out for prayer. A thought delayed his answer – if fighting men had to spend so much time on their knees there would be no time for war, and then what use would any of them be?

'Highness, I travelled as quickly as I could, thinking I was summoned by the King,' said Blackstone, daring to probe for an answer to Isabella's presence.

'Don't fish with me, Sir Thomas. I'm no toothless lamprey to take your meagre bait. You do so at your peril. I am a pike that devours others in this murky pond.' She saw that her rebuke cut through his dogged fatigue. 'You thought the seal to be that of your King,' she said.

'I did.' He paused. 'And then it was shown to me that it belonged to his father.'

'By the good priest Torellini, no doubt.'

'Yes, my lady.'

'An eye as keen as his brain. A trusted go-between. So a dead King summons you and you came. Why?'

'A King's seal is enough. I thought my lord might have wished to disguise the summons,' Blackstone answered as simply as he could. There was no point in trying to offer clever answers. Not to this woman. But he could not resist trying once again to see what her connection was to him being brought to this place. 'I serve the King,' he said.

She studied him. The clenched sword of defiance stitched onto the bloodstained jupon, grime on face and hands and his scar cutting a valley across a stubbled face. She could imagine him in battle, remembering the stories told to her of how he had thrown himself into the fray, an action that saved her own grandson. She ignored his statement of loyalty. 'And the coin?'

'A fine talisman, highness. Its inscription blessed my journey.'

'And I'll wager our friend Torellini translated that as well. Your lack of education serves you badly, making you depend on others,' she said, her gaze as unrelenting as her criticism.

'I am no stranger to my own shortcomings, my lady,' Blackstone answered respectfully.

'Are you not? Then you share the same understanding with the rest of the world,' she answered, her voice laden with sarcasm. 'Which of my messengers reached you?'

'Master Samuel Cracknell, highness.'

She considered his answer for a moment. At least one had got through then. 'And what of Master Cracknell?' she asked.

'Dead of his wounds, but he clung to life long enough to deliver his message.'

Isabella blinked and looked away for a moment and it seemed to Blackstone that news of Cracknell's death was not something she cared to hear.

'That saddens me,' she said as if to herself, confirming Blackstone's instincts. 'He was a favoured sergeant-at-arms. His family will be rewarded for his courage and loyalty and you shall give a full account later. My command went beyond words on parchment. Did you realize that? Did he?'

Blackstone was no closer to finding out why he was standing before a Queen who had once seized the crown, and who still seemed to have great influence. 'St George's Day,' he said. 'I had to get here before then.'

She smiled. Blackstone had seen beyond the simple message. Her instincts were still as sharp as a blade and she had been correct in choosing him.

'We are both exiles, you and I, but I am a daughter, sister, mother and widow of Kings. I was a child when I was betrothed; a young woman when I seized the crown to make this country strong. I choose men carefully, Sir Thomas, and I have chosen you.' She stood and Blackstone bowed. 'And in serving me you will serve your King.'

Isabella the Fair left the antechamber flanked by her ladies-in-waiting. Once out of sight her resolve gave way and she faltered; her ladies stepped forward quickly to support her arms. There was little hope for her own future, but bringing the outlawed knight home might well serve that of her country.

Blackstone and his two companions were taken to rooms much better than a common dormitory for soldiers. Their clothing was taken by washerwomen and they were fed meat and pottage, with white bread whose burnt base had been cut away. Guards were placed at their door – which remained unlocked – who were there, said de Marcouf, for the men's safety. The Norman knight made no attempt to have them disarmed and instructed the men to sleep before they left for Windsor and the great tournament.

'We'll find you armour,' he told Blackstone.

'I don't fight in tournaments,' he answered.

De Marcouf was as tired and irritable as a man could be who lacked sleep and was exhausted by the journey back from the coast, yet was still expected to await Isabella's command. 'You will do as she instructs,' he said edgily.

Blackstone tore off a chunk of the bread and soaked it in the thick pottage, then sucked the moisture from it until the mush squelched in his mouth, but he kept his eyes on the older man. It would be too dangerous to antagonize such trusted confidants.

'With respect, my lord, she did not summon me all the way here to fight in some extravaganza that has no meaning and value to anyone other than the King and his noblemen. It's a damned party piece and I have no interest in being part of it.'

De Marcouf glared at him, but knew the argument would be lost if he continued. No one could force Blackstone to take part. And the fighting man was correct – it was an expensive piece of showmanship.

'Get some sleep,' de Marcouf told them and pushed past the sentries, who closed the heavy door behind him.

John Jacob took a slice of meat. 'The food's good,' he said, 'and the mattresses look as though they have enough straw in them to settle a horse. We're being cared for, Sir Thomas. You're going to piss them off, so we should eat and sleep while we can, before they throw us into a damp cell.'

'They won't cause us harm. Not yet, at least. Perhaps when we've served our purpose; not before,' said Blackstone.

Caprini ate delicately, choosing the lesser cuts and slicing the bread where the top crust was browned darker from the oven – a humble man who allowed others to eat better than himself. 'What purpose could there be for your presence here?'

As yet there was no answer being offered by anyone. Blackstone shook his head. Jacob worried a piece of bread in his fingers. 'Do you think the King's son is behind this? Maybe using his grandmother to get you here? He's the one who exiled you and took everything from you. A man carries a grudge long enough and it grows bigger every day. A trap can be sprung in a dozen different ways.'

Before Blackstone could answer Caprini asked, with a quizzical look at him: 'The Prince holds a grudge against you?'

'Sir Thomas tried to kill the King of France,' said Jacob. 'At Poitiers.'

Caprini's hand faltered before the bread reached his mouth. 'The King of France will be at the tournament. He is a royal prisoner of the King of England, an honoured guest.'

In his desire to reach England it had not occurred to Blackstone that the man he had vowed to kill would be present, but the Italian knight was correct. Caprini leaned forward, elbows on the table. 'I have heard that King Edward keeps lions and leopards in the Tower of London. Perhaps, Sir Thomas, you have been lured here to fight like an ancient gladiator.'

'Perhaps, Fra Stefano, it's time for you to go on to Canterbury and prostrate yourself at the place where Thomas Becket was slain.'

'And miss such a spectacle? I think I will stay with you. Someone will have to pray for your well-being or bury what scraps are left of you.' For the first time in the long journey to England, Caprini's face broke into a grin and the three men laughed. Blackstone raised the goblet of wine in a toast.

'Lions and leopards,' he said. 'Long may they reign.'

The air was dry and light, high clouds veiled the sun's glow when Blackstone was escorted next morning across the bailey towards the postern gate. The castle yards buzzed with activity as liveried servants and household staff made final preparations for the journey south to Windsor. From what Blackstone saw in the confines of the yard there must have been a hundred or more coming and going, all to serve Queen Isabella. He had known Norman lords to show their wealth by having households of servants, but now that daylight had come to Hertford, valets, huntsmen, grooms, squires, clerks and stewards scurried like rats in a hay barn. Isabella's wagon carried her standard of a shield divided bearing on one side the arms of England and on the other the fleurs-de-lys of France. A hierarchy of servants fussed silk cushions embroidered with flowers and birds into a day-bed arrangement and tied back woven curtains behind a voile drop to afford Isabella privacy on the road. Soldiers attended their horses as sergeants-at-arms barked orders. Blackstone looked at the activity and thanked God that when he rode anywhere it was just him and the bastard horse.

De Marcouf and the escort strode across the footbridge towards the meadow where a dozen or more courtiers hovered like marsh flies around the King's mother, who sat on a cushioned chair. Her huntsmen stood to one side with a brace of dogs as her falconer gazed up, pointing something out to Isabella. Blackstone's eyes found the fast-moving silhouettes against the sky's white veil as the raptor found its target, and when it struck the hapless pigeon Isabella slapped the arm of her chair in triumph. By the time Blackstone was escorted to her the hunting bird had been retrieved and settled back on the falconer's arm.

'Sir Thomas,' Isabella said, 'you slept well?'

A crispinette held her hair neatly, balancing the beauty of her face and the make-up that accentuated her cheekbones and the red stain to her lips. Like the veiled morning sun, she projected a muted glow of health. Her cloak was open despite the morning chill and she seemed in good spirits.

He bowed. 'In great comfort, highness.'

'Good. We have two days on the road, but I could not resist an hour's pleasure. Falcons are my indulgence and I am spoiled with gifts of them from my son and those who still profess to admire me.'

'I am certain that your highness has many admirers who are genuine in their affection for you.'

She gave him a knowing look. A lifetime of fawning servants and courtiers had encrusted her heart with a brittle disregard for such compliments, but at times there was someone who found the right words and spoke them plainly as had Blackstone.

'You have learnt that flattery to a woman, even a queen, does not go unnoticed or unappreciated. You were taught manners by a Norman lord's wife,' she said, the tone of her voice telling Blackstone that she knew exactly who had nurtured him from common archer to man-at-arms.

'My lady the Countess Blanche de Harcourt,' Blackstone answered.

'Her husband was a loyal supporter in those days. She taught you well.'

A memory of a Norman castle and a lasting friendship that ended beneath a falchion's blade on the orders of the French King flashed into his mind.

Her eyes lingered on him for a moment. 'You look a different man than the one I received,' she said. His jupon and breeches were laundered, his boots cleaned, his beard trimmed. 'You look better groomed than my dogs.'

'I have been spoiled by your highness's generosity.'

'So you have,' she said.

She saw the goddess Arianrhod at his throat. 'I have seen her amulet before. Our Welsh archers have her as a talisman. They say she protects them. It's a pagan belief. You're no Welshman.'

'I am not. But years ago a dying Welsh archer pressed her into my hand at Caen.'

She nodded knowingly. 'Where much slaughter took place. No matter. A soldier seeks protection wherever he may find it.'

She stood and a lady-in-waiting stepped quickly forward, but was waved away. Isabella needed no helping hand in public; besides, the sleeping draught had taken her through the night and her morning prayers had strengthened her, and the joy of her early hunt had lifted her spirits. She stroked the hooded falcon.

'I have twenty birds – falcons, goshawks, tiercels, lannerets – an expensive indulgence. It costs a penny a day to feed each of them.' She faced Blackstone. 'But their ability to strike so silently and effectively is worth paying for.'

Blackstone waited but her gaze made him lower his eyes.

'Not so defiant after all,' she said. 'You have good sense not to challenge me, young Thomas Blackstone.' She made a slight gesture and the courtiers backed away out of earshot. 'Are you worth paying for, I wonder?'

'I have always served the King, highness. I ask for nothing in return.'

'But your loyalty comes at a cost to others. I know what happened after Poitiers. I am a Frenchwoman who has family and friends in France. I know the ladies of the courts, I know the rumours and the gossip and the truth of what happened. You fought and won your battle but you lost your wife and children. And you did not force them to remain with you. A man's affection betrays his heart, Sir Thomas. You are a confusing man to me, and I like things to be clear. How else does one make decisions?'

She walked a few paces and then pointed at the ragged pigeon that lay on the ground. Blackstone bent and picked it up. She took it from him, its limp neck and opaque eyes a sad sacrifice to a queen's pleasure.

'You strike your enemies with the same ferocity. You kill efficiently. You leave women and children weeping.' She put a finger beneath the dead bird's head and lifted the almost weightless neck. 'And yet you give comfort to those who seek it. And mercy to those who beg it.' She dropped the dead bird. 'Where does a killer find such compassion?'

'Perhaps, my lady, it was there first and the killing came afterwards.'

She nodded. 'A good answer.' She lifted her arm. 'Help me to my chair.'

The gesture almost caught him by surprise but he quickly levelled his arm for her to grasp and in the instant she took it he felt her weight to be little more than the bird's.

'You trust the men with you?' she asked as she settled onto the cushions.

'John Jacob has served the King and me with fierce loyalty. The Italian Knight of the Tau was unknown to me but he saved my life from assassins and fought at my side on our journey here. Every man I have with me I would trust with my life. And that of my King.'

'Then what I tell you is for you alone, for now at least. You will decide when the time is right to share it and with whom. Do you see how I extend my trust to you?'

He nodded, but felt that she had already lured him into her web. This woman could entice the devil to forswear Satan.

'Then treasure it, because it can be easily squandered and my grandson's life could be at risk.'

And with those words the cage door fell and held his loyalty captive.

CHAPTER TWENTY-SEVEN

The tournament on St George's Day was to be a great celebration before the two Kings reached agreement on the treaty that would give Edward much of what he desired from France. He would renounce his claim to the French crown provided his sovereignty over widespread fiefs and counties was recognized. King John the Good's ransom had yet to be paid and there was great concern that it would be further delayed because of the strife that still tore across France. The Dauphin held Paris, but civil violence and class hatred were being stirred by Charles of Navarre, the French monarch's duplicitous son-in-law, who had escaped from prison the year before and who wanted to be King. Taxes could not be raised and the ransom would not be forthcoming unless order was re-established and the violence quelled – and who would succeed in doing that was far from clear. If the treaty were not ratified, the demand not met, the ransom not paid – England would go to war again.

'A king and queen are divine, Sir Thomas. We have the hand of God on our shoulder and we have great responsibility to heal a nation and secure its future,' Isabella said.

Blackstone waited patiently. He knew parts of France were in turmoil, but what did it have to do with him? Paris and the Seine were the key to the heart of France and whoever held those controlled the country.

'Last year you helped common townsmen and villeins rise up against the Duke of Milan's soldiers.'

'I did, my lady. The Visconti's troops were contracted men who committed atrocities.'

'France bleeds from civil strife and routiers; wounds fester into poison. A king can lay hands on the sick and if God wills it they will be healed – or He, in His wisdom, lets the afflicted die. Until we know God's desire we must strive with the attributes He has blessed us with – our instinct and intelligence. Your King stands back while France turns on itself. It suits him. It suits a King who waits for a treaty to be signed.'

Blackstone saw the logic of it. While a nation tore itself apart the English King sat back until a victor emerged. John the Good would be desperate to agree terms that would at least leave him a country to rule.

'Then the King lets others do his fighting. It places great pressure on King John and the Dauphin. It makes sense, my lady. It's what any good general would do. Loose the dogs at the bear and see who wins.'

Isabella looked suddenly tired. 'France and England are one. We inflict this on ourselves. It will become a hollow victory.'

'I see no role for me to play in all of this, highness,' said Blackstone.

'You will. And I will instruct you later. Your mother was French; your wife is French. You are suited to my plan. But first it is enough to know that you must take part in the tournament. That is my wish and you will fight with shield covered and without your coat of arms displayed. The King and the Prince must not know you are here. Not yet.'

She stood and he watched as she hid the pain. He took a half-step towards her and she rested her hand on his arm. In an instant he saw in her eyes not the most powerful woman in England and France but a dying woman, who feared for her family and the country they ruled.

'You cannot see the future, Thomas Blackstone, but I tell you that one day it will be more than a dying queen who relies on your strength.'

She withdrew her arm and walked bravely past the courtiers, who stepped clear of her path and lowered their heads in respect.

* * *

The cortège rumbled slowly southward on roads the King of England had vowed would be repaired. Blackstone and his two companions rode on the verge, easing the horses' amble. It was a slow, laborious ride that demanded patience and reminded Blackstone of the baggage trains of war. How a woman in pain endured the rocking wagon he did not know, but royalty were not the same as ordinary people. They were chosen to rule. Divine. And that gave them what? he wondered. The ability to hear the voice of God? The money to buy His grace, more like, Blackstone reasoned. Common men fought in blood for holy benevolence. He silently thanked the great mystery of it all for a King and his son who had built the bridge between themselves and their soldiers. A warrior king was blessed by God and his people. As the journey progressed there were frequent stops as Isabella gave alms. One day he counted 170 poor being blessed with her largesse. At each place they stopped Isabella beckoned him and used the strength of his sword arm to help her from her wagon. Each stop she spoke carefully to him and drew him in further. As his horse shadowed the royal wagon he knew that Isabella the Fair had enticed him to her more as an enchantress who cast her spell than a queen who commanded.

Blackstone had not been summoned again but on the second night, as they approached Windsor, he saw in the distance hundreds of burning torches illuminating the castle's great walls and tournament fields that fluttered with pennons and banners.

'Do you think we'll ride in tonight?' asked Jacob. 'It's a murky business, all of this, Sir Thomas. And there's a kingdom's worth of armed men down there.'

'A Queen arrives in daylight so that she may be noticed,' said Caprini.

'Aye. Tomorrow, John, she'll not skulk in. Not she.'

Voices drifted across the distant fields. Entertainers were singing as their music beat its rhythm in what sounded like a county fair.

'Well, King's tournament or not,' said Jacob as they gazed down at the burning fields, 'there'll be whoring and drinking.' He smiled. 'At least I hope so.'

Blackstone turned to Caprini. 'There'll be a monastery somewhere around here. Perhaps you'd prefer to find lodging there. Knights and the nobility can be as drunk and raucous as a tavern's villeins.'

'What others do is no concern to me, Sir Thomas. I live my own life.'

'As you wish,' said Blackstone, 'but when a man wades through a swamp some of the slime always sticks to him.' He nudged his horse forward.

Servants had gone ahead to pitch Isabella's pavilion for the night's rest. Blackstone and Jacob lay in silence on the damp ground watching as stewards controlled the camp's never-ending activity. The intemperate horse was hobbled and fed and kept close by. Until Blackstone knew what was being asked of him he wanted the chance to escape if danger loomed out of the night. Liveried staff scurried this way and that, cooking fires burned, food was prepared and served and ladies-in-waiting came and went from the Queen's pavilion. The two men lay beneath a tree and rolled themselves in their blankets. Caprini had gone beyond the pickets and found a hermitage to pray at. Across the camp a boy servant, little more than six or seven years old, was cuffed round the ear by a cook for dropping something. He made no sound of pain or complaint and went on with his duties with the cook's scolding voice following him.

'You miss your lady, Sir Thomas?' Jacob said unexpectedly.

The question took Blackstone by surprise. Men seldom shared their feelings with each other. Their actions spoke louder. Though perhaps it wasn't such a strange thing to ask, Blackstone thought. It was John Jacob who had killed the man who had raped Christiana and who had kept silent to protect her name. And when Blackstone fought the Savage Priest before they were exiled it was Jacob who had scaled the castle walls and brought her and his children to safety. Jacob was a strong man; with his cropped hair and stubbled face he looked like someone who would not be troubled by a fight, and on many occasions Blackstone had been grateful for the man's stubbornness. No task was too great for this captain.

'Yes. I think of her every day.'

'Rightly so. She's a fine woman and that boy of yours, Henry, he's a lion's heart inside of him. Bit uncertain of some things, I grant you, but he's a son to be proud of.'

Jacob was one of the chosen few whom Blackstone trusted without question. The men seldom spoke about their families, if they knew of them, preferring to remember whores who gave pleasure and drink that smothered memories. But John Jacob was quieter than most.

'You have family,' said Blackstone. 'South, aren't they? Near London?'

'Once,' said the captain, without any hint of regret. 'They died.'

'The pestilence?' Blackstone asked after a pause trying to remember when last they had spoken of home and hearth. What little there was of either.

John Jacob shook his head, still gazing to where children ran back and forth carrying platters of food. 'The famine, back in '50. Stored rye went mouldy; crops failed. All they had was drawk and darnel, and them weeds don't keep a body alive. My girls died first. Two of them. Then the three lads. I don't know what happened to Beth. Neighbours said she wandered off into the woods after she buried them. Wolves probably took her.' He spoke matter-of-factly, as if telling of something simple instead of a great loss at a time that had taken the lives of many.

'You weren't there?'

'No. King's business in Flanders after Crécy. My belly was full.'

They lapsed into silence again, the moment past.

Soldiers formed an outer picket as Marcouf's captain with thirty men stood guard closer to the royal quarters. Blackstone and Jacob had been fed, but no summons had come from Isabella.

'It's a bugger not knowing what's going on,' said Jacob after a few minutes. 'She's enough men here to protect a king. I've never been this close to a queen before. And she spoke to you. Personal, you say, with no one there? No chamberlain, chancellor or household controller? No one?'

'No one,' said Blackstone, taking the last bite out of a flaccid-skinned apple. The horse lowered its head and snuffled his hand, lips back, teeth seeking the fruit. Blackstone gave it a gentle slap, making it pull back its head, but then it scuffed the ground with a hoof and repeated its demand. Blackstone relented and opened his hand, letting the horse take the core, turning his palm to cover its nostrils. It swung its head away, needing no comforting hand once it had what it wanted.

'Until we find out what's going on, John, we'll keep watch between us. There's bait being dangled, but I don't know why. Not yet.'

They pulled their blankets up and propped themselves against the tree. There were enough shadows flitting through the torchlight for anyone to move in the darkness with a knife in hand. Within a few hours' ride was the Prince who had outlawed him and stripped him of his towns in Normandy. And with him was the captured King John who had slain his friend Jean de Harcourt and whom Blackstone had sworn to kill. Whatever lay over that hill on the tournament fields, there was enough hatred and distrust to be the cause of Blackstone's death.

The movement was slight, a will-o'-the-wisp that came through the night mist, a candle's dandelion glow followed by the soft rustle of a woman's brocade. Isabella had not sent a captain of the guard or the grizzled de Marcouf, but a young woman who attended her. She appeared like a vision and for a moment Blackstone thought he had fallen asleep on his watch and was dreaming.

'Sir Thomas?' she said, keeping her distance, fearful that if he slept he would react with a knife in his hand.

Blackstone didn't move. 'Yes,' he answered.

'My lady awaits you.'

John Jacob half rose as Blackstone got to his feet. 'It's all right, John. They've sent an angel for me.'

Jacob grunted when he saw there was no danger. 'I'll stay awake. Angel or not, priests say women are Satan's gate. And they should know. Tread carefully.'

The captain of the guard stood aside as the woman led Blackstone into the pavilion. A rich orange glow from candles placed around the carpeted tent offered a false sense of warmth. Isabella sat, wrapped in a fur-lined cloak. A stool was placed ten feet away. Isabella smiled and nodded to the angel. '*Merci*, Jehanne.'

The angel glided away, back into the night mist.

Blackstone had kept his head bowed until the elderly Queen spoke.

'The stool is pitifully small for a man your size, but I need to see clearly the face that earned its scar from saving my grandson. The eyes betray the truth of what someone really thinks, and what I have to say to you will leave me in no doubt about your thoughts.'

Blackstone eased Wolf Sword's scabbard and squatted on the stool to face her.

'For some time our spies have been telling us that an assassin has been sent to England. Here, to kill the Prince. You are suspected of being one of those assassins.'

It was an opening gambit meant to throw Blackstone off guard. He said nothing for a moment, thinking of those who had tried to kill him – an Englishman at Lucca, Visconti's men on the Via Francigena. 'An assassin would kill the King,' he said.

'If a protracted war takes place even a warrior king may not sustain the effort demanded. Look what my grandson achieved. It would be he who went to war in the vanguard. Kill the Prince and you leave a bereaved King, weakened by grief – perhaps reluctant to go to war.'

'Or inflamed with an anger that would burn down the world in revenge,' said Blackstone.

'Neither result benefits England.'

'Then it was the King who sent men to kill me?'

'More likely those close to him.'

'How would they know I was sent for?'

Isabella made no show of regret. 'Because someone in my court betrayed me.' Betrayal and conspiracy were a daily fact of life among the labyrinthine passages of court.

'Do you know who, my lady?'

'Not yet. It will be someone privy to my sending Master Cracknell. I will find out in due course. I always do.'

'Who holds the seal that you used, highness?'

'I hold it. Had I used my own, Father Torellini would have known immediately it was I who summoned you.'

'I think he knew anyway,' said Blackstone, trying not to look too obviously into the Queen's eyes, but as determined as her to seek out the truth or catch any fleeting glimpse of lies.

'But he did not divulge it to you, because why would you trust a disgraced Queen? An old woman who stays in the shadows?'

Torellini, you devious old bastard, Blackstone thought. There were confidences shared between the Florentine priest and the English throne that he would never know. 'The assassins? Who were they?' he asked.

'The King pardoned and released many criminals when he went to war. They are known to his advisers. It is not difficult to find men who kill for money, Sir Thomas. You are such a man yourself.'

'I'm no assassin.'

'A distinction that will not be considered when they discover that it was I who sent for you.'

'They think that you would kill your own grandson?'

'There are those who believe I had my own husband murdered. What difference in their minds between killing a King and a Prince?'

For the first time Blackstone realized that the Queen of old was obliged to vie for power with those close to her own son. How much trust had been lost over the years? How much affection remained? 'Then you will be under suspicion.'

'Yes,' she said matter-of-factly. 'And you will be killed when they discover you are here.'

They had tried and failed so far but he knew that once he showed himself in the open, defenceless without his men or any other protection, then they would have him. 'I'm in a bear pit, aren't I? What do I do?'

She turned her wrist in a small gesture of distraction, twirling one of the gold bracelets that was loose on her thin arm, as if considering her answer.

'My lady. I'm a common man, but I'm no fool. You have not brought me this far, to this moment, without knowing what is to be done.'

He saw the truth in her eyes as clearly as the written message that had been sent to him.

'You go into the lists and beat the Prince in combat.'

If she had planned to catch him unawares she succeeded.

'I cannot! I've seen bravery in men, but the King and my Prince are the lions of England. I cannot challenge them. In battle men stepped forward into an overwhelming enemy because of them.'

She saw the anguish on Blackstone's face – his admiration and love for the King and the Prince was genuine. But she made no concession to his feelings. 'You will yield when he knows you have beaten him. There is no need for him to suffer humiliation but he will know when the better fighter has won the day.'

Defeat squeezed Blackstone's chest. 'I cannot.'

'This is the only way your name can be cleared and the journey I plan for you be completed. I will be able to convince the King that what I see lying ahead is to his benefit. His and England's.'

Blackstone stood, as something more fearful than facing any enemy gnawed at him. 'My lady, when I fight, I fight to kill. There's no other way I know. My fury unleashes itself without my knowing it. I cannot do it,' he said, as if confessing a mortal sin to a priest.

'Cage your demons, Sir Thomas, grasp them by the tail and do not let them loose.'

'There is no control of them once they are set free, my lady. They slip their bonds and carry me into the fight.'

Isabella turned her eyes away from the scarred knight. His loyalty was beyond question. She understood that no command of hers would ever force Blackstone to fight. It would take more. 'Then you may never see your family again,' she said quietly.

Blackstone felt as if a mace had struck him. He blinked. 'My family? Where are they?'

'Safe for now. But only as long as you do as I command.'

Defiance edged his voice. 'Tell me and I'll do as you wish.'

'You do not bargain with a Queen!' she bit back. 'You bend your knee and offer thanks that she gives you the chance to save their lives.'

Blackstone went down on his knee and bowed his head. A surge of hope for his family was beaten down by a sudden distaste for the woman who manipulated him. He would do anything to save Christiana and the children.

Even defeat a King's son.

CHAPTER TWENTY-EIGHT

'I'm in a shit pit,' said Blackstone to John Jacob. 'I've never used a lance. Never trained with it.'

'I thought your Norman lord taught you the use of arms,' said Jacob.

'I refused the lance. You know as well as I do they're useless in battle, except for ramming into the ground and spearing horses. Tournaments are for show, not for killing.'

'That might not be true after today,' said Jacob.

'Your faith in my death is touching.'

Jacob shrugged. 'All I'm saying is the Prince and whoever fights with him are well practised in the use of every weapon and have been trained since childhood. You wouldn't expect them to be a skilled stonemason or archer. I don't think a shit pit is deep enough.'

The two men remained silent. Blackstone was unafraid of combat but fearful of being injured through his lack of skill with a lance. And if he could not beat the Prince and prove his worth then Christiana and the children were at risk.

'If you go down will she speak for you?' asked Jacob.

'Isabella? I doubt it. She'll wash her hands of us. I'll be the assassin everyone says I am. You keep yourself well away, John.'

'Running from a fight isn't something I care for.'

'If I'm beaten, you're taken. Get down to the river and try to reach Calais. Tell Sir Gilbert what happened and ride back to Italy.'

'As much chance of that as a whore giving herself for free,' he said keeping his attention on the armour that had been brought for him to strap onto his sworn lord. Every knight of worth had his armour fitted to his body. Ill-fitting plate chafed and slowed a fighting man's skills, which was another disadvantage for Blackstone. Damned near eighty pounds of uncomfortable armour and a belligerent horse unused to riding in the lists seemed to be an insoluble problem. Jacob rubbed a piece of frayed strapping on the armour's breastplate between finger and thumb. 'All those who saw us safely across France will be used to hunt us down. No, Sir Thomas, for everyone's sake you've got to see this through.' He tossed the old armour to one side in disgust. 'And whatever you do, hold back enough so you don't kill him. Even your pagan goddess won't save us then.'

A cloaked figure stepped from behind a tree. Jacob's knife was quickly in his hand making the approaching man stop.

'Master Jacob,' said Caprini as Blackstone laid a hand quickly on Jacob's arm, recognizing the shadow's form. 'I wish to return to my bedroll.'

The Tau knight had moved remarkably close to both men without being seen or heard. Blackstone and Jacob exchanged a brief look.

'Fra Stefano,' said Blackstone, 'the ground's wet tonight; you should have stayed at your prayer.'

Caprini came closer to the small fire and helped himself to a spoonful of pottage. Jacob cut a piece of bread and offered it.

'I am grateful. Thank you,' Caprini said. The firelight from the pavilions faded across the meadow. 'The trees drip unpleasantly; we should have brought a tent. The trouble with England is that God must see it as a garden that needs constant watering.'

'A dribble of rain down a man's neck is barely a problem worth considering,' said Jacob as the Tau knight ate slowly, chewing each morsel as if it might be his last meal.

'I heard what you were talking about. Your Prince will only fight at the end of the day when the last two men have fought; then he will take to the lists. Three tilts of the lance for each challenge unless the challenger is unhorsed.'

'How do you know that?' asked Blackstone. No one had told him the order of the contest.

'May I?' Caprini asked, extending his hand for another slice of bread. 'I know this because I am a foreigner. Because I am ignorant of this ritual. And I ask a man called Roger Mortimer –'

'The Earl of March? You spoke to him?' said Jacob, interrupting his bread-cutting. The man was no older than Thomas Blackstone, but held one of the highest ranks in England. 'He's to proclaim the jousts. You don't just walk up and ask him. He's the Marshal of the Army.' Jacob look disbelievingly from the Italian to Blackstone, who looked bemused at the hospitaller's lack of formality.

'But I did because when I was at prayer I saw him with others going to their own chapel. Men who pray, Master Jacob, share the same joy. A Knight of the Tau is not unknown in this country.'

'I beg your pardon, Fra Stefano. I meant no disrespect.'

'How could any be taken?' he answered gracefully and then spoke to Blackstone. 'Take the blow on the first pass and go down. Why take three tilts? Sooner or later he will unseat you. Once you're on your feet he'll be obliged to dismount and face you.'

'He's as strong as I am. And if the fall doesn't knock me senseless he soon will after I tumble.'

'All right. Take the strike, and then knock him down,' said Caprini.

'It makes sense, Sir Thomas,' Jacob said, adding his weight to the argument. 'This armour is so poor it may come apart after the first hit. I've seen the power of two horses at full tilt. Use that horse of yours to barge him. It's a foul beast at the best of times. In fact, I've never seen a creature so keen to meet the devil on his own terms.'

CHAPTER TWENTY-NINE

The Visconti's man, Werner von Lienhard, had insisted on a hot bath before being dressed for the tournament by his esquires. Servants had boiled water for hours, but their sleepless night had earned them no gratitude. His pennant fluttered above his pavilion, joining those of other knights from across Europe who had been given safe passage to attend and fight in the tournament on St George's Day. Hundreds of English, German, Gascon and Flemish knights put aside old enmities and pitched their tents and pavilions next to each other within sight of the royal standard and the dais where the King and Queen would sit with their honoured guests. Now, as the contest began, a dazzling array of blazons milled around as knights and their squires paraded the lists to the cheers of hundreds of spectators. Knights rode their caparisoned tournament horses, wearing ornate plate armour, emblazoned with their arms. Crested helms and pennants vied for attention like peacocks showing off to the ladies of varying ranks dressed in their finest bright colours and jewelled garlands. They watched each other, a knowing look in their eyes, because a feast of adultery would be committed over the next few days and nights.

Von Lienhard had already identified three or four women he would sleep with before the tournament ended. There would be time before the royal warrant of protection ran out, forcing him back to the Visconti. There was prize money to be had as well as women but the Visconti offered random slaughter, which suited his tastes more. Such killing would be denied him during this friendly tournament where lances would be capped and fatal blows forbidden. Prowess would rule the day and von Lienhard was determined that he and the other German knights would ride home victorious from this spectacle. Friendly jousts or not, men died or were injured and he had sworn to the Visconti that, given the chance, he would kill Thomas Blackstone – if he appeared. He had asked others whether the Englishman had made himself known, but no one knew of Blackstone being present. Perhaps, he speculated, Blackstone had not survived the mountain pass.

The cheering crowds of spectators were silenced as trumpeters heralded the Earl of March's announcement that each combatant would fight on horseback and on foot armed with any weapon of attack and defence except for devices of evil design or those enchanted with charms of spells that were forbidden by God and the Holy Church to all good Christians. On the cloth-of-gold-draped dais Edward and his Queen sat with the French King and other noblemen, as Isabella was fussed over by a lady-in-waiting. Blackstone watched the tender expression on his King's face and admired the difference between his demeanour with his family and his rousing aggression with his troops on the battlefield. His sharp features were softened by his berry-brown hair and beard and he was dressed far more richly than when Blackstone had seen him go to war. A design of wildfowl and falcons with open wings was embroidered in coloured thread into his tunic and gown, and his belt was stitched with drakes and ducks that cowered from the hovering falcons.

When Blackstone had been first brought before Isabella her clothing was modest in its decoration. He paid little attention to women and their dress, but today Isabella could not be ignored. She was the grandest of queens. Blackstone had seen enough precious jewels, seized from Italian merchants unfortunate to be on the wrong side of the conflict. They brought a good price to help feed and arm his men over and above their contracted payments. Today, however, it looked as though Isabella the Fair could pay the French King's ransom simply by donating her jewellery. Alms to the poor. Her gold chaplet was studded with diamonds, rubies,

sapphires and pearls and these precious jewels were repeated in
her slender gold crown that glistened in the light. Isabella the Fair
outshone King Edward and his Queen and all the richly clothed
nobles and guests in the royal stand.

'No wonder we are peasants,' said John Jacob. 'Not all of us,
perhaps,' he added quickly, looking at the Italian.

'Do you see any finery on me? My own rosary is as plain as
black peas. I was a soldier before I became a hospitaller,' he said.
'Only kings and nobles have the right to wear such luxury. I am
happy with plain woven cloth. Who among us needs anything
more?'

Jacob grunted. 'True enough. I'd feel like a court jester dressed
in woven colours,' he muttered.

'Perhaps we're all the King's fools, John. We don't need fancy
dress to make us so.'

They stood well back from the swirling colours that seemed
even brighter against the grey sky. Painted lances and fluttering
pennons added to the spectacle. It was obvious to Blackstone
that the King still showed favour to his treacherous mother. He
reached for her hand and kissed it and then waved aside the lady-
in-waiting as he settled her cloak comfortably about her, nestling
her cloak's fur collar snugly into her neck. Had time healed her
treason, Blackstone wondered, or had she never been committed
it? Perhaps, as she had told him, she cared only for England in
everything she did and let nothing stand in her way. Not even
Blackstone's family. They were the means to make Blackstone
yield to her will. He gazed long and hard at the russet-haired,
unsmiling French King who sat, square-jawed, next to Edward
and his Queen. Edward was showing off. Splendour such as this
was costly and was being paid for by the French – from taxes
raised from ransoms paid for Edward's prisoners. King John was
indirectly paying for Edward's party; no wonder the English King
laughed and cheered as loudly as any commoner.

For the better part of the morning Blackstone and the others
kept their distance, denying themselves the spectacle in case any

of them was recognized. They kept their cowls over their faces and busied themselves like servants cleaning Blackstone's weapons and adjusting the old armour. Roars of appreciation or despair soared and dipped as favoured knights won or lost their contests. A mêlée of horsemen staged a thrilling assault of sword and mace that saw the Duke of Lancaster fall wounded, and as others were beaten and yielded the crowd's excitement rose, muting the trumpets and drums. Blackstone edged his way around the lists feeling the same apprehension he experienced before battle. Most men felt it. All kept it hidden. And Thomas Blackstone was no different. Whatever it was that drove men into the turmoil of war became their friend when steel clashed and the desperation to survive gave them strength. It was the waiting that churned a man's stomach and let the sweat trickle down his spine. But, Blackstone chided himself, this was to be no fight to the death. It was a spectacle in which knights and squires who loved the contest showed off their prowess – little more than a training session – and his family's safety depended on his waging a convincing fight. However, if the Prince fought as hard as Blackstone had witnessed on the battlefield then there was a chance that Blackstone could be beaten. He spat out the stale taste that crept into his mouth. It was not the conflict that troubled him, but rather that he would once again be within striking distance of the French King.

Blackstone carefully edged along the rear of the crowd and studied the man he had sworn to kill. The French monarch half rose from his seat as a Burgundian knight unseated a Gascon. Any small victory for the French over an English ally was a cause for rejoicing. King John clenched a fist in victory. Had he done that when his executioner hacked off Jean de Harcourt's head? Blackstone wondered, remembering the moment when he had called across that Field of Mercy and sworn vengeance. As the Gascon yielded beneath the Burgundian knight's assault amid more muted cheers than would have gone up had the Gascon won, King John glanced across the crowds and in that moment Blackstone felt a shudder. His own archer's eyesight was keener than most and he saw the French King's eyes narrow for a second. Had their eyes met fleetingly? Blackstone dismissed the thought. He was too far away to be recognized, but he saw the King's face as clearly as the day he had cut his way through the field at Poitiers and got within ten paces of killing him.

The moment passed. The French and English Kings applauded. Drumbeats and whinnying horses demanded attention.

A deafening roar of voices swelled over the tournament field. A pair of knights stood like gatekeepers at each end of the lists, barring entry through the gates to anyone not fighting. They held lances down across the entrance as behind each of them the next two fighters came to the mounting benches. A herald's voice was suffocated by the wave of excitement as the Prince of Wales's pennon was shown at one end. There was no need to announce who was next to joust. His horse was swathed in a black trapper that bore the Prince's tournament colours of three white ostrich feathers. A friendly tournament such as this meant his royal coat of arms would not be displayed. The same three ostrich feathers were blazoned against a black background on his shield. His helmet was adorned with the boiled-leather crest of a lion. In the centre of the lists the tournament marshal raised his arm, readying the combatants. As if on command, the crowd fell silent – so silent that the snorting horses and the snap of closing visors sounded loudly. Attendants held the horses' bridles, aiding each rider to control the power that now demanded to be released, and handing each man his shield. The marshal's arm dropped as his voice carried the command to let the horsemen go.

'*Laissez-les aller!*'

The gatekeepers stepped back quickly out of the way, raising their lances, letting the surging horses through. A gasp of expectation rose up, turning from awe to blood-lust. Edward of Woodstock, the great Prince, victor of Poitiers and captor of the French King, crouched, lance steady, hurtling towards his opponent across the seventy yards between them; seventy yards that were devoured in six seconds. The Prince's opponent struck the Prince's shield a blink of an eye before the Prince found his target, but the Prince took the blow at an angle and his own lance splintered as it struck with such accuracy that the impact lifted his opponent out of the saddle. The combined weight of horse, man and armour and the bone-crushing momentum carried the man across the saddle's cantle. As his body thudded into the ground Blackstone already knew that the man's shield arm must have been broken. His eyes had followed the tip of the blunted lance from the moment the Prince had lowered it. Edward's aim had not wavered, even when he had taken the glancing blow on his own shield. It was the strike of a highly trained knight. This was no sport. The Prince meant to be the victor and Blackstone understood the cold, deliberate intent meant that he, too, was likely to fail in this contest of arms.

'He will not rise,' said Caprini. 'He is too badly injured.'

They watched as ushers ran forward to aid the stricken knight and from the way his body sagged Blackstone knew the man's shoulder was snapped. The Prince retired beyond the gate to await his next opponent, applauded by King and commoner, cheered on by a crowd who revered their heroic Prince.

'Sir Thomas,' said Caprini. 'You cannot beat this man in the saddle. Angle your shield high, like so.' He bent his arm to demonstrate. 'Deflect the blow, push forward in your stirrups. Get him on the ground with you. Then you can overcome him.'

'You have a lot of confidence in me,' said Blackstone.

Caprini kept his eyes on the Prince as he was fussed over by attendants. 'I see a fighter's weakness and his strength. He was aiming for the other's head. Strike the helm and such a blow can snap a man's neck at worst. At best he is in darkness for a long time. Your Prince is known to be a generous benefactor, but not here; not when he fights.'

John Jacob had taken his time in dressing Blackstone. After Blackstone had bathed he tugged on a linen shirt and then a padded tunic to help protect his ribs. Blackstone had reined in his impatience as Jacob fumbled with straps and the layers of clothing and armour. To save his sworn lord's strength from bearing the weight of the armour on his chest and shoulders he dressed him from the feet up, adding the weight piece by piece. Over Blackstone's leather shoes he fitted the sabatons of mail, then plate armour for the shins, knees and thighs. He eased a sleeveless mail haubergeon onto his torso and cinched Blackstone's waist with a leather belt.

'Christ, John, I'll split like a squeezed worm,' he muttered as Jacob found an extra notch.

'Keep your guts in place,' Jacob said, attending to his duty, determined to give Blackstone as much protection as possible. 'When was the last time you had to do this?'

'Never,' said Blackstone.

'Merciful God, I hope you've had a good breakfast,' Jacob answered without halting his ministrations as he fitted a breastplate and then added pieces for Blackstone's shoulders and arms. 'Too tight on the arms?' he asked.

Blackstone lifted and swung his fighting arm. 'No. It's good enough.'

'It'd better be. Our Prince will have the very best armour. Catch the flat of your blade on it and it will slide like water off glass. Stroke hard and put your weight behind it. Hard, Sir Thomas. You have to beat him with your strength.'

'He's no weakling.'

'But he hasn't been running up and down those accursed mountains in Italy for nigh on two years and fighting bastard Hungarians who take a lot of killing.'

Jacob checked his work, looking Blackstone up and down as a concerned mother might dress a child. 'It'll do,' he said as he tugged on the plated gauntlets with their leather lining for grip onto Blackstone's big hands. Blackstone was obliged to bend down so his captain could tug a leather cap onto his head and then, before fitting the helm, slipped a mail coif over him to protect his neck and shoulders. There was to be no surcoat showing his coat of arms. He settled the uncrested helm on Blackstone's head.

219

'Your own mother wouldn't recognize you, Sir Thomas. Come to that, neither would I if you came at me dressed like this.'

Jacob wiped the back of his hand across his mouth and spat in satisfaction. He was sweating from attending Blackstone. God knew what it was like in that metal coffin. 'Near enough time, Sir Thomas. Lads have brought your horse to the mounting bench. I've hobbled him and kept him hooded. Don't want him running amok and bringing attention on us.'

Blackstone nodded as the figure of the French King merged back into the rich colours of nobility on the dais. 'Good enough. Keep my blazon covered on your jupon and shield and when I go down it's up to you to get my horse.'

'Aye, me and a dozen more. It'll be done, though I'm not sure how.'

Blackstone turned to Caprini. 'You gave your word not to mention my name, Fra Stefano.'

'It stands. And if there are those who wish you harm, then Master Jacob and I will guard your back. It is my intention to take you to Canterbury. I sense that a pilgrimage would be good for you.'

The thunder of hooves rumbled across the ground and the clash and roar of the crowd signalled that the Prince had taken another prize.

'He's getting warmed up,' said Jacob. 'His muscles will be loose now, but he'll be hot. He'll have sweat in his eyes. One more chance when he goes back and takes off his helm for a servant to wipe his face. He won't take off them gauntlets and do it himself. He wants his third victory and then he can sup and do whatever heroic princes do after a joust. Piss in a gold jug and turn it into wine, for all I know.'

Blackstone felt the crumpled linen shirt between his shoulder blades twist like rope from the sweat that soaked him beneath the padded jacket, mail and armour. He had forgotten how cumbersome it all was and why he and his men chose to fight without the plate.

Caprini came to escort him towards the enclosure. 'Did you hear that? The crowd? A German knight, the best I've seen. He cleared the field. We see the best of them all today, Sir Thomas. Remember what I said and you will come through this with honour.'

'And still be able to walk, I hope,' said Blackstone. 'I've no joy at the thought of fighting the Prince.'

As they approached the mounting bench the bastard horse raised its head, scenting his master's approach despite being hooded. 'Christ help us both,' Blackstone muttered. Had he been able to reach the silver goddess at his throat that now lay tucked beneath the steel collar he would have invoked her blessing. Jousting horses were as well trained as the men who rode them. Blackstone's horse was a fiery instrument of war. And it seemed as irritated as Blackstone at having to wear such protection. The beast was caparisoned over a quilted blanket, a chanfron headpiece of jointed metal pieces had gaps for its eyes, ears and nostrils, and curtains of mail protected its flanks, while a strong, boiled-leather covering protected its chest.

Trumpets blared, the marshal's voice drifted through the pavilions. An unknown challenger was to take the field. Rumour had it that it was to be one of the King's closest friends disguised as a poor knight – a jest, just as when the King and his son dressed in the guise of city officials at jousts and took on all comers. Others said that it was the Gascon lord, Jean de Grailly, who had returned early from the crusade in Prussia. Those who professed to know from reliable sources said it was a famed Spanish knight. Rumour after rumour had failed to uncover the name of the knight who would soon appear without a coat of arms. It was an added excitement and one that fuelled the crowd's interest. A fine way to end the first day of the ongoing tournament.

Wolf Sword was held in a ring tied to the saddle's pommel; axe and mace were tucked into and tied onto his studded belt. John Jacob steadied the horse's steel bridle as its yellow teeth snapped and champed at the bit.

Blackstone nodded and Jacob eased off the hood. The horse shivered, ducked its head, tugging against the reins, testing Blackstone. His legs held its body firmly, not too tight – not yet – because whatever Blackstone needed from this beast it would be commanded through the pressure from his legs. 'I have him,' he told Jacob.

Caprini stepped in and took the leather-bound, unmarked wooden shield from an attendant, lifting it so Blackstone could hook his bent arm through its straps.

'I think you have a chance. Rise up when you strike,' said Caprini. 'Rise up and lean forward the moment before impact. He will do the same, but the man who gets the blow in first will suffer the least. He crouches but you will have extra power to strike a downward blow. It might save you because he will find his target on your shield. Then, take yourself to the ground when you are ready.'

Blackstone wondered if the old broken bone that bent his shield arm would take such an impact. Another attendant handed him the unwieldy ash lance, near enough fourteen feet long, thick at the base to tuck beneath his arm with a carved place for his gauntleted fist to grip behind the simple crossguard. A crown-shaped, three-pronged cronel covered the lance's tip. He felt awkward – trapped like a coiled snake in an iron casket. 'Thank Christ they're blunted,' he said, meaning the lance. He eased its base into the well-worn pocket of the fewter on his stirrup to hold it steady until it could be brought to bear.

A persistent throbbing drumbeat of his heart pounded through his helm. John Jacob stood on the mounting stool and raised a wineskin to Blackstone's lips. 'Wine and water, Sir Thomas. You take the fight to him. You'll need this.'

Blackstone swallowed, grateful that his dry mouth had been eased.

He held the great beast ready, its plain caparison as dull as its singed-looking hide. Two unmarked creatures, their identity camouflaged by drab covering, about to hurl themselves into the riot of colour that fluttered in all its pageantry.

He calmed his breathing, felt the horse settle and knew, from whichever of God's angels hovered at his shoulder, that he had nothing to fear.

Jacob and Caprini stepped away. Now that Blackstone was armed and ready no further contact was allowed. He dropped the visor and sucked in the claustrophobic darkness – the narrow slit barely wide enough to see directly in front of him. A fleeting memory of thousands of French knights bearing down on him and the other archers gave him a moment of imagined horror. How they had slain those poor bastards trapped in these coffins. What terror must they have known? Yet still they had come on.

The horse snorted, lowered and then raised its head. Ears cocked forward. Muscles bunched and quivering. Eager to fight. Blackstone could not contain the moment of anticipation that mingled with joy. He laughed. 'You have the strength and balls of a bull,' he said to the horse. 'And I thank God for it.'

The guards at the gate raised their lances and stepped quickly away.

The marshal's voice carried. '*Laissez-les aller!*'

CHAPTER THIRTY

Blackstone grunted with effort, desperately sucking air in the dark confines of the helm. Everything felt wrong. Something chafed in his groin against the saddle, bunched linen rubbed beneath his armpits and the jolting, uneven gait of his horse bobbed his vision up and down. With shield and reins in his left hand he pulled up his horse's head, fighting the unruly beast that seemed only to want to attack the other stallion that bore down on them. Blackstone cursed and tried to keep it on course, but between the bellicose horse and the wavering lance he struggled to keep his opponent in sight through the helm's narrow slit. His frustration rose to anger. *Goddammit! For Christ's sake! Come on! Straight! Straight, for Christ's sake!* a voice in his head bellowed as he used his legs to try to bring the aggressive horse onto the right course and not too close to the Prince who hurtled towards him. He had seen knights badly injured when horses collided, and also that it was not always possible for the knights to get a clean strike against the shield because of the wavering mounts. He held the lance right to left across his chest, angled just off the near edge of his shield. Its tip wavered uncontrollably and he could feel through his anger the despair that he would be unlikely to strike the Prince's shield. An archer's instinct always let the bowman guide his arrow shaft onto his target and that instinct rescued him in the final moments before the combatants closed. He eased the reins through his fingers, letting the belligerent horse turn its head as if to attack the other as he angled his shield. Raising himself forward from the saddle he took the weight and strain onto his hips and thighs, letting the bunched muscles in his back transmit their strength into his shoulder and arms. Instinct, anger and defiance let his eye take the tip of his lance onto the black shield.

Wood splintered. The impact smashed his shield against his ribs and threw him back across the saddle; only the strength of his legs held him onto the horse. Pain shot through his shield arm and blood roared in his head; somewhere beyond that was the bellowing of the crowd. He was glad of the extra notch John Jacob had cinched on his belt as he pushed his stomach muscles against it and came upright in the saddle. He pressed one leg into the war horse's side and kicked it around with the other. As the horse turned he saw that the Prince had not yet regained his stirrups and his own mount was floundering. He had made the first pass but he had no wish to do it again. The beast had struck the Prince's mount on the pass and now all eyes were on the Prince. Blackstone desperately wanted to pull free the visor and gulp air, but he gathered the horse, exerted his strength against its will and brought it to an impatient halt, letting it bellow and snort its exertion and frustration. His own lance was splintered two thirds of the way down its shaft, as was the Prince's, and following the Prince's example he tossed it aside. Blackstone was about to feign injury and allow himself to slip from the saddle but he was saved this humiliation when he saw that the Prince's horse was limping, injured from the contact. Blackstone watched the man he had last seen at Poitiers climb down from the saddle as attendants ran forward to seize its reins. Cheers and applause greeted the Prince's recovery and Blackstone could tell that he had winded the King's son. But that did not disguise the Prince's anger that came fast-paced towards him after drawing his sword from its saddle ring. Blackstone pulled Wolf Sword free and dismounted. John Jacob led four ushers at the run to take his horse. Blackstone said nothing as his captain took the reins from him, barely hearing his utterance.

'God's blood, you rattled his brain, Sir Thomas. Finish him.'

Blackstone was already striding away towards the royal stand with Wolf Sword's comforting grip in his hand. Now that he had survived the joust he knew he could do what came more naturally to him. The man wearing the crested helm and dark, burnished armour covered by his tournament surcoat strode towards him, but Blackstone could see there was a slight imbalance in the Prince's stride. Perhaps, he thought, the impact had wrenched muscles. Blackstone felt exhilaration as he quickened his pace, knowing the crowd now applauded with approval at his eagerness to engage the Prince of Wales.

Neither man waited for the other to strike first but barged their shields, hoping the other would be pushed off balance. The instant they clashed Blackstone realized, despite the Prince being nearly as tall and muscled, that he had the advantage of Edward, who rocked back half a pace. It meant nothing to the crowd, merely that the Prince braced his legs and brought his sword down, catching Blackstone's helm. Like a church bell's hammer the sword's clang reverberated inside. Neither man yielded another pace backwards, but kept striking their opponent with tireless blows. Each could hear the other grunting with exertion and both ignored the rousing cries from the crowd. Blackstone forgot his promise to Isabella. All else faded into a blurred memory as he hammered blow after blow against the heir to the throne. Edward had fought with youthful joy at Crécy and as a more experienced warrior at Poitiers, and a lifetime of zealous ambition to one day be a warrior king like his father brought him on to attack Blackstone. Yet every strike he made Blackstone parried, every manoeuvre that turned body and shield Blackstone blocked. Neither man could best the other, but Edward was tiring, his strength weakening. Blackstone sensed it as surely as he knew, when he had been an archer, that his arrows would find their target.

Blackstone saw the Prince shift his weight onto his back foot as he sought a firmer stance against the ceaseless attack. Blackstone had him. At that moment the Prince realized that the knight who faced him was stronger. And lethal. Blackstone bore down on him and felt him take two faltering steps backwards. Sweat stung Blackstone's eyes, his mouth was dry from exertion and a nagging pain crept up his old injury into his shoulder. Ignoring the discomfort he closed with the Prince. He heard the man's wheezing breath, as desperate as his own. This was a tournament no longer. It was close-quarter battle that made a man take desperate measures to survive. Blackstone's mongrel blood swept aside any jousting code of honour – he and the Prince had committed themselves to a fight that could lead to either of them being badly injured. Their ferocious desire to survive bled into the men's muscles. Blackstone would ram him with his shield, then take his legs from beneath him and the Prince would be unable to rise with the weight of his armour and the by then draining exhaustion in his muscles – the fight would be won.

Beyond the Prince's helm Blackstone saw a stripe of blurred colours that resolved into those on the dais who leaned forward in anticipation. The fury that possessed him to fight would be his undoing. The thought of his family lay beyond a distant horizon. He saw his adversary and only him. Nothing else mattered. But then, as if the pagan goddess had reached into his heart, a glimpse of Christiana flashed into his mind. Her beauty caught him off guard. As it always had. She was calling to him. Taking a half-pace backwards he deliberately raised Wolf Sword in defence rather than attack. Seizing the moment the Prince struck hard and fast, delivering a swinging blow that shuddered against Blackstone's helm. A lesser man would have been brought to his knees. Blackstone tasted the blood in his mouth and with a gesture allowed his head to drop in submission and his arms to splay in surrender. The bitterness he tasted was not due to blood alone.

Both men stood heaving with exertion. Prince Edward pushed up his visor; sweat glistened on his face and Blackstone saw that he too had bitten hard on his tongue, blood running from the corner of his mouth. Through heaving breaths the Prince made his demand. 'Show yourself.'

Blackstone ignored his aching body and cumbersome armour and knelt before Edward. 'I am here to serve you, my Prince, not cause you harm,' he said and extended Wolf Sword towards him in a gesture he knew the Prince would recall from the day at Calais when he gave Blackstone his coat of arms – the sword, held like a crucifix, grasped by a gauntleted fist.

The Prince's eyes widened.

Neither man spoke. Blackstone cut free the leather covering from his shield, exposing his coat of arms. Then he pushed back his visor. What he saw was a seething anger held in check.

'Your defiance has no bounds. You defy us, you return marked as an assassin, and you defy yourself in order to allow us to best you.'

'No, my lord. You took advantage of my hesitation. I gave you no quarter. You won.'

Edward spat blood from his mouth. 'Get up, damn you! Show your colours to our father.' The Prince bowed his head towards the royal dais. 'Sire! The day is over. We have been victorious. We beg permission to retire from this field.'

King Edward smiled, raised a hand in a small gesture of permission, and as the Prince walked towards the end of the lists, rousing cheers acknowledged his success. The King's eyes fell on the man who had come so close to beating his son. Who would have beaten him had he not yielded. Blackstone turned his shield. And bowed his head. There was no need for the King to see the scarred face that was hidden beneath the helm. The warrior King was less aggrieved than his son to see Blackstone and he allowed him an indulgent smile.

'Sir Thomas Blackstone,' he said, enjoying a hidden delight as the French King at his side flinched from the Englishman's name. 'You dispel the lies we hear about you and confirm your bellicose defiance. *Défiant à la mort.* We have a thought to see you arrested but your efforts here have pleased the crowds,' he said, then paused. 'And we hear you are a champion of the common man. It befits us to be merciful.'

Blackstone raised his eyes. It was obvious that the English Crown had been kept informed of his exploits in Italy. 'God bless you, my liege.'

'We are divine, Sir Thomas; you, it seems, are coveted by His angels. Either those ascending or those who are fallen. How, we wonder, did you find the path to our door?' He glanced at Isabella, who did not meet his eyes but stared resolutely ahead at the fighting man who had yielded to her wishes. 'No doubt that secret will be made known to us in time,' he said.

The King studied him a moment longer. He had not seen Thomas Blackstone since that day at Crécy when his torn body lay cradled by a priest, surrounded by the greatest knights of England, who all swore to the boy's prowess and courage. From that bloodied state a knight had risen with a reputation that could not be ignored – or denied. The King stood to leave, but before bowing his head Blackstone looked into the French King's eyes. He would not yield to him. One determined throw of Wolf Sword could reach John the Good's chest. It would tear apart his heart and Blackstone's promise of revenge would be complete. But that would not save his family.

He bowed as deeply as he could despite the damned armour and cinched belt cutting into muscle and flesh; like a flagellant monk he pressed hard against it to pay for his broken promise.

Penance.

The Tau knight helped John Jacob ease away Blackstone's armour and mail. The ill-fitting plate had chafed his skin and his ribs were already discolouring into purple bruising.

'What of my horse, John?' he asked the captain, who tossed aside the last piece of armour in disgust.

'Aye, we've got him tethered and fed. Flared-up he was, took half a dozen of us and another hood over his head to settle him. He quietened some when we stripped him down. There's barely a mark on him, though how in God's name he didn't have your legs crushed I cannot say. I thought he was going to bite the head off the Prince's horse. Sweet Jesus, Sir Thomas, they'd have disqualified you even before you got in the saddle had they known what a mean bastard he is.'

'But he's not injured?'

Jacob shook his head. 'Not a mark, as far as I can see. His hide is tougher than yours. I've hobbled him again because he's kicking anything that comes close. We should take the iron shoes off him. That might save any other horse from being hurt,' he said as he swabbed Blackstone's back with a cloth soaked in brine to clean the abrasions.

'No, leave him be, but tether him and the other horses close by. I don't know how long we'll be welcome here.'

Caprini took balm from his saddlebags and administered the sweet-smelling paste across Blackstone's ribs, insisting Blackstone raise his bent arm against the pain so he and Jacob could bind him with a linen bandage.

'Not too tight or I'll not draw breath,' he complained.

'Loose enough to let you swallow the frumenty I've cooked,' said Jacob. 'Bit of decent pottage will do us all very nicely.'

Blackstone glanced at the clay pot nestled in the fire's embers and the herb-scented steam emerging from it. 'If Will Longdon was here he'd have found some white cuts or shot a pigeon and found some decent bread. Is there ale?'

'Between you and that horse I've barely time to draw breath m'self. What's in the pot will fill our bellies.'

'So it will, and I'm grateful for it, John,' said Blackstone apologetically, his irritability calmed by the stalwart Jacob's practicality.

Caprini tied off the bandage. 'You gave your Prince bruises to remember. But that was all. You could have beaten him. Why did you not? It was obvious to me that you held back.' The Tau knight stepped away and repacked the jar of balm. He studied Wolf Sword's pommel, and then balanced the hardened steel in the palm of his hand. 'I've seen you fight, Sir Thomas. He was no match for you.'

It seemed for a moment that Caprini favoured Wolf Sword. His fist curled onto its grip, the blade unnervingly close to Blackstone's neck. The two men's eyes met. Blackstone realized with a shock how easily someone could get so close to him and with one thrust take his life that had been so carefully guarded. The moment passed. Blackstone took Wolf Sword from him and eased it into a scabbard. 'He was a match for any man.'

Caprini made a gesture of surrender. 'As you wish. Loyalty is a fine trait, but victory today could have made you the tournament's champion.'

'Sir Thomas does not seek glory,' said John Jacob. 'He serves the King.'

'Well spoken, Master Jacob. 'But your sworn lord is not a man to yield – not without good cause,' the Italian answered.

'I'm no fool, Fra Stefano. I could see that,' answered Jacob, and turned his back so his questioning gaze did not fall on Blackstone.

Blackstone eased himself into a fresh shirt. 'I am blackmailed by Isabella,' he said. 'There, now that I've told you, your lives may also be at risk. The Queen may not like the idea of you sharing our secret.'

'Then you yielded at her command,' said Torellini.

'My family is in danger. The King plays for time while France burns. I am being used by her, but I'm caught up in something I don't understand. I was thought to be an assassin brought here to kill the Prince. It's a shit pit of stench and I want no part of it – but I have no choice.'

Jacob and Caprini remained silent until the captain offered him a bowl of steaming food. 'Best to eat while we live, Sir Thomas. They say there's ambrosia in heaven, but I'd miss a decent hot meal.'

Blackstone took the bowl and the hunk of rough bread being offered.

Caprini warmed his hands at the fire as Jacob dished out another serving. 'And what word of this assassin? Is he known?' he asked.

Blackstone shook his head. 'No doubt a rumour to trap me is all it is.'

Caprini swallowed a mouthful of food. 'Then you are still in danger from those who spread it. You face men who are jealous of their position with the Prince. You are not wanted here and if the Prince is still your enemy even though you have tried to prove otherwise, then I doubt even his grandmother can protect you.'

'Her concern is for me to stay alive until she has no further use of me. We are safe for the time being.'

John Jacob spooned another dollop of frumenty into Blackstone's bowl. 'It's never the wolf's pups who'll savage you, only the she-wolf.'

Dusk settled across the meadows as spring mist caressed the river. Hundreds of rushlights flickered ready for the contest to continue once prayers had been attended to and food taken. No one had yet approached Blackstone, so in the half-light they smothered the fire and struck their camp, carrying weapons and bedding to another site. If there were unknown enemies anxious to cause harm before Blackstone could discover Isabella's true purpose it was best to hinder their efforts by moving to the outer area of pavilions and tents. Months before this tournament the King had enjoyed a torchlit joust at Bristol and he wished to continue the spectacle of combat in the same manner. He and his guests would return in another procession to thrill the crowd, alms would be distributed to a chosen few while for most the chance to glimpse the warrior King and his family was deemed sufficient largesse. None had filtered away in the gloom to their villages. St George's Day was as much their celebration as that of the nobles. Soon, like creatures from a minstrel's fable, knights would ride in the shadows, their decorated and plumed helms bobbing and weaving as horses pranced and torchlight was reflected in burnished armour and illumined the colourful surcoats.

The three men on foot led their horses through the pavilions, avoiding those whose coat of arms suggested they belonged to those who might have been given lands and title by the Prince. Smoke from campfires and torches swirled upwards, dispersed by a forest of banners and pennons flapping lazily in the cool night breeze. Blackstone recognized many of the blazons; others were unknown to him. One banner, smaller than its neighbour, was held open easily by the small breeze; then, as a gust of wind rustled treetops, the second, heavier banner suddenly flared open.

An avenging angel.

A bare-breasted woman crowned with gold, eyes glaring across the defile towards him, teeth bared, wings and talons spread-eagled as if to swoop and carry him off. Harpies were the destructive spirits of the wind, baptised with names of storm and blackness; fierce and loathsome, they were thought to dwell in filth and stench. These harbingers of divine vengeance were despatched by the gods to snatch the souls of evildoers. The figure of the harpy bore down on him, tearing its way into his memory and the dying moments of a bloody battle a dozen years before. Mayhem's deafening roar pounded through his ears, his pulse quickened as once again he saw the coat of arms loom at him, powered by the knight's strength behind the shield and his vicious attack. A shattered mirror in his mind's eye reflected jagged battle scenes and the pain and horror of seeing his brother fall like a slaughtered ox beneath the swords at Crécy, the man who had done the slaying riding, harpy-painted shield high, sword hacking a bloody path towards the Prince. That glaring chimerical monster, both woman and beast, had swooped down on him as he lay, wounds bleeding, in the Crécy mud, and the attacking knight had taken his hardened steel sword to Blackstone. Blinded by his own blood, and close to death from his injuries, God's miracle and the blessing of the Celtic goddess Arianrhod had given Blackstone the strength to slay him. He had taken that knight's sword with its running-wolf-etched blade and wore it to this day.

And now that vile bitch taunted him again – an emblem of death, bringing with it other ghosts that clung like a silk cloth impaled on a thorn bush. Something that could not be removed without further damage or pain.

CHAPTER THIRTY-ONE

The King had begun restoration of the royal lodgings in the upper ward of Windsor Castle. His temporary apartments were sumptuous enough for the brief time he would spend there and although the obligation of hospitality would still stand, his own quarters were private. A divinely appointed king never entertained his inferiors unless they were of very high rank or blessed with his friendship. The French King was his prisoner, but was treated with great respect. Not only was he housed at the Savoy Palace but he was given the comforts and retinue that befitted a king. He was as a free man – except that he was not. He was the key to even greater riches and territory. He and his young son Philippe were equals to the English King, so there was little cause for Edward to feel anything but victorious. The tournament was a spectacle whose fame would reach across Christendom and yet a rowelled spur of discontent now stung his success. His son was raging, his mother was silent and his wife, Philippa, betrayed no emotion at all. The good woman from Hainault remained stoic and had the grace to smile at Edward as he listened patiently to his son's outburst.

And a good meal was about to be ruined.

'He was exiled!' fumed the Prince of Wales with barely contained anger. 'And I was humiliated.'

'You won the contest. There was no disgrace. You were the better fighter. Everyone saw that,' said Edward gently. 'And you will lower your voice in our presence,' he added with an inflection that brooked no disobedience.

The King's various counsellors who hovered constantly about his presence had been ushered away by his Chancellor and,

234

retreating to the shadows against the royal apartment's walls, they became blind and deaf to what was said between their liege and his family.

Rebuked, the Prince of Wales bowed his head. 'Sire. Forgive me.'

'It would seem that forgiveness will need to be dispensed to all before the night is out,' he said and turned to face Isabella. 'Perhaps your grandmother can explain how an exiled knight has appeared at our celebration without his King's permission.'

Isabella's gaunt features reflected the pain she was in, but Edward would not yet offer any further sympathy or care. Mother and son were still close, but a king required respect and obedience from everyone. Isabella took the gold and silver enamelled cup of wine to her lips. Enough potion had been poured into it to keep her from collapse. This was no time for weakness, even in front of her son, for it was not sympathy that she wished to draw from him, but his sound judgement, to help him take the next step towards securing the territories in France – even, perhaps, the French crown, if John defaulted on his ransom of more than six hundred thousand pounds – a sum that seemed impossible to raise.

'I sent for him,' she answered simply.

'I wonder why I am not surprised to hear that confession,' he said.

'It is not a confession; it is a statement of fact. I sent for him because you need him, but he obeyed the command because he thought it came from you.'

The King stroked his beard from his gown and sat opposite her, keeping a respectable distance that maintained royal status. 'My dinner will be cold, madam, and my knees ache from prayer. If I am to end this day with anything but an empty stomach and pain I would ask you to explain yourself. Quickly. For both our sakes.'

He had noticed her wince momentarily, little more than a twitch of an eye, as she subdued her pain.

She lowered the goblet, replacing it on the ornate stand at the side of her chair. 'When the tournament ends you will finalize the draft treaty with John.'

Edward wondered briefly whether it had been a mistake to allow her to be visited by the French King and others in his retinue; it had been a chance for Isabella to reacquaint herself with friends and cousins from France. Information was a weapon.

'I will. Most of France is ours. Or soon will be, once the Dauphin accepts the terms,' he said.

Isabella's voice was calm and assured and she spoke directly to her son as if he were the only other person in the room. 'France is burning. Routiers bleed her dry. Some of whom are encouraged by you – perhaps not openly, but it serves you well to observe the chaos. The great and the good have yet to decide whom they will support, be it John's son the Dauphin, or Charles of Navarre. You play one against the other, because whoever succeeds in bringing the people of Paris under their control will wield the power.'

'I see no connection between the politics of France and Thomas Blackstone,' said the King, trying to guess what he had missed but which his mother had foreseen.

'The turmoil is spreading. The peasantry arm themselves and even the lower ranks of nobility join their cause. There is murder and brutality and you offer no assistance,' she answered, urgency in her voice.

'Madam, I am playing a long game. There is a ransom and a country at stake.'

Isabella nearly forgot herself, the irritation bitter on her tongue. 'There will be no country!' she said too sharply. The King tilted his chin as if to rebuke her but she quickly lowered her voice. 'John and the Dauphin fear for their families! How can either accept your treaty when their attention is diverted not only by the back-stabbing Navarre but by a peasant army that burns and loots its way across the countryside?'

She knew the King was aware of the payments she made to couriers who travelled back and forth between her and Charles of Navarre and others who were embroiled in the violence in the country of her birth. Information could be used either for or against Navarre, depending upon how she saw the great game changing.

'You have your ear close to the ground,' Edward said.

'I have it close to the hearts of those who are threatened,' she answered. Always quicker, always sharper, always better informed.

'John's family is his concern. His duty, as laid down by God, is to protect his country,' said Edward testily. 'Where he fails I shall succeed.'

Isabella gazed at her son, letting her eyes rest on him. He was the greatest King England had known and she had played her role in making it so. She answered with genuine tenderness. 'You are a benevolent King. You are gracious and kind and you curb your anger towards your enemies when you have them on their knees. If your family were hunted by the mob what would you wish?'

She watched his face change from one of attentiveness to that of a man who could well imagine the horror of his own children being slaughtered. Then his face hardened.

'I am not John's keeper. I have yet to wear the crown of France. Let the Dauphin find the means to protect his own family.'

Isabella rallied her waning energy. 'And you believe his fear will not influence his judgement in the treaty? He will try to strike a bargain. To buy time. I would ask you to save John's daughter and his son's wife and family. Benevolence will be met with gratitude. Your treaty will be less argued over. And King John will regain control over his son and Navarre – and his country. Thanks to you.'

Edward remained silent. He knew as well as the Prince that Blackstone could have beaten him, but had not. The rumour of his being an assassin had turned out to be just that – false accusation. Isabella had brought him to the tournament to prove his loyalty and thrust him to the fore – thrust him down the Prince's throat, more like. And the devil would play advocate between King and Prince, father and son, when the time came, because Thomas Blackstone was a thread that ran through all their lives. So now Edward knew what Isabella wanted. Whether she was correct he could not know. Not yet.

He stood, annoyed that he was being manipulated. A small, albeit temporary, victory was needed over Isabella.

He beckoned his chamberlain. 'Arrest Sir Thomas Blackstone.'

Like everyone else, Werner von Lienhard had been eager to watch the King's son fight. The avid crowds bellowed their approval of the anonymous knight who showed no colours and who had nearly unhorsed the Prince of Wales, their great English hero. Von Lienhard had pushed his way to the front and watched the contest. By the time Blackstone revealed his identity to the King, the Visconti's champion knew he could beat the scarred-faced Englishman: Blackstone's fury could be subdued by cold-hearted skill learnt over the years from the best swordmeisters in Germany.

As Blackstone and the others picked their way clear of the pavilions towards the darkened meadows eight armed men moved out of the shadows. Each was a knight who had no compunction about slaying Englishmen – especially as they were being paid by von Lienhard. Conrad von Groitsch and Siegfried Mertens were two knights who were close friends of von Lienhard. Each came from landowning families, but when their wealth had been squandered by an incompetent father or stolen by an older brother they had been forced to sell their fighting skills to those who paid the highest. For these three men the Visconti of Milan had been a generous benefactor. Others in the group had suffered humiliation on the lists or on battlefields. They were Germans and Frenchmen, and all were prepared to transgress the code of chivalry demanded by the St George's Day tournament.

Blackstone had been distracted by the coat of arms that glared down at him. At no time since the slaughter at Crécy had he had any interest in knowing whom he had slain. Wolf Sword was his through victory, but now he realized it might be someone else's by birthright.

The knights' sudden appearance alarmed the horses, making Blackstone and the others instinctively grab their reins. Before he could pull Wolf Sword from its scabbard that was secured to the saddle's pommel, the horse had ducked its head, throwing him off balance. Its rear hooves lashed out and the heavy thud of iron shoes meeting mail-encased flesh and bone was plain to hear. Caprini had swung his horse between himself and the attackers and quickly engaged the first two men who struck at him. Blackstone released the reins and within moments he and John Jacob stood close enough together to deter the attacking men who wore mail but no surcoats, their open bascinets enclosing snarling faces. Without shields or armour Blackstone and the others were at a grave disadvantage. They parried a quick surge of attack, edged towards Caprini, and quickly formed a defensive wedge like a broadhead arrow, back to back. The horses ran loose, then settled beyond the first line of pavilions. Von Lienhard attacked Blackstone, a man with him at each side, forcing Caprini and Jacob to flatten their defensive line. Sword blades clashed and clanged, but then Blackstone took two strides forward, caught one of the men as he made a clumsy strike, and rammed Wolf Sword into his thigh. As the man fell Blackstone lowered his weight with him, keeping the blade rammed into muscle. The man dropped his sword and clawed at Wolf Sword's blade, to no avail. Blackstone had seen fighters make the mistake of withdrawing a blade too quickly, allowing their adversary to regain his feet and strike a low blow that could gut a man. Strong and violent men could withstand such agony as their hearts pumped energy and hatred into their muscles. In the seconds it took to press the blade firmly another of the attackers caught Blackstone across the back of his head and shoulder with a flat-bladed blow deflected by his mail. Fireflies danced behind his eyes and he felt his knees give way. Wolf Sword fell from his grasp. As he staggered to one side the wounded man lunged with a knife, but John Jacob kicked him in the face and then pushed Blackstone away as another struck downwards with a blow that would have cleft Blackstone from collarbone to hip. The Tau knight rammed his blade from a low angle, forcing it upwards through the man's raised armpit, its honed blade cutting through muscle and bone and out through his lower jaw. Blood and tiny fragments of bone sprayed from his head. The shattered jaw, in the throes of death, emitted a final vomiting retch.

Four of the attackers were sprawled, writhing in pain from deep wounds, the fifth was dead and, as Blackstone clawed himself to his feet, von Lienhard bent and picked up Wolf Sword. His eyes were held by the running wolf etched on the blade below the crossguard. In that moment a memory struck him as firm and violent as a mace. The sword was his elder brother's, ten years his senior, given by his father when he had come of age. He had carried it when he rode with the King of Bohemia at Crécy. Those who bravely charged the English that day gave their account of his brother fighting towards the Prince of Wales. He was within paces of killing the heir to the throne when he fell. Butchered by a common archer. An ignominious death at the hands of an unknown, low-born man – who now carried the sword.

The shock of it held him too long. Blackstone took a few quick strides and as von Lienhard looked up from the etched blade Blackstone's fist clubbed him behind the ear. It felled the German to his knees as Blackstone seized Wolf Sword. The three defenders turned to face von Lienhard's remaining men. Three against two. The night should have been theirs, but the fight had caused a commotion and squires from the surrounding pavilions had armed themselves with flaring torches and swords. Tent flaps were thrown back as half-dressed knights emerged to see what was happening. They were not concerned. What they – mistakenly – saw was three ruffians fighting knights, who would be dealt with by the squires and the constable when he was summoned.

Von Lienhard was on all fours, shaking the dizziness from his head, unable yet to stand, as the two surviving attackers held back while Blackstone and his companions readied themselves for an attack from the gathering attendants. It was obvious that the Englishman and those with him would not dare face down so many and, seizing their chance, they dragged a groggy von Lienhard away from the fray.

'Shit pit again,' said John Jacob as the three of them circled, readying themselves for a rush from the gathering men. Caprini slipped off his cloak and twirled it around his shield arm as four of the older squires warily nudged their torches closer.

'It's Sir Thomas Blackstone!' one of them cried, his West Country accent, broad and gentle, carrying across the pavilions. Blackstone realized he must have been a senior squire among them because he half turned to address the others behind him – a gesture of trust that Blackstone would not take advantage of. 'Lower them swords! It's not Sir Thomas as would start this.'

The men who followed did as the older man instructed. There was enough light now for everyone to see the three beleaguered men clearly. There were many squires, mature in years, eligible for knighthood, but who either did not care for the responsibility or did not have the means to support all that knighthood demanded, and Blackstone reasoned that this squire might be such a man.

'There are wounded men who need attention,' said Blackstone, 'and one who is beyond help.'

'Aye, my lord, it'll be seen to. I am Roger Hollings. I serve my master, Audley.'

Blackstone stepped forward. 'Our greatest knight,' he said, remembering the honour Sir James Audley had gained at Poitiers.

'Finely spoken, Sir Thomas. A great knight indeed.'

'He's here?'

'At the castle. He's an honoured guest of the King.'

'And rightly so,' said Blackstone, thankful that Audley's squire had been on hand.

Von Lienhard and the surviving knights stood their ground warily, knowing the moment for their success had passed.

'And these good gentlemen?' Hollings asked. 'Is there business to be settled?'

Before Blackstone could answer a murmur of voices carried from beyond the men. Twenty torch-bearing guards led by a sergeant-at-arms pushed their way through the crowd.

'Sir Thomas Blackstone?' the arresting officer said, moving close to Blackstone, unafraid of any violent response against the King's command. 'You will surrender your sword.'

There was no need for Blackstone to ask on whose authority the command had been issued. He turned Wolf Sword's bloodied blade away and offered the hilt to the sergeant-at-arms, who took it and passed it to another at his shoulder. Caprini and John Jacob followed Blackstone's example.

'I do not think this will end well,' said Jacob.

'Have faith,' said Blackstone, placing an arm on his friend's shoulder.

'We must hope that the good knight here can pray on our behalf as well as he fights,' Jacob answered, looking to the Tau knight, who unfurled his cloak and covered his shoulders, making the distinctive symbol plain for all to see.

'I pray better than I fight, Master Jacob, but it can take time for prayers to be answered.'

'Then I'll not hold my breath – while I still have it,' said John Jacob as the three men were ushered away.

CHAPTER THIRTY-TWO

The King had spent little time at his dinner, sufficient only to play the gracious host to the French King and his honoured guests. Now that Isabella had involved herself yet again in affairs of state he needed time to deliberate how best to indulge her while considering her advice, knowing that her political and diplomatic skills had always been astute. He decided to approach one of his most trusted advisers, and under the guise of discovering how the Duke of Lancaster was recovering from the injury he had sustained in the tournament, he visited his close friend, who was now confined to his quarters under the care of the King's personal physician.

Henry of Grosmont, Duke of Lancaster, had been Edward's closest friend for more than twenty years. He was one of England's greatest knights, who had fought and won battles and sieges that had brought fame and glory to his King. Lancaster was a man of impeccable integrity and for the past five years had been Edward's chief negotiator in his search for peace with the French, even dealing, against his will, with the duplicitous Charles of Navarre. Now this great-grandson of Henry III lay confined to his bedchamber, sweating with pain from his injury.

Lancaster had dismissed his attendants when the King had entered his chamber and now Edward wrung out a wet cloth and tenderly laid it on his friend's fevered brow.

'Do not shame me, sire,' said Lancaster, 'I am your servant, you are not mine.'

In the company of his close friends, the earls of England who had helped him achieve success, Edward was able to relax the formality his crown demanded. 'We soothe the brow of a friend and we serve loyalty. And require the counsel of a man who has a common touch.'

Lancaster relented, letting him wring out the cloth again. He sighed. 'Ah, my lord, because I always preferred the embraces of common women to those who were more refined means rather that I prefer *their* common touch. They were more willing.'

Both men smiled, and Edward rested his hand on his friend's shoulder, fussing his nightshirt at his neck. 'You have always dressed well, drunk the finest wines and loved music and dance. You have always known what road to travel.'

'In my youth. I am now too pious for the joys of life.'

'And you have fought more bravely than any other.'

Edward related what Isabella had done and her reasons for acting as she had. King and friend eased into a comfortable silence as Lancaster considered what Edward had told him and, despite his discomfort, thought clearly of the events that were unfolding across France. 'Thomas Blackstone might be a sign of the divine presence. Were it not for him you would be denied your son and heir. Isabella is right.'

Edward sighed. 'Dammit, how often has she been wrong? An infuriating woman, our mother.'

Lancaster smiled. 'It does not matter who lives and dies in any of this, only who decides it,' he answered. 'And that is your prerogative. Blackstone can be more use under your command. He has proved himself. And his loyalty,' he added in a whisper, his throat rasping from dryness.

Lancaster eased himself on the pillows at his back and allowed Edward to help him sip wine. As the King eased his friend's head back, Lancaster placed a hand on that of his sovereign lord. 'Blackstone would not willingly go against the Prince. She made him. She holds something over him.'

Lancaster's exhaustion was evident. His wounds and the sleeping potion the apothecary had put in the wine lowered him into sleep and, as his eyes closed, the King of England tenderly drew the fur-lined bedclothes over him.

Isabella the Fair had seen it all clearly. The King, and England, could only benefit from Blackstone's attempt to rescue the French family. And if God willed it, he might even succeed.

But Edward had sent many men to their deaths in his time. If Thomas Blackstone needed to be sacrificed so that his treaty was seen to be negotiated in good faith, then so be it.

Stefano Caprini was treated no differently from Blackstone and John Jacob. His devotion to God and to His pilgrims meant little to his jailers. It would not be the first time that a hospitaller had turned to violence, and even though they knew nothing of his background they had heard of others who followed the Order of St James who led mercenaries. The three men were held in an antechamber near to where the King was undertaking renovations to the castle. Scaffolding and stonework lay nearby and Blackstone had run his eye over the masons' work. The skill was apparent and a part of him wondered whether, had he not been arrayed for war, he too might have found work as a skilled stonemason. But twelve years of fighting and war had given him different skills and had assuredly earned him more money. Builders, no matter how good they were, would see many a cold winter without a fire in the hearth. Work was hard to come by. Fighting was not.

De Marcouf was their jailer, flanked by half a dozen armed men. His orders were not to shackle the prisoners, but to keep them under spear and sword point – and under no circumstances was Thomas Blackstone to be harmed. Through the low doorway was a passage leading to another chamber from where Blackstone could hear the muffled voices of a man and a woman, but the thickness of the wall and the stoutness of the door made their words indistinct.

Caprini eyed the Norman knight. 'You served as our guardian and now you hold us at sword point. We are unarmed and yet you fear us. If we were to be harmed your sergeant-at-arms had enough men to wound us. Are we such dangerous beasts?'

'I am not here to engage in conversation with you, Fra Caprini. If a messenger comes through that door and tells me that you are to be slain then it will be done without question,' said the Norman.

A wooden latch slid back and the door was opened by one of the King's attendants, who nodded at de Marcouf.

'Sir Thomas,' de Marcouf said and gestured with his sword for Blackstone to go through the doorway.

Blackstone turned to Caprini. 'I have not yet heard a prayer uttered.'

'We pray with our hearts, Sir Thomas,' said the Italian.

'Little comfort for others,' Blackstone answered. 'Try moving your lips.'

Blackstone stooped through the low archway, de Marcouf at his back, the light from the cresset lamps and the attendant leading him to the next chamber. No man could go before his King and not be humbled. Battlefield exhortations to strengthen courage as he rode along their ranks were as close as most common men got to their sovereign lord. The blessing for the English was that Edward was a warrior king and knew how to reach out and seize their loyalty. He had fought at close quarters and put his own life at risk. A soldier's heart understood why men killed and it was a King's divine right to bless them for doing so.

Blackstone saw the flames first – huge, curling tongues devouring the hefty logs in the gaping fireplace that held bundles of faggots stacked to one side. The warmth struck him as soon as he entered the small chamber. A broad-planked table stood to one side, its dark wood glowing from years of beeswax and servants' efforts, and which now had the unsheathed Wolf Sword lying across its dull sheen. Beneath his feet was a thick, woven rug and beyond him, close to the fire, a figure whose features were half lit by the flames. A hanging tapestry depicting a white hart being brought down by huntsmen covered the stone wall behind her. Despite the rug it was not a room for comfort, but rather a place where outsiders could be received. Isabella sat in a high-backed wooden chair, its single cushion untouched by her back, which was as straight as a yard-long arrow. And Blackstone thought when he saw her that the glint of the half-light in her eyes looked like blood-tipped bodkins.

Two other men stood in the glow of candlelight. One was as tall as the King, but older, with the hard, scarred look of a weathered oak. Gilbert Chastelleyn was a knight of the royal household; a key figure in Edward's life; a man prepared to serve as ambassador or warrior, as the King required. The second man stood opposite him, half-turned from the fire, one hand on the back of the Queen's chair, the other resting casually on the pommel of the dagger at his belt: Stephen Cusington, captain of the garrison at Saint-Sauveur-le-Vicomte, the great citadel close to where Edward had invaded France, was a battle-hardened knight who kept his King's possessions free of routiers and Frenchmen alike. Blackstone remembered him fighting with the Prince of Wales at Poitiers. Neither man looked pleased to see Blackstone; their animosity was barely concealed. Chastelleyn made a slight movement with his head. Beyond the Queen, in almost complete shadow and twirling a precious stone ring on his finger, was the King. Other than the gentle worrying of the adornment he did not move. He was watching the broad-shouldered man who still had mud streaks on his breeches and a darker spattering of something else on his jupon. A dried trickle of blood ran from his hairline, down the side of his ear and disappeared behind his collar.

Blackstone half turned towards him and went down on one knee, keeping his eyes focused on the carpet's intricate pattern woven by a skilled hand at some time in history in a land he could not know. He concentrated so that his mind would not lead him astray and begin a dialogue with the devil as to what punishment might be inflicted on Caprini and Jacob. He had made the challenge on the Prince and he had been the cause of the death and wounding of his attackers. Their guilt was by association, his by command. The devil won.

'Sire, I beg your indulgence for those who accompany me. They served me and I am to blame,' he blurted out. The damned pattern had blurred before his eyes.

De Marcouf laid his blade down the side of Blackstone's face, close, so he could see it next to his right eye. 'You do not speak until spoken to.'

'All right, all right,' said the King. 'Get up.'

Blackstone stood and raised his head.

Edward strode forward and stood closer to the knighted archer. The English and Welsh bowmen had been his greatest weapon, but at Poitiers the witnesses to the battle described how it had been raw courage – man against man, sword in hand – that carried the day.

'Sir Gilbert Killbere encamps outside Calais,' said Chastelleyn unexpectedly. 'With a hundred of your men.'

'Sire,' Blackstone answered in confirmation, unsure how the King had gained the knowledge so quickly – but of course the English-held city of Calais would have messengers travelling regularly.

'Very well,' Edward said impatiently. 'It is our desire that you are welcomed back to your native soil. You are pardoned from exile.' Clemency granted in a simple utterance.

Blackstone felt the surge of relief and began to bend his knee again but was stopped by the King's command.

'Enough of that. We know of our benevolence. Our son, the Prince, will be aggrieved, but that is not your concern. Greater issues press us.'

He paused, letting Blackstone remain perplexed at his good fortune. 'We desire France to be ours,' said Edward. 'The Marshals of the Army urge us to make haste and seize Paris. Then it is done.' He looked at Blackstone, a silent command to speak. Blackstone searched for an answer. How best to please the King? He could offer his men at Calais, and if necessary break his contract with Florence and bring several hundred more. It would be a worthless gesture. The King's plan was too ambitious.

'Do not try to take Paris, highness. You have neither the time nor sufficient siege machines,' said Blackstone.

Edward's enthusiasm for war had never diminished. The warrior King would finally take the crown of France. 'We'll draw him out. No need for any siege!' the King answered. 'It would be the end of France. We hold King John, the Dauphin is a boy and the people of Paris are unsettled, ready for revolt, caught between Charles of Navarre and his ambitions and the Provost Étienne Marcel. The timing is perfect.'

Blackstone defiantly held his King's gaze. 'If the Dauphin is still in the city you cannot entice him. No favour, no promise will make him leave the safety of Paris. Only if there is conflict within the walls and he is threatened will he leave it.' He saw the King's irritation smothered by his desire to have Blackstone agree to his strategy. Cusington and Chastelleyn would have berated Blackstone, but a slight gesture from the King stopped them.

'Let us have no pessimism here,' said Edward. 'Not from you. The civilized world knows what you did at Crécy. Scribes have it down; monks have copied it. What you did then – and since – travels at your back like a gathering storm. You put God's fear into your enemies but treat those deserving of mercy with a tenderness that could put a mother to shame.' He watched his scarred fighter, perhaps expecting a show of pride, a tilting of the chin in acknowledgement of his generous flattery, but Blackstone gave no sign other than to keep his gaze focused.

At a nod from the King, Cusington poured a glass of red wine for him. An edge of disappointment crept into Edward's voice. 'You are a mystery to us all, but we are glad that your sword is on our side of the lines – is it not, Sir Thomas? That Wolf Sword of yours fights for England?'

The question broke Blackstone's gaze, and he dipped his head in acknowledgement. 'Sword and war bow before it, highness.'

'We believe it. And our mother, for all her intrigues and chess moves, insists upon it,' he said with another glance towards the stoic Isabella.

Blackstone waited a moment; the mention of the King's mother had brought a brief softening to the monarch's brow and a glimpse of a smile. There was affection there despite, as he had said, the former Queen's intrigues.

'Highness, the Dauphin is weak and indecisive, but he has a resilience to him. He won't come out and fight,' insisted Blackstone.

'Why ever not?' Edward barked. 'He's a King-in-waiting! He must prove himself!'

'He has no need to, lord. He has Paris. I have run the gauntlet of its alleyways, and have seen the belligerence of its people. Paris would suffocate an army should they ever manage to breach its walls. He won't come out. And you cannot get in – should not even try.'

Silence was a weapon effective against those of lesser rank, and King Edward used it wisely, punishing Blackstone with it. After what seemed an interminable time, and during which Blackstone stayed unmoving, eyes lowered, in front of his King, Edward finally spoke.

'Very well. Perhaps for now you see a situation of which we have no knowledge. Events move at a pace that race ahead of us. Our army is not yet ready and we cannot know how the boy will react.' Edward laid his finger against Wolf Sword's blade. 'But we are aware that the French royal family might be threatened. You are to seek out and find your enemy's family and secure their safety for the Dauphin. How you achieve this is of your own choosing.'

Blackstone knew his own family's safety was of no interest to the King of England, but impertinence was a breath away. 'And my own family, sire? What of them?'

Edward turned on him, but by a miracle did not condemn him. He would have, Blackstone felt certain, had not Isabella placed her hand on her son's arm.

'I gave him hope that he might find them,' she said and then turned to Blackstone. 'We believe they are east of Paris. There are noble ladies under the protection of local lords, but that protection falters under the increasing weight of violence. The Dauphin's family joined those noblewomen. Find them and you may well find your family.'

Blackstone dipped his head in respect and thanks.

Edward held out his hand towards Cusington, who seemed to

know exactly what was wanted. He lifted Wolf Sword from the table and gave it to the King. It had been wiped clean of blood before being brought to Edward, who gazed at it, remembering the night he first saw it.

'You clenched this to you in what we thought to be a dying archer's grasp,' said the King. He ran the tip of his bejewelled finger across the etched swordmaker's mark of the running wolf. 'A few hours ago you were attacked by a German knight. His name is von Lienhard – the same name as that of the man who tried to slay our son at Crécy – and whose sword you took that day.'

'I know that now, sire, but I had not realized the fact until I saw his coat of arms tonight.'

'It was his older brother.' Edward waited. 'You know something of having a brother killed in battle.'

'I do, sire,' Blackstone said, knowing the matter of the night's fight was still to be resolved.

'He is the Visconti's man, and might well have been declared tournament champion had he not broken tourney rules. He approached us and wished to claim judicial combat against you. We understand what drove him to break the tournament's pledge, but as no crime has been committed against him, he could not be offered satisfaction. He and those with him have departed.' The King paused. 'Be aware that revenge will unleash a man's baser instincts,' he said.

The King's words were a judgement against Thomas as surely as they were a warning to be on his guard now that von Lienhard was free to act as he wished. Edward, ever the King who valued a warrior and a masterly crafted weapon, offered him Wolf Sword, letting Blackstone feel the comfort of it nestling in the palm of his hand.

'What is taken in battle cannot be denied,' said the King, and then after a moment added, 'be it a sword or a country.'

Nothing more was said. This time the silence was the command for him to leave. As de Marcouf ushered him to the door the King spoke.

'Sir Thomas, you nearly killed our cousin John on the

battlefield. A common man does not kill a king.'

Blackstone did not hesitate in his answer. 'He butchered my friend and your ally, Jean, Count de Harcourt, sire, without trial or priest, and he went unshriven to his grave. I slaughtered the Norman knight who betrayed him and swore protection for his family and justice for his murder.'

'Your presence here has caused our honoured prisoner upset,' Edward said.

Blackstone was glad of it but he kept the thought to himself. 'Fear in an enemy's heart weakens him, sire.'

Edward held back his smile. This belligerent bastard before him was a killer who struck fear into even a King's heart. A French King. Not his own.

'It would be advantageous for you to show contrition. Debase yourself before him and seek his gracious pardon.' Edward saw the ripple of dissent before Blackstone even opened his mouth to answer.

'Sire, I do not have your benevolent spirit, nor am I obliged to be agreeable for the sake of future treaties. I will kill your enemies and my own. There is no distinction for me.'

It was a clever answer – one that flattered the King and made clear his loyalty – despite its edge of disrespect for the French monarch.

'And if I command it?'

'I obey.'

But Edward did not wish to humiliate the man who had carved a path through the battlefield and saved his son. Blackstone's defiance was too great a weapon to blunt in such a manner. Blackstone hesitated. No command came. He bowed and followed de Marcouf from the room. As they entered the dimly lit passage he turned before the door closed behind him and he saw the King of England bend and help his aged mother to her feet. She suddenly seemed very frail. No longer was there a great king in that room, only a caring son attending his mother with concern and affection.

The door slammed shut.

The way forward lay beyond the end of the passage.

PART THREE

THE TERROR

CHAPTER THIRTY-THREE

The Captain of Calais, Sir Ralph de Ferrers, was an honoured knight, a man who had long fought for his King, and who could barely conceal his contempt for those who sold their swords. Right now the two knights who stood before him looked to be little more than ruffians, swordsmen who would brawl in taverns and make trouble for a provost and his men. But they were more than that. Both had reputations. Both were men of renowned courage. Killbere was a ferocious knight, the man who had stepped forward at Crécy and whom all others followed. Blackstone was a name that had grown in legend and the man's physical stature could well live up to it, de Ferrers decided. But he also knew that men like these could be the cause of bloodshed. He examined the document embossed with the King's seal. As yet there had been no proclamation issued bearing the Great Seal, a command issued under the King's hand, confirmed by the Chancellor of England, that Sir Thomas Blackstone was granted immunity and that his exile had been rescinded. Bureaucracy was a baggage train to a fighting man's war. No matter; this decree for safe passage through English-held territory was genuine enough, and until such time as messengers arrived with the court document this piece of linen bearing the King's command in a clerk's neat hand and the wax impression of Edward's personal seal was more than enough for the Captain to assist Blackstone – as far as his duty allowed. The gruff-voiced de Ferrers folded the pass.

'I've no taste for brigands; we've a plague of you bastards here. Now I suspect you're going to cause me further aggravation,' he said, knowing full well that Blackstone was not acting in self-interest – if indeed he had been pardoned by the King. 'As Captain of this city I hold jurisdiction over soldiers here.'

Blackstone ignored the man's contemptuous manner. There was little time to bandy words with an old knight who governed a city of merchants and garrison soldiers. 'Do you have any contact with the Dauphin's forces?' he asked.

'We go no further than the walls. I have two hundred acres of city to defend, and a garrison sorely stretched to man the walls. But I can tell you there are English routiers raiding up and down the Seine valley, so Paris holds the Dauphin's attention.'

'But you and the seneschal share responsibility for the marshes. You've authority outside these walls to see that the King's land is kept profitable and in good repair,' Blackstone said, determined to probe for any knowledge that might help him.

'Do not presume to lay down my duties, Sir Thomas. I know them well enough.'

'Then you know I have had my men on the hills,' said Blackstone. When he had arrived at Calais he had soon found Sir Gilbert Killbere encamped on the Sangatte heights beyond the marshlands surrounding the city. 'Did you ever challenge Sir Gilbert or ask why he was there?'

'I know of Sir Gilbert. His men did not attempt to enter the city. There was no cause.'

'You know the King's pledge. If Calais is threatened he would send a hundred men and archers to aid in its defence. Did you not think that my men might have been part of a defensive force? Did you not think there might have been a threat? Did you think at all, my lord?' Blackstone asked this man who spent his days implementing ordinances and who had not held a sword in anger for years.

De Ferrers knew he should not have ignored the armed men on the heights; he had made enough excuses to himself. There was no threat from them – but now this lack of attention to his duty allowed Blackstone to challenge him.

For a moment he relented in his antagonism. 'The Dauphin is being squeezed and he will be lucky to keep any control beyond Paris.'

'Then you have no idea where his family might be?'

'I don't give them a moment's thought. Why should I? Calais is the portal to France, and if the King invades then I will make sure the gates stay open. Beyond that, these French bastards are of no interest to me.'

'And Navarre's troops? Are they helping the uprising? He has a crown to gain. Where is he?'

'That turd slithered from the devil's bowels. You want to find him, look to where the flies gather. Your kind should have no trouble following the stench,' de Ferrers said.

Killbere could hold back his impatience no longer. 'You're a damned turnkey, and nothing more,' he said to de Ferrers, who scowled at the insult. 'Aye, you can bristle like the hairs on a hog's back, but, dammit, Sir Thomas Blackstone has earned enough respect for a civil answer. You think he'd be here wasting time with you if there were not some urgency? He's on the King's business, for Christ's sake! Even a common jailer can see that!'

'He has safe passage. Nothing more!' de Ferrers replied angrily. 'You'd do well to remember *your* place. I have authority enough to have you jailed!'

'Which is all you are fit for – though you would do well to remember that it wasn't so long past that Sir Thomas and his men protected these precious walls when the French thought to take them back. You hold this place, then you must know what your enemy is doing. We need to know.'

De Ferrers wanted nothing more than to have these men away from Calais, so he suppressed the desire to respond to the perceived insults and rolled out a map across the table. 'The Dauphin struggles to rally support and the Parisians support the Provost of Merchants, Étienne Marcel,' he said, his forefinger tracing a circle around Paris. 'They murdered the Dauphin's marshals in front of him. Word has it they said they were protecting him from

257

them.' He grunted. 'They were showing him how vulnerable he was in the city.'

'Then he's not there, is he?' asked Blackstone. 'He can't be if his family is in jeopardy.'

De Ferrers began to realize that Blackstone's presence might somehow be connected to the French royal family. 'No...' he said hesitatingly. 'He withdrew to Meaux and we think he's made his headquarters there, but where his family is we cannot know.'

'Then we travel east of Paris,' said Killbere. 'Forty, fifty miles or so. What about skinners?'

The Captain of Calais drew his finger across the map. 'There are mercenaries here and... here, as far as we know, but they are so widespread it is impossible to be exact.'

Blackstone's eyes stayed on the map, reading what he could of the countryside. Rivers and canals were better marked than many roads, some of them little more than tracks that could be washed away in storms. 'What of these peasants? How organized are they? Are they anything more than lynch mobs that will burn themselves out once they have what they want?'

'They are called Jacques, or the Jacquerie, led by a man called Cale, from somewhere near Clermont. He seems to have some education. He's no arse-in-the-mud peasant, but they've turned to him for leadership. They swarm to the north and east of Paris,' he said, running his finger across the map. 'Far enough from Calais not to cause trouble, but close enough for Paris to see flames on the horizon.'

Blackstone and Killbere studied the map. They knew the routes from Normandy into Picardy; both had ridden and fought their way across it years before, but how they were to avoid the raiding bands of routiers was uncertain. No matter where they looked, the brigands were as big a threat as the marauding Jacquerie.

'Come on, my lord, let's not squeeze a dog's bollocks until it yelps and bites. How do we reach Meaux? Due south and east, or can we ride around these murdering bastards?' demanded Killbere.

'Who knows? The mob swarms. More to the east, the last we heard.'

'Damn. There's no avoiding them, Thomas. We'll have to ride right through them.'

'You won't get through,' said de Ferrers. 'It's an area more populated than elsewhere, so they have little trouble recruiting. God knows why they've taken to slaughtering on that side of Paris. Those are rich agricultural domains held by tenant farmers and there's little reason for the violence to take hold there.'

'He's right,' said Killbere. 'Tenant farmers prosper from buying land and employing their own peasants. Why destroy that?'

De Ferrers's knowledge of the rampaging peasants gave him a brief moment of superiority. 'Thousands of Jacquerie have gorged themselves on murder and looting with their women alongside them. The women are no different; you'd be a fool to think otherwise. They urge atrocities against their own sex and children. These women are not like ours, they're enslaved to hardship even in their own homes. They breed like vermin and, if they don't have enough food for another mouth, they think as little of suffocating their own newborn as of relieving themselves. Once the rampage had begun their brutality became as violent as the men's.'

Blackstone's stare made the man avert his eyes. He was in no mood for a gatekeeper's opinion. 'A mob surges; a man throws in his lot. These people are tired and enraged. It's a blood-lust against the nobility. As simple as that,' said Blackstone.

Killbere glanced at him. Was Blackstone saying he understood their grievance? Blackstone knew that questioning look, but this was not the time or place to argue. Killbere turned his attention back to de Ferrers. 'What's their strength?' he asked.

'Rumour has it that they number in their thousands and grow stronger every day,' said de Ferrers, 'but they split and re-form. Hundreds into thousands and then fracture again as they seize and burn.'

Blackstone thought deeply for a moment. His task was impossible. A hundred men could not fend off thousands. 'I have thirty-three mounted archers with me. I need extra arrows. At least two sheaves a man. Can you sell them to me? A penny for every shaft.'

'The going rate is a penny and a half and arrowheads are five a penny,' he said.

Blackstone nodded. 'All right. I'll take what you can give me.'

De Ferrers looked through the window that gave him a view of his domain. He might hold the keys to France for his sovereign, but he knew that Calais was not impregnable, no matter how quickly the King could send reinforcements. What if brigand and peasant joined forces? Would Charles of Navarre bring them together? That would be a formidable force. Double walls and two ditches that could be flooded with seawater were his main defence. The vital harbour was formed by a piece of land jutting east, which served as an additional defence to the north. At the extreme north-west was the castle whose fortifications merged with the town walls. In the centre was the marketplace and outside, a suburb stretching east, south and west. If ferment stirred within the walls how quickly would he be able to suppress it? The arrival of these two knights had now nudged him into doubt. No merchant was allowed to bear arms, not when his garrison consisted of only nine knights, forty squires and thirty archers. Archers were the gold in a king's crown. It was not beyond the realm of his bureaucratic imagination to know that such a small force could be overwhelmed. He should be more forthcoming with Blackstone and Killbere, but not with vital arrows.

'I have no surplus,' he said, and rolled the map. 'But I will tell you that they are not simply an unruly mob, despite their blood-lust. They have help,' he said. A man's betrayal of his class was always a bitter thing to admit. He was familiar with many French knights who had shared crusades and tournaments, and it was not unusual for some families to have common ancestors. 'Allegiances can no longer be trusted. The peasants have military skills that can only come from educated men – noblemen, minor noblemen. I have heard that when they burned the castle at Beaumont-sur-Oise there were knights who were part of the mob. Men have turned themselves into devils to save themselves from death at the hands of the Jacquerie. The Duchess of Orléans barely managed to escape to Paris; more than sixty castles were destroyed in her area alone.'

Killbere ran his tongue over his teeth. 'God's blood! I thought we had slaughtered enough of their nobility over the years. Now there's more to be done. Come on, Thomas, let's get out of this dank place and leave the clerks to their scribbling and Sir Ralph here to his ordinances. Time spent here can make a man old,' he said, looking at de Ferrers. 'Old before his time,' he added for good measure.

Before de Ferrers found the wit to answer Blackstone raised one more question. 'Have you seen a German knight by the name of von Lienhard? A big man, fair-haired above the shaved sides of his head, wears his beard short. He bears a harpy on his coat of arms. He and others like him had safe passage for the King's tournament, but he broke the code of conduct and fled England.'

De Ferrers shook his head. 'There is so little honourable behaviour left,' he said with a disapproving look that had not altered since Blackstone had entered his quarters. 'We've had many knights travel on the King's safe conduct, but no one of that name. If he has lost his honour he'll no doubt be found with the routiers. What else is a man like that to do?'

The meaning was not lost on Blackstone but there was little more to be gained from staying any longer within the walls of Calais. Von Lienhard would one day want his revenge, but not anytime soon, Blackstone reasoned. There would be little chance of the German tracking him down amid the present chaos. Savagery gripped France, tearing at it with a ferocity that spared neither life nor honour, and if King Edward wanted to inherit a nation that had not bled to death, then the Dauphin's family might serve as the balm to heal its wounds. And where the nobility gathered to hide from the terror was where he might find Christiana and his own family. Beyond that he could not say what lay ahead.

261

CHAPTER THIRTY-FOUR

Christiana stumbled along the roadside ditch, dragging an exhausted Agnes behind her. The nine-year-old child had listened to her mother's desperate explanation that they had to escape the rampaging hordes of murdering Jacquerie.

Earlier, they had sought shelter in a knight's manor house, but when they reached the turn in the road the acrid smell of the burnt-out buildings told her she was already too late. She had foolishly dismounted and left Agnes with the horse as she carefully made her way through the ruined house in search of food. There was nothing to be salvaged. In the wreckage she saw scorched bodies curled like sleeping children. She had known those who lived there and she could only guess that the remains were those of the knight's wife and offspring. As she dragged her dress through the charred timbers she tripped and fell headlong into the burnt and mutilated carcass of the knight himself. She cried out, recoiling from the roasted meat that still clung to his ribs and the black mess of the man's innards. Terror snatched at her and the acid surge of bile forced itself from her throat. She choked and retched.

Her cry had startled the horse, already nervous from the smell of death, and it tore itself free from Agnes's grip. Christiana heard her child's shout of distress and ran after the galloping horse. Blackened, muddied and exhausted, she turned her anger on the tearful girl.

'I told you to tie the reins!' she shouted at the wide-eyed Agnes. 'I told you!' she yelled again, knowing that she was being unjust. As her daughter's lip quivered, trying to hold back a sob, Christiana knelt and pulled the trembling girl to her. Everything they had in the world was tied to the horse's saddle: food enough for two more days, a wineskin and a bedroll. That was all they could salvage when those first men had torn through the palisade around her own house and her steward had fallen beneath staves and knives. It had been a modest home to afford her independence and yet stay within easy riding distance of her friend and mentor Blanche de Harcourt. The Countess had lost her Norman lands when her husband was executed, but she was a countess in her own right and held title in the county of Aumale. It had been by God's grace that Blanche and the younger of her children were away from home when the killing started.

Miles away from Christiana's house a ploughman had returned from the fields to find his lord's bailiff and three of his soldiers stripping what few sacks of grain the ploughman held in his barn. It was a command that had come from Paris, because the Dauphin had closed off routes into the city. The waterways had been blockaded to stop provisions coming into the capital; the supplies were to be taken instead by dozens of fortified garrisons to stop the savage hordes of routiers under Charles of Navarre's command getting any closer to the city. The ploughman heard nothing – he was deaf to the reason, his spirit broken. His wife lay ill; his children had barely enough to eat to carry them through the day's work, let alone the approaching autumn. It was as hollow an existence as the permanent hunger in his belly. And when, finally, the family withered and died the lord of his manor would seize all that remained. Every tool, bowl and animal they had. Under the right of *morte-main*, everything, including his labour, belonged to his master. The Church already took its tithe in kind, demanding grain, hens and eggs – it was a tax owed to God, he was told, and then he was threatened that his soul would burn in eternal hell if he did not also obey the demands of his own domain lord. On that fateful day when the bailiff arrived, the ploughman's flailed soul consumed him.

He said nothing as the last of his hens and jars of lard were loaded and his breeding sow was tied to the back of the cart. He stepped and raised his hand that held the scythe. The three soldiers ignored his approach, but as he hacked the bailiff to death they cursed and turned on him. It was not the first killing of a peasant family, but it sparked a fire that took hold as quickly as had the ploughman's thatch.

Across the countryside the peasants' discontent had been slow to erupt, but the years of suppression had festered; their plight had been made worse by the ravages of the routiers. It was bad enough that they could barely feed themselves, but the roving brigands took what they wished and killed anyone who resisted. The French King was still a hostage in England and their cries for protection fell on the deaf ears of lesser nobles who had few means to aid them and who seized what they could for themselves. And those who could not help joined forces with the brigands. The peasants' distress found its release in anger and accusation at the cowardly knights and lords who had betrayed them by surrendering to the English Prince, and made their lives an even worse hell than before. No priest's threat could be worse than what they now endured.

The lynch mobs grew and those knights and their families whose homes stood in their path were the first to die. No one was spared.

A horse whinnied. 'Get down!' Christiana said quickly, pulling Agnes into the ditch. Someone cried out in the distance, perhaps at the sight of the galloping horse. There was no chance of running across the track towards the forest. The land between had been cleared of trees over the years and stumps and brambles would have ensnared them, holding them helpless for whoever was approaching. She cradled Agnes in front of her and pulled her muddied cloak over them both, gripping the knife in her hand as hoofbeats thumped along the track. She heard a voice cry out.

'Too late!'

More hoofbeats rumbled and then slowed as men halted their horses close enough for her to hear their snorting and the jangle of bridle and bit. The men's voices were muffled. She held her breath as one of them dismounted. Agnes trembled and began to whimper; the cold water at the bottom of the ditch was soaking their clothes, making them both shiver. Christiana pressed her lips close to her daughter's ear and whispered for her to be silent. The man's boot scuffed the stony path and she heard a sword drawn from a scabbard.

The squelch of the man's footfall came along the ditch. The terror in her mind coiled her muscles; she was barely able to control her own trembling, but one thing was certain in her mind – she would not allow her child to be raped and then butchered as had happened to others. The man was almost upon her when she heard his gasp of surprise.

'Here!'

Christiana pushed herself up and thrashed blindly with the knife towards the man's legs a yard from her. He cursed and sidestepped as she lost her only opportunity to inflict a wound to buy her time. The soldier moved quickly and pinned her knife hand, twisting her wrist to make her release the blade.

'Run!' Christiana yelled as Agnes clambered up the side of the ditch and wove between the legs of the startled horses. As Christiana fought the man who held her, another of the four men jumped down quickly from the saddle and snatched the wriggling and screaming child.

Christiana cried out, despite the man who struggled with her saying something that she could not understand. 'Don't hurt her! I beg you!'

Another of the soldiers quickly came down to help the man holding her as she fought and kicked. The second man gripped her face, hard, making her cease trying to smash her head against the other's chest.

'Stop!' the man shouted, but Christiana spat at him, twisted her body, and kicked out. The sudden shock of the man's slap made her taste blood. There was no way to stop the men raping them now; she was too weak to fight. *Dear Christ*, she prayed, *don't let them harm my child*.

Tears stung her eyes and the pulse of blood pounding through her head muted the man's words as she watched him mouth words at her. His rough hand pulled away the wet hair plastered over her face. Was this an act of lust before she was thrown to the ground and her skirts ripped away from her? *Whatever happens, do not let me see my child raped and killed. By all that is holy, I beg You.*

'My lady, listen to me. You are safe. We are Sir Marcel's men. Sent to search for you. Do you understand?'

It had been an act of tenderness. The man had brushed the hair from her face as a mother would do for her child – a small gesture to soothe away fear. Christiana blinked, felt the strength seep from her. Her blurred eyes sought out the small crest on the man's jupon. It was the badge of Sir Marcel de Lorris, a minor lord who held lands in trust for her friend and mentor Blanche de Harcourt. It was where Blackstone's son Henry had been placed as a page to be trained in arms and to serve the knight and his household.

The man repeated his question again. Christiana nodded and felt the man's hold loosen. The soldier lowered Agnes to the ground as Christiana staggered against the bank, soaked, cold and exhausted. She held her daughter to her and wiped the tears from her dirt-caked face. The men stood back, waiting for her to gather her composure. She dragged her sleeve across her running nose and, holding Agnes at her side, looked at the rough-hewn men who could just as easily have been routiers.

'I beg your forgiveness for hurting you,' said the man who had slapped her. He was older than the others, wisps of grey in his beard, his helmet enclosing a weather-beaten face that now looked remorseful.

Christiana nodded and spat away bloodied phlegm. This was no time for delicacy. 'They have killed those in the house. We must bury them,' she said without thinking.

The man was uncertain for a moment, knowing she was of higher rank than him. 'My lady, we do not know where the mob is. They swirl across the countryside like a flock of starlings. There's no telling. We must leave those poor souls as they are for now. My lord commanded me to find you and your child. We found your horse some way down the track. Can you ride? You and the girl?'

'We should go,' one of the other riders said.

The man raised his arm to silence him, waiting for Christiana's answer. 'If need be we can give you food now, but we should ride if you are able.'

The violence summoned up to defend her child had left her. She nodded. 'I can ride.'

'Then one of us shall carry the child,' said the man.

'No. She will stay with me,' Christiana told him and extended her hand so that the man could help her clamber up the muddy bank as the other quickly lifted Agnes up onto the track. 'I am no stranger to danger,' she told the man, as if convincing herself that she would confront whatever lay beyond the curve of the road.

He cupped his hand for her to step up into the saddle, its low pommel allowing him to lift Agnes into her lap. She gathered the reins in one hand and held Agnes to her with the other.

'My lady, I have no doubt of your courage. We all know who you are,' said the soldier.

Is that what was known of her? she wondered. Did her estranged husband's reputation still confer respect and protection on her despite his selling his fighting skills to Florentine bankers? Was he now any different from the brigands who tore France apart and opened the gates to a peasant uprising? She had abandoned her marriage, but it had not yet released her.

'Does my son still serve your lord?' she asked.

'He does, my lady.'

'Then take me to him,' she commanded.

Smoke from burning houses and great estates plumed on the horizon. The advancing peasant army crept its way across the landscape without any fixed goal, twisting this way and that like a river. As soon as they slaughtered one noble family they moved on to the next. The route Christiana's escort took bore them away from those tell-tale signs of destruction and as they rode closer to their lord's demesne, the countryside seemed as it should. Crops and meadows were undamaged and livestock grazed. Her arms ached from holding Agnes to her, but she made no effort to ease the burden of the sleeping child. It would not be long before they were all safe, although a nagging uncertainty refused to leave her and she could not place what it was that teased her mind. Everything was as it should be here; perhaps the mob had swept across the horizon, leaving de Lorris unscathed.

Relief flooded through her when they turned along the track and she saw the manor house. Palisades were pulled aside as the men escorted her past more armed men into Sir Marcel's courtyard, where she was warmly welcomed by the armoured knight and his pregnant wife, Marguerite.

'Christiana, thank God you were found. The blessed Virgin has seen fit to cloak you in her protection,' said de Lorris. 'Take the child to a bedchamber. Bathe and feed her,' he instructed his steward.

The servant reached up and took the sleeping Agnes. Christiana struggled to ease herself from the saddle. They had ridden hard, her escort relentless in their desire to return to the safety of their master's fortified manor. She saw that, as well as the four riders who had accompanied her, there were another six men-at-arms, and a half-dozen crossbowmen who manned the low walls. There was no sign of Henry.

Christiana could barely keep herself from leaning into the knight's arms, in gratitude not only for her rescue but also that her son had been sent to this devout man as a page and under whose tutelage he would soon be a squire. 'Where is my son? Is he safe?'

Marguerite de Lorris put her arm around Christiana. 'He is. He works in the tunnel to clear it for our escape should we need it,' she said. 'Come now, let me find you clothes and have a bath drawn for you.'

Christiana eased herself from the woman's embrace. Her hair was twisted and matted from mud and water, her skin caked with dirt. She was as bedraggled as a peasant woman. 'A tunnel? Are we not safe here?' she asked.

'We have no idea how many are out there,' said de Lorris. 'The tunnel leads to the chapel. No one violates the sanctuary of the church. It will be a final refuge should we need to abandon the house.'

Christiana nodded, trying to grasp through her exhaustion how desperate their situation was. 'Is there no news at all?' she asked.

De Lorris glanced quickly at his wife, uncertain how much he should tell a woman who had barely managed to escape with her life.

'The Dauphin faces insurrection in Paris,' said Marguerite, making the decision for him. 'Tell her, my lord – we all need to know how things stand.'

De Lorris eased the two women towards the door, out of earshot of his men. 'The last we heard was that the Provost, who is against the Dauphin, has seized the moment to urge the peasants to rise up south of the city. If they cut off all the routes into Paris who knows what might befall us.'

'Then we have nowhere to go,' said Christiana, her mind chasing possibilities of further escape.

'If too many come here then you and Marguerite will be guided through the tunnel while I and my men hold back the mob as long as we can. Christiana, none of us is safe as long as this murder continues.'

Christiana felt the hollowness of despair. 'Why don't we leave now?' she asked, looking towards the soldiers who manned the walls. What had seemed to be a stronghold moments before now seemed to be completely inadequate. 'Surely we should go to a town? Any town. They will resist. We need higher walls than these.'

Sir Marcel's lips tightened. The lands he held extended for miles around and she had drawn comfort from the fact that those who worked the estate had not risen up against him. And then she realized that there had been no sight of anyone in the fields. No smoke from the hovels, no barking of dogs or cries of children.

The land was empty. This had been the unrecognized discomfort she had felt when they first approached.

'Your villeins have run off and joined the mob, haven't they?'

'Yes. I can only pray they remember that we did not rule them with anything other than a harsh word.'

Panic quivered in her stomach and chest. She forced it away. The mob would come, she was sure of it. Now she had to think clearly. Her son and daughter must survive even if she did not.

'Will you take me to Henry?' she asked.

Beyond the entrance hall an iron-studded door gave way to steps that led down to the cellar. Its chilled darkness held haunches of smoke-darkened venison and the cleft carcass of a pig hung in two halves, a meat-hook piercing its thick skin. The room was large enough for wine and foodstuffs to be kept cool and beyond it was a low door that allowed flickering torchlight to seep into the cellar.

The steward who had led her below the house went ahead with a burning torch. 'My lord's father once used this passage to meet his mistress in the chapel. He did not respect his family or the church, as his son does. Sir Marcel thought it wise that it be cleared and readied...' He caught himself and quickly assured her: '... should it be needed.'

Christiana saw that pieces of old armour and moth-eaten, threadbare carpets and tapestries had been stacked against one of the cellar's walls. Cobwebs sizzled in the torch's flame as he led her deeper into the gloom, to where a candle burned in a copper holder hooked onto the wall.

'Be careful, my lady,' said the steward, half turning towards her, as he pointed out the uneven ground beneath their feet.

She muttered her thanks, but there was a question that needed to be answered. If the mob came those in the house could buy their lives by betraying the whereabouts of the tunnel. 'Why have you stayed?' she asked.

The man faltered, hesitating before he took another step. 'I am a Christian man who has served his master since childhood. If there is a more devout knight then I have not heard of him. My lord has shown kindness and humbled himself before his King and God. It would be wrong for me to abandon him in his hour of need. Death will come when God sends that dark angel. Who am I to run from it?'

She saw the glimmer of a smile in the torchlight, one of resignation and sadness that his death might be imminent. Christiana reached out and took the candle from the wall. 'Go back to your master. I can find my way,' she said and, without waiting for his answer, pushed past him. She was not willing to let death's angel go unchallenged.

The air was heavy, veiled with smoke from the steward's flaring torch. She thought she had gone about a hundred yards, one hand outstretched to help guide her against the rock wall, when she felt the fetid atmosphere lighten and the coolness of fresh air touch her skin.

A shadow fell across her path as a figure scuffed the ground and she almost dropped the candle as a knife blade caught the light. She had not seen her son for more than a year and the figure of the boy – only three months short of his eleventh birthday – was still as she remembered him, but he had grown and she could see strength had gone into his limbs. She called his name.

The boy faltered. My God, he looked like his father, she thought, as he suddenly smiled at the sound of her voice. He stepped forward and lifted her hand to his lips.

'You're safe! And Agnes?'

'Yes,' she nodded, eyes stinging, 'with me. She's sleeping.'

The candlelight exposed her streaked and torn clothes and through the grime on her face the tracks made by her tears. Without embarrassment he palmed them away. 'My lord said his men would find you.' And then guilt crept into his voice. 'I wanted to go, but I'm only his page, so I had to obey him.'

'And he sent you here so that you could ready our escape.'

271

He sounded relieved. 'Yes. And I've made it safe for Lady Marguerite and the children. And now for you and Agnes.' His eyes searched her face and clothing. 'Has it been terrible?'

'More than I imagined,' she admitted. He was no longer a child; there was no need to hide the truth.

He gently pulled her another few steps forward. A sturdy chestnut beam lay against the end wall, crosspieces nailed across its length. He pointed upwards. A flush of air came from the space above. 'That hole leads into the chapel. I've already put two wineskins and a satchel of food up there. There are blankets and clothes for the children. We shall be safe. I can push the stone in the floor across it. Did you know that my lord's father used this for...' He bit back the word. '... fornicating.'

'I know what it was used for,' she said, and smiled. A boy training to be a squire heard soldiers talk and, no matter how devout his master, those around him would speak about the rougher aspects of the world. It would do him no harm, she thought; the world would test him soon enough.

She suddenly felt tired and leaned against the wall. He reached out for her.

'Mother, you're exhausted. Let me take you to the house.'

'Are your duties done?'

'Yes. More clothes and food perhaps, but I can do that afterwards.'

She eased herself free from him. 'No. Finish what you must do. Our lives may depend on it. I'll go back to Agnes; come to us when Sir Marcel gives you permission. He has trusted you with the responsibility for us and his family.'

Henry nodded. 'I thought it was a lowly task because of being a page.'

'No. He honours you and expects you not to fail him.'

He looked older now. His chin lifted. 'You don't have to worry. We'll be all right. You'll see.'

In another life, before he was born, she heard the echo of another young man she had nursed back to life – whose strength had become hers. Together they had survived, bound in a fate that carried them across a great river, clinging to each other as an enemy chased them down. She had known terror before and Thomas had killed the man who inflicted it. But her husband was not here now. Henry was his father's son, but he was not yet his father.

'Get a rope, make it fast to something in the chapel,' she told him.

'I have this ladder for the ladies and the children –'

'It's not for us,' she interrupted. 'If we have to escape through here then they might try to seize us from this passage. You will use the beam to block the door from the cellar. The rope is for you to climb into the chapel. Henry, you will be the last one down here.'

He swallowed hard. The mob had so far been a distant problem, but now these past eighteen months' weapons training with his lord and his squires would imminently be needed. His mother's appearance had shocked him and the reality of the looming danger dried his mouth. 'Then... they will come,' he said, trying to disguise his fear with a half-hearted smile.

Henry wore a sheathed dagger in his belt. It had once belonged to her husband's squire and he had given it to Henry before he was brutally killed. She tugged it free and tucked it into her waistband.

'They will come.' She reached out and touched his face, drew it to her and tenderly kissed his forehead. 'Be ready, my son. We will have to fight for our lives.'

Werner von Lienhard had left Windsor with his tail between his legs, shamed that he had not been permitted to face Thomas Blackstone in single combat. But reason subdued his despair. It had been his skill and practicality that made him a captain of men with the Visconti. He would wait. The time would present itself again – revenge should burn long and slow like an Italian vendetta. It was still a matter of honour to kill the man who carried his brother's sword, but now it would be on von Lienhard's terms and the grievance would never be relinquished. Perhaps back in Italy, when Blackstone returned, a public trial might be contrived – an appeal to the *Signori* that he had the right. The Visconti would like that. They would relish the thought of seeing the Englishman beaten on their own territory. It was all he wanted – to swear the oath publicly before bishop and lord that his cause was right and just before God.

Now, he contented himself with the knowledge that he had the skill to beat Blackstone when the time came. He and the two other knights who rode with him from Windsor had made their way from the French coast towards the city of Senlis. On the way they witnessed the surging mass of peasants, a thousand or more, who swept over a knight's abode. Watching from high ground and partly hidden by trees, they saw the family slaughtered, falling under the frenzied attack of scythes and woodcutters' axes. The Jacques threw the small child screaming into the air and then impaled her on their pitchforks. After the men raped the knight's wife their women hacked her limb from limb. And then the horde stripped the house like a plague of locusts.

He turned to the two knights who had watched in grim horror as members of their own class were slaughtered.

'There is nothing we can do to stop this killing. If we are seen we would be overwhelmed. And I will not die at the hands of scum,' he told them. He had seen enough slaughter in Italy to know that a peasant was little more than a dog: soulless, ignorant and incapable of rational thought.

Conrad von Groitsch turned his face away from the slaughter. He crossed himself and spat. 'To see such a good, fine lady and her child butchered by a rabid mob sickens me,' he said.

The other murmured in agreement, but all three kept their eyes on the murderous horde. Von Lienhard watched the retreating villeins swarm away from their attack, carrying the goods they had found. The house was set ablaze and the smoke from this funeral pyre swirled and was carried by the breeze, fluttering like a battle standard. The peasant uprising had its own flag of war.

'There were a couple of men-at-arms who rode with them. You saw it?' he asked, passing a wineskin to his companion.

274

The third man, Siegfried Mertens, swilled wine around his mouth and spat it free. 'And they took no part in the slaughter, but they helped themselves to the silver,' he said to von Lienhard. 'If we're to cross France back to Lombardy, we could make the journey more prosperous. Silverware and riches are wasted on peasants.'

'I want no part of, it' said von Groitsch. 'Killing peasants is one thing, slaughtering our own is quite another. I'm no pagan.'

The three men looked out from their vantage point. The horde had changed direction. A cry went up and the ravening mass looked up towards them. One of the mounted men-at-arms had caught sight of the colours on the Germans' shields.

'Christ's blood,' said von Groitsch. 'Let's get away from here.'

'Wait,' said von Lienhard. 'We're German. They have no quarrel with us.'

'We're knights, Werner; for Christ's sake, see what's coming towards us. They mean to kill us,' said von Groitsch.

Von Lienhard pulled himself into the saddle. 'If we want silver and plate we'll ride to them, raise a hand in greeting and offer to show them how to fight like soldiers instead of the shit-legged scum they are.'

His companions winced at this foolishness, but von Lienhard had always been one to seize an opportunity and – as the fair-haired knight spurred his horse forward, helmet free, sword still in its scabbard and with a hand raised in greeting to the first of the horsemen who galloped towards him – they heard him laugh.

'These villeins are a festering rabble of rats!' he called to the men-at-arms. 'But I can show them how to fight when the time comes!'

The horsemen pulled up and twisted in the saddle, checking the labouring mob swarming three hundred paces behind. 'As do we!' one of them said.

'Better to catch the devil's tail than his fangs,' answered von Lienhard. 'We split them and lead them. What do you say? More booty for us all. They can have the fine furnishings,' he said, and grinned.

It was the moment of truth as the horde came within fifty paces. The first horseman nodded. Having another three knights at their backs would give them a better sense of security, even if it were a false one. The man-at-arms wore his colours as brazenly as a tournament knight and turned his horse to face the villagers and townsmen who wielded an assortment of weapons behind him.

'They're with us!' he called. 'Good men who hate these fat landowners!'

The mob of peasants were so caught up in their own heady success that they roared their cheers and then wheeled like an army, skirting the horsemen, their rampage not yet sated.

'Pig-shit stupid,' said von Lienhard.

'Aye,' said the horseman. 'And we are glad of it, otherwise we'd be taken ourselves. But they're learning. They fashion swords from scythes and billhooks and there's one from Picardy who can read and write.'

'He's here?' von Lienhard asked.

The man-at-arms shook his head and made a vague gesture towards the horizon beyond the forests. 'Thousands of them out there. He's with them. Name's Cale. Bastard must fancy himself as a peasant king.'

Von Lienhard let the horsemen ride off on the flanks of the peasants. He would wait until the mob had seen him and his blazon so that they would recognize a knight who supported their cause during their next slaughter. As the heaving mass passed him, he raised his hand like the Pope in blessing to the wide-eyed grinning monkeys, drunk with bloodletting and power.

'Satan awaits you, you turds,' he said, knowing they could not understand him, and smiling as he kept up the pretence of solidarity with the peasants. 'Retribution will come and you will cry out to a deaf God. And you will know the wrath of the nobility, who will peel the skin from your backs, rip the tongues from your mouths and put your families to the sword.'

His companions eased their horses up alongside him.

'Their stench alone is enough to make a horse retch,' said von Groitsch. 'Werner, this had better be profitable.'

'Conrad, trust me. We shall ride the tide of terror home in a vessel of gold and silver,' he said, nudging his horse to follow in the Jacquerie's wake as great hooded crows glided and flapped through the pall of smoke, and then crabbed their way towards the tattered flesh that lay across the French knight's courtyard.

CHAPTER THIRTY-FIVE

Blackstone and Killbere made their way down from the citadel's room, watched by a relieved Sir Ralph de Ferrers, glad to rid himself of two of Fortune's men. They would find whatever reward the King had promised in the fields of blood, far beyond the walls of his jurisdiction.

Killbere was anxious to challenge Blackstone's lack of condemnation in front of de Ferrers. 'A word or two against these lice-infected peasants might have eased his manner. A barrel of arrows wouldn't have gone amiss.'

'And you were as gentle as a mendicant monk begging for alms, were you?'

'I am who I am, but you could have brought him around.'

As they eased past sentries and clattered down the stone steps to the inner ward and their horses, Blackstone blew his nose with a finger and pulled on his gloves. Their journey had not yet properly started and already the odds were heavily stacked against finding his family alive.

'Who's to say they don't have a reason?' said Blackstone.

Killbere looked incredulous. 'You think you understand these turds?' he growled.

'I was a free man and never a serf, Gilbert, but you crush those you rule long enough and it's more than their bones that break.'

'Mother of Christ, they slaughter worse than the damned routiers. These aren't aggrieved peasants at Santa Marina you can sway, Thomas. These devils have crawled out of the pit and rake their talons on the innocent.'

'You think I side with them?'

'I served my sworn lord when you were a snot-nosed peasant working in a quarry, living in a hovel. I *know* you, Thomas. Sweet Jesu! You see every man's tortured soul as if it were his blazon. Scum, Thomas! Vile, vicious, evil, shit-stinking scum is what they are.' He drew breath and grabbed the bigger man's arm. 'You were never that.'

'And the noblemen who ride with them?'

'Worse! I don't know what's worse than shit but they are. And when I find the word I will tell you. They should be hoisted and gutted and their entrails dragged from here to the end of the world by dogs. And I'm the man to see it done.'

They reached their horses. Blackstone raised the stirrup strap and kneed the bastard horse in the belly. Standing this long would have let it bloat and when they rode the saddle strap could loosen and make the saddle unstable. The horse shook its head, rattling the bridle, half glancing backwards, ready to snap its yellow teeth given the chance. Blackstone tightened the strap another notch.

'If Christiana and my children are in their path, Gilbert, I'm already too late. If the Dauphin's family is at Meaux, then that's our best chance to find them. These peasants might have just cause – I don't care – but the King has bartered my pardon and family so that I can help him seize this godforsaken country.'

Sir Gilbert sighed. 'When you were a boy I was charged with taking you to war and instilling anger in your blood and love for your King in your heart. Perhaps I didn't do it well enough.'

Blackstone's voice softened. 'Gilbert, you are a cynical old bastard who did it too well. I serve our King whether he bartered or not. He is my sworn lord as you were once. One day his victories will give us all a chance to rule ourselves. But not as a mob.'

Killbere grunted. 'Then we kill as many of these Satan's imps as we can.'

'I know my duty, Gilbert.'

'Good! Because that's what gives us honour. That and sending these vile bastards back where they come from.'

A gratified Killbere spurred his horse forward across the drawbridge and urged it into a canter along the track leading through the tufted marshlands and the heights where the men waited.

Killing was a profession best honed by practice.

Blackstone gathered his men around him. He told them of his plan to try and reach the Dauphin's family.

Perinne rasped his palm over his crow's-foot-scarred head. 'I might know how we can get down to Meaux, Sir Thomas,' he said. 'I passed through it when I was a boy.' He scratched a curve in the soft earth. 'Town's on the bend of the river. There's a bridge, or was as I remember it, across to the stronghold. The walls are thick enough, and reinforced with towers and bastions. If they're in there they'll be as safe as lice in Will's crotch.'

'Nothing is safe near his cock,' said Gaillard.

'It's a weapon of war,' said Longdon.

'By all accounts it's outflanked by Brother Bertrand,' Blackstone told his gathered captains, allowing them the moment of humour. 'Good. Then Perinne will lead us. Gaillard knows the marshes around Calais so he will take us beyond them. The trick is not to be caught by the Dauphin's forces, the routiers or the mob.'

Meulon poked the fire with a stick. 'What about Charles of Navarre?'

'Him too,' said Killbere.

None of the men had a suggestion as to how a hundred of them could travel through countryside that teemed with potential enemies.

'Why don't we find Navarre and join forces with him? He must want to get hold of the Dauphin and his family as much as our sovereign lord,' said Will Longdon.

'And use them to bargain his way to the crown or have them on a gibbet,' said Blackstone. 'Our Lord Edward wants them alive; Navarre plays a game of his own choosing.'

'With many an English mercenary at his back,' said John Jacob.

'Perhaps it's the King's plan to use him to seize Paris now they support the uprising,' said Meulon.

'None of us can know who to trust,' said Blackstone. 'Navarre wants the crown, as does our King. One force plays against the other, but whoever plays the game the best will win.'

'Some game it is then, Sir Thomas, if the French crown is being tossed in the air like a fairground prize,' the big Norman answered.

'Aye, and we're in the middle of it,' said Longdon.

'It's no bad place to be,' said Gaillard. 'The middle of a wheel is what makes it go round. We can control what we need to.'

'By the sweat of Jesu's brow, Gaillard, I swear you do not see it,' said Longdon. 'What goes through the middle of a wheel? A shaft. What is a shaft other than like a spear or...' Longdon poked him with the feathered end of an arrow shaft, whose fletching he was carefully repairing. 'An arrow?' He circled thumb and forefinger and then poked a finger through it. 'Middle. Shaft. Us.'

Blackstone squatted by the fire. It would soon be dark and no progress would be made travelling through hostile territory at night. 'Will, see it as a wheel if you must, but let it be a wheel of fortune. We'll ignore them all and seek out the Dauphin's family. All we have to do is save them from the mob and see them secure somewhere. Once word gets back to our King then we decide what it is we want to do.'

Killbere stood and looked around him. They were in a good defensive position, and an attacker would be hard-pressed to make his way through the tufted, uneven ground of the marshlands at night, but a local peasant could sniff them out and lead anyone wishing to do them harm.

'Captains, get the men fed, the horses hobbled and tethered. Keep them saddled. Set pickets through the night. No fires. As Sir Thomas said, we don't trust anyone.'

'Not even the Captain of Calais?' asked Longdon. 'He's the King's man.'

'Not even the King's mother,' answered Killbere.

'Especially not her,' said Blackstone under his breath.

* * *

The men rolled themselves into their blankets, finding what meagre comfort was to be had on the forest floor. Killbere watched as Stefano Caprini, who always kept himself on the edge of the camp, knelt in prayer; then Sir Gilbert spread his blanket and kicked leaves and moss to make a passable hollow for his hip. Blackstone was already stretched out, sword at his side. It would not be long before the darkness covered them and neither man would be able to see the other, no matter how close they were.

Killbere jerked his head towards Caprini. 'Why is he still here?' he asked

'Canterbury was a disappointment. No discomfort or misery to be had,' said Blackstone.

Killbere's brow furrowed, and then he realized that Blackstone was jesting. 'Ah, right. Now that he has the pleasure of a damp forest, cold food and the joy of Will Longdon's complaints – I ask again: why is he still here?'

'He confessed his sin,' said Blackstone, turning onto his side so that his words might not drift further than Killbere next to him.

'Don't tell me he's another damned Brother Bertrand who has found fornication to be a greater delight than self-pleasure,' said Killbere.

'Where is *he*, by the way?'

'Kept with the horses. Thank God we have no mares. He fetches and carries and does it well enough. He has a permanent grin on his face, so he's a happy bastard.'

'Gilbert, only idiots smile all the time.'

Killbere sighed in agreement. 'We pulled him from a peasant's hovel two days after we arrived, suckling like a piglet on the swineherd's wife's teats. We had to pay the man off with a handful of salt.' He unwrapped a half-loaf of bread and cut a piece, which he handed to Blackstone. The stillness of the forest deadened most sound, but here and there a man coughed, or a murmur gently

282

carried. The quietness of the place made it seem obligatory to speak barely above a whisper.

Blackstone glanced into the near-darkness where the Tau knight prayed. He shook his head, remembering. 'A strange fellow. We reached Canterbury,' he said, tugging the crust with his teeth. 'The place was tight with pilgrims – and he spent a half-day at prayer while I had the horses newly shod. And then...'

Killbere sensed his friend's uncertainty and stayed silent while Blackstone found the words.

'And then he returned from the cathedral, and knelt before me saying that Father Torellini had told him to stay at my side until my journey was done.'

'Back to Italy?'

'I don't know,' said Blackstone. 'He said he had intended only to get me safely across the mountains and to Canterbury, but he was to be granted indulgences by the Pope for every day he was away. And then... then he told me that a man must die with his sins cleansed, without regret in his heart and as poor as Christ.'

'No sharing of the spoils for him, then,' said Killbere with a satisfied grunt.

'It was strange, Gilbert. I value his fighting skills and I couldn't deny him his duty. And then he said that he'd had a vision when he'd prostrated himself where Thomas Becket was slain.'

'Holy men and visions make me more fearful than witches and their familiars. What kind of vision?'

'He didn't say... only that I would need God's comfort.'

The two men fell silent. After a moment's thought Killbere cleared the congealed bread from the roof of his mouth with a fingernail and sucked it free. 'Priests, friars, monks and soothsayers: they all dabble in the black arts. Steer clear of them all and pray to Christ before a fight is what I say. That's the best men like us can do.'

'And trust the men at our shoulder and back. You taught me that,' Blackstone answered. 'And it's brought us this far.'

There was no answer other than Killbere's rhythmic breathing. He was already asleep.

Blackstone turned into his blanket and, as he settled his face into the sweet-smelling moss and leaves, he saw the darkness move. The blazon on the Tau knight's cloak had caught the glow of filtered moonlight as he rose from his prayers, and then the darkness took it like a magician's spell. No sight, no sound. As if Fra Stefano Caprini had been a dark angel come to count the souls he was owed.

Blackstone pulled Wolf Sword closer to his chest and then kissed the silver goddess Arianrhod. The question he had not asked at Canterbury was: whom did the Tau knight mean when he said a man must die cleansed of his sins? Caprini or Blackstone?

CHAPTER THIRTY-SIX

The terror came across the broad moonlit fields. There was no need for torches as the mob moved with slow, relentless determination: at first in no formation, but as if blown by the wind, like dandelion seeds across the low-cut meadows; then, as if drilled, they gathered in a great arc – a bull's horns to entrap the unfortunates within the manor house, their approach the more frightening in its silence, with only the steady sound of shuffling footfalls. As some trampled their way through the vegetable gardens, others came ant-like down the corridors of the vineyards. They slowed and then halted as they reached the low walls and saw the glint of moonlight on armour. The mob's leader raised a fist clutching a billhook, and more than four hundred peasants behind him followed his example.

'Renounce your nobility and your status and swear allegiance to those you have oppressed during your unnatural life as lord of this demesne,' the man cried, his voice echoing across the courtyard.

Christiana and Henry stood in an upper-storey room, pressed against the wall, hardly daring to peep around the window opening. Agnes was further back, wide-eyed with a child's fear, wondering why her mother and the brother she had not seen for so long held knife and sword at the ready. The man's voice had resounded through the house and she saw her mother turn towards her and smile in encouragement. She had been told to be brave, but she found no comfort in her mother's words. For days they had hidden from those who wished to harm them and she did not know why they were being hunted.

The ghostly figures that had come across the landscape had taken those in the house by surprise, but the sentries had seen the fields waver in a tide of shadows and raised the alarm, snatching those in the house from their sleep.

'Be ready to go downstairs,' she had warned Agnes. 'Stay silent and hold back your tears. We will be all right. Lady Marguerite and her children will be with us,' her mother had added. But Lady Marguerite was not with them. She was in her chamber in the wing of the manor house, where firelight gave them light and warmth. Here in the cold, unlit chamber there was nothing but the ghostly shadows cast through the window opening, and bare boards that smelled of dog and lavender seeds. She shivered and wished she was with the other two children, huddled by the fire with their mother.

Christiana dared to peer around the opening.

'Mother!' Henry hissed at her. 'They'll see you!'

The chill that Christiana felt was not from the night, but from the cold understanding that they would not survive the night unless they reached the cellar. And it would have to be done in darkness, because the moment the mob saw a torchlight they would swarm after it. She hesitated as, below, Sir Marcel made his appeal. Could the knight's name and reputation be enough to hold them back? Would they bypass the manor and take their terror elsewhere? Sir Marcel stood on the low rampart, resplendent in his armour, but unable to hide the uncertainty in his voice at the sight of such a vast mob.

'I am Sir Marcel de Lorris. And there are those among you who know me and who have been favoured by my family's goodwill. Take what livestock and food you need but leave my home and my family in peace, I beg you, in God's good name.'

Christiana watched fearfully. There had been no assault against the walls, no roar from the mob – instead there was the most terrifying sound. Laughter. Their leader laughed. And Christiana knew it was already too late. She turned and ran to Agnes with Henry a couple of paces behind her when a scream of utter terror squeezed a mailed fist around her heart. They were already in the house.

'Downstairs!' she hissed, catching Agnes's hand.

Behind her she heard a woman's sobbing. Marguerite! There was nothing she could do. The mob had infiltrated that wing of the house, drawn by the firelight. And then the mob bellowed from outside.

Cries of pain came from the courtyard as soldiers loosed their crossbow bolts and the men-at-arms slashed at the ghostly horde. As she ran past the windows towards the stairwell she glimpsed the uneven fight and wished there had been a contingent of English archers in the yard. They would not be able to stop the hundreds but they would have brought so many down in such a short time that the attack might have faltered.

She stopped suddenly. Noises from downstairs meant they were already below; they had rushed past the feeble defence and were already stripping out the house's wealth. More voices carried, harsh and commanding, as the mob's leaders called them to halt and bear witness. Sweat ran down her back and she cursed the layers of clothes that hampered her. Her daughter began to gulp great sobs and she went down on one knee to quickly assure her.

'No noise. Bite your tongue if you have to, but do not cry out.' With trembling hands she cupped the child's face and kissed her, then took a tight grip of her hand.

'Mother.' Henry's urgent whisper made her turn. Her son stood at a window, back against the wall, sword still in hand but with a look that told her the screams she heard belonged to his master's wife. She dragged Agnes with her, desperately unwilling to let the child go. She held the girl to her as those she had heard in the lower hallway scuttled like rats to witness the atrocity inflicted on the lord of the manor.

From what she could see, most of the men-at-arms, those hardened men who had rescued her, were already slain, their bodies stripped naked and smeared with blood and dirt as they were desecrated underfoot. Lady Marguerite's clothes were being torn from her by peasant women; they grabbed her hair, their knives slashing away her fine clothes, uncaring that their blades cut through fabric and into skin. Christiana watched the woman's humiliation and terror and felt the blood drain from her face. Sir Marcel, bloodied and wounded, was held bound by a stave behind his arms as he was forced to watch the sickening assault on his pregnant wife.

In front of the parents was the battered and bloodied body of their fair-haired daughter, two years younger than Agnes. They had thrown the child from the window into the courtyard below. The mob leader spat into Sir Marcel's face, and yelled for him to renounce his rank, and his privilege, and to turn his lands over to the people. Sir Marcel nodded, his body shuddering from the tears.

Christiana saw half a dozen men-at-arms on horseback at the gate, and for a moment there was a flutter of hope. And then one of them raised himself in his stirrups. He was bareheaded, his sword still in its scabbard. Neither this knight, nor those with him, would raise a voice to protect them. He was young and she saw his fair hair and the shaved side of his head as he cried out to the mob's leader.

'Be done with it! He will say anything now. It means nothing. Be done with it!'

The women had forced Marguerite to her knees and she had tried through her sobbing grief to reach forward to pull the battered body of her daughter to her. But a woman grabbed a handful of her hair, wrenching free a bloodied fistful. Sir Marcel was trying to say something to his wife when one of the men stepped forward and cut her throat. Her body convulsed as the women kept a firm grip on her, the pulsating blood soaking her bulging stomach. The horror was not yet over – men pulled his son through the crowd. He had obviously tried to protect his mother and Christiana could see he had been wounded: his left arm hung limp and he staggered, barely able to stay on his feet. He was little more than a child, still at home being taught, like all seven-year-olds, the joy of verse and the meaning of honour. He trembled, his fine clothes soiled with his own fear. A massive bruise covered half his face. No sooner had his eyes sought out his father than the mob's leader slashed down viciously and slew the boy. A cheer went up as the child's head was thrown into the crowd.

Christiana's strength deserted her and she slumped to the floor, her face pressed against the rough cold wall. It would be better to be torn apart by wolves, which would kill more quickly and with less cruelty than these peasants. Someone grabbed the front of her dress and shook her. It was Henry, slapping her face.

'Get up!' he hissed. 'Get up now!' She smelled the vomit he had spewed from his own terror before her own had cast her into darkness.

Reaching for him she found her strength and then fear and instinct made her run for the stairwell. There were scant seconds for them to reach the cellar as the mob bayed for Sir Marcel's death. As she went down the staircase, her back pressed against the wall, a firm grip on the knife, she saw the crowd part, exposing the heaped bundles of kindling. Two of the attackers struck flints and lit tallow torches and dragged the helpless de Lorris to where the fair-haired knight stood with a lance rammed into broken stonework. They bound the barely conscious man to the makeshift pyre and thrust the torches into the dry tinder. The flames quickly took hold and held the mob's attention as Sir Marcel raised his face to the night sky and screamed in agony.

Footsteps thumped back and forth above them, carpets and furniture dropped past the window – they were already looting. She dragged Agnes behind her as Henry watched their backs until they pushed into the cellar. She could smell the intruders before she saw them. A rancid stench of stale sweat and excrement that clung to clothes and skin. A candle flickered in the near-airless room as a man and woman gorged what food there was while shoving oatcakes, jars and cuts of meat into a sack. Their mouths were full, distorted gargoyles, when they saw Christiana. The man spluttered, reaching for a falchion he had laid on the table in his haste to seize supplies. As he lunged Christiana released Agnes's hand and grappled with him, knowing in that instant that he would overpower her. Without thought she rained down knife blows on his neck and shoulder and saw blood spurt as she severed an artery. He fell back, legs kicking out across the blood-wet stone floor, choking on the food, hands to the wound that would kill him in minutes. The woman had thrown a clay pot at Henry, and then backed like a cornered feral cat as he and Christiana threatened her. The peasant slashed a short-bladed knife in front of her, sweeping back and forth, disgorging the food so she could cry for help.

'Kill her!' Christiana cried as she lunged, forcing the woman to face her attack. Henry hesitated, but only for a second, when the woman's knife nearly caught his mother's face, and then he drove down his sword into the woman's back. She fell, taking his sword embedded in bone and muscle. He gazed, wide-eyed, at the first person he had slain.

Christiana stepped on the woman's shuddering body, her foot pressing her weight onto the neck, her voice a slap, breaking his hesitation. 'Get it!'

Henry yanked free the blade. The babble of voices from outside came closer as the mob came into the house. Christiana snatched the candle and led the way into the passage as Henry shouldered the door closed. They bumped along the rough-hewn wall, stumbling and grazing skin. Uneven rocks punched and bruised them; their breath rasped with exertion as terror drove them on to where the beam lay ready. She waited, trying to calm her breathing, listening in case any of the mob was already in the chapel. She pulled a bloodied sleeve across the sweat on her face. She could barely make out Agnes in the poor light, but she saw that Henry's face was daubed with dirt and gore. He had taken responsibility for their safety – as his father had once done.

'I'll go up with Agnes. Block the door with the beam; can you do that on your own?' she said.

'I can do it. The rope's up there. I'll need the light.'

Christiana handed him the candle. Her torn hem caught a cross bar; she ripped it free, then clambered up into the darkness. She eased herself into the sullen chapel. It was empty. Windowless, it had only one door. She turned around and lowered her hand to Agnes. Henry waited until his sister's ankles kicked free of the beam and then he carefully placed the candle into a recess of an empty cresset lamp and manhandled the beam away from the hatch. As he dragged its weight towards the doorway he could hear no sound from the cellar. The mob must have been more interested in what lay in the house, but he could smell smoke. They were burning down the manor. Henry wedged the beam at a low angle, felt its foot bite into the rough stone floor and turned back towards the escape route.

Complete darkness blanketed the chapel. The dull spluttering glow from the candle in the underground passageway barely offered enough light for her to see Agnes.

'The rope!' whispered Henry from below the hole.

She lowered the rope whose one end was tied around a pillar. It was eight or nine feet to the floor below. Henry speared the point of his sword beneath the candle, reached up, twisted the rope around his left arm and hauled himself up far enough for his mother to wrap the torn strip from her dress around the palm of her hand and reach down to grasp the sharp-edged sword and its life-giving light.

As Henry climbed up she reached down and grabbed his belt to haul him onto the chapel's floor. For a moment he lay with his face pressed against cool stone. Christiana laid a hand on his head.

'Your courage never failed you. And it saved our lives,' she said.

Henry got to his knees, his hands trembling after the blood-rush of the killing during their escape. 'I was frightened, Mother – so scared of what they might do to you and Agnes. They're burning the house. I smelled smoke when I blocked the door. What should we do now?'

'Wait here a moment. Agnes, hold Henry's hand.'

The chapel was barely big enough to hold twenty people. As she raised the candle she could see wooden benches that straddled the chapel's width and a plank table that held the silver crucifix, a small casket and silver candlesticks. She made her way to the iron-studded door and prayed it had not been locked from the outside.

'Mother! Don't take the light away, please,' whimpered Agnes.

Henry eased her to him, and put his arms around her. 'Hush now – be brave, little sister. Mother has to see if we can get away from here.'

The child had known terror like this before, when a killer had held them on a castle's battlements and threatened their lives. Since then there had been safety and the warmth of a home with her mother. There had been no menace, no frightening voices except those that came in her dreams. And when she woke kicking away the bedclothes and crying in fear, her mother's soft arms cuddling her, and the warm smell of her mother's body, comforted her and soothed away the memories. Her father had killed the man who had threatened them, but then he had left them, and she did not know why. She remembered a field of flowers and the snow-capped mountains that day when he held her in his strong arms and promised to return and fill her bedtime with stories. But he had not yet come back.

'Is Father coming?' she asked Henry as Christiana took the light further away.

'I don't think, so, sister. He does not know we are here, so how can he come? Mother and I will find a way. I promise. But we cannot do it without you.'

'What must I do?'

'Be brave, and say a prayer.'

Agnes thought about it, and nodded, words failing her.

Henry tried to see his sister's features in the near darkness. She was nine years old, but she was like a child. Perhaps it was different for a girl. He had heard the men-at-arms and the squire say such things when they talked about women. Sir Marcel had been a kindly mentor and although his squire beat Henry at times for failing in his duty, the gentle knight had always explained that it was a man's duty to protect women. Now Henry hoped he had done his best.

Christiana turned the iron ring that lifted the latch. Before she pulled open the door she hesitated, worried that the dull glow from the candle might give away their hiding place to those in the manor house. Yet if she extinguished the flame the darkness would be complete and fear could strangle them. She placed the candle a few feet from the door so that when it opened there would be the barest glimmer of light showing. She eased back the door and breathed in the night air, sweeter than the dank chapel. She dared herself to step out further, and de Lorris family gravestones rose up from the ground, throwing cruciform shadows towards her as flames began to eat away at the manor house roof. She saw the dark forms of the mob as they began to filter away from their destruction, but two embers of light were bobbing their way up the path towards the chapel. She recognized one of the torchbearers as the knight who had called for the mob to kill Sir Marcel.

There was no escape.

She pushed her weight against the door and wished there had been a key in the lock. That at least would stop these rogue knights from coming into the chapel. Picking up the candle she moved back quickly through the benches to her children.

'We have to go back down into the passage. Men are coming.'

She saw the fear in her daughter's face. Christiana smiled bravely, and glanced quickly at Henry, a look that told him not to contradict her. 'They might be coming to help us,' she said. 'But we have to wait and make sure. Do you understand? We have to be quiet, and we will have to wait in the dark.'

She felt the child stiffen.

'Remember what I said,' Henry told her.

Her bottom lip trembled but she nodded, and reached out to grip his hand.

'There might be smoke down there,' said Henry. 'We must tie cloth around our mouths and noses.'

Christiana pushed the knife blade into the stitched seams of her dress and tore back the material, then fashioned it into a mask around Agnes's face. Then she and Henry did the same. It was awkward trying to climb back down the hole. She took the weight on her forearms until she could grip the rope between her feet. Henry held on to her arm, took some of her weight and then watched as she went down the rope hand over hand.

He lowered Agnes down after her as he heard men's voices outside; their words had a guttural edge. Then the iron latch turned in the lock. Henry blew out the candle and grasped the side of the hole, felt the rope as his mother took up the slack and lowered himself down. As he did so the door of the chapel swung open with a heavy thud.

They huddled together like creatures fearing for their lives when hunting dogs sniffed them out. The voices were indistinct, but the scrape of armour against stone grated on their nerves. Christiana tried to listen to the sounds beyond the hammering in her head from her heart's pounding and to picture what the men were doing. Their laughter was a sharp echo from the vaulted roof. She heard the sound of objects clanking and realized they were taking the silverware. And then one man said something and the others fell silent.

She tightened her embrace around her children, squeezing hard to contain their panic – and her own.

'You can't smell that?' said von Groitsch. 'It's candle wax.'

'It's smoke from the house,' replied von Lienhard.

'No, he's right,' said Martens. 'Candle wax. Someone's here.'

Von Lienhard lifted the burning torch higher as the other man tied off the sack holding the chapel's silver.

'There's nowhere to hide in here. They killed everyone in the house and there'd be no priest this far from any village.' He sniffed the air, lifting the smell of the burning tallow away from his face, throwing the light further. He saw the edge of a raised stone slab just behind the pillar. He stepped towards it, knocking aside a bench.

Christiana heard the unmistakable sound of a sword being unsheathed from its scabbard. They cowered from the imminent threat, taking slow, shallow breaths as the smoke seeped around them from beneath the barred door of the cellar.

Light spilled down the hole.

They couldn't be seen unless someone was foolhardy enough to clamber down into the passage.

They held their breath.

And then Agnes coughed.

Von Lienhard scraped the edge of the hole with his sword blade. 'Come out, or I seal the passage and you can choke to death in the darkness.'

He heard hurried whispers from below and then saw a woman, whose auburn hair caught the flickering torchlight. She looked to be no more than thirty years old, and although her dress was not of such fine quality as that worn by the nobility he could see she was no servant woman. She was petite, and her face was splattered with blood specks and dirt. Her dress was torn, and in her fist with scraped knuckles she gripped a knife. What he saw was a she-wolf protecting her cubs, as two children appeared at her side and gazed up at him. He glanced back at the other two knights, who made their way towards him; now all three gazed down at the survivors from the slaughter.

Christiana had whispered her instructions quickly to the children. She had made Henry pull off his jupon that bore Sir Marcel's badge. There was no choice but to seek mercy from these rogue knights. She pressed Agnes's face close to her own. 'Do not speak to these men. They must not know who your father is. Do as I say.' She turned her head and whispered so that only Henry could hear her. 'These men are with the Jacques. Say nothing.'

Before Henry could question her Christiana looked up at the knights. 'We are afraid,' she said, gazing directly into the fair-haired knight's face. 'It might be better for me and my children to die down here.'

One of the men spoke quietly to this knight, but she couldn't make out the words.

'Who are you?' the other knight demanded.

'I am the widow of Sir Guyon de Sainteny,' she lied, giving her deceased father's name. To have mentioned Blackstone would either incite violence or elicit respect – she could not take that risk. No sooner had she brought up her father's name than the memory of who had been responsible for his death stabbed at her. She quickly shook the image from her mind, determined not to let the truth that still haunted her expose her lie.

The men looked at each other and turned their faces away for a moment.

'You heard of him?' von Lienhard asked.

The other two men shook their head. There were thousands of knights across France.

'We should leave them down there,' said von Groitsch. 'Let the rats have them. I've no taste for rape or using my sword on them.'

'We can use them,' said Martens. 'How long do you think that mob will go on? There will be a reckoning. We've seen a dozen places burned down now and taken enough silver to see us through.'

'She's a nobody,' said von Groitsch.

'No, wait a minute, Siegfried is right,' said von Lienhard. 'We can use them to buy ourselves time. This silver is no great haul. We keep the rest hidden and use this as a token of our good intent to the Church.'

'And if they know we're involved?' asked von Groitsch.

Von Lienhard, sighed and shrugged. 'Then we do what must be done.' He looked down at Christiana. 'We don't know of your name.'

'My... husband was a poor knight from Normandy. He died at Poitiers.'

'We're German knights,' said von Lienhard. 'We too fought with the King of France... Where were you when the mob swarmed?'

'The cellar.'

'And the blood?' he said, pointing the sword tip at her.

'Two peasants attacked us. My son and I killed them.'

'You saw the mob approach then?' he asked, trying to establish whether she had seen him and his companions.

'No. We were travelling... to... Paris but we were told it was held by the Provost who supports these Jacques. The lord of this manor gave us overnight shelter. When he heard the attack he sent us to the cellar. And we found this tunnel.'

'You saw nothing then?'

'No, we only heard the screams.'

Von Lienhard looked at his companions. They considered their decision for a moment. Von Groitsch shrugged; Martens nodded and whispered. 'They can serve as our own safe passage. The nobility won't let the mob have free rein much longer. They'll find a way to stop them. Best we should be on the winning side.'

Von Lienhard looked down at Christiana's upturned face. There was a beauty to it and she had spirit. A widow young enough to need a man for protection. Who knew – she might even have a dowry or land that might be worth considering? 'We saw the flames and got here too late, not that we would have been able to save the good knight of this house. We thought to at least secure what silver there might be for the Holy Church. So, my lady, we will escort you on your journey.'

Christiana knew it was a terrible risk to accept but to refuse meant certain death. 'Then my children and I are grateful for such honourable men to rescue us,' she said, and forced a smile of gratitude.

Von Lienhard put aside his sword and lowered his arm into the hole.

'Then take my hand, Lady de Sainteny. My name is Werner von Lienhard.'

CHAPTER THIRTY-SEVEN

Two days later, three hours after daylight, as distant church bells rang for terce, Blackstone and his men continued to ride south-east at a steady canter, keeping the weak morning sun behind their left shoulder. They had forded streams and eased their way across rivers that gave them a better direction than roads. Rivers were carved in the landscape forever. There were occasional signs of horsemen on the horizon, but no great body of men had shown themselves and, if routiers still plagued this area, then it seemed they had taken what they could and moved on. Half a dozen hamlets had been burned days, if not weeks, before Blackstone and the men eased their way past the destroyed hovels. Squeezed between grasping landowners and savage raiders there was little wonder the peasants had taken themselves south to join the mob, Blackstone thought, but this understanding of the peasants' plight was soon dispelled.

A road curved down into a belly of land, an area rich for crops and livestock, but the meadows were trampled and the vines smashed. What had been chicken and goose pens were torn down and the smouldering, skeletal remains of a manor house bled smoke into the morning air. They halted, watching for any signs of ambush around the distant manor.

Killbere pointed to the bodies scattered in the manor's yard. 'Can't be more than two days since this happened. I'll go down.'

'No. I'll do it,' said Blackstone.

Killbere reached out for the horse's rein. 'Thomas, there's a woman and child down there among the dead. Let me go.'

'If it's them then it makes no difference when I find out,' he said.

Will Longdon held back the archers, placing them on the edges

of the meadow and ruined vineyards. If any intruders attempted
to surprise the men they would be halted far enough away to
allow the men to counter-attack. Blackstone and the others eased
their horses into the yard. Scavengers had already been at work.
The naked men's flesh was pockmarked with crow pecks, and
foxes or feral dogs had gnawed their private parts, tearing off the
softest flesh first, then their faces and buttocks. It would not be
long before wild boar deep in the forest caught the scent and then
muscle and bone would be devoured. Blackstone dismounted and
walked towards the child's broken body. She lay face down, fair
hair matted with blood and dirt, arms splayed, showing that she
had fallen while running. Close to her was the blood-soaked body
of a woman, her blackened throat cut, her face puffed with decay
and maggots, making identification impossible. Blackstone slipped
his hand beneath the child's body and tenderly tried to lift it. It was
as rigid as a wooden crucifix, but he managed to ease her over.
The girl's eyes were open, opaque, the broken bones disfiguring
her beauty. He felt the shudder of relief that it was not Agnes.

Blackstone eased the child down and turned to where Killbere
stood watching. He shook his head. It was not his child.

'Praise God and his angels, Thomas,' the grizzled veteran said
with as much kindness as he could muster. 'Over here,' he added,
turning back to where the charred remains of a man lay like cooked
meat in the cinders. 'The man has good armour on him. Probably
the knight, and these were his family. The woman, the girl and a
headless corpse of a boy who's dressed well enough – most likely
his son. Bastards must have tormented him first.'

John Jacob and Meulon had sent the men into the ruins of the
burnt-out house. 'No bodies inside. Everything either went up in
flames or was taken. They left a clear enough trail,' Jacob said.

Meulon pointed beyond the fields where the trampled ground
was signposted with abandoned pieces of pottery and furniture.
'They couldn't carry everything.'

Caprini had clambered beyond the house towards the chapel.
He called back, 'In here, Sir Thomas.'

Blackstone gestured towards the fallen men and family. 'Meulon, you and Gaillard go among the dead, have the men drag them together. Not the peasants, only the others,' he said; then he pushed through the stench of death towards Caprini, with Killbere and Jacob a pace behind.

When they reached the chapel, Caprini struck a flint and lit a fallen torch, holding it aloft inside the gloom. 'If there was silver here, it's gone, but that was the only desecration. There are benches kicked aside. Nothing has been broken. And there is this,' he said as he led them to the open hole.

'An escape tunnel,' said Killbere. 'It'll lead back to the house. Perhaps someone got out in time.'

'Or lies wounded,' said Caprini, loosening his cloak and lowering himself down, pushing his shoulders through the narrow passage. Moments later he emerged and clambered free of the claustrophobic space. 'The end is blocked, masonry and a door brought down by the fire. I saw no blood. And there is none here on this floor,' he said, sweeping the torch across the stone slabs.

'A manor house with armed men. Far enough away from Paris to be considered safe. Could the Dauphin's family be those outside?' Killbere suggested.

'Was his wife pregnant?' John Jacob asked.

'I don't know,' said Blackstone. 'We've all been witness to murder and killing, but this was a torment as bad as the Hungarians in Italy.'

'These weren't routiers, Sir Thomas,' said Jacob. 'You saw how much ground was trampled out there. There weren't many horses. These were men on foot. Hundreds of them. And some of the bodies – they weren't fighting men.'

'I know, John. We've found the peasant army, or one of them,' said Blackstone.

Caprini made the sign of the cross. 'What you have found is Satan's host.'

* * *

Blackstone rested the horses, allowing time to feed the men and bury the dead despite his impulse to ride on after the sight of the pregnant woman's corpse and her murdered children. It pleased Caprini to offer prayers for the dead and he made the failed acolyte, Bertrand, serve penance by dragging more than his fair share of the bodies to their shallow, hastily dug graves. The unknown knight and his family were brought together in one grave and covered with stones gathered from a pile on the border of a tilled field. Blackstone refused to bury the twenty or so scattered peasants' bodies brought down by crossbow and sword. Even Caprini made no objection to them being left for the beasts.

Blackstone's men left the manor behind them, following the trampled ground until it petered out into pebble-strewn riverbanks. There were no mudflats or riverbanks to show where the horde had gone, but John Jacob had taken Meulon and Gaillard ahead as scouts and they had found tracks, half obscured by the water, on a mudbank in the centre of the shallow river. Blackstone led his men onto a broader road towards the fringes of the vast forests that lay across the horizon. It was better to be in the open where they could see others approach rather than enter unknown woodland where horse and man could be easily ambushed. Within hours the torn ground told its own story of hundreds of men and carts having gone before them – although the tracks led not from the burnt manor house but from the opposite direction. Blackstone brought the men to a halt. The open plain would not conceal fifty men, let alone hundreds.

'This is more than sheepherders,' said Meulon. 'And we are close on their heels.'

'They'll be in those woods,' said Blackstone. 'There's nowhere else.'

They gazed towards the fringed treeline more than a thousand paces away.

'There's colour there that shouldn't be,' said Jack Halfpenny

301

from halfway back in the column where the archers rode behind the hobelars. 'You see it, Sir Thomas?'

A thousand yards and the lad saw a colour in the dark scratch that etched the skyline. Blackstone's archer's eye sought it out but failed. 'Where, Jack? I'm damned if I can see it.'

'A fistmeil left from the forest's edge,' said Halfpenny.

Blackstone and the others clenched a fist and extended a thumb. A dab, little more than a bird's speckled feathers, moved in the darkened treeline.

'I have it,' said Blackstone.

'No peasant, then,' said John Jacob. 'Knights most likely.'

'And not routiers. Holy Mother of God, it's likely to be a gaggle of Frenchmen hunting while their neighbours burn,' said Killbere, turning in the saddle to Blackstone. 'Christ, you don't think it's the Dauphin and his army, do you, Thomas? Then we'd have a fight on our hands.' He grinned, relishing the thought of slaughtering more of his sworn enemy.

'I hope not; we're caught in the open here and a hundred of us fighting an army is a distraction I can ill afford, despite your wishes, Gilbert – though we might exhaust them on the run.' Blackstone raised himself in the stirrups. 'Not that there's anywhere to run or hide. They hold the advantage, whoever they are.'

'We might soon find out, Sir Thomas,' said Gaillard. 'Some of them are riding towards us.'

'Scouting party,' said Killbere. 'Fifteen, twenty perhaps.'

Blackstone saw the flutter of pennons and the spread of horsemen. 'Eighteen men. Knights or squires?' he said.

'Sniffing us out, Sir Thomas. Shall we knock a few from their perches?' said Will Longdon. The archers followed his lead and pulled their war bows from the waxed linen carrying bags.

'Not yet, Will, there's no need to antagonize a swarm if there's only a couple of bees buzzing. Meulon, you and Gaillard take ten men, ride ahead a couple of miles, see that there's no one coming from our flank.'

The two Normans turned their horses, calling for the men they named to follow.

'Shall we ride out to them?' asked Killbere. 'If there's a horde of the bastards in those trees and we've to outrun them, it would be better to test their intentions sooner. A few insulting words should see to it.'

'Let's do that,' said Blackstone and turned to Jacob. 'John, hold back. If there's trouble ride for that gap between the two forests. Will! Ready yourself and six others to cover our arses if we run into trouble. Fra Stefano, this isn't your fight, so choose your own ground.'

'It has been chosen for me,' said Caprini and spurred his horse forward with Blackstone and Killbere.

As they approached the horsemen drew rein, but made no sign of aggression as Blackstone slowed the eager horse until they halted thirty paces from the waiting men, who wore a mixture of mail and armour and were confident in their numbers. These three men who had ridden towards them could pose no threat.

One of the eighteen urged his horse forward and halved the distance. He could not yet see the men's shields slung on the side of their horses, though to him these three horsemen looked like routiers with their mud-splattered jupons and cloaks, yet their manner was confident, which made him doubt this first impression.

'I am Louis Mézières, squire to my lord, Sir Philippe de Guisay,' he said with the haughtiness that French nobility carried like a banner for all to see. A declaration of superiority.

Blackstone said nothing, and leaned against the saddle's pommel. He let his eyes wander over the other squires, who seemed to bristle, making their horses edgy. It was an act of indifferent insolence on Blackstone's part.

Killbere hawked and spat. 'You look like peacocks on a lawn. You and your friends are dressed up for a tournament. Is there a party somewhere?'

Mézières recoiled as if he had been struck with a gauntlet.

'I hope you will excuse Sir Gilbert Killbere,' said Blackstone. 'His last squire bled to death from his tongue-lashing,' he added, letting the squires knows they were in the company of a knight.

Mézières looked confused. The man who spoke to him showed as little respect as the English knight at his side. 'You are not his squire?'

'I am not sufficiently trained to serve as a squire,' answered Blackstone.

The Frenchman looked from one man to the other. The third man in the black cloak, darker in skin and beard, had remained silent. 'With respect, Sir Gilbert, your man is as impertinent as a stable-hand.'

'He is worse on his bad days,' said Killbere. 'If he doesn't kill three or four men a day he gets very irritable. He favours French blood.'

Mézières's jaw opened and closed a couple of times. He glanced back towards his companions before, in a vain attempt to establish some authority, facing the three men again. 'We are required to question you. And your intentions in riding here.'

'On whose authority?' said Blackstone, straightening himself in the saddle. The inflection in his voice left no doubt that he was to be answered. It made Mézières suppress his irritation – it was obvious he could not be dismissive of this man.

'My Lord Charles, King of Navarre, leads troops against the peasant uprising.'

Navarre. The great liar and manipulator who plagued the royal houses of both England and France. Blackstone had no intention of being caught up in the usurper's show of strength to impress the nobles. It was likely to be little more than posturing to gain support in his bid for the crown.

'How many men do you have?' said Blackstone.

'There has been a coming-together of several hundred noble lords and knights to halt the vile slaughter,' Mézières said, showing sufficient respect. 'May I ask your name?'

If they weren't to be hindered in their journey Blackstone had to identify himself. 'I am Thomas Blackstone,' he answered and pushed his knee against the shield strapped to his saddle, turning it enough for the squire to see its blazon.

The man licked his lips. Blackstone's name was known well enough among the knights of France. Rumours of brutality and murder curdled stories of his exploits like sour milk. Blackstone – the Englishman who had tried to kill Jean le Bon, King of France, at Poitiers. The very crown that Navarre now sought. He was an ally.

'My lord,' said Mézières, dipping his head. 'I am honoured. I am certain you and your men will be made most welcome. Our army rests in the forest behind me.'

'Barely an army. More like a midsummer dance,' said Killbere.

Blackstone leaned to Killbere and whispered: 'If Navarre learns we are to secure the Dauphin's family, he'll set the dogs on us. They're our prize, not his.' He eased the horse forward, closer to Mézières. 'And the Dauphin? Where is he?'

'Burgundy. Far from here, trying to raise an army. It is a futile effort, Sir Thomas. Once we inflict justice on the mob we will take Paris. There will be no resistance from the citizens once the uprising is put down,' said the squire confidently, as if fired by a quest to find the Holy Grail.

'Master Mézières, you say your lord, Navarre, has several hundred men?'

'Six... seven hundred,' the squire answered. 'Enough to defeat the rabble.'

'I have heard they number in their thousands,' said Blackstone. 'Unless you can find small groups of them in their hundreds, your army will be pulled from their saddles and their own weapons used against them. I am on... *family* business. Give your lord my best wishes, Master Mézières.'

With that Blackstone heeled the horse around and turned back. He had gathered useful information. The Dauphin was in Burgundy and Charles of Navarre was playing at being a general.

If the mob did not lie before him and had not breached the city walls then the road to Meaux beckoned.

He could see Will Longdon and his archers standing ready with bows strung and a half-dozen arrows per man stuck into the ground in front of them. Bodkins, Blackstone thought to himself, barely able to suppress a smile. Goose-feathered shafts a yard long that would whisper through the air, causing it to shudder as they fell, pinning man to horse, piercing plate, driving their pile through any armour a nobleman's wealth could buy.

A part of him wished those behind him would try to exert their authority so that he might hear the war bow's song again.

CHAPTER THIRTY-EIGHT

Thousands of men moving across the countryside did more than leave trampled meadows and their burnt-out victims: they left a stench of excrement. No latrines were dug; those on the march stepped a few paces from where they slept and squatted.

'There is shit from here and beyond,' said Perinne when he returned with a scouting party. He and his men had found two peasants, abandoned by the others because they had collapsed in a stupor, drunk from a nobleman's looted wine. They were foul to the eye as well as the nostrils. 'And these two must have rolled in most of it.'

'Keep them well back,' said Killbere, gesturing the men to haul the two unfortunates further back. Their wrists were bound with a length of rope and they had been forced to keep up or be dragged by the horsemen. By the look of them they had not kept up too well.

'Did you question them?' asked Blackstone.

Perinne nodded. 'They are from Picardy. I barely understood them, Sir Thomas. Their dialect is like a dog with its throat cut. It seems the mob's got itself a man who can read and write to lead them. These are pig-ignorant shit dwellers. Inbred with goats. What little brain they have is soused with wine.'

Haunted eyes stared up at Blackstone from unshaven faces caked in filth, bruised and battered from their ordeal. They trembled, sinking to their knees, uncaring about their stench or what it was that clung to their rags.

'Are these part of the mob who burned that manor house down, do you think?' asked Killbere.

'Does it matter? We're going to hang them anyway,' said Blackstone.

'It doesn't matter, Thomas, so why waste good rope? Cut their throats and be done with it, but if they know anything, anything at all, then we should give them a chance to talk. There are a hundred castles, walled towns and fortified manors and we cannot search every one of them. It would be easier to find a celibate monk in the whole of Christendom than the Dauphin's family in this ravaged country.'

Blackstone turned to Will Longdon. 'Give them food,' he said. The centenar widened his eyes.

'Me, Sir Thomas? I'd catch the plague if I went downwind of 'em.'

'You snared and cooked coneys yesterday. They're in your bags. They're only coneys, for God's sake, Will.'

Longdon moaned as he undid the satchel tied to his saddle. 'Still, Sir Thomas, why send these buggers to the devil with our food in their belly?'

'A knife in an eye would get them talking, Thomas. Longdon's not wrong,' Killbere said quietly, though loud enough for only Blackstone to hear.

'I know. If there are thousands of these Jacques, then no matter what they've taken from a nobleman's house there still won't be enough food for them. They've gained nothing from these killings – neither meat or freedom,' he answered.

Killbere grunted. 'No meat? They've herded swine, cow, chicken and goose. How many smoked hams or cheese and fruit have they pilfered? These peasants will be as fat as ticks on a dog's belly.'

'Gilbert,' Blackstone said patiently. 'They own none of it. They have secured nothing. They are as they have always been; only now they will pay a price that far exceeds what little they have gained.' He turned to Longdon. 'Give it to them.'

'Bertrand!' Longdon ordered the failed monk. 'Here. Take it to them. You heard Sir Thomas.'

The archer's rank gave him command of the lowest in their group, and Bertrand stepped carefully forward as if approaching chained dogs; then, when close enough, he tossed the roasted rabbits to the prisoners, who fell on them like ravening dogs, the one fighting the other for the scraps.

'Are we afraid of two shit-caked and starving peasants?' Blackstone muttered.

Killbere shrugged. 'Do not complain, Thomas. Your order is obeyed. It's your own goodwill towards them that causes your despair. That and their stench.'

'Sweet Jesus, forgive these men,' said Caprini. 'That they are brought down below the level of animals.'

'You pray for their forgiveness, Fra Stefano? For the state that God has already placed them in? Prayer won't help them. Would you care to offer them water to quench their thirst?' said Blackstone.

Caprini didn't shirk from the challenge and slid from the saddle, then took his water skin to the two creatures. He stood over them and they cowered as if he were the Pope.

Killbere said quietly. 'Perhaps they think he's the angel of death with that cloak.'

'I had that thought myself one night in the forest,' Blackstone admitted as he watched Caprini administer the water. The men drank thirstily, their tied hands clasped as if in prayer, eyes raised towards the Tau knight.

'I do not speak their language,' Caprini said, turning towards Blackstone.

'Perinne, ask them what they know of the peasant army. Where it goes next. Is there any plan to their killing?'

The men became animated when the hardened soldier swore and threatened them in something that was as close to their own dialect as he could muster. Food and spittle competed for lodgings in their beards.

Perinne shrugged. 'Sir Thomas, they don't understand numbers, they say the peasants are as many as ants in a dung heap.'

'I could have told you that,' said Killbere.

'Sir Gilbert, all I can understand is that they were heading towards the town of Mello near Clermont to join a bigger group. Looking at all the shit we found out there, that means a lot of villeins with an urge to kill driving them on like a spear up their arse.'

'You know this Clermont?' asked Blackstone.

Perinne nodded. 'If it's where I think it is, we'll have to go through them, sooner or later. We could keep avoiding them as best we can, Sir Thomas, but they're bloody near everywhere.'

Blackstone spat. Damn. Thousands of peasants coming together would be a formidable army and he had no desire to get caught up trying to fight his way past them. Better to let someone else do that.

'We're riding back to Navarre,' he said to Killbere.

Killbere grunted. It made sense. 'Let the French slaughter the bastards. That's all they're fit for.'

'The French to kill or the peasants to be slain?' asked Blackstone.

'Both. They deserve each other,' said Killbere.

Blackstone tugged his rein and nodded at Perinne. 'Hang them. They need to be seen.'

Blackstone waited as Charles of Navarre looked across the open countryside that lay before him towards the gathered peasants. Blackstone could see the concern crease Navarre's face. Was it fear or dumb stupidity? What did he think awaited him in the valley below? Blackstone wondered. It was obvious that Charles of Navare was shocked by what he saw. The horde looked more like a trained army than the undisciplined mob he had expected. Trumpets blew over drumbeats as they waved tattered flags and raised fists clenching weapons. Navarre had sworn to destroy the uprising, a political manoeuvre to show support for the nobility, because the Dauphin had abandoned the aristocrats to their fate when he went south-east to raise an army to seize back Paris. Navarre's promises had drawn seigneurs and knights from Normandy and Picardy determined to finally put up a shield of resistance against this horde.

'If he's to keep these nobleman at his back, he had better do his killing well,' said Blackstone as he watched the look of uncertainty on Navarre's face.

'He's no fighter, Thomas, look at him,' said Killbere. 'His arse pinches tighter than his lying lips. How in the name of Christ have we ended up here?'

'We use him as he intends to use us,' answered Blackstone, studying the army that had formed up in front of them in their strong defensive position. 'They've chosen their ground well,' he said.

It was no vast army such as the French had fielded at Crécy or Poitiers, no heaving body of knights and war horses, but the thousands of peasants before them, who held the plateau near the town of Clermont, looked to be well organized. And men with weapons forged with a village smith's skills had enough steel to bring down horses. Peasants armed with crossbows joined those in the front rank; armour could be pierced as easily as an aristocrat's arrogance. Several hundred horsemen held the rear; and in between a couple of thousand armed men stood in line. There was military know-how in this peasant army – and Blackstone was not the only one to see it.

'He's a clever-enough bastard, this leader of theirs,' said Killbere. 'Those trenches he's dug and the wagons protecting his flanks will make it difficult to dig his men out. Like scraping shit out of a horse hoof, you have to be careful the beast doesn't kick you in the face.'

'Navarre has the numbers – just – but we've both seen how men on the ground can stop horsemen,' Blackstone said.

'Aye, but if Cale has any military sense he'll let Navarre throw himself at them and then swarm over us like rats from a burning barn,' answered the veteran knight. 'You heard what Will and Halfpenny said. They could take Cale out of the saddle when he's in range. Wouldn't take a dozen bodkins to punch through his miserable skin.'

'Killing Cale would be short-sighted, Gilbert. He's got three armies elsewhere, and information we could use.'

'God's tears, Thomas, you still think we'll find the Dauphin's family with a turd like this?'

'Which turd? Cale or Navarre?' Blackstone answered and smiled. 'A good fight is worth the effort, but I have no wish to risk wounds and death to any of my men on these murdering scum. We've better causes waiting for our risk.' He gathered the reins. 'Remember my orders, Gilbert. My life depends on it.'

He spurred his horse along the low ridge to where Charles of Navarre waited, still undecided how best to attack the ranks of peasants, who now seemed eager to fight.

The army of peasants had burned their way across the landscape as effectively as any king's troops plundering in war. Ranks were swelled with minor noblemen and landowners who saw advantage in attacking those with richer domains, whose wealth could be stripped from them. Long-standing vendettas could now be settled by using the mob in their favour.

News had reached them that the Provost of Merchants in Paris had sent a separate mob of citizens south of the capital to join their cause. Who could stop them now? The Jacquerie army to the north, and another to the east, would soon control every approach to the city, and once the citizens rejected Charles of Navarre and closed its gates to the Dauphin, denying him governance of his kingdom, then the villeins would hold the nation for themselves.

They were led by men who knew how to fight. Guillaume Cale was a local man who had taken them to victory with the promise of greater prizes awaiting them – once they had pulled down these knights of Charles of Navarre.

Two long ranks of peasants bayed an incoherent war cry extolling their excesses, and crying for the blood of the noblemen who waited in the distance. Who could stand against them? A peasant's delusion had become a chimera let loose.

When Blackstone had returned to Navarre's men he was greeted coolly, but his information as to where Navarre's enemy might take a stand had proved correct and the emblazoned knights curved their way across the countryside like a glittering rainbow. If grandeur and pomp could have won the day then no sword would ever need to be drawn. The gathered knights were ready to strike, the mass of horsemen, flags and pennons, surcoats and horse trappers a surge of colour that was meant to intimidate.

Now Blackstone rode to where Navarre gazed out uncertainly at the gathered mass.

'My lord,' Blackstone said as he snatched the bastard horse's reins, stopping it from barging the war horse of a wealthy knight in Navarre's entourage. Navarre looked faintly surprised that Blackstone had addressed him directly without permission, but his worry about the possible humiliation at the hands of the peasants facing him swept aside his irritation.

'Is the Englishman impatient to kill more Frenchmen?' Navarre said, a thin smile advising those around him that this was an attempt at wit. A dutiful titter of laughter was offered up, but a few of those close to him remained grim-faced. These knights deserved better than Navarre. They had hitched their fate to his so that each might gain what he desired. Among them were Normans who still sought autonomy, hoping that Navarre would not renege on any surety given to their cause. Despite Blackstone being an Englishman he was considered one of them – his love and respect for Jean de Harcourt and his fight for justice at the Norman's death would never be forgotten.

One such veteran knight, the Norman lord Sir Robert de Montagu, his armour draped in a surcoat of azure and gold with a stag's head crest, sat on a destrier as grandly adorned as if in a royal procession. The horse's trapper copied the device and reached almost to the ground; the trimmed etched-leather reins were studded with silver – all denoting a man of high rank and prestige. By contrast Blackstone looked little more than a common hobelar, wearing his mail, jupon and boiled-leather breastplate for protection.

'Thomas, we're all impatient, but a decision has not yet been made. Be respectful of our lord's dilemma,' de Montagu said in

313

obvious warning, but with sufficient weariness to let Blackstone know that the Norman was tired of Navarre's indecision.

'You'll lose good men down there, my lord,' said Blackstone, ignoring him and addressing himself to Navarre. 'You'll win, but there'll be a price to pay.'

'Christ, Thomas, hold your tongue. We've no need for further doubt,' said de Montagu, alarmed at Blackstone's suggestion.

'You think we lack courage?' snarled the knight closest to Navarre. It was his brother Philip, the hot-headed younger man who would rather kill than negotiate with an enemy.

'No, my lord, I remember when you murdered the unarmed Constable of France four years ago. My friend Jean de Harcourt told me of your courage that night,' answered Blackstone.

Two of the Norman knights blocked Philip of Navarre's horse as he spurred it towards Blackstone, ready to strike at his insolence.

'De Harcourt was weak! As was his choice of low scum for friendship. We seized the moment!'

Taunting Navarre's brother gave some pleasure and it might snap Charles of Navarre into a more belligerent state of mind. Blackstone answered, keeping his eyes on Charles. 'My friend was intelligent and loyal and your actions spurred King John into retribution that cost de Harcourt his life and those of your brother's supporters. The murder you committed that night unleashed a vile killer against my family, so I know what comes from a bad decision.'

The horses fussed and were cursed at as they were brought under control. Charles of Navarre was devious enough to know when he had been offered an alternative disguised by defiance.

'What price do I pay, Sir Thomas? I have the support of the nobles. Men die in battle.'

'Would you exchange a denier for a gold crown? Or a rouncey for a stallion? There's no point in getting any man of noble birth killed, my lord. Any such death against these vermin will reflect badly. It weakens your cause and strengthens theirs.'

'Let's be done with this,' said Philip.

Blackstone remained unperturbed. Navarre's brother served only as the sword arm for the family's ambitions. Navarre raised a hand to quieten any further interruption and nodded consent for Blackstone to speak. 'And how do I avoid this?'

'Bring their leader, this Cale, to the table to negotiate. Without him they become rabble again.'

'Offer him a truce?' Navarre asked as the others murmured their disapproval.

'He has the status of a general. Or so he thinks. And you are King of Navarre.'

Navarre was a poor war leader, but his years of political deceit and intrigue gave him an instinct like a viper slithering from an entangled mass of snakes. He immediately saw what the others had not. 'Go down and bring him to me then, Sir Thomas.'

Blackstone had expected Navarre would want him to be the means of betrayal, then Blackstone's would be the name linked to duping the peasant leader. 'Sire,' he said, flattering the monarch of the small mountain province in the Pyrenees, 'I will convince him, but it needs a king to offer the truce and a nobleman to promise it.'

'And you will want something in return,' said Navarre.

'I want the right to choose how he dies,' Blackstone answered.

In that moment Charles of Navarre recognized the skill of the Englishman and the ruthless streak of a great commander. Blackstone would lay a trap and he, Charles of Navarre, was to spring it.

CHAPTER THIRTY-NINE

The peasants watched as Guillaume Cale rode forward to speak
to the two men riding at a walking pace to meet him in the space
that lay between the two armies. A parlay had been arranged
and perhaps, some muttered among themselves, they would be
paid by these frightened aristocrats to leave the field of battle.
More wealth, more possessions and the rewards for their savagery
lay within their grasp. Beyond them, beneath the glory of gold-
threaded flags, Navarre knew Blackstone had made a good choice
in choosing Sir Robert de Montagu to ride with him to meet the
peasant commander. The grandeur of the man and his horse
next to Blackstone made a sharp contrast, extolling the man's
rank.

Blackstone drew up his horse, leaving a half-dozen paces
between him and the peasant commander. Guillaume Cale would
have been considered handsome by some women: a strong-looking
man whose dark eyebrows curved like flared wings over his beaked
nose. His assortment of arms and armour gave him the look of
a fighting man and he showed no fear as he gazed at Navarre's
envoys. This was his home ground. The small town of Clermont
where he was born and raised was only a few miles away. A
man grew confident on his own territory, Blackstone thought, a
confidence that could blind him.

Sir Robert de Montagu held back, as had been agreed with
Blackstone, who would do the talking until Cale rose to the bait.
If Blackstone was correct Cale would demand that the reviled
nobleman debase himself by entering into the negotiation – believing
himself closer in rank to de Montagu rather than Blackstone.

'You're to be offered a truce,' said Blackstone.

'Whose puppet are you?' demanded Cale.

'I'm a fighting man. You can't win here today. I've seen better scabs on a dog's arse than those men behind you,' Blackstone deliberately taunted.

'Scabs that cover the wounds of France. You're an Englishman?'

'I am.'

'A routier,' Cale sneered. 'And you insult me? Behind me are common men and women that the likes of you rape and murder.'

'You don't need any lessons in that, general,' Blackstone said, tingeing his insolence with a casual deference. It had its effect. Guillaume Cale turned his attention to the richly dressed nobleman who obviously spent more money on his horse than a villein could earn in a lifetime. By comparison Blackstone's horse with its blotched coat and nondescript bridle reflected its rider's low rank. He was talking to the wrong man.

'Why am I spoken to by a man like this?' Cale demanded. 'Is it beneath your dignity to discuss terms with me when I'm the one holding this place with twice as many men as you have?'

The nobleman looked down, as if being shamed, keeping up the pretence that Blackstone had insisted upon.

Blackstone answered for him. 'You've some education, like me, general, and I hear you own land, also like me. We're different from these noblemen. I know what it means to be poor. I give you my word that –'

'Be quiet!' Sir Robert suddenly barked. 'This man leads an army, you do not.'

Blackstone looked suitably chastised, anger barely held in check as he continued the ruse. 'You pay him off when we can beat him!' he challenged the Norman.

'Neither of us wants unnecessary bloodshed,' de Montagu said in a reasonable tone, making Blackstone seem even more coarse than he appeared. De Montagu faced Cale. 'I can give you a King's word that you will be given safe passage and welcomed to discuss terms of truce that, he feels certain, will satisfy you.'

Sir Robert waited patiently as Cale considered the proposition. Charles, King of Navarre, was the French King's son-in-law who sought the crown. And to do that he needed to gain the support of the citizens of Paris, which meant bringing the Provost of Merchants onto his side. And the Provost had already despatched men to support the uprising. A treaty would benefit Navarre as it could the future of the common man. It might even secure rights that few had even dreamed of.

'I hold the field,' he answered. 'You will not defeat us today. And when noblemen fall under the billhook of a peasant your whole class bleeds.'

Sir Robert remained silent, but Blackstone fuelled Cale's confidence with a whispered plea.

'Don't do this, my lord, we can beat them.'

De Montagu played his part perfectly. He glared at Blackstone, and then shook his head. Cale grinned. He had them.

'We would need pardons for what has occurred in the heat of our unrest,' said Cale.

'Charles of Navarre believes we all should seek pardon for our deeds,' said de Montagu. 'Which is why he extends this offer of a truce to you.'

Cale looked a hundred paces beyond the two men, to where five squires and a knight waited, pennons aloft, ready to escort him to the parlay with a king.

Blackstone let his eyes settle on the man from Picardy whom the great swathe of murdering villeins had turned to as their leader and who now controlled their hate and the terror they inflicted. His thousands of peasants had burned and destroyed a dozen towns and might even, for all Blackstone knew, have slain Christiana and his children. So far they had broken the yoke of servitude and bested men-at-arms when those knights tried to defend their families and land. If Cale accepted the word of a king, even a king of such an insignificant and distant place, but who might one day wear the crown of France, then Cale's own vanity would seal his fate.

And if he did as Blackstone expected then he and Sir Robert might have only moments to live.

'We will stand our ground here until you return,' said de Montagu, gently closing the trap. 'As surety.'

He and Blackstone were no more than thirty long paces from the front line of peasants. They would be overwhelmed the moment anything happened to Cale.

Cale nodded. 'One sign of falsehood and you'll be dead,' he said, and then spurred his horse past them towards the waiting escort.

A ragged cheer swelled up from the peasants as Cale raised a clenched fist as if in victory.

Blackstone turned to Sir Robert. 'Keep a tight rein, my lord; don't touch your sword yet,' he said quietly. 'Be ready to raise your shield.'

His eyes watched the distorted faces in front of him. These peasants would like nothing more than to hack the two of them to pieces. Blackstone had seen those self-same faces as a boy when villagers dangled a cat over a dog pit for sport and then screamed their blood-lust as it was torn apart. Dark hovels and smoke-filled rooms caged such people, a lord's demands clawing at their backs like a flail. Noblemen, bailiffs, sheriff, sovereign and Church: all took their share of these creatures' pitiful existence. Their time would come – but not today. Not after what they had done.

How many breaths would it take before the snarling, debased horde cut them down? Without turning to watch Cale's progress towards Navarre, Blackstone listened to the retreating hoofbeats. Cale would be close to the escort now. When he and Sir Robert had walked their horses slowly towards the eager-to-kill mob he had counted out a man's pace mark in his mind.

'How many yards to their front line?' he had asked his centenar of archers before riding up to Navarre.

'Two hundred and four,' Longdon had answered.

'And nine,' the young Halfpenny had suggested.

His own archer's eye told him the distance lay somewhere in between – and when he had approached Guillaume Cale to offer the truce he had drawn up the bastard horse at what he deemed to be a hundred and seventy five yards from the archers.

There was a sudden cry as Cale was seized by the squires. No honour was lost when a pledge to a peasant was broken. It was whom you gave your word to that counted.

The shockwave that was about to surge towards them was the blink of an eye away.

Blackstone swore he heard the creak of a forest's trees bending before a mighty wind – but knew it was the sound of English archers drawing back their war bows. And when that wind swept down in a rippling storm it cut into the dangerous crossbowmen and those who tried to shoulder them aside to attack. They got within twenty paces. Sir Robert de Montagu held his nerve as the air ripped around them a second time.

The thudding of steel-tipped ash driving through bone and muscle sounded like a dog tearing flesh. The attackers faltered. Bodies lay writhing, effectively blocking those behind. A few of the crossbowmen loosed their bolts. One thudded into Sir Robert's shield, but he was already spurring his horse as a swarm of knights hurled forwards and archers loosed volleys from two flanks flaying a path for them. The peasants' hopeless attempt at attack faltered as hundreds died within the first few minutes. No man had got closer than ten paces to Blackstone. As Navarre's knights swept past Blackstone he kept his horse reined tight, holding back its desire to join the fray. Peasants were trampled, hacked and speared, as behind the horsemen dismounted knights walked through the field of blood, slashing at the wounded, hacking limbs, inflicting the noblemen's revenge. Navarre was well out of danger as he helped slaughter the wounded.

Will Longdon and his archers bent their bows and eased the cords from their nocks. Their part was over. They had held their ground, following Blackstone's orders not to join the fight. There was no booty to be had, no prize worth losing a valuable archer for. Blackstone turned his horse and saw Killbere where he had left him. There was no glory or honour in this slaughter. It was as simple as clubbing rats in an infested hovel. But to the peasants' rear a knot of armoured men spurred their horses away from Navarre's attack. A winged creature bobbed and weaved as the harpy-emblazoned shield glared from their midst. Those of the lesser noblemen who had joined the peasants' cause now sought escape from the disorganized rabble who refused to obey their commands.

Killbere watched as Blackstone raised Wolf Sword and spurred forward his horse. 'Sweet Jesus, what's he doing? He said to stay back,' Killbere muttered as his eyes followed Blackstone's attack.

John Jacob pointed with his sword. 'The harpy!'

Killbere had no time to ask the question; his baffled look was enough.

'We were attacked at Windsor,' said Caprini. 'By that knight and others.' He grinned at Killbere. 'It seems that Satan's horde shall not go unpunished!' he added, digging spurs into his horse's flanks, quickly followed by Jacob.

'Mother of God!' Killbere cursed. 'Will! Keep your lads here! Meulon! Gaillard! You and your men kill some of those turds before they swamp Sir Thomas!' The orders given, he urged his horse forward, following the Tau knight as the two Normans peeled away at an angle to drive a wedge between the swirling ranks of Cale's army.

Will Longdon was fitting his bow cord again. The fight might turn if those knights abandoning the field galloped towards them and managed to avoid Blackstone. He had faced armoured French cavalry before and knew how to bring them down.

The great horse trampled men flailing helplessly at Blackstone as he swung Wolf Sword up and down and then left and right, the blood knot biting into his wrist. Iron-shod hooves smashed bones as the horse barged through the men with Blackstone urging him on. Men screamed; others fell back wide-eyed as the shock of pain seared through their final moments. Blackstone saw Navarre's men to his right, but the harpy still gathered

321

others around it, its outstretched talons clawing its way free from the mêlée. Blackstone pulled the horse at a sharper angle in an effort to cut off the knight's escape. A blade slashed the greave on his leg, glanced upwards and tore a line across his thigh. The raw cut was insignificant, but he felt its stinging pain as he pressed the horse's flank to make him turn.

And then he was among them.

He barged aside a man-at-arms riding a big courser whose head yanked to one side as the muscled neck and misshapen head of Blackstone's savage horse struck it. A heavy thud, a wide-eyed stare. The man's sword was held too high as he half turned to strike. Blackstone swept his blade across the man's chest, slashing its razor edge against mail, knowing that it was useless as a cut but its force would rock the man back – letting him drive Wolf Sword's point into his groin. The strangled cry was swallowed in the man's helm; his feet slammed forward in the stirrups and he tumbled across the back of the saddle.

Other riders charged from Blackstone's blind side. It was Caprini and John Jacob forcing the knot of men to splinter, hacking into peasants and men-at-arms, leaving the German knight to pound through the gap. He was ahead of Blackstone and rode a faster horse. Sweat stung Blackstone's eyes. The leather grip on his gauntlet was wet with blood; he felt Wolf Sword's grip slip from his hand but it was saved by the blood knot and, twisting his wrist, he reclaimed it, letting the reins loosen, giving the bastard horse its head. He felt its energy surge like an arrow propelled from a war bow – it would need the devil and his helpers to pull it back under control.

The German tried to swerve, but the horses were side by side, Blackstone's shield covering his body from the smashing blows of the flanged mace being slammed against it. A glancing blow caught the top of his helm, whipping back his head; a burst of pain exploded behind his eyes and he rocked in the saddle, his falling weight slowing his horse so that it faltered a pace behind. Had it not been so mean-spirited a beast determined to bite the other horse Blackstone would have been carried away from the attack in a wild gallop. He lurched forward, brought back his shield arm and slammed it across the man's shoulder onto his helm. He too swayed as Blackstone used the horse's barging motion to bring a hammering strike down onto his helm. The German's horse veered; the man lost his stirrups and, despite the saddle's cantle, slid off onto the ground.

Blackstone let Wolf Sword dangle from the blood knot, grabbed the reins with both hands, pushed himself back in the saddle, and sawed the bit left and right in a harsh attempt to slow the horse. He pressed his wounded leg into its flank and kicked hard with the other. Like a lumbering cog trying to turn on a running tide the great beast curved around to face the fallen knight, who was on his feet again, mace thrown down, sword in hand. Blurred images swept back and forth as peasants fought a running battle with Navarre's men-at-arms. There was no order to their retreat; they stumbled and fell, craved mercy and were given none. Horses ran loose; torn flags fell into the bloodied field. Blackstone's horse finally slowed, flanks heaving, nostrils flaring as it bellowed air, while Blackstone tried to get it to face the man who now ran at him, sword raised for a blow that would take his leg off. It was impossible to turn in time to fend off the attack.

A horse swept into view; its rider, his sword raised, made a sweeping cut from on high, curving the strike down onto the side of the German's head. The man dropped like a sack of grain; a spurt of blood held for a moment in the air as delicately as a woman's torn veil and then splattered across him.

The retreat was in full flight and by the time Blackstone reached the fallen man Killbere had turned his horse back. He pulled back his visor. 'Tears of Christ, Thomas, you should rid yourself of that ox-of-a-horse!' he cried.

Blackstone yanked his helm free and tore off his gauntlet, pulling fingers through his sweat-soaked hair. 'It's not the horse; it's more likely the rider who can't handle it. Thank you for that.'

'Is he dead?' Killbere said.

'With half his head missing, he should be. Clean through helm and skull.'

'Good! It's as I intended,' said Killbere. 'The Italian said you weren't on speaking terms with this whoreson.'

Blackstone knelt and eased the split visor from the mangled remains of the man's head. The side and back of his skull were shattered but his face was plain to see.

'He's nobody's son now, Gilbert, whore or not. We barely spoke at all, but this wasn't him. It's one of the men who was at his side.'

'Ah,' said Killbere, as if he had failed.

'But,' said Blackstone as he looked across the field of slaughter, 'where one shows her talons so too will another. At least I know he's close.'

They used hot irons on Guillaume Cale's stripped body, laying the glowing tips across back and chest, pressing the searing heat onto the inside of his thighs and the soles of his feet, inflicting the most pain they could think of. They were practised in the art of suffering. They asked no questions and sought no confession; this was a simple exercise in torture to burn the man's screams into the townspeople's minds.

In Clermont's town square the bloodied man was forced to kneel before the terrified townspeople, flanked by Navarre's men, the gore not yet cleaned from their blades. A forge had been brought where a smith beat iron, taking the white-hot metal and shaping it as ordered by Navarre.

'We bring your son home!' Navarre called to the crowd. 'We return him to the whore that spawned him and this sewer that bred him!'

Blackstone and Killbere sat astride their horses looking across at the heads of the crowd watching the ceremony of humiliation. A rough-timbered platform had been quickly built and Navarre and those close to him stood on it as the bound Cale was forced onto a stool.

'Hanging witches was always good for business,' said Killbere, 'but there are no piemen or jugglers here today. Navarre has a cruelty to him that takes the pleasure out of public spectacle.'

'They're not finished with him yet,' Blackstone said, tasting the throat-clawing fumes from the forge mingled with the smell of burning flesh. He took the wineskin from his saddle and swilled out his mouth, spitting the foulness onto the ground.

'You waste good wine, Thomas. Why are we still here? I've no taste for this and neither have you.'

'I need him alive for a while longer. I made a bargain with Navarre.'

Killbere grunted. 'You can see how far that might get you.'

'It was given in front of the noblemen. He'll be obliged to keep it or lose their trust,' Blackstone answered.

Navarre beckoned the smith, whose tongs held the glowing metal in the coals. 'There were those who thought this man could be a King of the Jacques,' he told the crowd. 'Their wish is granted.'

Guards tightened their grip on the ropes holding Cale.

'Behold your King!' Navarre shouted as the smith clumsily placed the band of hot iron onto Cale's forehead. Flesh and hair burned, and even Navarre was obliged to cover his face with a linen cloth as Cale screamed and writhed.

'Kill the poor bastard and be done with it,' Killbere muttered.

Cale slumped forward, the pain too great to bear, as Navarre and his entourage stepped down from the platform, leaving Cale's blistered body to regain consciousness and ready itself for the final horror. The crowd tried to turn their backs on the spectacle but soldiers prodded and jabbed them to face the pitiful sight. Blackstone pushed his way through to the platform.

'Not too close, my lord,' said one of the soldiers. 'There's enough shit and piss come out of him to make a pig faint.'

Blackstone ignored him and clambered up onto the platform. The guard snatched at his arm.

'Take your hands off me or you'll know the pain that he feels,' Blackstone said.

The guard hastily withdrew his hand and turned back to the peasants where his authority lay. Knights like this Englishman held sway over common soldiers and he had no desire to end up like that poor bastard on the platform.

Blackstone eased himself closer to the slumped man. He reached down and took the smith's leather pail of water, soaking the cloth Navarre had discarded. Squeezing the water over the man's burnt head he waited until Cale muttered something, his shoulders hunched as he gritted his teeth. Hot irons were an agony that grew worse as the flesh continued to fight the pain. Blackstone tilted back the man's chin, letting the water run into his parched lips. Cale's eyes opened and focused on the man who had tricked him and who now gave him comfort.

He nodded. There was no pride left to sustain him; arrogance had been scalded from him. 'Thank you,' he rasped.

The stench around the man was as foul as the guard had warned, but Blackstone used the bucket to sluice the man's waste away and then knelt close to him. The iron crown, now cold, squeezed Cale's head like a vice, the cruel symbol scarring his face beyond recognition.

'You are going to be hanged soon,' Blackstone told him unhurriedly, making sure that his words were heard clearly, holding the man's attention. 'They will hang you by the neck and then draw you, spilling your guts into those coals so that they'll burn in front of you. Then each limb will be hacked and tossed to dogs. Then they'll take your head.'

Cale's body shuddered, its pain settling ever deeper. From somewhere in the darkness within he drew up the strength to answer Blackstone. 'You... torment me... further.'

'No,' said Blackstone, 'I can end this suffering. It will soon be Midsummer's Eve and the celebration of St John the Baptist. You can die like him. Tell me what I want to know and Navarre will behead you. There will be no more torture.'

A tear welled in Cale's eye and spilled down his fractured cheekbone to join the phlegm from his nose that soaked his beard.

He nodded.

'Do the Jacquerie seek out the Dauphin's family?' Blackstone asked. He gave the man time to answer, letting him ease the words from his cracked lips.

Cale nodded. 'They do,' he whispered.

'Who leads the mob?'

'Vaillant. Jean Vaillant. From Paris. And... Pierre Gilles...' Cale said slowly.

'Where?'

'East... to Meaux.'

Blackstone did not wish to put words into the suffering man's mouth. If the royal family were there he had to hear it from the one man who knew for certain.

'Why? Why Meaux?'

They... and many other... noblemen's families... Meaux. They go... for them.' His body trembled, his voice cracking.

Blackstone had his answer. He needed nothing further from this broken man.

'We could not stop...' whispered Cale.

Blackstone hesitated, waiting for him to finish what he was trying to say.

'We... had seized... a lion's tail... We did not... know how to let go.'

Blackstone made no reply. There were still thousands more out there who were not afraid of their grip on terror.

PART FOUR

BLOOD OATH

CHAPTER FORTY

Christiana followed the two German knights through the narrow, crooked streets of Meaux, her thoughts only of escape. Exhaustion had tugged at her over every yard, and she had slept in the saddle, jolting awake when Agnes nearly tumbled from her arms. Von Lienhard had tried to engage her in conversation in an attempt to tease out information, but she begged his forbearance for her tiredness and the German soon became bored with her. She served a purpose for them and beyond that they had no interest. They had travelled in near-silence for the better part of the day and then they came upon the great curve of the river and the walled city that stood on its northern bank. Before the city gates were opened to them she saw the towers and battlements of the fortress rising up in the background and knew that once inside they would at last be safe. The labyrinth took them, turning this way and that along streets only wide enough to accommodate a laden donkey, where daylight barely reached because of the density of the overhanging windows and roofs.

As they rode slowly, one horse behind the other, she saw no way to avoid staying with the two men who had pretended to rescue them. The killers would go into the fortress with her and who there would believe her story of their part in the slaughter of Sir Marcel de Lorris and his family? It would make no sense. Why would they risk their own lives to bring her to safety and why had they turned over the silver from de Lorris's chapel to the bishop? She knew that gratitude and honour would be afforded them. Until she could relate the images of their part in the killing she would have trust in her own instincts, because once the accusation was

331

made there would be a judicial hearing and then her own life and those of her children would be at risk.

Women sitting outside their houses raised their heads from their sewing as the horses ambled past them. Christiana was bedraggled and bloodstained. She was obviously another nobleman's woman rescued by knights. Another one to be locked into the fortress where they thought themselves to be untouchable.

Their indifferent glances told Christiana that escape could be more dangerous than staying with the killers in the stronghold known as the Marché. There would be no welcome or hiding place among these old houses that sagged, timbers creaking, almost touching each other from either side of the thoroughfare. Their doorways opened into near-darkness where children picked hems from scavenged cloth in light from hearth-fires barely bright enough for visibility, their fingers close to their faces. Beeswax candles cost money and only the Church and noblemen would indulge in such extravagance. For families crammed into one room, animal fat was scraped and saved then turned into pungent candles by a chandler.

Agnes squirmed in Christiana's arms as the small procession pushed aside street hawkers and water carriers. She looked this way and that along city streets that clanged and hammered from the noise of furriers and shoemakers, coopers beating metal rings into place and locksmiths tapping away diligently at their trade. This small city was prosperous. At each narrow side street she strained to see how they might fare if for any reason they had to run. Artisans' signs competed with each other outside the wooden houses. A vintner's board, as big as a door, with its painted symbol of a bush, proclaimed a cellar to drink in; an apothecary's sign of three gilded pills glistened in the rays of sunlight that managed to penetrate the narrow street and she glimpsed the white pole, striped red, for a barber-surgeon. There was wealth here. That was good. That meant these people had something to lose and would resist if the mob descended. The city gates would remain closed.

Women haggled at poultry stores as chickens and ducks, their legs trussed, floundered on the ground with rabbits and hares. Five *deniers* for a rabbit, four for a chicken. The stallholders' cries fought each other. Down another street a butcher's offal swarmed with flies, the beast slain in the street, its blood pooling in the gutters. Harness makers, spice and salt sellers: all of these trades would surely fight for what they had. She felt a growing sense of confidence. Wealth and food. These townsmen were no part of the Jacquerie; they would not sacrifice what they had.

The sky opened again as they emerged from the cluttered streets. The stone-built fortress rose up before them across the narrow stone bridge on the opposite bank. It was a strong defensive citadel, cushioned from attack by the outer walls of Meaux itself, and surrounded by water on all sides. As the horses clattered across the bridge, the portcullis cranked upwards. Christiana kissed Agnes's hair and turned in the saddle to give Henry an encouraging smile. Safety, food and warmth lay within.

She put a finger to her lips.

Stay silent.

Once behind the stronghold's walls Christiana and Agnes were accommodated in the vast dormitory made ready by the Marché's commander. She soon learnt that hundreds of women had been given safe haven, many of whom would never see their husbands again, nor their burnt-out homes. The lesser noblewomen were obliged to suffer the indignity of being herded into rooms and corridors, even though their status might have normally afforded them the comfort of their own chamber. But they were alive, witnesses to horror, and that kept any such discontent unspoken, but they all still felt their vulnerability, no matter how thick the walls of the fortress or the rank they held.

Twenty or more banners and pennons fluttered but Christiana saw little sign of the noblemen whose coat of arms they were. She wrestled with the urge to confront von Lienhard now they were safe. An outburst would bring those noblemen running, but no sooner had they been accepted into the stronghold than she and Agnes were separated from Henry and taken to where the women were billeted. Von Lienhard was welcomed and praised for his courage in bringing her and the children to safety and, as other women ushered her away to their quarters, Christiana's final sight of Henry was of him being ordered to join other young pages and squires who had survived – though from what the women had said, their numbers were few. He would be given weapons to clean and other duties to perform: she hoped one task would be to serve on tables so she might have the chance to see and speak to him again. Von Lienhard had glanced her way and with a noncommittal expression placed a hand on Henry's shoulder. There had been enough fear in her life these past days but the thought that von Lienhard might suspect that she or Henry had seen his acts of brutality closed around her like bands of steel. His gesture had been obvious.

If Henry was to live – she must remain silent.

CHAPTER FORTY-ONE

Perinne scratched an inverted triangle in the dirt as Blackstone and his captains gathered around him. He placed a stone at each corner and then pointed out what knowledge he had of the area.

'Up here on the left, that's Beauvais, and from what we've been told, Sir Thomas, that's swarming with these peasants. Across here,' he said, hovering a stick to the right, 'this is Compiègne, and we're between the two.'

'Paris is there,' said Blackstone, pointing to the bottom of the triangle, 'and Compiègne is a stronghold for the Dauphin. They have held firm against the Jacques, and we don't need to stir that nest – we'll have problem enough getting down to Meaux,' he added, jabbing in the dirt a few inches to the right of Paris.

Gaillard extended his spear shaft and gently curved a line that extended from the east of Meaux and then let it taper off as it nudged below Paris. 'Sir Thomas, we cannot go directly south – if the Parisians march as you have been told we will ride into them and I heard a man-at-arms say he was from a stronghold of Navarre's men at La Ferté-sous-Jouarre on the river. But where that is I don't know.'

'Perinne?' Blackstone said.

The hobelar shrugged. 'No idea, Sir Thomas.'

Blackstone looked at Gaillard hopefully.

The big Norman shook his bearded head. 'Upriver from Meaux is all I heard,' he answered.

'The gap for us to squeeze through is getting tighter,' said Killbere. 'Peasants on the rampage, Dauphin's men in castles and Navarre's men close enough to get too nosey. It's tight.'

Will Longdon squatted, chin resting on his fists. 'Tighter than a nun's cunny,' he muttered to himself.

Gaillard eased his boot against him. 'No holy woman would let you close enough to empty her pisspot,' he said, tipping the archer over. Longdon instinctively rolled and came up with his archer's knife in his hand and a snarl on his face.

'You stupid ox! I'll geld you and then cut your fucking throat if you ever touch me again!'

Gaillard took a step towards him but Meulon was big enough to block him as John Jacob grabbed Longdon's knife arm. 'Drop the knife, Will. Drop it!'

The archer's forearm was corded muscle and it took a strong man to squeeze it that hard. Longdon's glazed eyes cleared for a moment. He had been one lunge away from stabbing the Norman.

In that moment Blackstone regretted not bringing Elfred on this mission. The older man had the most influence over Longdon. Will Longdon had been at Blackstone's side since they had first run across the invasion sands twelve years before. Before everything. Young men, vigorous and scared, sworn to Killbere and the King, sworn to each other, and Longdon had wafted their fears away with disrespect and humour.

'You grow mean in your years, Will,' said Blackstone calmly. 'There'll be no gelding done among my captains unless I wield the knife.'

The men fell silent, but the tension was still evident. The aftermath of killing stirred men's humours, and the bile took time to settle.

It would take only a moment of madness for a killing to occur in the oppressive summer heat, and then there would be a hanging. Which meant that two of Blackstone's men would die needlessly. Two of his best.

Killbere broke the simmering resentment that threatened to boil into violence. 'I loved a woman who was a nun,' he said quietly, a seldom-heard hint of regret in his voice.

The remark caused the men to look towards him in a moment of uncertainty. Sir Gilbert Killbere never spoke of his life or offered any glimpse into his past.

'An aristocratic lady placed in a nunnery by her father to keep her from me,' he said. 'I was prepared to take holy orders to stay in her embrace.' Killbere shrugged. 'Alas, it was never consummated. I was unworthy of the Church. And her.'

He had sacrificed part of himself so that the others might not take a step that would tear this close-knit band of men apart. But there was to be no intimacy beyond that. He grinned. 'Will's right: a nun would be tight and, as Gaillard said, none here are fit to empty their pisspots. We are who we are and we have only ourselves to blame for it.' He kicked away the scratches in the sand. 'I know how to get us through to Meaux.'

They rested beyond the forest, where a stream provided fresh water and the trees security from any groups of peasants who had escaped the slaughter. Free of mail and armour, Killbere swabbed his face and neck with a cloth soaked in the stream's cold water. The summer heat was already fierce enough to make them wring sweat from their shirts. Blackstone sat half-propped, with his wounded leg exposed, as Caprini knelt in front of him and prepared a dressing; Bertrand, at last given more responsibility than caring for horses, acted as his assistant, boiling a torn piece of linen in a pot over the fire. The Tau knight had cut a strip of bark from one of the trees, and carefully separated it from the moist sap behind it, easing the fibrous thread onto Blackstone's wound. The cut was six inches across his upper leg and was already discoloured, now that they had swabbed away the congealing blood and dirt. He then gently padded the wound with dried lichen scraped from the rocks by the stream.

Bertrand looked over his shoulder from where he attended the boiling water and linen. 'Sir Thomas, I have skills enough from my time in the monastery to stitch your wound.'

Caprini concentrated on laying his dressing into the gash.

'There is no need to stitch this wound. A week from now, with the binding of the clean linen the flesh will heal itself and there will be no risk of infection. And if you do not attend to the task I have set you, Bertrand, I will stitch your lips. You do not speak to me unless you are spoken to.'

Bertrand turned back to his task as Caprini stood and inspected his effort.

'It is done. Let the air get to it now, and when the linen is dry I will bind it.'

'I'm grateful, Stefano, but we need to press on.'

'And we shall, but man and horse need rest and food. A few hours will do more good than harm.'

Blackstone would have protested further, but he knew Caprini was right. He nodded agreement as the Tau knight stood.

'I have bound it with fern leaf and strands for now.' Caprini nodded in satisfaction at his work and turned away. 'Take away the soiled cloths,' he said as he walked past Bertrand. 'Once this strip is done, boil them. We'll have need of them again.'

Bertrand quickly bent to his task, lowering his eyes respectfully as he followed the Tau knight's command and seized the bloodied strips of linen used to clean Blackstone's wound.

When he had retreated out of earshot, Killbere spread his washing cloth across a boulder. 'I wouldn't let Bertrand sew a badge onto a jupon,' he said. 'He'd have your cock stitched to your eyebrows.'

Blackstone smiled, too tired to continue a ribald conversation. 'Was it true what you said about your woman?' he asked.

'Does it matter? It served its purpose. Thomas, the men have no care for the reason, they follow you because of loyalty. But when they risk their lives for you it brings instincts to the fore. Once this business is done it might be time for your captains to be separated and given their own commands.'

'I know. I see it.'

'Will's an archer, Thomas. He doesn't give a dog's turd for anyone other than you and old Elfred.' He thought for a moment and then smiled. 'Do you remember when he pissed in the river in front of the French at Blanchetaque?'

'And you telling him it would rust your armour. Christ, Gilbert, that was a time.' He let the memory show itself to him again. 'It wasn't Will. It was John Weston. He died in front of me at Crécy.'

'Ah. So it was. I had forgotten.' He grunted. 'So many dead over the years.' He swallowed his regret. 'You archers, your insolence obscured your names and your fear. And I was glad of it.'

'I've known fear before and since, but I swear the river ran with my own piss that day,' said Blackstone. 'Will's all right. He's taken to being made centenar. He thinks – and safeguards his men. He'll not do anything to betray my trust in him.'

'Be better for us all if we could follow a flag of war and fight the French as we did. That's what we're best suited for.'

It was unusual for Killbere to reminisce. And Blackstone had never looked back over his shoulder to that which he had left behind, but the mood took them for a moment.

'I despair, Thomas. There are no great battles to be fought any longer. I pray that Edward will never reach a treaty with the King of France or that his ransom is ever paid. If it were within my power to send out heralds, I would have them proclaim to every French nobleman that they should gather their arms and renew their allegiance to their sovereign lord. And then they would gather on some vast field in their thousands, with ranks of drums and trumpets, and raise their war banners and show their colours for us all to see. And then we few Englishmen would form ranks, tighten the blood knot on our swords and dig in our heels to fight our enemy. Will we ever again see thirty or forty thousand Frenchmen shoulder to shoulder, armour glistening, honour-bound to die on the battlefield? Sweet Jesus! I miss it – badly. It tears at me. It was the breath that kept me alive. Now what do we have? Skirmish and attack, seize a town, slay peasants in an uprising, and sell our swords to the highest bidder. I want a war, Thomas. It is what I was born for. It is how I want to die.'

Blackstone let the moment settle and then said quietly, 'I made a promise to the King that I would make the Dauphin's family safe. It means nothing to me and I know he uses our efforts to further his bargaining with King John. We are expendable, Gilbert; by now he may have already sent men to fight alongside Navarre and what we do has no meaning.'

'We serve the King,' said Killbere with a weariness born of long service.

'We serve the King,' repeated Blackstone. After a moment of considering all that such loyalty meant, he intruded again into Killbere's past. 'Gilbert, how do you know the Marne and the towns that lie on it? We've more than a hard day's riding and we're going to be lucky to slither our way through those who can cause us harm.'

'After I went under that horse at Crécy I was nursed and then wandered wherever my sword found employment. I made and lost money. I went east. Local lords fought; routiers pillaged. I covered some ground. When Gaillard mentioned La Ferté-sous-Jouarre, I remembered there was a fine brothel there. At least I think it was at La Ferté. Too many of these French towns have similar names.'

Killbere stood and extended his arm to Blackstone, who grasped it and pulled himself upright onto his wounded leg. 'I hope you're remembering the right brothel, Gilbert. Whatever I do for the King I also do in hope of finding Christiana and my children.'

They made their way through the trampled undergrowth to where his captains had made their fire. A tantalizing smell of roasting meat caught their nostrils.

'Will Longdon's snared and cooked something,' said Blackstone.

'As long as it's not Gaillard's balls,' said Killbere.

A great heaving mass spilled across the countryside from Paris, its citizen army dressed in their red and blue hoods. With cries of brotherhood and victory they joined forces with the surging hordes that still inflicted their terror. Word had not yet reached them of the defeat of Guillaume Cale at Mello or of his torture and beheading at Clermont. All they knew was that they were now strong enough to storm the Marché and seize the Dauphin's family.

'He was telling the truth,' said Blackstone as he and his men watched the horizon quiver with the dark tide of peasants shading the line between sky and land.

'They won't get there before tomorrow,' said Killbere. 'They've no horsemen, and they'll wait until everyone is at the gates, but I'll wager they won't breach the walls of the city, never mind the fortress. They'll be out of food in no time, and empty bellies make for a poor siege.'

John Jacob and Halfpenny rode towards them with a dozen of the archers. 'Nothing ahead, Sir Thomas. It seems they're all where you see them.'

'Let's hope,' said Blackstone and spurred the horse on, racing ahead of the gathering storm.

Blackstone's men faced the mayor and magistrates as they stood before the city gates. These wealthy burghers controlled the running of Meaux and it would be impossible to gain access without their permission. For so few armed men to attempt to force their way past these officials would be useless; narrow streets and those who lived there would punish them soon enough.

'I am Mayor Jehan de Soulez. The Dauphin's family are secure in the Marché,' said the mayor in answer to Blackstone's question. 'Wife, and child, protected by Lord de Hangest and a small bodyguard. There are nearly three hundred ladies who have been brought here and twenty knights – men of rank,' he said, the insult intended and understood. He glanced nervously at the rough-looking men. 'You understand that your men have no permission to be in the town. That will not be tolerated.'

'We understand,' said Blackstone. 'We wish only to enter the fortress.'

The mayor considered the request a moment longer. 'Your business?' he said, his tone changing, daring to take a few steps closer.

'My own,' said Blackstone.

341

The mayor's hand went to his lips, a small nervous gesture telling Blackstone that he had not yet decided to give them permission. 'Before he left I promised the Dauphin his wife would be safe. How can I know you do not seek to harm her?'

'You cannot know,' said Blackstone. 'But would I commit suicide by trying to harm her inside a fortress, where she has a bodyguard and with other men-at-arms at her side, and then try to escape through your city streets?'

The mayor saw the sense of it. 'Our promise has brought us a burdensome responsibility – one that we did not seek.'

'Then you had better prepare to defend your honour and your city. Barricade your gates, mayor, because there's an army of Jacques several thousand strong a day behind us.'

The shock registered on the magistrates and the mayor. He turned quickly to confer with his fellow burghers. A decision was quickly made.

'Ride through at the walk, do not stop at any tavern and do not cause damage or distress to our townspeople. The fortress is across the river. There is a gate each side of the bridge. The first will be opened for you, the second on the far side must be opened by those willing to welcome you,' he commanded tersely and then turned back with his councilmen into the city.

Blackstone urged his horse forward into another city that smothered a man's soul. Its confines closed in on him as he took in its threat. These people were surrounded by filth, and contagion could take hold in a man's mind as well as his body. When a threat loomed the city's closed gates sealed its citizens into a tomb of their own making. If a drinking well became polluted sickness would follow, and when rumours took in the threat beyond the walls then panic would grip the city. Fear and claustrophobia were an enemy's greatest weapons against those trapped within. Shared cookfires, cellars and rooms were all any of these people could expect, living in a city. They existed with each other's stench and when pestilence struck they could not avoid its agony. Blackstone shuddered and yearned for sight of a horizon.

By the time he and his men had made their slow passage through the narrow, teeming streets, the sun had begun to dip behind the high fortress walls. Every man's eyes took in its strength. An assault would need thirty-foot ladders to scale their ramparts, but with the river encircling the walls the only point of attack would be across the bridge. That was its weakness. Put enough flaming tar barrels there and the portcullis and the gates behind it would yield. Then there would be no escape from within and although the long summer night was a blessing that held the day's warmth and light longer, that same light allowed the mob to get closer, and it was unlikely they would be stopping to pray when the bell for vespers rang.

Blackstone led his column of men across the stone bridge, Killbere and Caprini at either shoulder. He glanced behind him and saw that Will Longdon and his archers were gauging the distance between the walls and the edge of the town across the river. Fighting in the town would make it difficult to use bows, but a broad expanse across the river could give them targets in the open should they need them. Blackstone counted the stanchions.

'Will? What do you make of it?'

'Two hundred and forty-three paces end to end and another thirty or so for the open square on the town side,' the centenar answered.

'Aye!' confirmed a few of the others.

Somewhere in the confines of the castle a guard commander barked out an order to raise the portcullis. A vast yard opened up before them. This citadel lacked any of the sophistication of the great castles of France, but there was no denying that it could withstand a siege provided its well did not run dry and there was enough food. And that depended how many had by now sought shelter from the uprising. Stable-hands and servants went about their duties, some running from the commands of a steward, others keeping their heads down, pitching hay in the open-fronted stalls that lay along one side of the castle walls.

'You there! Sir knight!' a voice beckoned.

Blackstone turned to see who called him and saw an older man hurrying over. Fingers of white flecked through his hair and beard, his cloak was trimmed with fur and his quilted jacket sufficiently embroidered to proclaim his status according to the sumptuary laws that dictated how a man might dress according to his rank.

'My lord?' answered Blackstone.

'No room at the inn!' he bellowed, but then guffawed at his own quip. 'Stables are full, man. You can see that for yourself. Have your men use the tethering rings on the walls; we've hay enough to feed the horses – for now! You and your two companions,' he said, waving a finger at Caprini and Killbere, 'inside with you.'

Without another word the older man turned on his heel, then halted and called back. 'Archers eh? Mercenaries? Brigands? Don't get any ideas in this place.'

'English,' said Blackstone.

'Same thing!' the man said. 'We need men and in here you'll behave yourselves or we'll throw you to the dogs – before we're forced to eat them!' He guffawed again and strode across the yard, shouting once or twice to amend a steward's orders, cursing the fact that the fortress was becoming little more than a dormitory.

'Whoever he is, he seems to be in charge,' said Killbere, easing himself from the saddle. 'I can smell food; perhaps they've hot water to bathe. My arse aches and my beard crawls' – he tugged his helm free – 'and I swear I've more lice than Jacques on my head.'

Blackstone ordered his captains to secure the horses and to roll out their blankets next to the wall; there would be no accommodation inside for them. They were English archers, despised and feared, and no one wanted them close.

'I'll sniff out the kitchens, see what I can find,' said Will Longdon.

'No thieving and no trouble, Will. I'll see to the food. Stay here with the horses. See to them first.'

Longdon made a pained gesture, shoulders raised and arms open.

'Will, we're caught in this place as surely as are prisoners in a gaol. We cannot fight our way out, not with the town at our back and these men inside. I want no trouble. And keep Bertrand away from any women – not that I've seen one yet.'

The fortress's servants would likely be men, in kitchen, chamber and yard, but if there were so many ladies sheltering, then there would be female servants with them – and a lascivious monk, even a failed one, could cause a conflict that would be certain to end in violence. Bad enough that the noblewomen had been brought here to avoid dishonour; to have it happen within these walls would spell disaster. Perhaps he should have the grinning idiot tethered with the horses.

The three knights walked across the yard. It was cobbled in places, paved in others. This was no poor knight's stronghold: money had been spent on it. Workshops and feed stores leaned against the far wall. Men patrolled the ramparts.

'If the Dauphin's family are in here, Thomas, then our work is done,' said Killbere.

'Let's see it to be true,' said Blackstone. 'Every refugee here will have information – perhaps they will know of Christiana.'

Killbere and Caprini kept their thoughts to themselves. Finding Blackstone's family amid the turmoil of a ravaged land would be nothing less than a miracle.

CHAPTER FORTY-TWO

As they clambered up the steps that led to the galleried loggia and chambers, Blackstone recognized one of the pennons among the flags: five scallops set against a black cross, the arms of Jean de Grailly, the Captal de Buch.

'Beyard must be here!' Blackstone said.

'Who?' Killbere asked.

'De Grailly's man at the alpine pass. He saw us safely across France,' Blackstone told him and turned towards a pair of heavy wooden doors from behind which he could hear voices. Before he got halfway, the doors opened and the older man from the courtyard stepped out.

'Come, man! Hurry. Did I not tell you to come to the great hall?'

'No, my lord,' said Blackstone, conscious that the stairs had pulled his leg wound and that he limped more than he would have liked.

'Then I should have done,' he said, without it sounding like an apology.

As the three men followed him into the room a squire on the other side of the doors closed them. Blackstone's attention was held by the two knights who stood looking at a rolled-out map spread across a planked table. The huge granite hearth behind them was stacked with wood, but remained unlit. The men's cloaks lay where they had been tossed and Blackstone immediately recognized one of them. It was not Beyard, but his sworn lord, the Captal de Buch himself.

'Sir Thomas,' said de Grailly. 'Fate brings us together again.'

The circumstances did not negate the fact that a high lord such as Jean de Grailly would not normally conduct an audience with someone of Blackstone's lower rank – that he did meant either that Blackstone was there under sufferance on the word of the older knight or that the Captal had seen him arrive and had broken protocol out of respect for the Englishman.

'I saw you ride in,' he said, honouring Blackstone. 'And asked my Lord de Hangest to bring you here right away.'

Blackstone bowed his head, and then introduced Killbere and Caprini.

'I know of you, Sir Gilbert. You have a ferocious reputation. Always in the vanguard,' said the Gascon.

'I am greatly honoured, my Lord de Grailly,' said Killbere.

'And although I am familiar with the great work of the Knights of the Tau, I do not know Fra Caprini. Let us hope these unfortunate circumstances allow us to better acquaint ourselves.'

Caprini, gaunt and monk-like, barely showed any sign of being honoured and acknowledged. As ever his dark eyes expressed no flare of emotion, and as ever, Blackstone wondered what turmoil and violence lay cloaked beneath the sign of the Tau. The two other knights in the room were robust-looking men, their cloaks concealing their blazons. One of them, squat and pug-faced, betrayed an arrogant disregard for those of lesser status, the eyes of the other, younger by a few years, quickly assessed Blackstone, as one fighting man does another.

'This good knight is Loys de Chamby,' said de Grailly, indicating the squash-faced knight, 'and with him Bascot de Mauléon, who rode with us on crusade.' They nodded a curt acknowledgement of the introduction. Blackstone did not recognize the fourth knight in the room, but it was clear by his clothing and his manner that he too held high rank.

'This gentle knight,' said de Grailly, turning towards his companion, 'is our cousin, Gaston Phoebus, Count of Foix.' Blackstone knew that de Grailly was two years or so younger than his own twenty-eight years and the nobleman seemed more or less the same age. Reputations preceded men and these two were known across Christendom, de Grailly for his loyalty and fighting skills given to Edward, and Phoebus for his family's loyalty to the French Crown. Gaston Phoebus, though, had parlayed with the Prince of Wales during his great raid before the Battle of Poitiers that rendered France inconsolable, bereft of its monarch and vulnerable to the violence that had swept across it since. He was a great feudal lord of two Pyrenean principalities whose father had been a staunch supporter of the Valois King. The son, though, wanted independence for his territories and his antagonism towards the French Crown was well known.

'The Captal has told me of your daring, Sir Thomas. You once delivered up a valuable stronghold to him.'

'Some years back now, my lord.'

'Not in the telling of it. He relates it as if it were yesterday,' said the Count, his charming manner easily camouflaging his reputation for ferocity in war.

The pleasantries over, the Captal nodded to the squire, who quickly brought beakers of wine. 'You and your men will have food as soon as we hear of what you have seen.'

Killbere and Caprini drank as Blackstone ignored his thirst and looked at the map drawn of the surrounding suburbs and countryside. Blackstone let his finger trace from where he thought his route had brought him.

'Here,' he said, 'further north at Clermont, Navarre destroyed two or three thousand peasants. Their leader is dead but he told me that the Parisians have sent men to bolster the Jacques.'

'Navarre will block them,' said the Count of Foix confidently.

'No, he won't,' Blackstone told him bluntly. 'He pursued survivors from Clermont, but has now gone back to Paris to try to secure the city. He'll change sides again, my lord, you know Navarre. He'll strike a bargain with the Provost, even at the risk of losing the nobles' support.'

There was no disagreement around the table about the reality that they and the few men they had were all that stood between the Jacquerie and a slaughter of the innocents.

Blackstone curved a track on the map. 'We came down this route here, and there're probably several thousand Jacques heading this way.'

'Then we must pray that the Dauphin, although our sworn opponent in all matters royal, returns with his army from Burgundy,' said Jean de Grailly.

De Hangest tapped the table. 'Do not forget yourself, my lord. I serve him and his family,' he said robustly. 'And I've no great affection for the English. I led the cavalry against Walter Bentley and his troops in '52 and we bled beneath their Lucifer arrows. Archers are on the dark side of creation.' The older man looked directly at Blackstone, who held his gaze defiantly. 'But times dictate with whom we must fight, and which devils we embrace!' de Hangest added, teeth bared in a grin.

'Our differences are already set aside,' the Count of Foix acknowledged. 'There is a mutual agreement to save these women and children.'

Blackstone sipped wine, and cautiously ventured a question. 'Then you will not be here in support of the Dauphin, but rather with Charles of Navarre.'

The Count of Foix looked shocked at the suggestion that he aligned himself with the house of Valois. The Captal smiled. 'Thomas, you tease a feudal lord. We were returning from a crusade in Prussia with the Teutonic Knights when we heard of these noble ladies' plight and that they were undefended except for my Lord Jean de Hangest's bodyguard.'

The old man had remained silent. These young lords and knights were the strength he needed to protect the royal family. His own efforts had sufficed so far but if the townspeople failed in their duty, then his would become impossible to honour.

'Can you get your bowmen on the walls?' he asked. 'We need to defend the Marché if it comes to it.'

'The Jacques would have the devil of a job reaching us in this stronghold, my lord,' said Killbere.

'I like to plan ahead,' said de Hangest. 'I have the royal

household to protect and fewer than twenty men to do it with. There are damned near three hundred women in this place now. The garderobes stink, there are not enough servants to cater for them, no one bathes, except the Dauphin's wife and a few of her ladies. We've kept the meat for the women; we men eat pottage, cheese and bread. A siege would see us finished and a concerted attack would make this place a charnel house.'

'You think they can fight through the townsmen and still reach you?' asked Caprini. 'The mayor has sworn his loyalty.'

'Good Fra Caprini, you hospitallers have an unquenchable belief in a man's word. My own grandfather fought with the Templars, much good it did him, and your brotherhood of Saint James will no doubt one day be destroyed by lords and kings who once offered you protection.' He slammed the empty beaker on the table to emphasize his point. 'Men are lesser creatures than incorruptible angels.' He turned his gaze back to Blackstone. 'Your archers. Can we use them?'

'No,' Blackstone said.

'You refuse?' de Hangest said disbelievingly.

'They are useless to you, my lord. The battlements are high; there are only rooftops beyond the bridge. The only place to stop an assault is on the small square on the other side of the river and that's close to a bow's range.'

'If the peasant army attacks, and I do not believe they would breach the city walls, but if... then they must be stopped before they reach the portcullis,' said de Grailly.

'My lord, these are English archers. Their bows are near seven foot long; they would not be able to angle them over the walls. They could blindly loose arrows high and try to bring them down on any assault, but they would not be enough to stop an attack of thousands.'

'But they would cause enough fear and terror to make the bastards think again,' said de Hangest.

'Aye, my lord,' said Killbere, 'those yard-long shafts will put the fear of God into any who hear their release, but our archers have precious few arrows to fly. We took back what we could from the dead at Clermont, but there's not enough.'

The men in the room fell silent.

'We must hope the Dauphin returns in time to sweep clean the countryside,' said de Hangest.

De Grailly said brusquely, 'He won't. He wants Paris before Navarre gets there. These ladies' safety is in our hands. We will make the best of it, when the time comes. Thomas, see to your men and what can be done.' He raised the beaker to his lips, his eyes across its rim looking directly at Blackstone. *Just in case*, they seemed to urge.

Blackstone and the others acknowledged the two feudal lords and turned for the door. 'Is there any word of my wife and children?' he asked, turning at the door held by the squire.

'They were in Picardy?' de Hangest asked.

'Yes. Somewhere... I don't know where. My boy's a page to one of the local lords... I think. Christiana is her name. My boy is Henry and my daughter Agnes.'

'There is no one bearing your name, here. I'm sorry, Sir Thomas,' said the older knight.

Christiana had settled Agnes with the other children. A hierarchy had been established within the various rooms of the stronghold. The Dauphin's wife, the Duchess of Normandy, with her daughter, and his sister, the Duchess of Orléans, were kept away from the other noblewomen, many of whom were wives who had these past few days become widows of knights loyal to the French Crown. The rooms could accommodate no more than thirty or forty women and children and so the corridors were also utilized for dormitories. It was here, with an opportunity to have light and air from the courtyard below, that Christiana chose to sleep with Agnes. The women possessed only the clothes they wore and cloaks for warmth; some of the more fortunate had blankets, but none – other than the royal family – had any bedding.

She had not seen von Lienhard since they had arrived and, although Henry had been put to work, she had glimpsed him occasionally in the yard below and called his name; he had looked up, searching for her, and then waved. He was all right. The boy was working hard and he would soon be tasked with bringing leather pails of water into the corridors for the women to drink; she could question him then. Knights and squires talked among themselves and Henry was intelligent enough to listen for any clues that might tell when the Dauphin's army would return, or where next the Jacquerie had swarmed.

Earlier she had heard horsemen clatter into the yard, but there were so many women who crowded the windows she was unable to see out. There was a sense of disappointment from the women, who soon turned away, complaining that it seemed to be a band of ruffians, most probably routiers here to sell their services. Their souls were already sold to the devil, one of the women said, garnering agreement from those around her. Back and forth the women complained. What they needed were knights like the Captal and his cousin the Count of Foix. Thank God de Hangest had been left to guard the royals. But a bodyguard was sufficient only for personal protection. The Dauphin could not have known that dissent and rebellion would rise so quickly. A scorched earth lay beyond the city walls. Abandoned they might be, but they were safe – for now. And tears were shed again and again as the women recounted the savagery inflicted upon their husbands and children. Stories of escape inflamed each group as women comforted each other, while others took children to their skirts, refusing to yield to their grief in public, each embracing what was perhaps the only survivor of her family. Children had been raped, tortured, butchered, and more than once a woman's memory caused an inconsolable cry of despair to shatter the stifling, airless rooms.

Christiana watched Henry carrying two pails of water from the well; a brief glance up and a smile as he balanced their weight, stepping quickly towards the entrance below. She saw men emerge from around the corner where the horses were stabled and a

lurching surge of hope forced its way from her chest to her throat.
Half a dozen hobelars were walking towards the well, two big dark-
bearded men with them, and ahead were four bantering archers,
their war bows bound and protected in their linen bags slung from
their shoulders, but still with their few arrows held in their belts.
Fletchings uppermost, bodkin points down. These archers had a
swagger to their muscled gait. Cocky bastards, Thomas had always
called them. Cocky hounds of war, tails up and ready to fight. She
knew these men. They were the curse of the French. Loathed and
hated by every noble house because almost every family had lost
a loved one beneath their arrows. And the women who sheltered
behind her would soon be screaming abuse when they saw them.
But not her. One of the men had helped rescue her from the alpine
fortress eighteen months before and his face was as clear now as
it had been then. Will Longdon.

She raced along the open gallery, trying to stay ahead of the
ambling men far below, so she could see their faces more clearly.
The two bearded men were the Normans, Meulon and Gaillard.
The others she did not know. These were men who had followed
Blackstone into Italy and now they were here. Thomas! Her heart
raced from a mixture of fear and excitement, confusing her. She had
lied about her name, used her father's, and now it did not matter.
Uncertainty gripped her. Was Thomas even here? Longdon and
the others were Fortune's men. Perhaps the women were correct
– they were routiers. She lost sight of them as she ran into the
stairwell. Three young squires struggled up the steps, slopping
water from the pails. At the far end of the long passageway de
Hangest and three other men stepped out of a room, its thudding
door echoing down the wooden-planked floor and stone walls. It
was a long, gloomy passage – small windows barely giving light
to see; it was where the knights were quartered – an area kept
free of women. The men walked briskly towards her, faces still
in the gloom, cloaks billowing, their weight creaking the boards.
She could feel the vibration shudder through the planking. At de
Hangest's left shoulder was a thin, angular man with close-cropped

dark hair and beard, and a black cloak that seemed too big for him. On the opposite side was a man, almost bow-legged, with wisps of grey in his beard caught by the light, creaking mail and huffing breath, as if quietly complaining at the length of corridor. Behind all three, but head and shoulders above them all, was the shadowed figure that she knew bore a scar from hairline to chin and more elsewhere on his body.

Feet scuffed and armour rattled below the pageboys who had thirty more stairs before they reached the landing. At the turn of the steps below them two knights emerged, their gaze catching sight of Christiana.

'My Lady de Sainteny!' von Lienhard called, his voice echoing.

Henry turned fearfully, pressing his back against the wall as he waited for the Germans to pass. Christiana looked from them to her husband, who had heard her name called and pushed past the others, striding towards her. The bitter memory of their parting was banished in that moment of relief at seeing him. Some part of her wanted to scream 'Murderer!' at von Lienhard, who had faltered on the steps, sensing something had happened, but completely unable to fathom what it was. He saw her pull back the thick russet hair from her face.

Christiana smiled at him.

And then Thomas Blackstone stepped into view and embraced her.

Von Lienhard felt his breath punched from his lungs and staggered back a step as the boy next to him dropped the pails of water and cried out:

'Father!'

CHAPTER FORTY-THREE

The knights were gathered in the great hall, seated in a half-circle, having listened again to Christiana's accusation against Werner von Lienhard and his fellow German knight, Conrad von Groitsch. She had levelled the accusation the moment Blackstone pressed his hands into her arms and pulled her to him. She had breathed in his smell of stale sweat and woodsmoke as if it were an elixir, reigniting the lust she felt for him. Her strength returned, banishing the burden she had carried for so long.

De Hangest, Killbere and Caprini had stepped into the void as von Lienhard had lunged up the steps, sword half-drawn and a curse spitting from his lips. Killbere had blocked his attack, and de Hangest had commanded his obedience as Caprini's sword was already in hand.

Lord de Hangest and Jean de Grailly were the senior men in the room, but de Grailly and the Count of Foix held the highest rank. It was de Grailly who spoke to Christiana standing in front of them.

'You have brought a damning charge against the men who saved you and your children. We have heard of the enmity between Werner von Lienhard and your husband Thomas Blackstone. We must consider that you make such accusations against him because of this bad blood.'

Despite her tiredness from the previous days, Christiana braced her shoulders; she knew full well her own life was now in danger. She looked directly at the Captal de Buch. 'I have sworn an oath of what I saw that night at Sir Marcel's home.'

'Why wait until now?' the Count of Foix asked.

'I was a woman alone without protection, not daring to challenge the man who threatened my child with harm if I spoke out.'

'No one heard this threat,' said de Hangest.

'No words were needed, lord,' she answered.

'You could have approached any knight in this room,' said de Grailly.

'And who would have been my champion?' said Christiana a little too fiercely.

De Grailly broke the embarrassed silence. 'I would have defended your honour, as all knights here defend the women caught up in the terror,' he said, not unkindly.

She bowed her head. 'I spoke too hastily, my Lord de Grailly, but it seemed to me that the threat outside these walls took precedence over my own misfortune and judicial combat is to the death. How could I expect anyone to bear witness for me?'

'But now you place yourself above such a threat,' said de Hangest. 'Come along, Lady Christiana, what's all this? Admit you're wrong and let's get about the business at hand and see to our defence. For God's sake, woman!'

Christiana refused to be cowed, and Blackstone half wished she would show some restraint, keep her head bowed, act as though she was contrite, and still keep the accusation in place. But that was not Christiana. She stood as defiantly as had he on many occasions.

The Count of Foix smiled at de Hangest's impatience. 'We must let words define our actions, my lord. We sit as a judicial court.'

The older knight grimaced. He had been sucked into a conflict between this woman and the German knight, and he had no wish for it to be prolonged any further. His duty was plain enough: protect the royal family. He cooled his irritation. 'You lied about your name, so why should we take this accusation to be anything than another falsification?'

'My father was Guyon de Sainteny. I sought protection in his name as I had done before...' She hesitated, barely managing not to glance at Blackstone. '... he was killed defending France. My husband has many enemies and I had enough trouble at my door. There were others who rode at the back of the villeins but it was that knight' – she raised her arm and pointing accusingly at von Lienhard – 'who helped murder Sir Marcel and it was he and two other knights with him who took the silver from the chapel.'

'And who returned it to the Bishop here,' said de Hangest. 'In a true and Christian gesture towards the Church.'

'I am certain there is other booty hidden,' she said. 'The third man rode away before we reached here.'

'Von Lienhard's denial is corroborated by his companion knight, Conrad von Groitsch,' said de Grailly carefully. 'Their word against yours. This places you in a fearful situation, my lady. Think hard and recant before this matter goes beyond the necessity of a simple apology for mistaken identity.'

'It was him,' she insisted.

'It was dark, madam. There were hundreds of peasants in the attack and the horsemen would have been some distance from you,' said de Grailly, trying to give Christiana a way to change her mind, even to show doubt. 'You risk death if this accusation is proven false.'

'The moonlight could not hide him. He wore no helm and urged the rabble to slaughter. He placed the stake for them to burn a good Christian knight to death while he still lived. You have heard of the horrors told by other women; mine is no less terrible. These vile men provoked violence. The peasants tore a child from its mother's womb! Do you not wish to see those who countenanced this action brought to justice? These men are dishonoured!' Christiana's voice had grown intemperate, blood flushed her face, and Blackstone knew that her fiery spirit would not be controlled much longer.

De Hangest scowled and pointed a finger, about to discipline her, when Blackstone spoke quickly, delaying the moment.

'My lords, when we faced the peasants on the plateau at Mello, I fought a knight who bore von Lienhard's arms. The harpy blazon cannot be mistaken. He rode with the Jacquerie.'

Von Lienhard responded quickly. 'You attacked a man who bore my shield. Who is to say it had not been taken foully by another? For all I know my kinsman had gone to help Charles of Navarre – it is possible a brigand slew him and took his armour. Blackstone attacked this man believing it was me!' he said brusquely, mindful of keeping the semblance of a respectful tone in front of his peers.

Jean de Grailly stared at Blackstone. He could not show any favour in this matter, knowing as he did that von Lienhard was a master swordsman. Blackstone drew strength from the fury that lay within him when he fought, but the German was known to be cold-blooded in his ability to kill.

Werner von Lienhard could beat Blackstone.

'Thomas?'

'Yes, I thought it was him. As this court has already been told, my King denied him judicial combat at Windsor. And he and this knight who stands with him attacked the Italian Caprini, John Jacob, who is my captain, and me. The third man was also at his side that night. Von Lienhard has no honour, my lord,' said Blackstone, driving home the accusation.

The German was in danger of losing his composure. 'Blackstone slew my brother at Crécy – the sword he carries bears the running-wolf mark. A brave knight treacherously slain by a common archer! I should be given the chance to retrieve my family honour,' von Lienhard insisted.

'And that was twelve years gone,' de Hangest reminded him.

'And honour is not bound by time,' von Lienhard answered quickly.

There were murmurs of agreement from the other knights.

De Grailly spoke calmly, sensing that the hearing might cause dissent among them at a time when they needed to stand as one. The peasants were swarming towards the city and every man would be needed. 'Sir Thomas's actions were witnessed by noble knights and the royal Prince at Crécy, and he was justly rewarded. This other issue bears the gravest of consequences. If you are proven to be dishonoured you will die; if Lady Christiana is lying then she will be hanged.' De Grailly sighed with the displeasure of the situation. 'All right. Bring in the boy.'

Von Lienhard took a step forward, eager to press his case. 'The boy will protect his mother!'

'Stay silent. There must be no intimidation directed towards him,' de Hangest instructed.

A squire brought Henry Blackstone into the hall. He looked uncertainly at the great knights who sat in a half-circle, his mother stood before them in the middle of the room, his father to one side of the lords, the German and his kinsman on the other.

De Hangest beckoned the boy forward so that the accuser and the accused were behind him.

'We know the terrible events that occurred at your master's house and your part in saving your mother and sister from the slaughter. There is only one question we have for you.' De Hangest's gaze went quickly from son to mother and then back to the young pageboy. 'Did you see this knight' – he pointed – 'bear arms with the peasants and commit atrocity against your master or his family?'

Henry Blackstone looked uncertain. His answer could save or condemn his mother. He dared a glance at his father, who showed no sign of encouragement but looked sternly at him. He hesitated again. All eyes were on him. He tried to find the courage he knew had been with him that night – disguised fear that had given him strength.

'Tell the truth, son,' Blackstone said quietly. 'On your honour.'

Henry felt his father's strength reach out to him. He turned to the inquisitor.

'I did not see it,' he said.

CHAPTER FORTY-FOUR

Firelight flickered across the stronghold's walls as groups of men squatted close to the flames, prodding the embers, worrying the flames with stick or blade. The contest was due to be held the next morning and the hobelars and archers cursed the bastard Germans for their vileness and slaughter that had placed their sworn lord's woman in mortal danger.

'I overheard the Italian talking to Sir Gilbert,' said Jack Halfpenny. 'He says Sir Thomas cannot beat this man.'

'And you believe an Italian?' said Will Longdon, his face crumpling in disgust.

'Hearing is not believing, Master Longdon, I am simply relating what it was I heard.'

'What you heard, lad, was the utterances of a fool. A man who believes a man's soul can be saved by pilgrimage, a man who slays a transgressor, a man who has a past as violent as any man's, I've heard. Shit for brains is what you have, Halfpenny. Do not listen to your betters' tittle-tattle.'

Gaillard stood by the fireside, his huge frame casting a giant's shadow. 'Sir Thomas has a spectre inside him, a torment that gives that sword of his a power of its own,' he said.

'See,' said Longdon, 'even a thick bugger like Gaillard can see that Sir Thomas will slice that bastard up like a roast pig after Lent.'

'A demon can't be slain, you short-arsed fool, but those Germans are masters of the sword,' Gaillard said.

'And now you contradict yourself, oaf! Sweet Jesus, where's your loyalty?'

'Do not question my loyalty to Sir Thomas! I rode with him when he first learnt use of the sword.'

'Well and good, but I served with him when we slaughtered your lot. I can hear their screams now. French bastards.'

Gaillard bent so quickly that Longdon had no chance to duck. The big fist seized his neck and lifted him. Longdon wriggled, hands to his neck, trying to release the grip.

Meulon suddenly stepped forward from the edge of the firelight. 'Leave him, Gaillard. Leave him,' he said sternly.

Gaillard would always be subordinate to Meulon, even though they now held equal rank. He released the choking archer.

'You are the centenar, Will, and Gaillard is a captain,' Meulon said. 'There is to be no conflict among us. We serve Sir Thomas.' He flicked his head and Gaillard turned, and then he waited while the big man took his slow-burning anger elsewhere. 'Whatever happens tomorrow I will never allow Sir Thomas or his lady to die. I will take the shame on myself if I must, but if Sir Thomas goes down, I will kill this German myself.'

Longdon swilled his mouth and spat wine. 'You do that and we're all dead. Trapped in this yard like fish in a barrel.'

'There are not many crossbowmen in the stronghold, and fewer than twenty knights. No more. You think about it. If we have to fight our way out of here we'll need your archers.'

Robert Thurgood watched the two captains face each other. 'Captain, that's a dangerous game. We would need to have a plan, and Master Jacob and Sir Gilbert would need to be brought in to it.'

Longdon turned and looked at the dozen men who gathered around the fire. 'An archer thinks on his feet, Thurgood. If Meulon makes his move we will be with him.' He faced the Norman. 'But Thurgood's right. Sir Gilbert and John Jacob will have no part of it.'

'If it happens, they will,' said Meulon.

'Christ,' Longdon muttered. 'We're inside a bear pit here. Thousands of peasants out there, and knights of glory in the stronghold. There has to be a better way.'

'Then speak to me when you have thought of it,' Meulon said. 'Stand vigil all night – if archers think better on their feet.' Then he turned away into the shadows.

The Knight of the Tau sat with his back pressed against the wall next to Blackstone, who fingered a crust of rough brown bread into a bowl of pottage. Caprini was slowly sharpening the blade of his dagger, stroking each side across the whetstone, each silent whisper honing its edge.

'Von Lienhard has fine armour. I suspect it is Milanese. There is virtually nowhere you can press a blade between the plates.'

Blackstone seemed not to be paying attention. Caprini looked for any sign that he had heard and that he might understand how the conflict which lay ahead was made more difficult by the quality of the German's arms.

'I suspect the Visconti gave them to him,' Caprini went on. 'The cost of armour like that is beyond most knights' means. You will need to put him on the ground and then find a way to slay him.' He balanced the knife in his hand, letting the firelight catch its steel. 'This is slender enough to get between those plates.'

Blackstone still ignored him, as if concentrating on scooping the remains of the food and seeing in his mind's eye the fight that would unfold the following day. Caprini said nothing more, but laid the knife between them. It was there if Blackstone wanted it. Blackstone licked the moisture from his fingers and wiped them on his jupon, then pulled his cloak around him.

'You saw him fight at Windsor,' Blackstone asked.

'I did.'

'And he saw me fight the Prince.'

'As did we all,' agreed Caprini.

'He is a better swordsman than I am, isn't he?'

'He is.'

'Then you believe I cannot beat him, having seen us both fight.'

'That is what I believe, yes.'

Blackstone curled himself into his cloak. 'Then I have no need of your knife,' he said, and walked away through the lurching shadows.

It would be a fight to the death. A judicial contest sanctioned by the authority of both the Captal de Buch and the Count of Foix. If Blackstone faltered then Christiana would be hanged, thrown from the open gallery with a rope around her neck. Her body would be left dangling against the wall until the crows had pecked the flesh from her bones. Her children would be separated; Agnes would go to a nunnery and Henry to a life of servitude as a common man.

Blackstone made his way into the castle and searched the rooms where the women huddled, doing what they could to make themselves and their children comfortable. Blackstone's hulking presence caused some of them to avert their eyes. The scar-faced man who strode among them, candle held high, looked fearsome.

'Agnes?' he called gently. 'I am looking for my daughter,' he said to some of the upturned faces. One of the women timidly pointed towards the corner of the room. Blackstone called her name again. 'I am the child's father,' he said. 'You have heard by now what is to happen tomorrow. I defend you all when I fight. Please tell me – is my daughter here?'

A fluttering movement caught his attention in the far corner as a young woman lifted her cloak and exposed a sleeping child. Blackstone stepped carefully over the others to reach her.

'I promised Christiana I would keep her with me,' said the stranger. 'Shall I wake her?'

Blackstone reached down and touched the warmth of his sleeping daughter's face. She was deep in slumber, nestled close to the woman, her own breath rising and falling with her guardian's. He wanted nothing more than to hold Agnes to him and nuzzle her hair. She would run her finger down his scar, wrap her arms about his neck and the years apart would close behind them. His hand trembled.

'I have asked that they let her see her mother in the morning. Will you keep her with you?'

The young woman nodded.

'Then let her sleep, and when she awakes, tell her that her father came to her and will see her soon.'

Following Henry's testimony, Christiana was escorted to the dungeon. The cells were nothing more than iron cages and the conditions were brutal – rough straw her only warmth other than her cloak against the stone floor and walls that glistened with damp, but blankets had been given to her on the orders of the Captal. There was no need for her to suffer further, he had instructed. In a further act of benevolence, she was granted a candle for the cell, and another to burn in the passageway outside the caged door, and a mattress so that the daughter of a loyal French knight and the wife of an honoured Englishman might have some comfort. She had already made the unwelcoming cell as comfortable as she could. The mattress and blankets were laid out; the candle burned on a stone plinth.

'You should have stayed silent,' Blackstone said quietly, holding her close, barely able to stop himself from pressing his hands and mouth against her as his fear for her fought his lust.

'I could not, and you know it. No more than Henry could lie to save me,' she said, regret tinging her answer.

Her face pressed into his chest as she tried to control the trembling in her body. Blackstone tightened his embrace. There were too many words dammed up in his heart and mind and he could not find those that would explain his feelings.

'You wrenched my heart from me when you left,' he said.

She lifted her face to his. 'And the thoughts of my father... froze mine,' she said. She spoke without bitterness, but her sadness could not be disguised.

Blackstone felt the moment hold them. War had cast them together and its cruelty had caused them both harm. Despite his love, despite the need for her, the last eighteen months had haunted him. Her lips touched his own, her finger tracing the scar on his face.

He knew that she needed to release the clawing thought of her father falling beneath the Englishman's arrow but he could not stop himself from feeding his own uncertainty.

'The child,' he whispered. 'Where is the bastard? Did it live?'

Her body stiffened. He almost choked on his own crass demand, but he had to know. He held her, preventing her from stepping away from him. 'Christiana,' he implored her.

She nodded, and raised her face so that he could see without doubt that she would defy him if he pressed her to abandon all thoughts of looking after the child. 'When the Jacques came we ran. I could not travel with him and Agnes, so I paid the nuns to care for him until I return. I paid them well.'

It lived. He could not halt the squirming twist in his stomach trying to reach up into his chest. He wished it was not there, begged his mind to discard the thought. But it stayed lodged like the broad head of an arrow. All he could do was nod.

'I could not forsake the child,' she said.

'Does Henry know?'

She shook her head. 'He was already serving with Sir Marcel when it was born.' She took a deep breath. 'It was a boy. As yet unnamed; unchristened. There you have it.'

Blackstone tried to find words to cover his feelings, knowing they were unjust, but they still persisted. He lifted the hair from her face and whispered close to her ear. 'You're headstrong enough to ruin a man's heart and cause more grief than a thousand cuts.'

Christiana would not allow him to leave her without an answer. She had abandoned him once, had forged her own way with her daughter and illegitimate infant, and had survived. Now her life was in jeopardy and in her husband's hands.

'Then what's to become of us, Thomas Blackstone?'

Had anything changed over the time since she told him of the rape? He had hoped the pain would have seeped away, but it lingered, an unhealed wound like that on his leg. It had to be ignored.

'Much will become of us. Let us be gentle with each other and soothe away the images in our minds,' he said tenderly.

Tears welled in her eyes. There was no sob of release as he kissed the tear on her cheek.

'Our lives seem bound by danger,' she said. 'You rescued me from the German horsemen once before.'

'And damned near drowned doing it,' he said, remembering the time when they had clung together as they forded the crossing at Blanchetaque. That was before the murderous battle claimed his brother, and cut his own body and face with wounds that took him to the feet of the angels. 'Had it not been for all that pain, I would not have you,' he went on, and felt the tension ease from her body.

The candle's glow shaded her dark copper hair as he eased her down onto the mattress. He kissed the halfpenny necklace on her neck, felt her heart beating against her breasts. The other half of the penny lay embossed in Wolf Sword's pommel. His voice was barely a whisper. His throat almost choked with his love for her. 'We cannot be denied each other, Christiana. We are bound by fate. Why else am I here? What circumstance brought me from across the mountains, from another country, to be summoned by a Queen and pardoned by a King to send me into this mayhem and through slaughter to find you and my children? My God, I cannot extinguish a love that lights my way.'

'Agnes,' she said, suddenly remembering.

He soothed the worry from her. 'She is with the young woman who cares for her. She's sleeping. You will see her tomorrow. We both will. This night is for us,' he whispered.

She half turned, allowing his fingers to undo the laces at the back of her dress. She shuddered with tears of joy at his touch. His rough-skinned hands stroked her with a tenderness that released her lust, denied since they had last slept together. No man had been near her since her rape, and she had never desired any other but her husband. Her dress fell and took with it the years of passion that had been held in check. As his mouth found her nipples they fought each other with a rage of urgency that demanded satisfaction.

By the time the candle flickered in its own pool of melted heat, Thomas and Christiana's lovemaking had renewed their vows and, like two newly found lovers, they lay, embraced in sleep.

CHAPTER FORTY-FIVE

Too soon, the summer night gave way.

'My lord,' said the turnkey who waited respectfully along the passage as Blackstone and Christiana dressed. 'If you please.'

Blackstone nodded at the man and held Christiana at arm's length. 'We will be together before they ring the bell for nones.' He turned away from the woman he had loved since he was a boy sent to war. She waited for him to turn back. A glance. A smile. But in all his life Thomas Blackstone had never looked back.

The sun had not yet risen high enough to cast its warmth over the high walls as John Jacob helped Blackstone dress for the impending duel. The shadows were deep and still held a chilled dampness, and a quietness seemed to have settled over the yard. Fires smouldered where soldiers had slept; Blackstone's men came and went to the latrines and washed at the well. Horses whinnied, their weight shifting at their tethering rings; stable-hands filled feedbags and fussed them over the horse's heads.

'Who's attending to my horse?' Blackstone asked as Jacob tightened the leather strap on his lord's shoulder plate.

'Who else but Brother Bertrand?'

Blackstone grunted. The promiscuous monk had a strange calming effect on the aggressive horse that allowed him to attend it without injury.

'Good for something then,' Blackstone admitted, shifting his shoulders to allow the armour to fit more comfortably.

Killbere bit into an apple, grimaced at its sourness and spat the pulp from his mouth. 'Damned food will be getting scarce and these bastard townsmen are hoarding for themselves.' He lifted a wineskin and drank thirstily, and then allowed himself a low, slow belch. 'You'll wear full plate; arm and leg protection is not enough, Thomas. He'd cut through mail and with your injured leg you're already at a disadvantage.'

Killbere propped himself against the wall as Blackstone ignored him.

'Make sure Bertrand finds the best oats for all our horses,' said Blackstone. 'If the Captal has good fodder then we must get our hands on it as well. Have Will and some of the men steal it if we must.'

'Sir Thomas,' Jacob said, standing before the man who had once trusted him with his family's safety. 'You must –'

'No armour, John. Open helm, arms and legs only. I'll not fall face down in a damned iron coffin. I'll move faster than him this way. That's my advantage.'

Blackstone saw the look on his friend's face as he glanced at Killbere.

'Ah. No advantage, Thomas,' said Killbere. 'Judicial rules of combat. Both men equally dressed and armed. You're to wear armour. This is how gentlemen fight, not like a tavern brawl or a raid across the hills. Tournament rules! Time you accepted them. Bind his leg tight, John.' Sir Gilbert then scrubbed a hand across his stubble. 'I need a piss.'

Blackstone watched the old fighter saunter across towards the latrines as Jacob readied the heavy plate.

'Sir Thomas, if anything happens, I swear to you I will save Lady Christiana.'

Blackstone gazed up at the open gallery that ran along one side of the wall. It would not be long before Christiana would be brought out ready to be hanged should he fail.

'Don't let her hang, John. I don't want her choking and kicking her life away. There will be no time to reach her. Have Will put an arrow into her, and then protect yourselves.'

John Jacob nodded. It seemed Blackstone understood how poor his chances were against von Lienhard. 'You'll beat him, Sir

Thomas,' he said. 'You and that Wolf Sword have cleaved many a man from this life and that bastard deserves no less. Now, let's get this plate on you.'

Before Jacob could begin dressing him in armour both men heard the low rumble of what sounded like bees trapped in a barrel. They drummed and hummed until one sound rose louder than the others – a trumpet blared, and then another. Discordant and irregular, the hum became a roar and then one of the sentries cried out in alarm.

'The Jacques!'

The impossible had happened and the warning took a moment to sink in.

'Get the men and horses! Archers to me!' Blackstone commanded and ran for the ramparts. By the time he reached the narrow parapet he could see in the far distance beyond the city a dust cloud stirred up by thousands of shuffling feet. Closer, though, were angry voices echoing through the narrow streets, rising up against the stronghold walls. Beneath the town's overhanging buildings the darkness heaved back and forth and then spilled out like a burst gut, spewing armed men and women into the clearing across the river.

'Christ, they've breached the city walls,' one of the sentries said.

Blackstone turned back and saw Jean de Grailly buckling on his sword; the Count of Foix and the other knights, von Lienhard too, were running down the steps from the great hall. This was no breach – there were no flames, no cries of terror – the mayor had opened the gates to the thousands of Jacques.

Blackstone met de Grailly and de Hangest in the middle of the bailey – the place where his judicial contest would have started had it not been for the unexpected assault outside. Now men ran for their horses; swords and lances were being gathered by servants and squires, stable-hands saddled horses while shrill cries of fear from the hundreds of women rained down from the gallery on the men below.

A voice carried from one of the men on the ramparts. 'Bundles of kindling being brought to the end of the bridge!'

'They mean to burn us out,' said Killbere.

De Grailly was calm, his hesitation barely noticeable before he issued his orders. 'Thomas, your archers must buy us time. There are twenty knights here and with our few squires and your hobelars we number a hundred horsemen or so. We split the field. Lord de Hangest and I will take our men left with the Count; my Lords de Chamby and de Mauléon and...' He looked at the men and hesitated briefly again. '... von Lienhard and von Groitsch will ride to the right, and you, Thomas, with the remainder, cleave them down the centre. Drive through them to the city gates, beyond if we must. Spare none.'

'My lord!' de Hangest interrupted. 'I will lead. Blackstone may follow! My duty lay here before your welcome arrival.'

De Grailly was obliged to acknowledge the older man's right. 'Quite so, my lord. As you wish. Thomas, once a path is cleared have your archers move into the streets.'

'Their war bows are no use in streets that narrow,' said Blackstone. 'Sword and buckler is the best they can do.'

'Very well. Have them follow in our wake. Let them kill those who are left and burn down every house.'

'The city?' asked Loys de Chamby, the pug-faced knight.

'My friend,' said the Count de Foix, 'they opened their gates so that we and these good women might suffer the worst of fates.' The Count looked to Blackstone. 'Burn and kill, Sir Thomas. We must put an end to this uprising. Spare the cathedral and the religious houses.'

The knights settled their helmets and pulled on their gauntlets as de Grailly looked to the two adversaries. 'And the matter between you will be settled when this is done.'

Blackstone and von Lienhard exchanged glances and then each turned to attend to their duties and face the immediate threat.

Brother Bertrand ran forward with the bastard horse's leading rein. Its ears were perked, the boiled-leather breastplate hugging its chest muscles. The archers had raced to stand ready as Will Longdon gathered with the other captains around Blackstone.

'Hobelars with me. Meulon, Gaillard: Sir Gilbert will lead you and your men. Will, when the gates open we will strike across the bridge. There will be too many crammed on it to resist; before we reach the other side loose what you have on the far end. You know the range. You'll be shooting blind; have someone watch on the parapet for us below. That will give the horsemen time to cut through and into the streets. Then you and your men leave your bows, take up torches and sword and burn every house.'

'And them what's in 'em?' Longdon asked.

'None can be spared now,' Blackstone said grimly.

'They have brought the wrath of God upon their heads,' said the Tau knight.

'They've brought Sir Thomas Blackstone and his avenging angels onto them is what the ignorant bastards have done,' said Will Longdon.

There was a rising panic among the women, but Jean de Hangest went among them and reminded them of their rank and that their behaviour should reflect it, and vowed that no harm would come to them. The Dauphin's family were still secure, but it would make no difference if the twenty or so knights and Blackstone's men-at-arms could not halt the surge that would soon swamp the bridge. They would all die. Although the men numbered a few more than a hundred they had the advantage of being on horseback and well armoured, and the peasants in their stupidity were no more than an enraged mob. Blackstone had shouted across the yard where he saw Henry, sword in hand, and told him to stay with his mother and sister, to stand with the other pages and the frightened women.

A sentry on the wall cried out his warning. 'They've opened the far gate! They're coming onto the bridge!'

Blackstone looked to where Will Longdon's archers stood in ranks of three – a formation to lay down arrows across a narrow but deep killing zone. He steadied his horse, its withers rippling, head tipping forward, tugging at the reins in his left hand, eager to lead those horses that stood on its flanks.

The men-at-arms bristled with tension, crowding behind the Marché's gates.

The sentry shouted his warning again. 'Halfway! Hundreds of them jamming the bridge!'

Blackstone and his men were the vanguard; it was they who would drive the wedge through the mob and they who would be most at risk. He tightened Wolf Sword's blood knot on his wrist, saw Fra Caprini cross himself and smiled as Killbere hawked and spat, as unperturbed as if he were about to go on a day's hunting. He watched as Will Longdon and the others braced one leg forward, their first arrow balanced on the stave. He felt their readiness. Remembered being shoulder to shoulder. They would bend forward and then arch their back muscles to get the extra flight from their arrows as if their bodies themselves were bows – and then *Nock! Draw! Loose!* Sinew and strength and a skill honed since childhood.

He grinned.

Will Longdon saw him and nodded.

Dear Christ, it was good.

A rumbling thunder of the hundreds pounding across the bridge rose up over the stronghold's walls. De Hangest called for the gates to be opened.

Blackstone saw the mob in his mind's eye.

'Wait! Forty paces!' he called out. 'Give them forty paces! Then open the gates!'

De Hangest was about to protest, but saw the sense of it. At forty paces they would still be surging forward, the weight of those behind forcing those in front onward; to then open the gates allowed the knights to spur their horses. The clash of the opponents would drive the horse's hooves over them in a bone-crushing impact.

De Hangest looked up. The sentry raised an arm. And then dropped it.

'Now!'

The gates swung open and de Hangest dug his heels into his horse. Blackstone, with John Jacob at his side, and Caprini and

Killbere barely a stride behind, followed, gathering their killing instincts into a snarling cry. Those in the first ten ranks of the mob's wave faltered, their terror-etched faces mouthing curses, arms raised helplessly to protect themselves against the huge beasts.

For twenty yards Blackstone and his phalanx did not strike a sword blow, their horses' weight and their iron-shod hooves smashed through the body of men and women, whose cries were drowned by those horses behind Blackstone. Astride the war horse he felt its awkward gait adjust to the smashed bodies. Blood spattered high onto his legs and then, as the horde tried to turn and run, Wolf Sword began to swing in its rhythmic and graceful murderous arc.

Twenty yards from the end of the bridge wholesale panic gripped the mob as a flight of arrows suddenly descended into the bottleneck. The thud of steel-tipped bodkins, the fist of God hurled from the heavens, claimed fifty or more peasants. Screams and shouts echoed across the river as the cut of sword and axe made the bridge a butcher's yard of misery. The bastard horse snorted, its head down, straining to run faster, needing to be controlled, as, nostrils flaring, it smelt the blood.

Ten yards. Another whisper of arrow shafts.

Close, Will! Not too close! We're on them! Blackstone's mind yelled, fearing his centenar's miscalculation, his shoulders tightening unconsciously, expecting a yard of ash and goose feathers to run him through.

Five yards! The bodies jumbled and the three layers of arrows fell again.

Dear Christ! Too close! But fear became exultation – to be so close to the lethal storm, almost feeling their whisper on him. It enthralled him as the arrows struck and smashed their targets. And then he was among those who had no place to run except to turn and face the knights in a desperate attempt to fight with their backs against the buildings' walls, in the narrow streets choked with heaving panic. The taste of terror soured their throats as Blackstone and his men forged straight ahead into the city. Out of the corner of his eye he saw de Grailly lead his men to the left, their horses being urged across the dead and dying and the harvest of arrow shafts that rose up from the bloodied furrows of the slain bodies.

Will Longdon had timed his archers' strikes perfectly.

Blackstone felt the wound on his leg split when he and John Jacob jostled each other as they plunged into near darkness of the narrow streets. Red and blue hoods mingled with the rough cloth of the Jacquerie as the Parisian militia tried to escape with those they supported. Men were crushed against house walls as the horses pressed them; others could not stumble over their fallen comrades in time before Meulon and Gaillard rammed spears into them. Fra Stefano Caprini raised his voice to God and called for his past sins to be forgiven as he slashed man and woman beneath his sword.

Women and children screamed in terror. Mothers abandoned their young as fear erased any feeling other than self-preservation. The vengeful horde swept down on the townspeople who had opened their gates. A price had to be exacted. Children tried to run between the horses and were clipped and crushed by their iron-shod hooves. Skulls split and limbs splintered. Killbere plunged into a small square, cobbled and dark, where clothing hung from lines, and dogs ran yelping before the terrified mob, and somewhere in the dark houses babies cried for their absent mothers. He heeled his horse, an almost continuous movement in a circle, yanking rein and digging in spurs. The beast spun in its own length as Killbere lashed the Jacques with his chained flail, its vicious spikes tearing scalps from heads and crunching bones. So swift were his strikes that none could reach up and haul him from his horse, and he grunted with satisfaction at the efficiency of his 'holy-water sprinkler'.

The men-at-arms forced their war horses into the narrow alleys, their heraldic devices looming from the shadows, a final torment for the wounded and dying. No mercy was shown, no act considered too violent. The noblemen regarded vengeance and retribution as their God-given right against these peasants who had torn apart the fabric of their brotherhood. This uprising already lay bleeding on the plateau at Mello, its leader tortured and beheaded in Clermont, and now it would be crushed to death in the streets of Meaux.

Von Lienhard and von Groitsch fought alongside four others and then separated as they sought out those who had run into blind alleys, then turned back to pursue others in flight. Loys de Chamby forced a group of men into a boxed side street and was hacking them down; von Lienhard and his fellow German saw that he was in no need of help and rode into a forked street. Too late they saw the crossbowman step from a doorway and level his weapon at the French knight. Von Lienhard cried out a warning; de Chamby wheeled his horse but his shield was down, leaving the side of his face unprotected. The quarrel slammed into his helmet, punching through his skull, shattering teeth and blinding him. He swayed and fell, allowing the peasants to take their chance and escape. Von Groitsch spurred his horse after them as von Lienhard forced the crossbowman into a doorway. Unable to reload the weapon in time he threw the useless crossbow at the knight and drew his sword, but the German deflected it with his shield, leaned from the saddle and rammed his sword point beneath the man's chin.

Archers, each one carrying a sword and a burning reed torch, had run across the bridge, jumping over contorted corpses, cursing as they stepped and slithered through their gore.

Will Longdon gave his orders. 'Halfpenny! Men with you, others with Thurgood and the rest with me. Torch the bastards. Don't get separated!' he yelled as he ran into the nearest house and spilled tallow onto straw bedding, setting it ablaze. From house to house they went, the flames following them, casting the men's shadows higher. Longdon rammed his sword into a man huddled into a doorway, whose arms were outstretched for pity, a whisper for water barely escaping his lips as the burning took hold and snaked from floor to floor, seizing a foothold on each overhanging house. Like snarling lions the flames leapt across the void, clawing onto the dry timbers.

Will directed the men at his shoulder to go left and right. Kill and burn was his chant as he raced towards the sounds of screams and fighting. Breathless and sweating, he saw two knights beating off a mob of peasants, the savage cuts hacking limbs from those who raised their arms in a hopeless act of self-defence. One of the knights turned his horse and then fell without a sound as a crossbow bolt struck his helmet. Slivers of light cut the gloom and Longdon saw the German slay the peasant archer. Then the horse was spurred on and away into another side alley. Longdon ran forward. The French knight was dead right enough; what was left of his shattered mouth hung from his skull, eyes gaping, the bolt protruding through his pug-faced skull. Longdon reached for the sword, a fine weapon, but to seize a French knight's weapon when they fought as allies could lead to accusations of murder and looting. He thought better of it and crouched, seeking to find where the fight had taken the men-at-arms. Smoke began to choke the passageways. Longdon knelt to draw breath, wiping the grimy sweat from his brow; cries echoed and screams drowned all but the loudest cries of pain. Steel clanged and horses whinnied while somewhere ahead he heard a German's derisive voice barking at those he killed.

Houses were burning fiercely, forcing Longdon to duck and weave as a tapestry of flames licked across the walls. In the veils of smoke a horseman was slashing this way and that at any peasant who dared strike at him. Men wearing the parti-coloured hoods of red and blue seemed to be everywhere but the horseman was cutting them down efficiently, using his horse to wheel and crush. Some tried to claw their way into a smouldering house but could not escape his blows.

A baby wailed in the doorway. Longdon hesitated as he tried to keep the knight in view through the thickening smoke, but the baby's piercing cries finally proved too insistent to ignore. The battle-hardened archer dropped his torch and reached into the entrance and plucked the infant from the ragged bodies that lay on the threshold. Another few minutes and flames would lick down the narrow passage, drawn by the air, a beast that needed constant feeding. A dead woman's body half covered the child; perhaps she had tried to protect it from a sword slash and died herself instead. Longdon held the child to him, picked his way clear of the bodies, and took it a dozen paces away from the burning house. He could do no more than take the infant away from the flames and nestle it against the bodies of slain men and women. It would die, but at least it would not suffer the torment of the fire. He quickly ducked away as he realized what must be done to save Thomas Blackstone from the challenge of the superior swordsman. No arrogant-bastard knight would bring down his friend and sworn lord if he could stop it. A dead militiaman sprawled on top of those slain by the German, who now urged his horse down another street. Longdon sheathed his sword, pulled the man's crossbow from beneath his body and found the quarrels in the man's belt. Ignoring the dead body's sagging resistance he put his foot into the weapon's stirrup against the man's chest, hauled back the cord, settled his breathing and then the bolt.

Clambering over the corpses he reached the street corner, pressed his shoulder against the wall to steady his aim and brought the weapon up to his master-archer's eye. The swirling smoke funnelled upwards from the narrow twisting lane to cloak the German, who half turned, shield high, thirty feet away, the wide-eyed harpy's mouth screaming its silent delight at the slaughter, her talons seemingly reaching down to claw at the desperate peasants falling beneath the sword. Longdon felt a brief moment of admiration for the simple weapon that allowed a man to kill so easily at close range. The bolt slammed into the back of the German's neck, its impact throwing him forward across the horse's withers, startling the horse forward, deeper into the gloom.

Will Longdon threw aside the crossbow and turned back to find his men. There was no need for more slaughter: the men-at-arms had inflicted a biblical revenge worthy of any crow-black priest's exhortation. What he needed now was a drink.

CHAPTER FORTY-SIX

The day's killing ceased when the Captal de Buch and his knights swept beyond the city walls and into the surrounding countryside, where the peasants scattered in disarray, making it as easy to kill them in the open as it had been in the narrow streets. Once through the city Blackstone led his men in a great flanking curve that halted any retreat and forced many of the defeated Jacques onto their knees, pleading for mercy. The noblemen's code of honour did not extend to the murdering peasants and their retribution against those in the uprising was savage. Bodies hung from trees; every village in the surrounding area was razed to the ground. Some of the leaders who were betrayed by their own followers were hamstrung, left to crawl for what remained of their pitiful lives.

Blackstone turned back his men once he saw the rout was complete. He felt no thirst for revenge against the Jacques; they had taken their chance to seize their land and failed, and their punishment had been swift, their threat crushed. It had been a long day of slaughter and his leg needed attention. He sat on horseback with the Tau knight, their blood-splattered jupons testament to the close-quarter killing. None of his men had been killed; some had taken light wounds, but a barber-surgeon could treat those who needed it. Blackstone preferred Caprini's administrations.

'That will burn for a month and a day,' said John Jacob as the three men watched the thick smoke rise from the city. 'It'll stink like a damned hog roast in there.'

'A funeral pyre for the damned,' said Caprini.

'A stench you can't wash from your nostrils,' Blackstone told him. His leg throbbed and blood oozed through his breeches, staining darker and wetter than the blood of his victims. 'The nobles will gather their forces now. Let them finish it.'

Killbere rode towards them as Meulon and Gaillard gathered the men.

'Thomas! These noblemen have inflicted God's justice on the poor bastards, and I've no taste for it. It's not sport and it's not battle and I'm tired of it. We should get drunk and be on our way.'

'That we should,' said Blackstone and, ignoring the wrench on his wounded leg, eased his horse forward.

As they approached the city walls, they found the gates still open, and this time, instead of being met by the mayor and his officials, they were greeted by his body swinging from the gibbet alongside his officials.

'Arrogant shit,' said Killbere. 'Didn't like him the moment he opened his mouth. Let's hope he choked slowly.'

Making their way through the streets, they found a route that was not blocked by fallen timbers and flames, or choked with bodies from the assault. As they rode through the gate at the far end of the bridge Will Longdon's men were retrieving what arrows they could from the dead. Some shafts could be reused, but damaged fletchings would not fly well, and patient, skilled work from the archers would be demanded to repair them.

'You loosed so close to me I thought I was going to be shaved,' Blackstone said to Longdon, who was carefully examining a fletching.

Longdon grinned. 'You moved too quickly. I thought you would be doing more killing with that blade of yours.'

Blackstone nodded, looking about at the others, counting the men quickly. 'All safe?'

'You didn't leave us much to do,' Longdon said and began the walk back to the stronghold alongside Blackstone's horse. 'Most of the knights had themselves a fine day. Some of them are back and they're exhausted.'

'I hear sympathy in your voice, Will. Slaughtering the multitude is a hard day's work for some of these men.'

Longdon handed a wineskin up to Blackstone, who drank deeply.

'Plenty of food and drink to be had, though much of it's gone up in flames. Should've left some of 'em alive though, to clean up the mess.' He grinned again and reached up for his wineskin, but it was already at Killbere's lips. 'You're welcome, Sir Gilbert, it was only a drop to wet the throat of a hard-working archer.'

'Longdon, you haven't worked a hard day in your life and this wine is piss-poor. Find some ale, for God's sake.'

'Burning down a city takes time and effort, Sir Gilbert. And it's dangerous. There were times I near took a wrong turn and got myself trapped. Damned near cooked I was,' said Longdon with enough sarcasm to earn him a spew of wine from Killbere that he quickly sidestepped.

'Aye, we'll get you in the kitchens then if you're that good with lighting a fire.' He tossed the wineskin to the Tau knight. 'But your archers did a half-decent job at the end of the day,' he said. 'Make sure they know it. You're their centenar. Give them praise where it's due.'

The horsemen moved ahead, but Killbere turned in the saddle. 'And use that tone with me again and I'll have you cleaning the shit drains!'

Longdon watched the horsemen move past him, a curse on his lips but pride in his heart. His men had done all he asked and these horsemen knew it. Arrogant shits. Not Thomas Blackstone though, he told himself. Not him. Killbere's threat was nothing. It had to be said, was all. He burned with the desire to tell Blackstone that he had seen von Lienhard go down in the streets with a quarrel through his brain. More than anything did he wish to tell his friend that this was one fight that did not need to be fought and that he, Will Longdon, had seen to it. It had surely been God's plan to see Blackstone and his family reunited. And he had been chosen to see it done. Perhaps, he thought, he should find a priest and tell him that. An archer chosen by God to do His will. Now that would have Killbere choking till he dropped.

Blackstone turned to Killbere. 'He's an archer's man, Gilbert, don't chastise him too much.'

'You're too damned friendly with them, Thomas. They're archers, they need to know a man-at-arms cares little more for them than their skill.' Killbere grinned. 'I wish we had more of them and that's the truth. But you will keep silent on that.'

'You believe I would?'

Killbere sighed. 'You damned near pissed yourself when those arrows fell so close. And it wasn't through fear. I saw that. Christ, given half the chance you'd be back in their ranks whoring, drinking, fighting and killing the French. But using the sword is what you're bred for now, Thomas. What we need is a proper fight. Stepping forward and hearing the drums and trumpets. We'll die old men in our beds, shitting ourselves like mewling infants.' His frustration bubbled over. 'We need another war, and if Edward doesn't come at the Dauphin now and seize the crown then he never will!' He looked apologetically at Blackstone and shrugged. 'Is how I see it.'

'I will be sure to let him know your feelings when I see him.'

'I always knew there was something of a gossiping woman about you,' said Killbere with a grin.

They rode into the yard where exhausted knights sat where they had dismounted. Horses stood head low from hours of giving chase. Men's blood-flecked faces stared at him and he realized he probably looked no different. Servants and pages brought refreshments to their masters as knights dipped their heads into pails, flicking the sweat and water from their caked hair, dragging fingers through bloodied beards. Swords were unbuckled, gauntlets dragged from aching hands; horses remained as yet unsaddled. Blackstone had seen men as tired as this after battle and it told him how much killing had gone on over the past hours. Brother Bertrand ran forward to take the horse.

'Two knights killed, Sir Thomas, but there are dead as far as the eye can see from the ramparts. We are blessed by your return,' he said with his usual idiot grin as Blackstone eased himself from the saddle. He needed Caprini to dress the wound again. The monk noticed. 'With respect, Sir Thomas, you should have let me stitch that wound.'

Blackstone saw the cuts on the horse's flanks. One deeper than the other. Its muscles rippled as he laid a hand on it, its head turning, but held by Bertrand.

'Apply your skills to him,' he told Bertrand. 'Do it properly and you'll be rewarded,' he said.

'Reward enough to be with you, Sir Thomas,' said Bertrand, leading the battle-scarred horse away.

Killbere handed his reins to a stable-hand and muttered. 'That stain on his face is from kissing your arse.'

'Is there anyone you have a good word for?' said Blackstone.

'My King. I love my King. Who else is worthy?' he said and laughed, placing a hand on Blackstone's shoulder.

As they walked into the bailey the gathered knights turned their attention towards him. The Captal and the Count of Foix had emerged from the great hall. Blackstone's instincts warned him of an impending threat. De Grailly had no smile of welcome on his face.

Will Longdon led his men in from the bridge and saw Blackstone and the others crossing the yard towards de Grailly and the Count of Foix. The Captal de Buch said something, shook his head and gestured towards a knight who stood at the far side of the yard.

It was von Lienhard.

He had killed the wrong man.

Longdon's stomach knotted as the German looked towards the archers and then raised an arm and pointed towards him. His mouth went dry. Had there been a witness? Everyone in the yard turned to face him and he thought of how he might run. Murdering a knight was a crime that would see him swinging from a rope in the next few minutes. Panic gripped him. He turned to push his way back across the bridge when he saw the dead German's horse and the knight's body laid across the saddle being led into the bailey. It was the dead knight being brought into the stronghold they were looking at, not the archer. He sucked in breath. His panic subsided and was soon overtaken with bitter self-recrimination. He had failed Thomas Blackstone and now his friend would likely die.

'Sweet Christ, there has been enough bloodshed this day,' said the Captal de Buch to an insistent von Lienhard.

The blood-smeared German hawked and spat the sourness from his throat. His own blood was up from the day's killing, and he could see the Blackstone fared worse through his exhaustion and wounded leg.

The Captal looked with some disdain at the German. 'It is customary for those who fight a judicial contest to fast and attend a vigil through the night.'

'My Lord de Grailly, these are extraordinary circumstances. There are still Jacques to be hunted down and punished. There is a kingdom at stake and this matter is trifling in comparison. I insist it is fought.'

De Grailly knew von Lienhard had a good point. There was still work to be done beyond the walls. 'I have fought with Teutonic Knights and admired their courage and honour when on crusade against the pagans. But you would have this matter settled today, when the light is failing and we have done our duty? Sir Thomas's wound must be attended to. It would be honourable to withdraw until such time as he is healed.'

Von Lienhard seemed as gracious as if he had been invited to a summer feast. 'If he wishes to retire then I shall step aside.' He smiled at Blackstone though his eyes did not. 'I do not need him to be bear any injury in order for me to beat him. But his wife must recant her accusation.'

De Grailly fumed, almost forgetting his superior rank and succumbing to a verbal brawl. 'Well, Thomas? Will she? I'll not have her harmed if she does. And then this matter is closed.'

If he could convince Christiana to drop her accusation then von Lienhard would be free with his honour intact. Blackstone looked directly at each man in turn. These men did not know his wife, and Blackstone would not try and convince her to recant. 'This vile knight inflicted a foul death and instigated worse on a good man's family. My wife is prepared to risk her life and orphan her children to see him punished. There is no need to delay our contest. I will have my leg bound and take food and drink, if my Lord de Grailly permits it.'

The Captal nodded. Everyone was weary after the day's killing, and although the clear summer evening would last for another hour, the darkness would then be upon them. 'Have torches readied, and fires lit,' he told de Hangest. 'This matter will be concluded tonight. Bring the Lady Christiana out, prepare her.' He cast a glance at Blackstone. 'Make certain she has her cloak. It's a warm night but... she will be chilled,' he said.

Blackstone was grateful for his consideration, and inclined his head in recognition.

De Grailly stepped away from the two combatants and looked up to where the women stood in the colonnade. It did not matter that he privately believed Christiana, there were rules that bound men to their honour – at least in a matter such as this. The men below and on the ramparts watched him as he turned and faced the walls that separated the stronghold from the city beyond the river, where the sky still churned with smoke. If the night went badly, and the wind of good fortune shifted, they would be smothered by it.

'The wager of battle will commence in one hour when compline is rung! Let a priest be called and the oaths taken!' de Grailly called across the stronghold.

It was all that needed to be said. A man was going to die and a woman's life might be forfeit.

'Bind it well, Fra Stefano, I'll need it as strong as it can be made,' Blackstone told the Tau knight.

The Italian had cleaned the wound and applied a dry linen dressing, and then carefully fashioned the boiled leather from an archer's bracer and bound it to give the leg rigidity. 'You should pray before the oath,' he said. 'I cannot do that for you.'

'You can pray for my family.'

'I can pray for the world but sometimes God chooses to let His plan unfold without intervention.' He paused as he attended the wound and looked up at Blackstone. 'You will die when the time is determined.'

For a moment Caprini's grim countenance made Blackstone feel that the Italian man of God had a direct communication with the Almighty.

Brother Bertrand brought food and drink, and then washed Blackstone's back, dried him, and helped him into a fresh linen shirt. The padded jacket was still wet from the day's exertions but the fresh cloth next to Blackstone's skin would refresh him. The two men attended to him as Will Longdon and the other captains sat a few feet away.

'We can fight our way out of here,' said Killbere. 'There's no need for this, you know, Thomas. There are enough of us.'

'My men will be standing by the gate and I have Gaillard on the ramparts with others ready to raise the portcullis,' said Meulon. 'Sir Thomas, I will ram my spear down any man's throat if I see you fall.'

Blackstone stayed silent, letting Caprini and Bertrand fuss at their duties.

'Bertrand, did you rub down my horse?' he asked, ignoring the others.

'With handfuls of dry straw, Sir Thomas. I cleaned his hooves of flesh and mud, and fed him the best oats that Jack Halfpenny stole from the grain store. Your horse is an ungrateful beast. He bit me here,' he said, pulling up his cassock and showing the bruise and outline of the horse's teeth on his buttocks.

'That's him poisoned, then,' said Will Longdon, glad for the fool distracting them from the business at hand.

'You cannot die from a horse bite. We all know that,' said Gaillard derisively.

'The fucking horse! Gaillard. The horse!' Will Longdon said in exasperation, his own nervousness simmering beneath the surface.

How could the Norman still not understand an Englishman's humour?

The captains laughed, but it was forced, and even Gaillard nodded and grinned sheepishly. 'I knew that, Will,' he said giving the moment to the archer, and allowing it as a truce between them.

Blackstone was already fighting von Lienhard in his mind. The first strokes were vital. Caprini had told him of the German's efficiency, those calculated and well-rehearsed guards, each held for a blink of an eye, high guard, low, cut, strike and the turn on the balls of his feet as if he wore little more than a linen shirt rather than armour. His gaze followed the men stacking bundles of wood at each end of the yard that would be lit as bonfires so that the combatants might have more than torchlight held by men in the arena. A trestle table had been paced in the middle of the yard and a priest laid out a crucifix for the oath-taking. The *judicium Dei* – the judgement of God – would soon be decided.

Blackstone kissed the pagan goddess at his throat and stood up. The leg felt good; it hurt but the binding was tight. John Jacob elbowed Bertrand out the way and began to dress Blackstone.

'Gilbert, did you speak to Henry?'

'I did. He will be with his sister. He's a good lad. He'll not let you down.'

'I have no doubt of that. See to it that he finds a good knight to serve if this does not go well.'

'It will go as well as you expect, Thomas. You've fought better men than him, for Christ's sake. He fights like a girl with a wooden stick!'

The men laughed and Meulon stepped forward with Wolf Sword. 'I have honed it, Sir Thomas; its edge will split a hair.'

'Let's hope it will do the same for the head beneath it,' said Blackstone as Jacob strapped the armour to him. Meulon's beard opened and exposed his grin.

'I won't let him kill you, Sir Thomas. I'll hang for it, but your King and your men need you.'

There was a murmur of agreement from the gathered men.

'No. You will be hunted down wherever you go. I've told Sir Gilbert and John what's to be done if I go down.'

Killbere spat in the dirt. 'Thomas, we'll not interfere in this. You will stand your ground, Meulon. Sir Thomas must face his own demons, like every man here. But if he kills you, we'll kill him. Pure and simple. We'll pincushion the bastard with a dozen bodkins. It won't help you, being dead, but you can look down and see his tormented soul wrestling with the devil.' He took a breath and embraced Blackstone. 'I took a boy to war once, and then I rode with a man. You can beat him, Thomas,' he said emphatically. 'You and that damned pagan goddess will see him despatched to hell – helped on his way by Fra Caprini's prayers. Eh?'

The day's light had eased from the clear sky and men rammed burning torches into the stacked wood. The great red glow lit up the yard. In what remained of the city a church bell rang out for compline. The end of the day.

The Captal de Buch and the Count of Foix sat foremost on the benches that had been set up on the edge of the contest area. Bascot de Mauléon sat behind them with the other surviving knights and their squires. Jean de Hangest stood to one side. He had duties to perform before the contest began. An almost ghostly whisper went among the women who gathered at the colonnaded gallery as Christiana was brought out and helped to stand on a stool with her back braced against a pillar. Blackstone watched as her hands were bound and a sergeant-at-arms eased the noose around her neck, then looked down towards the Captal and nodded. When Blackstone was killed or forced to admit defeat through his wounds, she would be pushed over the edge.

'Right, lads, let's take position,' said Killbere. The old fighter would have the men placed around the yard. If they were forced to kill von Lienhard then they would need to be in control of the castle.

Killbere eased Will Longdon to one side and whispered in his ear. The archer looked up towards Christiana, his face ashen, but Killbere's stern look made him nod his understanding.

As Brother Bertrand was of no use to the fighting men he was instructed to wipe the smile from his face and carry Blackstone's helm as the Tau knight stood with him carrying the unsheathed Wolf Sword. Von Lienhard had a squire assigned to him and a servant who carried out the same duties as Caprini and Bertrand. They had not yet put on their helms and wore only their padded leather caps. Each stared unflinchingly at the other as the priest signalled them to stop before the makeshift altar.

The sky's deep blue mantle closed over the castle. Flames from the fires lurched higher as the priest instructed the two knights.

'Your mortal souls are in danger,' said the priest. 'You will both swear a solemn oath damning yourself to forsake the joys of heaven should you be proved liars by the outcome of this challenge.'

'I so swear,' said Blackstone and von Lienhard.

Both men were then signalled to kneel, ready to kiss the crucifix. Blackstone felt the wound tear; his balance wavered slightly, a slight movement that did not go unnoticed by von Lienhard. As was customary in a contest of mortal combat both men knelt opposite each other, left hand, unencumbered by its gauntlet, extended across the makeshift altar grasping the other's bare hand. Their right hands touched the crucifix ready to swear their cause to be just and to call upon Lord God Jesus to witness his proclamation. Blackstone felt the man's grip exerting its strength, a small act of dominance before the eyes of God, pressing the bones in his hand. He let it tighten and offered little resistance. If that was how the German wanted to impress him then so be it. Jean de Hangest, as marshal of the contest, laid his palm across their bare hands. The final oath was to be spoken so that all those in the yard and the women above heard their voices clearly. Blackstone tilted his head and looked over his opponent's head towards Christiana. His voice rang out across the void between them.

'My cause is to defend my wife's honour and to prove that her accusations against this knight are truthful and that his foul actions and deeds are evil, and that he is unfit to live in God's eyes.'

Von Lienhard could barely keep the sneer from his lips, and kept his gaze directed at Blackstone, uttering his oath like a direct threat to the man he intended to kill. 'I swear that the accusation levelled against me is false and that I have just cause to defend myself. I shall prove my innocence by this man's death.'

De Hangest raised his hand. 'Let it be in God's hands.' He stepped back, allowing the two men to get to their feet; the priest turned, made the sign of the cross, replaced the crucifix and began a quiet incantation as the German looked past Blackstone at the two men who stood a few paces behind him. The Tau knight and the monk stared back at him, as defiant as the man they served. There had been no occasion for von Lienhard to have seen either man closer than this before. They were many who milled about the yard, but he could swear he had seen one of them before – but where? He could not place the man and his mind gnawed at the thought. He was dressed differently than he remembered, he knew that, but it was more than the man's clothes that shielded his memory from remembering. It made no difference. It was one of those things, unimportant now. Once he had killed Blackstone he would approach the man.

The priest turned to face them and began to relate the psalm often spoken for the night-time prayer at compline. 'In te, Dómine, sperávi, non confúndar in ætérnum; in iustítia tua líbera me. Inclína ad me aurem tuam, accélera, ut éruas me. Esto mihi in rupem præsídii et in domum munítam, ut salvum me fácias.'

Blackstone had heard it in his childhood from the village priest. He never understood it, but had learnt over the years that it had something to do with putting his trust in God and justice. And, he remembered, it asked God to rescue the supplicant. He looked at von Lienhard. He had a light in his eyes that was more than the reflection from the fires. It was one of confidence.

Of victory.

CHAPTER FORTY-SEVEN

Caprini eased Blackstone's helm onto his head and tightened the double straps at the back to make it sit correctly, while Bertrand held the gauntlet for Blackstone to push his hand deep into its leather palm. He flexed his grip feeling the tightness of the metal joints that extended across the back of his fingers and hand. Wolf Sword's blood knot slipped over onto his wrist.

'He has raised studs on his gauntlet, Sir Thomas,' said Bertrand. 'They will tear apart your face if you lift your visor.'

'Since when did you know about fighting?' Blackstone said as he readied his crooked arm for Caprini to ease on his shield. The monk dropped his eyes at the rebuff.

'A warning is all, Sir Thomas,' said Brother Bertrand, chastened.

'I have eyes of my own,' said Blackstone, keeping them on von Lienhard as his helm was adjusted and the locking pin for its visor tested.

Caprini fussed with the helmet, and faced Blackstone as he satisfied himself it was as good as it could be. 'I cannot help you in this matter, Sir Thomas, and I am in danger of failing to keep you from harm,' he said, helping to settle the shield on Blackstone's arm. 'He is very quick with his feet, strong in his chest and arms, and he will attack first. I saw it at Windsor. And in the instant of you raising your sword arm to strike, he will come beneath the blow and use his shoulder to throw you to the ground. It will happen suddenly. Prepare yourself because your leg will not be able to resist.'

Blackstone took a final glance towards his men. Killbere and John Jacob had positioned themselves on each flank of the archers, who stood, bows strung, some resting their hand on their belts a fingertip away from their arrows. On the opposite side Christiana was held by her executioner, a grim look of forced courage on her face.

Everyone sensed that von Lienhard was the more skilled of the two men.

In a final plea Caprini put his face close to Blackstone's, his dark eyes locking onto the Englishman. Blackstone heard not the words of an avowed hospitaller knight, but those of a man more used to slaughter than to prayer.

'I vowed to protect you. Save my honour and take the knife I offered. Slip it between the joints of his armour, low, thrust up through his chest, use your weight, drop your sword at that moment and force the blade into his heart with all your strength.' His gaunt face tightened in its urging.

Blackstone gazed back into the man's dark eyes. 'I'll kill him my own way,' he said.

Fra Stefano Caprini raised an eyebrow, but said nothing more. Blackstone knew he would need a sorcerer's spell to be lucky enough to kill the German. He was a killer spurred on by the desire to revenge himself for his brother's death on the battlefield. He wanted Wolf Sword in his own hand and his honour restored. He was the Visconti's man and there were many defeats, also, to be avenged. No matter what cause or reason goaded von Lienhard on, Blackstone had too much to lose other than his own life. Much could go wrong in a fight and it would take only one hesitation, a single moment of uncertainty to allow a telling blow to break through the German's defence. All he had to do was survive long enough for such a moment to present itself.

And chivalry would die the moment the first blow was struck.

As the priest hurriedly moved away Blackstone and von Lienhard moved onto the unpaved area of the bailey, a place where livestock would once have grazed. The ground was now bare, trodden underfoot into compacted dirt, with what little grass remained pressed hard into the surface, ready to grow when the rains came and the hundreds of men stopped trampling it. Blackstone and von Lienhard stood five paces apart, each with sword and shield, each with a knife fastened to his belt. Their iron shoes scuffed the dirt, telling them where it was uneven, where an unbalance might be forced. The huge fires cast their light across the yard; shadows raised high onto the walls, the heat from the flames adding to the night's warmth and the sweat that already trickled down the combatants' spines. Blackstone clenched Wolf Sword's grip and tried to draw his opponent in, quickly looking down as if to see that the tuft of ground would trip him. Von Lienhard lunged, head and sword low, with no intention to bring down a strike from a high guard, as Caprini had predicted, the expectation being that his opponent would instinctively raise his sword, allowing the German to barge his shoulder beneath the raised arm and throw Blackstone to the ground.

Blackstone sidestepped, brought his injured leg back a pace, and slammed his shield into the harpy's demented image. Von Lienhard had the momentum and strength, but Blackstone's half-turn and shield defence forced the man past him, and as he went by Blackstone slammed Wolf Sword's pommel down on the back of his helmet. He felt the blow connect, knew it would startle for a moment but would force the German to bend at the waist, half turn, slash backhanded, cover with his shield and expect his blade to connect with the Englishman's thigh. Blackstone's guess was correct, but he was too slow to move out of the way of the scything blade and he was lucky that it was only the flat of von Lienhard's sword that smacked against his wound. Inside the suffocating visor Blackstone grimaced as the pain flared. It was a non-lethal strike, the pain could be borne and used to spur him on, but von Lienhard was already attacking again. Blackstone heard him grunting, forcing out his breath as he hacked and swung in a flurry of blows, his muscular build propelling strength into his sword arm. Blackstone parried his blow with his shield, deflected the blade with his own, felt the hardened steel bite as von Lienhard twisted, and somehow, more quickly than

DAVID GILMAN

Blackstone realized, brought the sword down, almost striking his
shoulder where even his armour would have been crushed and
weakened. He caught the hardened steel on his shield, felt it bite,
and twisted, hoping the blade stayed embedded. But von Lienhard
stepped back, ripped it free, swung from the shoulder, a great arc
aimed at a joint. Blackstone turned on the balls of his feet, the
blade tip whispering past his neck, and, as he tried to regain his
balance, von Lienhard struck again and again. The two massive
blows forced Blackstone to take the strikes on his shield, once
again rendering his own sword arm useless. Von Lienhard was
beating down blows. The blade's edge would not be the killing
strike; these were weakening attacks to smash away resistance
and destroy his opponent's shield. Von Lienhard was seeking the
opening, ready to thrust the sword's tip in and sever arteries and
muscle, bringing his opponent down so that he could be finished.
Blackstone could not move quickly enough. The leg's binding held,
but the wound protested. He knew there would come a moment
when he would blink the sweat from his eyes and realize that
the man attacking him would kill him in a few more strikes. He
was outclassed and everyone, including Blackstone, knew it. The
crowd was hushed as steel clashed and the dull thud of sword
meeting shield became a steady rhythm of unrelenting assault as
both men grunted and swore from their effort.

Killbere shuffled his feet, shoulders twitching as he fought a
constrained battle of his own. 'Jesus Christ, Thomas has not made
one decent strike. Come on, man. You can see what he does now.
You've tested him enough,' he muttered.

As if Killbere's whispered frustration reached him Blackstone
seized a moment as von Lienhard's sword swept past his head
and could not be raised quickly enough for another attack. Wolf
Sword arced down in a lethal strike that would have cleaved the
man from shoulder to hip had he not worn plate. Von Lienhard
sucked in air, twisted from the waist, took the strike mostly on his
shield, deadening the effect as half the blade caught his shoulder.
The blow cut through the harpy's outstretched wings, severing her

394

naked breasts. Von Lienhard's arm would have broken from the force of the blow and was saved only by the strength of his now useless shield. He tossed it aside and in the same instant threw himself at Blackstone, trying to smother him. Blackstone, still encumbered by his shield, turned on the balls of his feet, threw his shield arm around von Lienhard, pulling him close and beat Wolf Sword's pommel against his helm. They wrestled as if in a tavern brawl, Blackstone bringing all his strength to bear.

'I slew your brother!' he hissed. 'And I'll send you to him!' he goaded the German, trying to force more errors from him, but von Lienhard wrenched free, steadied himself, the ringing in his ears clearing although sweat near-blinded him. He shook his head, saw Blackstone rid himself of his shield and attack.

'Now he has him!' John Jacob cried.

Blood pounded through Blackstone's mind. A vendetta was being fought: two men, each fighting to revenge his brother. Blackstone heard the surge in his ears and the welcome strength from the urge to kill overtook him; this time he would not hold back as he had done with the Prince. He ignored his slow-moving leg, forced it to do things no wounded leg should be asked to do. Wolf Sword struck every blow with a power that should have brought von Lienhard to his knees. But the German's skill, powered by hate and evil, kept him alive. He deflected a strike and swung his studded gauntlet against Blackstone's head. His shoulder was behind the blow and Blackstone felt his teeth rattle and his tongue bleed. The sour, metallic taste filled his mouth and he spat within the confines of his visor. His breath rasped, but he feinted his next strike and as von Lienhard shifted his weight Blackstone's bunched fist came down like a mace, striking the side of von Lienhard's head. The spectators cried out as the German stumbled from the massive blow and Blackstone brought Wolf Sword up, ready to deliver a lethal strike.

A gasp went up from the crowd as Blackstone lunged and his leg buckled. One of the huge fires spat a cloud of sparks into the night sky – an omen of the devil's breath. Blackstone recovered, gripped his sword's blade halfway down with his left hand, used it to block von Lienhard's strike, turned it to pound him with the pommel, using Wolf Sword like a two handed-club, then jabbed its point into his armour, desperately seeking a weakness that would yield to its sharpness and allow its lethal point into flesh. The blade skidded and bounced off the fine armour. The moment had been lost. And Blackstone knew it.

Von Lienhard counter-attacked.

Blackstone stood his ground. He could no longer move lightly on the balls of his feet. The wound would not let him. It was only a matter of time now before the more agile knight cut his legs from beneath him and the moment he was on the ground von Lienhard would find enough gaps in Blackstone's poorly fitting armour to pierce. Both men heaved from exertion and heat, desperate to yank back visors and suck in air, but both denied themselves the temptation. As flames and shadows competed across the yard, faces in the crowd turned expectantly towards the German, anticipating a kill. Von Lienhard would take fewer than a half-dozen strokes to finish it now that Blackstone could not move quickly. The clash of steel was dulled, his own thudding heart and rasping breath closing out whatever cries came from the spectators. Men stood, fists clenched; women raised their hands to their mouths; other faces showed the rapture of conflict, as lustful as a man who desires a naked woman. Von Lienhard struck once, twice, half turned, three times, another, then a fifth. Blackstone couldn't field the blows quickly enough. He went down on one knee as von Lienhard's momentum took him a few strides past him.

Wait! Blackstone's mind told him. *Let him come!* His sword lowered as if from exhaustion. His head drooped, half turned so he could glimpse von Lienhard's attack as he moved, feet shuffling, gaining ground, finding balance, muscles pumped.

Von Lienhard came in for the kill. Blackstone was before him – helpless, finally succumbing to the inevitable. Through the narrow slit of his visor he glimpsed the man whose face he knew but could not place standing with Blackstone's men, looking directly at him. As if he knew what was about to happen. His face. That face. Where had he seen it?

And then it came to him. A half-lit passage in Milan. A meeting with Galeazzo Visconti and his mad, twisted brother, Bernabò. A door closing behind the man who had been summoned earlier. A half-glance in shadow. Those eyes. It was the knowing eyes that he recalled. That brief moment, less than a breath's worth, caused him to hesitate.

The man who had gained Blackstone's trust was the Visconti's assassin. A man of God!

It was the hesitation Blackstone had waited for. Hurling himself at von Lienhard, he bore him to the ground; the men grappled, but Blackstone's weight was on top. Swords were now redundant. Von Lienhard was jabbing with his dagger but finding no entry, while Blackstone yanked savagely at his opponent's visor. The locking pin had jammed. He straddled von Lienhard's chest, pinned his knife arm and rammed the heel of his hand beneath the visor. Once, twice, and then it gave, slamming upwards, revealing the spittle-covered and snarling face. Von Lienhard was strong and now he had air. He sucked it in, arched his back and nearly threw Blackstone off, but Blackstone balanced his weight, urging his mind to revel in the pain from his bent leg.

'Confess!' Blackstone cried.

Von Lienhard twisted his head back and forth in denial, raising his legs, trying to kick Blackstone's weight from him.

'Admit your guilt!' Blackstone yelled again.

Von Lienhard had lost. He would be taken and hanged. But where there was breath there was hope. With a desperate surge of energy he rolled his shoulder, pushed up his arm, forcing Blackstone's visor up, his fingers clawing inside to rake his studded gauntlet into Blackstone's bloodied face. Blackstone pushed aside his arm and hit him. The punch unleashed from an archer's shoulder muscles slammed into von Lienhard's face, splintering bones. He convulsed, gurgling blood through his shattered mouth. His skull was crushed. His arms flailed and then stopped. A shudder went through him. One blow had killed him, like a beast felled with an axe.

Blackstone pulled his gauntlets free and desperately sought to release his helmet, his fingers unable to undo the fiddly straps. He gave up, and rolled free of the German's body. His men were running towards him, faltering and then stopping, because the fight had yet to be declared. He heard a muted cheer from the spectators, and then eased onto his good leg, almost too tired in that moment to stand. He forced himself onto his feet, faced the senior lord and addressed the Captal de Buch. 'I have discharged my duty, my lord. I beg you to release my wife.'

De Grailly stood and signalled to the guards, who eased Christiana down from the parapet. He strode towards Blackstone. 'It is done, Thomas. Dear Christ, I thought he had you a dozen times.'

'He did. But there was not enough hatred behind his sword. I would have dragged him down to hell with me had he cut me.'

De Grailly and the Count of Foix looked at the battered man who stood before them.

'Let us hope there are no other brothers in the von Lienhard family,' said the Count.

De Grailly smiled. 'It's been a long, day. Thank God it has ended as it has.' He placed a hand on Blackstone's shoulder and then turned away to join the other knights, who followed him into the castle.

Killbere and the others gathered around Blackstone. Caprini undid the straps of his helm and Blackstone gratefully pulled back his leather coif and with his fingers combed the sweat from his hair. Caprini gazed down at the battered corpse that would be stripped and hauled away to be hung by the ankles until it rotted.

'You should have taken my knife, Sir Thomas,' he said quietly, without emotion, and then smiled. 'Better to kill with less effort.' He turned away to allow Blackstone's men to offer their congratulations.

Brother Bertrand watched the Tau knight walk away, then picked up the German's torn shield. Why had Caprini offered him his knife? What was it he whispered? he wondered. A man with a background like Caprini's, who now employed violence in the service of God, had deadly skills of his own. Bertrand decided that he should watch Fra Stefano Caprini more carefully.

The battered shield's image glared back at him, the chilling gaze of the harpy, despite now being scarred, seemed as defiant as Blackstone. He looked up as Blackstone stepped towards him. All the skill and brutality in the world was of no use if you hesitated against him. One mistake had cost von Lienhard his life.

'You served God's will, my lord,' said Bertrand.

'I fought for more than that,' Blackstone told him, taking the damaged shield from Brother Bertrand's hands. The wild-eyed harpy had borne down on him twice in his life, and each time the man who carried that shield had nearly taken his life. He had now killed two brothers. One who fought for glory and the other who murdered for gain. Good riddance to both those gods of war. He tossed the shield into the flames. The chimera twisted in the heat, talons curled, teeth bared in a silent scream.

Let that be that, he thought. He had been spared, as had Christiana and his children. And for that he was thankful. He made the sign of the cross.

And then brought the silver goddess to his lips.

CHAPTER FORTY-EIGHT

Christiana bathed his wounded leg as he lay with a linen towel modestly wrapped around his waist to shield his nakedness from Agnes, who sat on a stool next to him, not daring to look at the cut. She cupped her hands around her face, staring at him, shielding her vision.

'Does it hurt, Father?'

'No, it's only a small cut.'

Henry stood at the foot of the mattress, watching his mother tease out the discoloured skin around the wound. The Captal de Buch had given over his own quarters – less an act of generosity than many supposed. He and the other knights would soon ride out to kill peasants who still roamed the countryside or who thought to escape the noblemen's revenge by returning to their villages.

'Henry,' said Blackstone. 'Have you cleaned my sword?'

'I have, Father. And have seen to it that your braies and hose are washed. Your shirt is almost dry. John Jacob had the monk squeeze them out and peg them near the fire.'

'His name is Bertrand. And he's no monk.'

'But he wears the habit,' said Henry.

'Have you seen his tonsure? Unshaven for weeks. He wears the habit because we would not give him any clothes until he proves himself. He's a servant, nothing more.'

Blackstone grunted as Christiana's probing went too deep. She raised her eyes in apology. He shook his head. It was all right. Fra Caprini had conjured up a balm and bark dressing, and if he was cautious for a few days then the wound would bind.

'Go and speak to Sir Gilbert. You know how to behave with a knight such as he?'

'I do, Father.'

'Good. Tell him I shall join him soon.'

The boy did as he was told, and Blackstone could not help but notice how strong and confident he looked. He was lankier, but already there were contours on his shoulders and arms, muscle forming that would grow with him. He would keep his son with him now. He could serve John Jacob and learn to be a squire and fight.

'Have you seen the royal family?' said Agnes.

'I have seen the King of England,' Blackstone replied.

'I meant the royal family who are with us in this castle,' she said, taking down her hands from her face, but still averting her gaze from her mother's ministrations.

'I have not,' said Blackstone.

'No one has seen them. They have quarters that no one is allowed to go into, except the man with the grey beard who shouts at everyone.'

'That is Lord de Hangest, and he is here to protect them.'

The child thought for a moment, and he watched as her eyes gazed into his own. She seemed momentarily uncertain. 'I did not think that we would ever see you again. I thought that you had forgotten us.'

Blackstone reached out and touched her face. 'I have never forgotten you, and I have always prayed for your safety. And I promised you, that day in the mountains, that I would come back.'

'You were not there to protect us, though. Henry did. He was very brave.'

'Do not say such things to your father, Agnes,' said Christiana.

Blackstone raised a hand to stop her berating the child further. 'I had to travel a long way, Agnes. Over mountains, through the snow, so that I might be brought by God's hand to your side again. I know you were frightened, but your mother and your brother were there to protect you, and they have both told me how brave you were. I will be with you from now on. Our family is together again.'

She nodded, the explanation accepted.

Christiana knew that sooner or later the child would start talking about the infant that had been left in the care of the nuns. 'Agnes, take this, throw away the water and bring fresh,' she said.

'Yes, Mother,' said Agnes, taking the bowl of discoloured water, and carefully made her way out of the room, slopping its contents as she went.

'There won't be much left in the bowl by the time she gets there,' said Blackstone, allowing the deep sense of contentment to comfort him. When the dirt and sweat had been sluiced from his skin and hair, the bathing felt like a baptism for a new beginning.

Christiana finished binding the wound. 'It's clean and if you don't ride for a day or so –'

He shook his head. 'We're leaving.'

Her uncertainty showed. 'To where?'

'I have men in Italy who will fulfil my contract, but now that I'm pardoned by the King we'll go to England. I'll find us a fine home, in a small town or village, and I shall be the Prince's man. There'll be no threat against you ever again. Before then I have to finish what I was sent here to do.'

He could see that his words rankled her. She had made her own decisions these past years and was now obliged to do as Blackstone instructed. England had never been her home and her discomfort with many Englishmen had never left her, bred into her as it was with a distrust and at times a loathing for their warmongering. *England.* The very word frightened her. An island fortress more forbidding than this stronghold. It was not that she resented his decision. Her happiness at being with him again was deeply felt; what rose within her was her independent spirit that disputed his right to decide where and how they would live. Relent, she told herself. God has saved us all by sending her lord and husband to them. There could be no denying such heavenly power. She crossed herself.

She was a mystery, this woman, thought Blackstone. Her passion for him was as wild as his for her, but her piety was a bridle and bit trying to hold her in check.

'Then we will be ready,' she said.

'You haven't asked what it is I was sent to do.'

'I thought you would tell me when you were ready, Thomas,' she said.

He sighed. 'God's tears, Christiana, you're not the kind of woman to timidly accept what I say. You never have been.'

'Perhaps I have changed,' she said unconvincingly, winding the cut linen into another bandage. He watched her for a few moments, until her own look of defiance eased. 'I am sorry, Thomas. I will happily go with you.' She knelt next to him and placed her hand across his chest. There were more scars than ever – a map of white tracks and discoloured blemishes – stretched by his muscles as taut as an oiled canvas scratched with a quill. She pressed her lips to his, her hand resting on his cheek. 'I am in love with you as I was once before, but I am frightened now because there is another child that you have never seen, and may never wish to see. Still he is mine and I must care for him. If you tell me to abandon him and leave him in the care of nuns then I will, but that will not soothe my guilt, nor stop me thinking of him.' She stood up and smoothed her dress, willing her shaking hands to be doing something.

'You have not yet told Henry. And Agnes soon will,' said Blackstone.

'What must I do? Swear Agnes to secrecy or tell my son? Am I to abandon the baby?'

Blackstone got to his feet; the binding on the wound was good. He put weight on it; there was little to worry about, but his actions were buying him time. He did not wish to be reminded every day of their lives of her rape. Nor the emotions it stirred. That she had been submissive that night to save her daughter's life was something he understood but that had never been enough to wash the image from his mind. This was the moment when his life would change.

'I will tell Henry about the child,' he said, and bent his head to the woman who had always meant more than he could find the words to express. 'And I will tell him that the child is mine.'

Christiana fought the tears. This was no time for weakness. She had fought and killed for her children; she had not backed down from her accusation against von Lienhard and because of it Blackstone had saved their lives and brought them together as a family again. He had come close to death and now pushed aside his own uncertainty. He could make no greater gesture of his love for her.

She nodded, and gathered the balm and mixture.

His own misgivings melted away when she smiled and her green eyes sparkled with hope.

They would soon be home.

Fra Stefano Caprini watched as Blackstone made his way from the room given him by the Captal de Buch. His eyes followed the man's long stride as he made his way down towards the outer ward. His leg seemed not to trouble him, and the sword that had brought the German's wrath and thirst for revenge slapped against his thigh in its scabbard. No one would separate him from Wolf Sword until he lay cold and dead. The sword, though, would not be the prize. Those who sought to claim Blackstone's death would seek the favour of the Englishman's enemies. And after defeating von Lienhard Blackstone's reputation would grow even more, but there would always be someone who wished to claim the glory of killing him. What though, he wondered as the figure walked along the gallery, would Blackstone do next? Would he ride back to Italy or perhaps ally himself with de Hangest and accompany the royal family to another place of safety, one that had not fallen to the Jacques? He studied the confident, striding man. It made little difference: Caprini's work was almost done.

Beyond the Marché, the city of Meaux still burned and would do for weeks to come. Deep-seated cores of fire, glowing timbers that refused to die, continued to flare up as the tumbled buildings' wattle and dried straw walls fed them. Acrid smoke lingered and the stench of burning flesh was becoming unbearable when the breeze shifted. John Jacob and the captains had organized their men to clear the bridge of the fallen Jacques, tossing the shattered bodies into the river. Once that was done they followed Blackstone's orders to do the same with one of the narrow streets so that the Captal de Buch could ride unhindered through the city.

Werner von Lienhard's body was stripped naked, his fine armour taken apart by the men, once Blackstone had refused it as a prize. He had no desire to encage himself in armour worn by a man whose spirit might still cling to it. Each of his captains took pieces as booty, then a rope was dropped from the walls and the German's corpse was hoisted by his ankles like a slaughtered pig. Blood drained from his body through his shattered face, which congealed into a purple mask. Those who had witnessed the fight would tell their own tales of it and when de Grailly sent a messenger south to Gascony to declare that the Jacquerie were routed, word of the Visconti's champion's fate would soon filter across mountain passes and eventually reach the Vipers of Milan. Von Lienhard's death carried little meaning in the scheme of things and would soon be forgotten – news of the failure of the great uprising would take precedence. And that too would be pushed from memory as the struggle for Paris gave warning that the fight for France went on. Those thousands who had died were little more than stepping stones across France's turbulent waters.

Blackstone's men had earned their rest. They were given looted ale from one of the cellars and after their labours in clearing the bridge and streets were allowed a brief respite before Blackstone gave them further orders. The danger was mostly gone and the bowmen knew they had got off lightly in the killing. For once they had not been threatened by an overwhelming force who could reach them. They bantered back and forth about who had done the hard work of killing the Jacques. The humid day made it too hot to argue and the ale, a few days away from being spoilt, needed to be drunk. Blackstone's men lounged, as do all soldiers in all armies, grateful to go almost unnoticed as they watched the activity that went on in the yard.

Horses whinnied and jostled as their riders cursed and brought them under control. De Grailly and his cousin had gathered the knights and regaled themselves and their horses in their colours. Surcoats of red and green; blue slashes against a red diamond; sheaves of yellow, black, silver and white that sported bird's wing; spear point and cross bars of gold. The big, muscled destriers looked even more formidable with caparisons bearing their lord's blazon blanketing their great bodies. The Captal and his knights were dressed as the mighty armies of France and England had always done when going to war, a spectacle to impress and terrify their enemy, a great swaggering of pride that reminded the common man of his place in the world.

'Like a bloody fairground,' muttered Will Longdon as he and the other archers leaned against the walls, keeping out of the horsemen's way.

'You think there's any need to get dressed up like a mummer to slay a few peasants?' asked Jack Halfpenny.

Gaillard sharpened his knife against the stonework, watching the lords and knights prepare for their departure. He snorted and spat. 'Better to have a glorious death at the hands of a great knight in all his regalia than be taken by the sweating sickness,' he said.

'He's right,' said Thurgood. 'I'd rather take my chances with one of this lot than something I can't see creeping up on me.'

Will Longdon looked from one to the other. Holy Mother of God. Gaillard's eyes twinkled. The bloody Norman was jesting.

'You arse, Thurgood!' said Longdon, playing along with Gaillard. 'Everyone knows you can see the sweats coming for you.'

'You can?' said the archer, his brow furrowing.

'When was the last time you pissed?' said Gaillard, realizing Longdon had caught on.

'Pissed?'

'Aye. When did you undo your jacket, pull down your hose, take out that poor excuse of a dick of yours and piss?'

'First light,' said Thurgood, now looking more worried.

'And?' said Longdon. 'It was all right, was it?'

'My dick?'

'Your piss!' urged Meulon, who had now caught the gist of the tease.

Thurgood's words stumbled as his brain tried to remember. 'I... I don't know... it was dark.'

'Your piss?' said Gaillard looking concerned.

'No! I meant it was still too dark to see.'

'Oh,' said Meulon with a tinge of regret, and a look between Gaillard and Longdon. 'That's never good. First light is when the sweating sickness first shows itself.'

'It is?' said Thurgood.

'Always with the first piss of the day,' added Longdon, looking equally concerned and giving a sad shake of his head.

'Bugger,' said Thurgood. 'I never knew that.'

'Sometimes you can see it when you piss again. Not always. Sometimes though,' said Meulon.

'Aye,' agreed Longdon. 'Sometimes.'

'And it itches. Your groin, it itches, does it?' said Gaillard seriously.

'No more than usual,' answered Thurgood uncertainly. Who among them didn't have crotch rot?

Longdon shrugged and the men fell silent. They went back to watching the great knights yank their horses' reins as squires ran from one to the other, adjusting straps and tugging horses' caparisons.

Thurgood looked worried, scratched his groin and edged away. 'I'll take another piss,' he said.

The others ignored him, except Longdon who barely gave him a glance. 'Good idea,' he said disinterestedly.

Thurgood nodded and walked on, then stopped halfway across the yard and turned. 'What am I looking for?' he called back.

'A fool with his cock in his hand!' shouted Longdon and joined the others as they guffawed.

Their laughter faltered when Blackstone and Killbere strode towards them.

'Here we go,' said Longdon, and then called to an embarrassed Thurgood. 'Get your arse back here!'

Blackstone stopped in front of de Graily to speak to the young lord, gripping the horse's bridle to steady it.

Killbere made his way to the men and spoke quickly. 'Sir Thomas will tell Lord de Hangest that we will accompany the royal family to Compiègne. It never yielded to the Jacques and the Dauphin's family will be safe there.'

'He's not coming for them, then?' asked John Jacob.

'If he couldn't bother his arse when the Jacques threatened them he won't be here now, will he?' said Will Longdon.

Killbere looked over his shoulder as the knights began forming into a column of pairs behind Jean de Graily and the Count of Foix. 'You lads listen carefully. These lords and men-at-arms are riding out and we don't know where the Dauphin's army is. It would have been better to have them with us, but each day brings its own troubles. We'll escort the women and children as far as we can, but if the Frenchies get behind us we don't have a rat's arse chance of outrunning them. And there's no guarantee that Lord de Hangest will even agree to Sir Thomas's proposal, but he's no fool and we outnumber him, so he'll go along with it, is my guess.'

Meulon spoke for the other captains. 'Sir Gilbert, if we take the Dauphin's family to safety, that would buy us mercy if we were trapped by his troops.'

'Sir Thomas once swore to kill the King of France. You think his son will forget that? Our own sovereign might have pardoned him, but Sir Thomas's life is still forfeit if the Dauphin snares him. We're of little interest to anyone. Sacrificing us is not worth a damn.' He looked from man to man. 'Who among us would not be hanged if caught? Our King still wants France. Those knights will go and slaughter until they tire of it, then they'll be at Navarre's side fighting for Paris.' He blew his nose and wiped his beard with the back of his hand. 'Keep a tight rein on your men. Outriders and scouts, and a rearguard of hobelars,' he said, looking at Meulon and Gaillard. 'We look to ourselves, lads. This business is not yet over.'

De Grailly leaned down from his saddle, his visor raised. 'You cannot stay here, you know that, Thomas. And my word can no longer protect you.'

'I am fortunate, my lord, that you were here. Without you we would all have fallen beneath the knives and staves of the Jacques.'

'It was a shared fight that's almost done. Join us, Thomas. I will find Navarre once we've strung up a few more peasants.'

Blackstone shook his head. 'Do not venture into Paris, my lord. I told Edward the same thing. While you go to kill more Jacques, Navarre will strike a bargain with their leaders in the city. You will be trapped in those streets.' He let the horse snuffle his hand, and smiled up at the Captal de Buch. 'Besides, I have yet to fulfil my task, set for me by the King.'

De Grailly nodded. This common man had a way about him that could scratch a high lord's pride. He was courteous enough, but his shield's device was a plain message to all, high lord or common man: *Défiant à la mort*. Well, thought de Grailly, impertinence and defiance were usually as necessary as a fist in a gauntlet. And that defiance, even knowing that von Lienhard had been the better swordsman, had enabled this Englishman – trusting in God, or his own strength – to defeat him. Blackstone had proved the better man.

'I've already spoken with Lord de Hangest. He's with the Duchess now. They know they must leave and that the danger has mostly passed, but he's afraid of Navarre. I have lent a few knights to escort the other women and children back to their homes – or what is left of them. They must salvage what they can of their lives. He and the bodyguard will escort the Duchess and the royal family elsewhere.'

'Compiègne,' said Blackstone.

409

De Grailly nodded. 'The most obvious place, but the safest.' He gathered the reins and settled his shield. 'You are encumbered by a duty that binds us all, but now you carry the added burden of a family.'

'No burden, my lord,' Blackstone said and smiled. 'I shall be back in England soon, and my family with me. Then we are all safe.'

De Grailly cast him a look that was almost of sympathy. 'We're none of us ever safe, Thomas. Not while we live.'

Blackstone released his grip on the horse's bridle and stepped back as de Grailly spurred his horse beneath the portcullis, followed by the Count of Foix and the other knights. Within moments the ward was desolate of men. Servants and squires had galloped behind their lords; the stronghold had only a steward and a handful of people left to see to its administration. Piles of steaming horse dung lay where moments before the great war horses had stood. The yard was eerily silent.

'There it is, then,' Will Longdon muttered. 'We're left with the shit again.'

CHAPTER FORTY-NINE

Within the hour Blackstone's men were ready to venture beyond the city walls. Supplies had been foraged and stowed securely in saddle panniers. Will Longdon's men had retrieved and cleaned what arrows they could. The goose feathers in the fletchings were damaged and it would take a skilled fletcher to repair them, so one had to be found. And Blackstone knew that sooner or later he would have to get back to Calais, unless he could barter a barrel of arrows from the English routiers who rode with Charles of Navarre.

What Blackstone really needed was to stay out of trouble.

De Hangest beckoned him to a door that led to the solar where the Dauphin's wife and family waited, being readied to leave the stronghold.

'You should have joined the Captal's men and escorted the other women away from this place,' he said. 'I have no desire to have a mixed force of English and Normans at my back.'

Through the gap in the door Blackstone glimpsed a child no older than Agnes, an embroidered lace cap holding her hair in place as she ran across the room to one of the ladies-in-waiting, who gently rebuked her for her excitement. The other women in the room turned at the sound of their protector's voice and, catching sight of the tall Englishman, quickly ushered the child out of sight.

'Was that the King's child Isabelle?' Blackstone asked.

'Those under my care are no concern of yours, Sir Thomas. I have no need of you or your men.' He pulled the door to, shielding the few women who accompanied the Duchess from Blackstone's gaze.

Blackstone glanced down as the survivors of the terror were helped into wagons by the remainder of de Grailly's men. 'The Duchess might be thought to be among those women who are being escorted. Was that the intention?'

'We are not using those innocents as bait for any Jacques who might remain.'

'But you are using one of the royal wagons,' said Blackstone as the slow-moving procession of knights and women trundled through the gates.

De Hangest watched them leave. 'It can do little more than attract attention from those who scout for Navarre. The Jacques are finished and I need a day's ride to take my charges to safety.'

'My lord, the King of England desires nothing more than their well-being, in a place of safety. It is why I came in search of them. Isabelle is the King of France's daughter and if she is safe then he will reach out to his people and raise the ransom demanded by my King.'

De Hangest scowled in disdain and turned away. 'You're a fool, Sir Thomas! Sooner or later the Dauphin will come for his family and his sister. She is close to the bosom of this family! You think the King of England cares about a nine-year-old child? He cares about the crown! He seizes Isabelle and he holds the key to a King's heart. There's a war to be fought, can't you see that?'

Blackstone matched his stride. 'What war? What armies? Navarre? He's as slippery as an eel and he'll bargain with the devil. Who knows how many troops the Dauphin has gathered from Burgundy? It's your King who will decide the fate of France.'

'It's yours who strangles us with sons of iniquity like you and your men and a self-serving Navarre who does your sovereign's dirty work. Navarre thinks he is grasping the French crown by going into Paris – he is doing what your King cannot do, but the strings are being pulled by Edward! Navarre and the routiers he uses are at the behest of your King! Yours! You won a damned battle and you seized our sovereign and we will pay. But you will not take this child!'

Blackstone watched as de Hangest stalked away.

'I will follow you!' Blackstone called after him. 'You have my word that I am commanded only to make certain they are in a place of safety. Nothing more!' His voice echoed down the passage.

De Hangest turned. For a moment Blackstone thought he had relented. His shoulders slumped; his head shook as if in defeat. 'Sir Thomas,' he said more gently, 'your word is your honour and there is no dispute in that. You are a warrior, and you see how a contest might be fought and a campaign determined, but you do not grasp the politics of it all.' He sighed. 'You will see.' He left Blackstone standing in the passage. The silence of the castle was broken only by the older man's hurried footfalls.

There would be no shame in riding back to Calais now. The Dauphin's family and the French King's daughter were in safe hands. The family would be in Compiègne within hours, behind walls that had not been breached, while the Dauphin tried to outmanoeuvre Navarre and regain Paris. Promises would be made and then revoked – broken by stealth or by brute force. De Hangest was correct. It was politics that would undo the fighting men. No soldier saw the great battles; he saw only those who lived and died at the end of his sword – as blinkered as the view through a helm's visor.

Seek out and secure their safety. The King of England's words whispered across France and through these darkened corridors. Blackstone was barely a day's slow ride away from fulfilling his duty.

It was nothing.

Everything was prepared. De Hangest led his men beyond the city walls, men each side of the two royal wagons. The Dauphin's coat of arms was hidden by draped sackcloth and, with no pennons or banners flying, the bodyguard left without fanfare, unlike de Grailly's departure hours earlier. Blackstone waited until they could see from the stronghold's battlements that de Hangest was a mile beyond the walls of Meaux. Killbere and Blackstone would

413

lead with John Jacob, Meulon and Gaillard, taking their men on the flanks with Will Longdon's archers bringing up the rear. Despite the scarcity of arrows, there were a half-dozen shafts per man and, with thirty archers, that could be enough to deter any small bands of Jacques they might stumble upon.

Brother Bertrand ran here and there bringing forward horses, tightening cinches, checking saddlebags, wanting nothing more than to please the men who had allowed him to accompany them. Tolerance was not always forthcoming. Killbere cuffed him around the head as he attempted to take in his horse's bridle a notch.

'You keep your cunny hands away from my horse!' Killbere said as Bertrand shied away from a well-placed kick for his troubles.

As the men mounted, Jack Halfpenny dared raise his voice. 'Best watch for crabs now, Sir Gilbert!' Those around him smiled, but none wished to tread too closely on Killbere's goodwill before they took themselves from the safety of the walls. The Jacquerie might be a spent force, but there were enough Frenchmen gathering into an army somewhere out there, and Killbere's mood was always uncertain at best.

'You'll have the right to jest with me when I've felt your blood splash across my boots. You say you were at Poitiers?'

'Aye, my lord. Me and Robert, both,' said Halfpenny nervously, nodding towards Thurgood at his side.

'Not with me you weren't,' said Killbere, gathering the reins. 'And not at Blanchetaque, nor Crécy. Will?' Killbere called to Longdon with uncommon friendliness. 'We were there, were we not?'

'We were, Sir Gilbert,' Longdon answered, basking in the great knight's benevolent tone.

'You think my horse is in danger from the unholy monk and his crabs?'

'I'd say they've already crawled beneath the saddle blanket and are nesting in your crotch.'

Killbere laughed, as did the others who had served together

over the years. Halfpenny and Thurgood smiled ruefully. It was nothing new to face the jibes of men who had fought shoulder to shoulder and lived to tell the tale.

Killbere twisted in the saddle. 'We'll keep well back from the French escort. They're nervous of us for some reason.'

The men jeered. Killbere's good humour served them well. After they had undertaken this final task, their world would be better because their sworn lord, Thomas Blackstone, would gain in stature, from which they too would benefit. Pride was a worthy companion when so few were chosen.

Killbere settled himself in the saddle, content as much as a man could be who yearned for a decent war. It might still come, he comforted himself. And probably before Thomas Blackstone dragged his hands off his wife's tits and joined them.

Blackstone embraced Christiana, indulging his senses in the warmth of her body and the scent of her hair. Hers was a sigh of contentment, his own one of ill-conceived desire.

'Go,' she said. 'Before I stop you.'

'And you could. Gilbert can do what must be done.'

'And you would resent me for it later. They are your men, Thomas. Go to them.' She sighed again. 'I am resigned to it.' She smiled, and kissed him. 'Finally.' She turned and beckoned Agnes to her. 'Come and kiss your father goodbye.'

Blackstone went down on his one knee, favouring the wounded leg. 'Agnes, I have so many stories to tell you, but I have to go now. I'll be back tomorrow.'

He looked into the eyes of his child and saw the wonderment that had always bewitched him. Her finger traced his scar, top to bottom, her mouth parted, the tip of her tongue touching her top lip, as if concentrating on drawing a chalk line on a slate.

'It's going to rain,' she said.

'Oh? How do you know?'

'Because you have been rubbing your arm. And you always did that when it was cold or when the rain was coming.'

A child's memory was like the flutter of a fairy's wings, he had once told her. Had the past two years been little more than that for her?

'You're right. It's been aching. And the weather is humid. Perhaps there will be a thunderstorm.'

She shrugged and reached her arms around his neck. 'You always smell of your horse, Father.'

Blackstone smiled, and kissed the top of her head.

Henry stood at the door. Jacob had found him a jupon, too big for his shoulders, but it was belted and bore Blackstone's blazon on its breast. He tried to suppress his pride, but could not. 'I should ride with you and serve Master Jacob,' he said.

'I know. But there are more years yet before you become a squire and we'll let you fight. Be patient. Do as your mother asks.' He glanced at Christiana. 'And there's something I will tell you when I return that's important for us all.'

Christiana smiled gratefully.

'Yes, Father,' Henry said obediently, not daring to ask what news it might be. He was trying hard to learn the patience demanded of him.

'Let him ride with you, Thomas. He's earned the right,' said Christiana. She nodded at Blackstone. The time to tell him would present itself; until then her son should be with his father.

'All right,' said Blackstone, seeing the boy's face light up. A mirror of himself long before. 'Get down to Sir Gilbert.'

Henry stepped quickly from the room without thinking of bidding farewell to his mother.

Blackstone was about to call after him in reprimand.

'It doesn't matter, Thomas. Let him be,' said Christiana. 'All's well now.'

Blackstone lingered a moment, wishing he could deny his duty. 'Until tomorrow,' he said. 'Bertrand will serve you; make sure he brings hot food from the kitchen and fresh water to wash. There are men on the walls and the gates and I have asked Fra Stefano to stay close to you all. Trust him; he has God on his side and protects pilgrims. And he seems to think I'm one.' He smiled. There was nothing more to be said. He stepped into the passage and half turned. Christiana's arms were draped across Agnes as she held the child to her skirts. He checked himself and felt a sense of puzzlement. He had never looked back before.

Blackstone walked down the gallery and saw the men below waiting for him. The silky layer of light cloud kept the sun from throwing shadows, but the sight of Caprini waiting at the end of the passage by the head of the stairs looked nothing more than the darkness that lurked behind a pillar. His black cloak swallowed his features, but his unflinching eyes caught the light from the stairwell as they watched him approach. His stern expression always reminded Blackstone of his childhood and the village priest who glowered at them as they struggled to learn under his tutelage, and was always ready with a hazel switch to sting them into concentration.

'I promised to accompany you until the end of your journey,' said Caprini.

'And I have felt your presence at every step of the way. Your duty is almost done now, as is mine. And then we can go our separate ways. I need my men with me, but someone of rank – someone I trust – must be here.'

The Tau knight was silent for a moment, then he nodded. 'I will pray for you,' he said.

Blackstone chased down the steps as Caprini moved to the gallery's balustrade and gazed down on the band of men who had shared his journey since Lucca. Killbere shouted something at Blackstone and the other men laughed. Blackstone raised a hand as if apologizing for their jest. What was said Caprini did not understand. The English used words that had double meanings. Better, he thought, to be a plain-speaking man; then each knew where he stood with the other. There could be no room for misunderstanding. A man prayed directly to God, and killed out of necessity without pity.

As the iron-shod hooves clattered out of the yard the Tau knight turned towards the room where Blackstone's wife and daughter waited.

CHAPTER FIFTY

De Hangest sweated in his mail, his filthy surcoat crumpled and stained like the other men's from the fighting and the fires at Meaux. There had been no time for the luxury of bathing; his was a responsibility he wished he could shed. Once in Compiègne he would relax – if they ever got there at this pace. He pulled back the mail coif from his head, willing what little breeze there was to strengthen. He hated this damned weather. It made women inconsolable and men bad-tempered, and the agonizingly slow pace of their journey added to his own stretched patience. The royal wagon was as slow as a man walking and he wanted to get beyond the open plain. He had denied them the route through the forests; it would have been cooler, but fraught with danger. The Duchess had complained, as she often did, but her husband had – praise God! – commanded her to obey all de Hangest's instructions.

He led the way, followed by the creaking wagon, flanked on either side by his own men. For the tenth time that hour he twisted in the saddle. A mile behind was the unmistakable phalanx of Thomas Blackstone and his men. They followed the tracks he had made, their presence as constant as the heat. And like the heat their presence lulled him into a false sense of security.

The riders appeared half a mile ahead, two of his scouts spurring their horses at the gallop over the gentle rising ground. He shielded his eyes from the sky's glare and then desperately looked around for any place that might offer better protection. If they galloped they did so to raise the alarm. A nearby hillock offered a modest vantage point, but the heavy-timbered wagon

419

would not make it even if they whipped the horses to death. His thoughts took too long. He heard the thud of hooves behind him as Blackstone spurred on his men to catch up. The Englishman had seen the two specks on the horizon before de Hangest. The scouts and Blackstone arrived almost together.

The panicked scouts twisted to point behind them. 'Less than a mile, my lord. Pennons. A large group of men.'

Before de Hangest could question them further a line of horsemen appeared in the distance. Tapered pennons flared on their lances, from the speed of their travel.

'Form up!' shouted Blackstone to his men as he pulled up next to de Hangest. 'My lord, have your men fall back behind us and protect your charges. There's nowhere to run. We defend ourselves here.'

Killbere and John Jacob had already galloped to the flanks as Meulon and Gaillard dismounted their men in an extended line. Behind them Will Longdon's archers took up position and rammed their meagre supply of arrows into the dirt at their feet. Bows were uncovered, cords nocked and shafts laid across their knuckles ready to bend and loose. The men's horses were held at the rear. De Hangest hesitated. Blackstone's men had moved with an enviable and practised efficiency, but those men approaching might be leading elements of the Dauphin's army from Burgundy. Or Charles of Navarre.

'My lord,' Blackstone said with steel in his voice. 'There's little time.'

'Is it the Captal? Has he turned back towards us?'

'Who knows?'

De Hangest quickly responded and brought his men and the wagon behind Blackstone's defence.

Blackstone called out to his men. 'French?'

The heat haze and the sweat in their eyes made it difficult to determine. The undulating ground allowed the pennons to stay in sight, but their slim tails offered little more than ribbons of colour.

'Can't make them out, Sir Thomas,' shouted Will Longdon and then deferred to Halfpenny's keen eyesight. 'Jack?'

'No blazon clear yet. Shields are down though. On their saddles.'

'He's right!' cried Meulon.

The approaching horsemen had extended their line across the gentle rising ground and slowed their pace.

'They've seen us right enough,' cried John Jacob. 'Spotted our archers.'

Blackstone rode ahead a dozen yards and stood as high as he could in his stirrups to gaze at the men slowly approaching. He caught a glimpse of a shield as a horse turned on the contour. A cluster of blue etched diamonds against a white shield, a red cross of St George in its upper left hand corner.

'They're English!'

'Is Navarre with them? Do you see his arms?' shouted de Hangest.

'No.'

The wary horsemen held back just beyond the killing range of the archers. De Hangest urged his horse forward.

'They mean to take us,' he said, pulling up alongside Blackstone.

Blackstone watched the patient men. No sword had been drawn, no lance lowered. They had not attempted to outflank them. 'Eighty men or so, my lord. Their visors are raised, and they wait for us,' he said. 'They don't know how many arrows my archers have. They daren't risk coming any closer. They want to talk.'

De Hangest looked behind him. Their defence was strong enough now that Blackstone's men had deployed, but a concerted attack could punish them, and the royal family were easy targets. 'Then let's avert bloodshed if we can,' said the older man, and spurred his horse towards the knights as Blackstone followed him a heartbeat later.

'Halfway,' he said to de Hangest. 'Let them come to us.'

They pulled up in the middle distance and four of the knights urged their horses towards them. They would parley. As they

421

came closer Blackstone recognized one of the knights. It was the antagonistic Gilbert Chastelleyn who had given him his orders at Windsor. He pulled up, glancing at Blackstone. His unsmiling face gave no sign of surprise at seeing him. Ignoring Blackstone he dipped his head to the Frenchman.

'My lord. I am Gilbert Chastelleyn. I serve Edward, King of England.'

'I am Jean de Hangest who serves Jean de Valois, King of France and his son Charles, Dauphin, Regent of France.'

The King's knights acknowledged the other.

'My Lord Cusington is not with you?' asked Blackstone. Both men were known to often carry the King's orders together. A fighting knight with a practised negotiator made a formidable pairing.

Chastelleyn considered for a moment. 'It does no harm for you to know that he is in Paris.'

Blackstone realized that if the King of England's negotiator was in Paris then he was using the usurper Navarre after all.

'Is Paris held by the English and their allies?' asked de Hangest anxiously. If the enemy had taken the capital then the French King might well have lost the crown.

Gilbert Chastelleyn hesitated. 'Events move on apace, my lord. But... no. We negotiate with Navarre who in turn makes promises to the Provost of Merchants who, now that the uprising is crushed, holds out for the Dauphin. The city is divided.'

De Hangest grunted. 'Navarre has English routiers with him. Which means there's no English army on these shores. There's no deal to be had between a turd like Navarre, with a bunch of cut-throats at his back, and the Provost. No one will open the city gates to your King.' He was canny enough to understand that Chastelleyn was alone. That no invasion force was at his back. 'What do you want?'

'The child,' said Chastelleyn.

De Hangest sat back in the saddle as if he had been slapped.

'King John's daughter, Isabelle,' Chastelleyn added.

De Hangest glared at Blackstone. 'You lied to me,' he said coldly. 'On your honour you said you had no desire to seize the girl.'

Chastelleyn answered. 'Sir Thomas knows nothing of this. He was sent to find the royal family, my lord. We did not know where they were held. He was ordered to take them to safety. I was sent to follow him.'

'And they are still being taken to safety,' said Blackstone. 'Only then is my work done.'

'Your work is finished now,' said Chastelleyn with barely a glance towards him. 'My King and yours desire the child,' he said, directing his comments to de Hangest.

'No!' said de Hangest, grabbing a tighter hold on his reins. The horse's head lifted, the bit cruelly yanking its mouth.

'You'll obey your own sovereign!' said Chastelleyn, tugging a letter from his gauntlet. Sweat-stained and damp, it still bore the French monarch's seal, which he thrust at de Hangest. 'Or I'll take her! Sir Thomas and his ruffians will never raise a hand against their own King's men.'

De Hangest fumbled to tear open the parchment, eager to read what was written.

'We have no interest in the Dauphin's family,' Chastelleyn went on. 'Only King John's daughter. You can take the others to wherever you choose. And for what it's worth the Dauphin is marching along the Marne valley with twelve thousand men. So time is snapping at my heels like a bloody dog in a bear pit.'

Chastelleyn glanced at Blackstone, was about to say something, and then did not. De Hangest needed to be convinced. 'For Christ's sake! A deal is in the making with the child. If we do not seize France then your King will sell his child to raise the money for his ransom.'

De Hangest read as much as he needed. There was a gentle sag to his shoulders as he folded the parchment and pushed it into his riding glove. He glanced at Blackstone. 'I told you that politics was beyond a soldier's understanding.' He faced Chastelleyn. 'The child cannot ride in this weather. She needs shelter.'

'We will accompany you another five miles to an abbey where there is a wagon waiting, prepared for her and her governess.'

'We'll still ride with you,' Blackstone said.

De Hangest nodded and turned his horse and Blackstone tugged his reins to follow.

'Sir Thomas,' said Chastelleyn. 'Wait.'

Blackstone faced him.

'I am no friend of yours. And I admitted to the King and the Prince that I was one of those close to him who tried to stop you coming from Italy. Queen Isabella was thought to be a threat. And word came ahead of you that you were sent as an assassin to kill the Prince.'

'I would never harm him.'

'He knows that. And he will be pleased that you are unharmed. Knowing what we know now.'

Blackstone frowned. 'My lord?'

'Did you find the man?'

'You have me at a disadvantage,' said Blackstone, a rising uncertainty twisting in his mind.

'Word reached us from Florence. There was an assassin, but *you* were to be his victim.'

Blackstone shook his head. It was too confusing to grasp. 'Then how would I know of him or uncover him if he hasn't struck at me?'

'He was with you from the start. Before you reached England. He's a man of God.'

CHAPTER FIFTY-ONE

It took less than an hour for the assassin to prepare himself. He walked quickly, knife in hand, towards Christiana's quarters. *Inflict great pain and suffering on Thomas Blackstone. Make him scream in agony, and let what he sees rip out his heart. He will die a slow death.* The words of Bernabò Visconti sang in his mind, as did the image of the Viper of Milan slavering with delight, teeth bared as he tasted the terror that would be inflicted.

The Tau knight eased into the room, knife in hand, held low, ready to strike quickly. He had heard a sound that made him cautious. The door was open, allowing a finger-width of light. A movement dashed across the gap. Mercury-quick. Shadows. Breathing that was unnatural.

He eased open the door with his free hand, as slowly as he could, praying the hinges would not betray him. He pushed his leg forward, letting the side of his foot roll onto the stone floor, a poacher's stealth, no noise of footfall, no warning for his prey.

There was another door that led to the next room. Another entrance. Damn. He had not realized there was another entrance.

Killbere held formation, keeping the men together as Perinne grabbed Henry's reins on Blackstone's command to stop him pursuing his father. The bastard horse near burst its heart galloping back to Meaux, surging through the twisting lanes and across the bridge. Once inside the stronghold Blackstone raced up the stairs, alarming his rearguard.

'Where is he?' Blackstone yelled. 'The Italian knight! Where is he?'

Confusion made them mute, and if they had an answer it would have been too late because Blackstone was already running down the length of the gallery, Wolf Sword in hand.

'Find him!' he shouted.

Christiana's door was closed but unlocked. He swallowed his fear and slowed his hand, then gently pushed aside the heavy wooden door and stepped inside a butcher's yard.

A ragged doll lay on the floor; it looked torn, its fair hair matted with blood, its blue eyes wide with fear, opaque in death. Blackstone's throat strangled. As he faltered a fragment of his brain warned him that the killer might still be in the room, but his strength ebbed as his daughter's blood trail took his eye to Christiana. She lay sprawled in the dark pool spread beneath her body from the stain that seeped from her heart. Her tender lips were parted as if taking a final breath.

Blackstone fell to his knees. He tried to find words, to call their names, but nothing came as bewilderment rendered him incapable. He reached out to touch Christiana, macabre, disfigured, the sticky pattern of blood streaked down her dress, her one shoe off, her bare foot lolling to one side, the palm of her hand open like a street beggar. Gazing at him. Asking why.

He leant in blood, flies buzzing, the warm summer light illuminating the room. The horror tried to make him scream, but there was nothing. No feeling that he could understand. The death was within him, its hollowness burying him. He vomited, bent double, guts retching until he could catch his breath and wipe the tears from his eyes. Not even Arianrhod could save him from the dark angels who crucified his heart and soul.

A sound scratched into his mind and he looked towards the other door that led into the room. Using the wall to support him, his hand left a trail of blood across its rough stone until he saw Caprini lying on his back, a knife rammed up to its hilt between shoulder and neck. Blood gurgled from his lips; eyes wide, arms unmoving. Bile gorged Blackstone's throat. Christiana had fought back. She had rammed his knife into him, but it had not been enough.

Blackstone snarled as he knelt and grabbed the Tau knight's jupon, feeling the blood-lust return. His free hand gripped Caprini's throat, ready to break the bones in his neck.

Caprini's lips were moving, his eyes beseeching Blackstone. Whatever angel guarded the Italian, it stopped Blackstone from killing him. He pulled Caprini to him, lowering his face so he could hear the words, wanting him to suffer knowing he was unshriven and would be in Satan's claws forever.

It was barely a whisper. 'Sweet merciful Christ... do not... abandon me. The pain... I could not know... such pain as this... I pray it pays my debt... for the sins I have committed...'

The two men's eyes locked onto each other. The last thing Caprini would see would be the hatred in Blackstone's face. The moment before Blackstone reached out his hand to crush the life from him, he mouthed something that Blackstone could not hear. Caprini shuddered with effort, blood spluttering from his mouth as his lungs filled.

'I... could not... save them... from him,' he rasped, clutching a bloodied fist to Blackstone's jupon, urgently trying to make him understand.

Blackstone's grip eased, his breath held tight in his chest. Caprini nodded, his grimace a smile as his last breath escaped from him. The Englishman understood who had murdered his family.

Blackstone's trembling hands gathered the reins. Those on the gates told him that Brother Bertrand had ridden out with some urgency to find him, and because he was Blackstone's servant they had sent him towards Compiègne. Like an army's drumbeats heralding slaughter the bastard horse's canter beat out its rhythm, but was unable to break the unforgiving numbness that held him in its grasp. The trap had been carefully laid and he had stepped into its spiked pit. The monk had played his hand well, an assassin who had waited until the greatest pain could be inflicted on his victim.

His men had followed his orders and shadowed Chastelleyn as he took the French King's child back to England. The dark-haired girl was the same age as Agnes, and a part of him wished she had died instead of his daughter. Wished that he had slain John the Good at Poitiers; had forsaken the promise made to Jean de Harcourt to revenge him; had never answered the summons from a Queen and had not slain a German knight's brother at Crécy. The memories of regret tumbled through him as a growling thunder warned of an impending storm. The curse had finally caught up with Blackstone. When he hanged the dwarf in Italy he had taken it upon himself. And now God's displeasure had been visited on him.

'And now, Thomas?' asked Killbere as Blackstone rode to the head of his men. 'What's this with Bertrand? Chastelleyn's scouts found him on the road south and brought him in. He's covered in blood and he's asked for sanctuary with the King's men.'

Blackstone watched as a hundred paces away Chastelleyn's men-at-arms formed a barrier between them.

'Father?' said Henry, who rode behind Jacob. 'What has happened?'

Blackstone saw the look of anguish on the boy's face. 'Perinne, take Henry to the rear.'

The stocky Frenchman nudged his horse towards Henry Blackstone.

'Father? Are we to fight?' the boy asked, suspecting that his role would be only to stay with the horses.

'Do as I say, Henry,' Blackstone told him. The cold, unemotional command had the desired effect. The boy had never heard such a frightening tone in his father's voice. He obediently rode with Perinne and once out of earshot Blackstone faced Killbere. He spoke coldly. 'Bertrand's the assassin. He killed Christiana and Agnes, and Fra Caprini who tried to save them.'

Killbere and John Jacob looked as though the most impossible act in God's creation had been committed. They were speechless for as long as it took the words to lodge inside them. Blackstone might as well have rammed a barbed broadhead into their ribs.

'Sweet merciful Christ, Thomas,' said John Jacob, the shock of it slumping his shoulders, the back of his hand pressed to his mouth.

'There is no mercy left in this world, John,' said Blackstone.

Killbere could not suppress his bitterness. 'Fuck Chastelleyn, Thomas. We'll take him and we'll flay the bastard. I want to hear him scream.'

Blackstone nodded. 'Wait here,' he said and urged his horse forward to where Chastelleyn sat behind the line of his men. He was expecting trouble. Bertrand sat on his horse a few paces behind the King's knight as Chastelleyn raised his arm.

'Close enough, Sir Thomas.'

Blackstone pulled up. Behind him Killbere had readied the men. Will Longdon's archers waited, war bows braced, arrows rammed in the dirt at their feet. Meulon and Gaillard held either flank, with Killbere in front, ready to order the assault.

Chastelleyn came forward. 'He has sought sanctuary under the King's protection.'

'Do you know what he has done?' said Blackstone.

'I do not. Only that he says that you wish him harm.'

'I am going to kill him slowly, my lord. He has murdered my wife and daughter in a brutal manner and slain a Knight of the Tau, a good man of God, who tried to protect them.'

Chastelleyn's expression changed. The doubt creased his face. He crossed himself. 'There's evidence of this?' he said, gathering his composure.

'The blood on him is theirs.'

Chastelleyn said nothing, but turned in his saddle so he could look at the monk. Blackstone watched Bertrand's face. It was different than he had seen before. There was no longer the idiot smile. His eyes were alert, startling in their glare. It was the face of a man who had shed the subservient role of a lascivious underling, a man who would take a kick and a taunt as part of his service so that he could slither into their midst and strike when none suspected.

He sat confidently in the saddle, upright. A different man. Untouchable.

Chastelleyn's shoulder arched with indecision. But then he shook his head. 'Sir Thomas. I cannot give him to you,' he said. 'You know I cannot. He professes to be of holy orders. He claims Benefit of Clergy.'

Blackstone searched for the violent fury that would hurl him through the English ranks and beat the murderer to death with his bare hands. But it would not appear. A winter god clutched his heart.

'He's an assassin,' repeated Blackstone with a chilling calmness. 'I will have him.'

Chastelleyn looked past Blackstone at the gathered men. Blackstone could raise a hand and his archers would loose their arrows with enough skill to miss their sworn lord and cut down his men. 'It must be proved otherwise,' he insisted. 'I am the King's knight, and he must be taken to the bishop to be tried by the Church. We have no jurisdiction other than to grant him that.'

Bertrand had not turned his face away. It was the final taunt that he wanted to see Blackstone humiliated or killed by the King's men. How far had Blackstone been broken?

Blackstone lowered his eyes and nodded his acceptance.

Bertrand smiled. Completely broken.

Chastelleyn had faced men's savage faces in battle but he felt discomfort under Blackstone's gaze. Whatever lay behind those eyes, Chastelleyn could not fathom, but he felt a ripple of ice water through his chest. Merciful Christ, Blackstone was intent on slaughter.

'God bless my King,' said Blackstone quietly, and turned his horse away, letting it amble back to his men.

Killbere waited for Blackstone's orders, sword in hand, ready like the other men to discard the King of England's goodwill and pardon.

Blackstone dismounted. 'Gilbert,' he said, 'we must not raise our hand against the King or his men. That's a promise I made a long time ago.'

Killbere said nothing as he watched the men-at-arms turn away to make their slow withdrawal. Bertrand was surrounded by Chastelleyn and a half-dozen knights in a protective shield.

Across the undulating plain, the heavy black cloud on the horizon speared the sky with a ragged lightning. Blackstone wished he could rage against the storm that threatened, but he could not: there was no rage in him; it was a steel-cold grief that caged his chest. He handed the reins to an uncertain Will Longdon, and took the bow from his hand. He chose a bodkin-tipped arrow whose goose-feather fletching offered the best flight, then walked forward a half-dozen paces. It was not impossible for a bent arm to hold a war bow; it could ease the immense pressure from the draw weight, but to use it was to tolerate the pain that came with it. His muscles had changed, bunched and knotted for sword and shield, but strength had never deserted him. Nor had the archer's instinctive skill of finding his target.

For the first time since he was brought down on the battlefield at Crécy, he nocked a yard-long arrow, felt the tension and pain in his left arm as he arched his back and drew the cord to him. His arm protested, but he held his curled fist vice-like, instinctively adjusting his body to compensate. A hundred and forty-seven paces from him, Chastelleyn eased his men aside, leaving the unsuspecting Bertrand exposed. The King's knight must have said something, perhaps a vitriolic curse, because Bertrand suddenly faltered, turned the horse and faced the distant Englishman who stood to the front of his men. Blackstone loosed the arrow, heard its whisper, felt the bow cord vibrate against his unbraced arm and watched as it arced and fell. Bertrand raised a hand, shielding his eyes, trying to see its fall. It pierced his thigh, pinning him to his saddle.

The monk screamed as his body contorted, eyes glaring in unbelieving horror at what had happened, mouth gaping in a desperate attempt to draw air into the pain that savaged him. The arrow shaft snapped in his thigh as the horse bolted and Bertrand crashed to the ground. The unassailable assassin had become a

431

feeble puppet whose strings had been cut. He lay twisted, one arm thrown above his head, legs contorted unnaturally beneath him, his eyes blinking as life clung on within him. He made a feeble plea for help from Chastelleyn, who stared down at him, watched the twitching fingers of the crippled man a moment longer and then, with a final glance towards Blackstone, led his men away.

Blackstone handed back the bow to Longdon and remounted. No words passed between them. Thomas Blackstone was still an archer despite what had happened to him all those years before at Crécy. He rode slowly forward and halted as he reached the stricken assassin. His eyes sought Blackstone's.

'Sweet Mother of God, Sir Thomas... I... swear I killed them quickly... The child... she knew nothing...' Bertrand squirmed, trying to put distance between him and the man who gazed down at him. Blood oozed, soaking his habit, which rode up exposing the wound and the shattered bone. Its ugly rent was still pierced with the broken arrow shaft, the goose feathers a dark, soaking mass. Bertrand begged for a knife across the throat to defeat the pain.

'There is more agony yet to be inflicted,' said Blackstone. 'Your journey to hell will take a thousand deaths. You will scream and vomit because of it – but I will break every part of you and your slime will be sucked into the underworld.'

Blackstone let the bastard horse nudge Bertrand's broken thigh bone with the edge of its hoof.

Bertrand screamed, stomach muscles crunching him into a protective ball, but the shattered leg resisted and he flailed, tears and spittle mingling in his mouth, which made an incoherent choking sound.

He sucked in air, shook his head, perhaps realizing what Blackstone intended. 'No... I beg you... let... it end... now.'

Blackstone nudged the great war horse slowly over his body, breaking his bones, starting at his ankles, hearing them crack, then moving upward to his shins. Bertrand's screams went beyond human agony as his body splintered beneath the iron-shod hooves. Blackstone never took his eyes from the tortured man, drinking in his terror, feeling nothing other than the cold satisfaction of the brutality he inflicted.

Bertrand's life lingered in a hell imposed by vengeance as Blackstone kept the horse's weight bearing down on pelvis and spine. His mouth gaped, spluttering blood as his ribs cracked. He could no longer squirm. His mind was beyond prayer.

When all that was left was the gasping, smashed body, Blackstone dismounted and knelt with one knee on the dying man's chest. Dark matter bubbled between Bertrand's teeth as his eyes held his tormentor's unrelenting gaze.

A desperate, whispered plea escaped from his lips. 'I... beg you... mercy... Finish me...'

Blackstone waited a moment, then stood and gazed down at the killer. 'No,' he said, and led the war horse's weight across him.

And so did every man and his horse who followed.

The storm rolled its grey veil of rain ever closer, pushed by an angry wind that carried Bertrand's final, pitiful cries across the bleak land. As death dragged the Viper's child to its lair the sky broke to soak the hard earth and wash away what torn and crushed flesh remained.

CHAPTER FIFTY-TWO

Blackstone bathed Christiana and Agnes, then packed their bodies with salt and swaddled them in linen. Killbere kept Henry away from the ritual and his father's wrenching sobs. Neither would be appropriate for the boy to witness. The sombre mood held the men and they kept their silence while their sworn lord stayed locked in the castle's rooms. Meulon and Gaillard did as Killbere instructed and prepared the slain Caprini for burial. He would be honoured as Blackstone had insisted.

When seven days had passed and a priest was found to offer prayers, Blackstone took Christiana and Agnes to the place that was once their home in Normandy and buried them there, as he did the good knight, Fra Caprini, who had tried to save them.

'I should have stayed with them, Father,' Henry eventually said, breaking a long-held silence.

'Their murder was not your doing, Henry, no fault lies at your door. How could it?' Blackstone answered, wishing only to reach for the boy and hold him, but there was a distance between them, a place he could not breach – the boy's will denied him that comfort.

'Father, I cannot kill like you. I have no wish to do so. I killed a woman to save Mother, and I would have fought to keep Bertrand from her and Agnes had I been there. But now...' He fearlessly raised his eyes to Blackstone. 'Now, I wish to do what Mother always wanted for me. I will study and become a learned man, and forsake this way of life.'

The boy turned away.

Killbere, who waited close by, shook his head. 'He's Christiana's child, Thomas. As stubborn as you and determined as her. Give him time. Let his blood settle. He'll find a place of learning brings no joy to a lad who's fought for life.'

Blackstone pressed a hand to the mound of dirt that now held the woman he had loved since first seeing her those dozen years before. She had shared danger with him and dared to marry an Englishman. An English archer.

'God turned his back on her, Gilbert. He has punished her instead of me.'

Killbere looked away, raising his eyes to an uncertain sky that threatened rain. 'I find no sense in it, Thomas. There is none. Your pagan goddess protects you better than a shield wall. Christiana and Agnes had their own angels at their shoulders. Who's to say when heaven needs them?' He waited a moment longer, leaving Blackstone to feel the dirt beneath his palm. 'There are no words,' said Sir Gilbert. 'But your son is alive. That counts for something. More than something. Let the grief settle, Thomas. And whatever anger lies buried let it find its way into your sword.'

Killbere turned away to where the men waited.

'Gilbert,' Blackstone said.

Killbere looked back.

'See to it that the boy does as his heart wishes. I'll not challenge or force him otherwise. Do that. For me.'

Killbere was uncertain what was meant, but he nodded anyway. 'I will.'

Blackstone kept his promise to Christiana. He and Henry sought out the bastard child. It was barely a year old, with a shock of black hair and dark eyes. It could easily have been his own infant. But he knew it was not. He paid the convent to raise and name him and then made his desolate way back to England.

Blackstone dwelt in a fog as dense as that which smothered the boat on its way home. A slow, nudging journey broken only by the creak and splash of the oars as the small craft was pulled through the glassy sea. A sailor stood watch holding a lantern, calling the depth, subduing his fear at the fog's sudden onset. Hours later, when others slept and the welcome sound of a church bell guided them onshore, Blackstone laid Wolf Sword, its scabbard wrapped in its belt, next to his sleeping son. Christiana's half of the silver penny now nestled below Blackstone's on the sword's pommel; the coin's ragged seam joined the two halves.

And then he slipped silently over the side.

There was no sign of his body and those who knew him swore he had swum ashore. Killbere and John Jacob searched fishing villages and towns trying to find their friend on the King's command while Meulon and Gaillard held the men together outside Calais, paid from the King's purse, waiting for news of him being found – but as months passed they feared for his life. Thomas Blackstone had disappeared as if embraced by that spectral mist.

Will Longdon searched the taverns, high and low, in riverside inns and city whorehouses, while Killbere and John Jacob scoured the countryside among the monasteries and religious houses where a man might disappear with his misery and search for the remnants of a lost God and son.

Queen Isabella the Fair enquired about her defiant knight before she took the heavy draught of medicine from which she never awoke. Blackstone never heard the pealing bells that signalled the death of the extraordinary Queen, or witnessed the solemn funeral cortège that carried her body from Hertford, dressed in the simple garments of the Poor Clares, to the Franciscans in London, where it was clothed for her funeral in the tunic and mantle of red silk in which she had been married fifty years before. When this era ended Blackstone lay, unkempt, in a dank, rat-infested room, unknown to those about him.

Winter came and went; no ransom for the French King was paid after Edward and King John signed the peace treaty. The Dauphin had inflicted his revenge on the leaders in Paris who had supported the uprising and had reclaimed the city, forcing Charles of Navarre to retreat and change sides yet again. The Dauphin granted remissions to others for their part in the terror and proved remarkably resistant to handing over vast swathes of France to Edward, as agreed by his father in the Treaty of London. When Isabella died Edward knew that her influence with the French had died with her.

He grieved and planned.

Clerks travelled around the ports commandeering merchant ships; fletchers and bowmakers had their stocks stripped and stored in the Tower of London, hauled there by carts and wagons seized from monasteries. Edward's commissioners of array ordered the recruitment of archers from all the southern counties and knights from their manors. The great lords of England gathered and the Church and Parliament came to an understanding that it was a just cause for Edward to pursue his right to the French crown by force.

Word reached those who searched for Blackstone that there was a mason who worked on a great bridge, cutting stone from a quarry, and that this mason kept to himself, labouring long hours until darkness and drink claimed him each night. No one would approach the scar-faced man and risk his sudden, unpredictable acts of violence. By the time Will Longdon and the others reached the quarry one cold dawn the man had left and made his way to London.

The crowded streets groaned from the passage of heavy carts, laden with supplies, as their iron-rimmed wheels gouged the dirt lanes and soldiers' tramping feet muffled the clanking harness of wagons carrying forges and bundles of white-painted war bows in their thousands. They jostled past cursing pikemen as hobelars forced aside the street sellers, and beggars and mendicant monks rattled their bowls and called on God and his angels to punish their King's transgressors.

Jack Halfpenny and Robert Thurgood shouldered their way through the crowds with an urgency that earned curses from those pushed aside, curses that soon died when it was realized that they were archers and the badge on their jupons identified whom they served. The Fletcher's Inn was down a narrow alley into which daylight barely reached, a rat-hole of a kind common enough in

London. The leaning façade was close to the butcher's yard, rank with offal and loud with the groaning of beasts as they sensed the violence about to be inflicted upon them.

Halfpenny lifted the wooden latch and stepped into the gloom. A tallow lamp threw its dull yellow glow across the room. The stench of barley ale and stale cooked food mingled with that of dog excrement and men's rancid sweat. The inn's cur dog whimpered and ducked away as Thurgood kicked aside a stool, ignoring the alehouse woman's admonitions. Rumour had reached them of a man who paid good money to hide. Outlaw or fugitive, there was always someone ready to betray a secret when a reward was offered. Up the stairs Halfpenny pushed open the door of a back room and saw a bearded, crumpled figure, soaked in ale and wine, who knew not what day it was, nor cared if the sky was light or dark. Tattered clothes exposed scarred, lean muscles wrought from hard work and battle and a silver necklace of a pagan goddess. Money had bought him secrecy for a time in this room above the foul streets of the city. Halfpenny kept guard on the door until Thurgood found Will Longdon, and he in turn sent them to find Killbere and John Jacob. Longdon waited outside the dank room's door like a mother waiting for a sick child to heal. He muttered a prayer or two and cursed the devil for snatching his friend's heart, and then cursed God for allowing it.

Killbere grunted with effort as he mounted the stairs. Will Longdon was grateful to see the flint-hearted knight, as pleased as a man could be who had stood at his side in the great conflicts.

Killbere pushed into the room and stood for a moment over Blackstone's slumped figure. 'Thomas?' he said gruffly. 'Enough of this.'

He hesitated, wondering if his words had been heard. Blackstone sat propped against the wall, remnants of food and drink around him, oblivious to the scuttling vermin that snatched at crusts.

'Your friends are here,' said Killbere more kindly and leaned towards Blackstone. A sudden lunge with a knife made him quickly step back. Drunk he might have been, but an animal instinct still lurked within Blackstone. Killbere bent forward again and waited for another knife thrust. It came quickly and between them Killbere and John Jacob disarmed Blackstone. He offered little resistance, his eyes glaring at the men who pressed close to him in a mirror of time. Killbere laughed and seized his face, turning it towards his own as John Jacob bent to help lift his great frame.

'You stink like a dog's arse,' said Killbere as they heaved Blackstone to his feet and took his weight. 'Thomas, look here, man, your boy comes for you.'

Blackstone stared towards the gloom-laden doorway where Henry Blackstone stood wearing a jupon bearing his father's coat of arms.

A spark flared in Blackstone's eyes – the boy seemed taller, stronger even, and he looked at his father with an unwavering gaze. Killbere beckoned the lad, who held a sword and scabbard. The old knight took them from him and thrust Wolf Sword against Blackstone's chest, forcing him to grasp it tightly. 'You're needed. By the King's command,' he said and grunted with pleasure. 'We're going to war.'

HISTORICAL NOTES

The opening attack on the hilltop town of Santa Marina reflected an historical event in northern Italy in 1358 when a large mercenary force – known as routiers to the French and *condottieri* to the Italians – was defeated by peasant militia. The mercenaries had passed near the town of Maradi and promised to pay for supplies – which they did not. It was unheard-of for unarmed countryfolk who might, at best, call themselves a local militia, to take on professional soldiers, but the villagers of Maradi in the central Apennines did just that. In that summer they sought revenge for Konrad von Landau's mercenaries – and they won by trapping them in the mountain passes and wearing down the soldiers' defences.

Following the great battle of Poitiers in 1356 thousands of soldiers were released from duty and, doing what they did best, they joined others as military professionals. The place to ply their trade at that time was Italy. In the Middle Ages Italy was not the unified country we know today but a number of independent states and princedoms. City-states were self-governing and hired mostly outsiders to fight their wars and protect their cities. Florence, Pisa, Rome, Milan, Genoa and other great city-states who offered a *condotta*, a contract for hire, had strict rules of employment for these men. Accounts were kept, food and weapons were supplied, but the soldiers were not allowed to reside within the city walls because they were inclined to commit acts of violence and theft against the civilians who were their paymasters. The English, in particular, were prized for their martial skills – as were the Germans – but the English and Welsh had by 1358 the greatest reputation as fighting men.

The Via Francigena is the commonly known route for pilgrims travelling between Rome and Canterbury. Several mountain passes could be used to connect with 'Francia', and the term 'Via Francigena' was used for different roads through these various passes that connected Italy and France. The so-called 'Lombard Way' became the Iter Francorum, or the 'Frankish Route' in the *Itinerarium sancti Willibaldi* of AD 725. The 'Via Francigena' is first mentioned in the *Actum Clusio*, a parchment in the abbey of San Salvatore al Monte Amiata (Tuscany), in AD 876. The *Anglo-Saxon Chronicle* tells us that in AD 990 the Saxon Sigeric was consecrated Archbishop of Canterbury and went to Rome to collect the *pallium* or the investiture mantle from the hands of the Pope, as was customary for that period. Sigeric's journey back from Rome after his investiture is recorded in a manuscript in the British Library, rediscovered in the 1980s by Italian researchers. The Archbishop's descriptions of places along the route have been shown to be very accurate though the tenth-century place names listed differ in many instances from their modern counterparts. This discovery has generated academic research, tourism promotion and, in some cases, restoration of the actual route for modern walkers. I used Sigeric's chronicle of distances between each landmark to gauge Blackstone's travel time in his return to England.

I walked for a couple of days along the beginning of such a journey – before it became too arduous – and I have published some photographs of the countryside. I have also included on this page some of my research photographs of Lucca: http://bit.ly/1j7V0XN. Of the many routes followed by pilgrims I used the area around the Maddalena Pass that connects Barcelonnette in France with Cuneo in Italy. It meant Blackstone travelling across the 2,000-metre range in winter. Historically it was also the pass through which Hannibal led his Carthaginian army towards Rome in 218BC.

The character Fra Stefano Caprini, a Knight of the Tau, otherwise known as the Order of Saint James of Altopascio – was a member of a hospitaller order who offered protection to pilgrims and also had their own hospitals. The brethren were knights and priests. During my research for this book in the wonderful city of Lucca the character had not yet been conceived, but as I walked the streets I saw a large fresco above one of the city gates showing two men of striking appearance. My guide explained they were Knights of the Tau and the role they played. I knew immediately I had to have such a man at Thomas Blackstone's side.

The Italian town of Pistoia, north of Lucca, was famous for its extremely sharp and deadly daggers. For centuries Pistoia supplied Europe's assassins with their weapon of choice. I had my anonymous assassin work in the Ceppo Hospital of Pistoia, founded in 1277, one of the oldest continuously operating hospitals in the world, which has underground passageways that extend for several hundred metres. This allowed my assassin to 'disappear' and find his master knife maker.

The Lords of Milan – Galeazzo II and Bernabò Visconti – murdered their brother Matteo in 1355 and divided his inheritance between them. These ruthless men let nothing stand in their way of gaining power and Bernabò's cruelty is well documented. He was declared a heretic in 1360 by Pope Innocent VI. Needless to say, the Visconti fought the Papal States – and Florence – for many years. Galeazzo was the more remarkable of the two brothers and was a patron of the Italian poet and chronicler Petrarch and also founded the University of Pavia. He was also known for the *quaresima*, a particularly sadistic form of torture that lasted forty days, alternating one day of excrutiating torment with one of rest.

Thomas Blackstone had to return to England in time for the great tournament at Windsor on St George's Day. The tournament was at the heart of chivalric culture and for the contest in 1358 the King had given safe passage to any European knight who wished to attend. I wrote that there was to be jousting by night during this tournament, but this is not historically accurate. I took this idea from a previous tournament held by the King at Bristol, and liked the imagery it conjured.

Juliet Barker in her book *The Tournament in England 1100–1400* claims, like other authors, that a knight's hand was protected on his lance by a vamplate, the inverted cone on the shaft that fits snugly over his gauntlet. However, Ewart Oakeshott, considered to be one of the world's leading authorities on the arms and armour of the medieval period, claims in his book *A Knight and His Weapons* (2ⁿᵈ edition) that this device did not come into practice until after 1425. He states that a lance had something that looked more like a sword's crossguard to protect a knight's hand. Oakeshott also mentions that the tilt, the long barrier of wood between two horsemen during the contest, also only began being used in the fifteenth century, quite some time after the St George's Day tournament in 1358 at Windsor. To show the danger posed by two charging horses rather suited my story. And although this was not a fight to the death, I chose to arm the Prince of Wales and Blackstone without the benefit of blunted swords.

When it came to the fight to the death at Meaux between Thomas Blackstone and the skilled knight, Werner von Lienhard, I took the ritual of prayer from *The Last Duel* by Eric Jager, who recorded the trial by combat of two knights in medieval France in the late fourteenth century. I chose von Lienhard's banner of a Harpy, or Harpie as it is also spelt, wanting it to elicit fear in the eyes of the beholder. In classical mythology the harpies were the spirits of the wind when it was especially destructive. Three were named Aello (storm), Celeno (blackness), and Ocypete (rapidity). Homer mentions only one of them, Hesiod two of them, and medieval writers describe them as very fierce, gaunt and loathsome, dwelling in filth and stench, contaminating everything within their reach. Greek mythology cast them as messengers of divine vengeance.

I am aware of the subjugation of women in the Middle Ages, and that those times dictated that they were controlled by men. But there were women of strength and character who, despite their 'subservient' role, ran vast estates, bore their children and at times went to war. I have written about Countess Blanche de Harcourt et Ponthieu in *Master of War* and *Defiant unto Death*: a woman who raised a band of mercenaries to revenge her husband slain by King John II of France. And Blackstone's wife, Christiana, who deserted her husband because of her sense of betrayal, but who fights for her children's survival during the Jacquerie uprising in *Gate of the Dead*. The women of these times were complex characters driven by fear, joy, desires and loyalty, and they had to find the strength to survive by any means that were open to them. It is too easy to see medieval women as downtrodden and abused caricatures. What about King Edward's mother, Queen Isabella, possibly one of the greatest women in English – and for that matter, French – history. She had guile and courage and was used as a negotiator between the French and English Crowns. She had a wide-ranging library that suggested a cultured woman. She owned religious books, furnished her chapel richly, gave alms and made pilgrimages; but if she did take the habit of Franciscan Poor Clares as reputed, it was only on her deathbed. She journeyed from Hertford Castle to the great tournament of 23 April 1358 at Windsor Castle to sit alongside her son and it seems obvious from chronicles that she and her son were not as estranged as some have suggested. During that great spectacle she was gloriously attired and enjoyed the public affection of the King. She had been ill for some time and died on 23 August, but records show that prior to her death payment had been made to a messenger going on several occasions to Canterbury for medicines and for the hire of a horse for Master Lawrence, the physician. On 1 August, payment was made to Nicholas Thomasyer, apothecary, of London, for spices and ointments supplied for the Queen's use. Among other entries is a payment to Master Lawrence of forty shillings for attendance on the Queen at Hertford, for an entire month.

Research reveals that Isabella – known many years later as the She-Wolf of France – always loved the husband she was supposed to have betrayed. She insisted prior to her death that she be clothed in the same gown in which she had been married.

The quest that Blackstone undertakes across France to rescue his family, and the life of the French King's daughter, meant he had to travel through a land of turmoil and violence. The Jacquerie was predominantly an uprising by peasants – who were commonly and contemptuously called Jacques by the nobility – but lesser lords and knights also threw in their lot with them and even provided some military leadership. Old scores could be settled while the Jacques tore the land apart, looting and killing. After the English had captured the French King at Poitiers two years earlier, the French nobility were discredited. France became virtually ungovernable. The Dauphin struggled to establish control while Étienne Marcel, the Provost of Merchants in Paris, seized control. Under their captain general, Guillaume Cale, the Jacquerie joined forces with Parisian rebels under Marcel. When the hordes reached Meaux, a city to the east of Paris where the French King's daughter and other ladies and children of the nobility had sought sanctuary under the protection of Lord de Hangest, a loyal supporter of the French Crown, the peasant army were let into the city by Mayor Jehan de Soulez. It was thanks to Jean de Grailly, the Captal de Buch, and his cousin Gaston Phoebus, Count of Foix, who had returned from a crusade in Prussia, that the women were saved. Naturally, Thomas Blackstone was going to be there.

David Gilman
Devonshire, 2015

I always welcome comments and can be contacted via my website: www.davidgilman.com; or on my author's Facebook page: https://www.facebook.com/davidgilman.author; and for those who are more fleet of foot: https://twitter.com/davidgilmanuk.

ACKNOWLEDGEMENTS

My thanks to Antonella Marcucci, professional guide, who gave me a personal tour around Lucca. Her knowledge was very helpful in the writing of this book and she kindly answered my ongoing questions once I returned home. Her enthusiasm and interest never wavered. Should anyone wish to gain an understanding of this wonderful city's rich history she can be booked at www.guidelucca. it. I am indebted to Dr Nelli Sergio and his staff at the Archivio di Stato, Lucca, for their assistance and for allowing me access to the early fifteenth-century manuscript *Le croniche di Giovanni Sercambi*. Maurizio Vanni, curator of the Living Museum, was very generous in opening the museum to me when he had a private function and photo shoot in progress, allowing me to explore the museum's basement where the original walls of the city are located and where I was able to place Thomas Blackstone in the medieval brothel – which is what these cellars were in the fourteenth century.

During the writing of *Gate of the Dead* I participated in a CLIC Sargent charity auction event. The auction raised funds for children with cancer and the highest bid would have a character in the book named after them. Neil Cracknell was the successful bidder and asked that his grandson Samuel Cracknell's name be nominated. By coincidence I learnt that Samuel's great-grandfather was Brigadier General Sir John Jacob Cracknell, and as readers of the *Master of War* novels will know, I have an existing character named John Jacob. A nice touch of synchronicity.

Much appreciation, as always, to my literary agent Isobel Dixon at Blake Friedmann Literary Agency for her unflagging enthusiasm and keen eye that improved the initial drafts of this

DAVID GILMAN

novel. Thanks to Nic Cheetham and the whole team at Head of Zeus for their passion and belief in the *Master of War* series; without their dedication to the project we would founder. I am grateful to my copy-editors and proofreaders, unsung heroes who diligently right the wrongs and to the art/design department for these wonderful book covers. My heartfelt thanks go to my editor Richenda Todd. Her suggestions always make a sentence more eloquent. She patiently and with much grace refused to let me get away with anything she thought to be questionable. Needless to say the liberties I eventually did manage to sneak past her are my responsibility alone. Thanks also for the efforts of my international publishers and editors who embrace translation and marketing with such commitment. Finally, my love and gratitude go to my wife, Suzy, whose support and understanding make the whole thing possible.